SAM CRESCENT

EVERNIGHT PUBLISHING ®

www.evernightpublishing.com

Editor: Karyn White

Cover Artist: Jay Aheer

ISBN: 978-1-77339-692-7

SAM CRESCENT

DEDICATION

To everyone who has fallen in love and fought the boundaries that had bound them.

AUTHOR NOTE

Lucia and Jack's story has been rolling around in my head since I was a teenager. Their story is all about love, about boundaries, about fighting for what you love, regardless of the consequences. Please, give Lucia and Jack a chance to show you their love, and what each other means to them.

SAM CRESCENT

MY TEACHER

Sam Crescent

Copyright © 2018

Chapter One

"That's enough from you, Connor," Mr. Parker said, glaring at his troublemaking student.

Lucia Deen tried not to look back at the guy who had just called her a fat bitch in front of the entire classroom. She hated coming to school for this very reason, but unless she wanted to hear her parents complain, she had no choice. It's not like the first time Connor or a few of the other *popular kids* had decided it would be funny to call her a name, or push her against the locker, or something else. She avoided the bus home from school, never went down corridors alone, and certainly made sure that her jeans fit snugly around her waist. There was a time she'd wear skirts that fell below her knee, but one of the jokes they pulled was to lift her skirt up and call her wobbly legs. Yeah, she stopped wearing skirts or dresses that day. The humiliation had been way too much for her.

She leaned on her hand and tried not to look at the rest of her classmates. They were all giggling at her expense anyway. If Marie was with her, then it wouldn't have been so bad, but for their senior year, they were in next to no classes together. It was pitiful that with all of her high school life so far, she had one close friend. That was it, one. Marie was her lifeline, and if it hadn't been for her, Lucia feared what her future would have been like.

Both of her parents worked all the time, so she rarely had any company. That wasn't unusual though. They had always worked, and they had always pushed her in the direction of being independent and making her own decisions.

It was why they didn't know the extent of the bullying. Why she could walk around all day completely naked and they still wouldn't see the bruises where another girl or guy hit her.

She was used to it and had been for the past ten years.

Yes, she was the fat kid in school. The one they always made fun of because she wore a size eighteen, not a size eight or zero. The girl that weighed more than anyone else, and everyone made sure she knew about it as well.

Feeling her cheeks heat, she listened as Mr. Parker got back into his lesson, comparing two poems by people she couldn't even remember the names of. English was her favorite class. She loved reading, but poetry wasn't for her. She didn't gel with it. The constant rhyming or when a poem didn't make sense because they used long words. She didn't mind books, stories, something fleshed out, and complete fantasy. They were her favorite, and she spent so much time reading that it helped her to deal with her life as it was now, or to deal with the loneliness as well. Some people would love her life with the lack of her parents' interest, but she hated it.

Tucking some hair behind her ear, she watched as Mr. Parker began writing notes on the board, and she copied them down in her notebook, being sure to be thorough. Just because she didn't like poetry didn't mean she wanted to fail at this.

Over and over he spoke about these two poems and all she saw was loss. The loss of a loved one and how people coped with it. Why did all poems that they were learning have to have some deep meaning or something? Couldn't they be completely stupid, like talking about someone breaking wind?

The bell rang, making her jump, and she didn't even realize that class was so close to ending. It didn't seem two minutes that she'd entered the room and now she was leaving it.

Classmates were already rushing out the door, yelling and shouting for lunch. Packing her stuff up, she was about to head toward the door when Mr. Parker called her name.

Hiking her bag up her arm, she turned toward him and stepped closer to his desk.

"Yes, sir," she said.

"You don't have to listen to the boys in my class."

"It's fine."

"It's not fine. I won't accept that kind of behavior, nor should you."

She nodded her head. "It's not a problem, Mr. Parker. It's not like it would be the first time or the last." She shrugged. "They get a good giggle out of it, I guess. No biggie."

"This happens in other classes?" he asked.

"When the mood strikes them. You can't tell me that you're not used to the fat kid getting bullied now. A few names here or there."

He tilted his head to the side with a frown. "You have any more trouble in anyone else's classroom, come to me. Do you understand?"

She nodded. "Sure." It would be the last thing she did. There was no way in hell that she'd bring this kind of mess out in the open.

Some of the other teachers laughed it off. Others tried to hide it, but she knew they were laughing at her as well. That was the way of life.

He shook his head. "Go on. Get to lunch."

"Thanks."

Turning her back on him, she made her way out of English to find Marie already waiting for her.

"You in trouble?" Marie asked.

They were the complete opposites of each other. Where Lucia was fat, with long, brown hair and dull brown eyes, Marie was slim, with long, blonde hair and blue eyes. They had become friends in kindergarten, and that friendship had grown strong over the years. Marie knew her situation at home, and how she spent a lot of time on her own.

"No. Why would I be in trouble?"

"Hello, you had to go and see Mr. Parker after everyone else left. I mean, only bad kids do that."

She giggled. "Nah. Connor said something mean, and he was just being nice about it. You know."

"Mr. Parker is one of the best teachers in the entire school. Let's face it, he's also the hottest."

He was the only teacher who didn't take any shit from anyone. Unlike some of their male teachers who kept their suits in pristine condition, Mr. Parker would roll his sleeves up, showing the ink that decorated his arms. In the height of the summer, the tie would come off and a couple of buttons would open up, revealing his chest. She was sure she'd seen a couple of marks displaying more ink.

Not that she thought of Mr. Parker in any way like that. She'd heard a lot of the girls in her class saying how much they'd love to fuck him and stuff. There were a lot of things some of their fellow peers would like to do to Mr. Parker, but he was completely off limits, and it wasn't something she allowed herself to think about at all.

In fact, it would be completely hilarious. Her and the teacher. There was just no way in hell something like that would ever happen.

"Look at you, having the hots for a teacher," Lucia said, wrapping her arm around her friend's shoulder.

"Please, so gross. He's, like, way old. Not going to happen."

They found a bench far away from the cafeteria.

Pulling her lunch from her bag, she handed Marie her cheesy fries and pulled out her sandwich of cheese and pickles.

"You think he's gross?"

"Don't get me wrong. He's hot, but he's old. We're still really young, and when he gets older we'd have to take care of him." Marie wrinkled her nose. "Not going to happen. We've got to live life to the fullest, and having an old dude, that's not living life. That's pitiful and boring."

Lucia laughed. Just a few minutes in her best friend's company and she felt a million times better.

"Are we going shopping this weekend?" Marie asked.

"I don't know."

"Don't your parents have that trip they're going on?"

"Yeah, they do." They were heading to England for some kind of conference, and just the thought of it depressed her. "I forgot about that."

"I already have it marked on my calendar.

Already told my parents I'm spending the entire weekend with you. I've rented some Brad Pitt movies. What do you think?"

"And you're grossed out by old guys but Brad Pitt is all the way?"

"Please, he's not that old, and he's so good to watch. I'm going to marry a man just like him," Marie said.

She rolled her eyes and giggled as her friend batted her eyelashes. Finishing her sandwich, Lucia packed her lunch away, ignoring the candy bar that was so calling her name. She was still hungry, but she wasn't going to eat anything else until she got home.

"You look sad again," Marie said. "You okay?"

"Yeah, of course. Nothing's wrong with me at all. You know. Just not with it today."

"Senior year will do that. College applications and lots of studying. Don't forget parties." Marie gave a little shimmy as if she was dancing.

Lucia wouldn't get invited to parties. Marie, maybe. She had been catching the eye of a certain jock lately, but she didn't know if her friend wanted that.

Senior year was proving to be just like every single other year. The same people were all in the same circles. Even now, sitting at lunch she knew the popular kids were all around the center tables in the cafeteria. Some of them actually sat *on* the table, and all of them were on their phones, sending messages, taking pictures, uploading them onto social media. The same old life.

There was a time she'd had an account where she posted updates to all of two people who friended her. After the skirt lifting incident and the nasty comments, she disabled her account and hadn't gone on again.

Marie kept talking about her Brad Pitt movie marathon, and it would be nice to spend the time with her friend. Forcing a smile to her lips, Lucia listened and laughed in all the right places that her friend needed.

Where Marie was taking senior year with fun and positivity, Lucia was struggling. Everything was the same. Nothing was different. Their last year of high school was supposed to the turning point of their life. She had so many high hopes, so many plans, so much riding on the final days of her life.

Did she have it all wrong?

She always imagined something amazing, something life-changing happening during her senior year, and in fact, it was the complete opposite. Only one week in and she was used to the horrible names, the usual routine of avoiding certain areas of the school.

Once they finished lunch, Marie had to be on the opposite side of the school, and Lucia walked her toward the art room before heading back to her locker. She had history, and as she stood collecting her books for the next couple of classes, she gasped as she was suddenly pushed against her locker.

Gritting her teeth, she didn't do anything, and listened as Rachel told her to lose weight.

"You can't even fit into the locker. We couldn't push you in, loser."

She waited for them to walk down the long corridor. Once upon a time tears would have filled her eyes, and she'd be sobbing, but right now, she kept them at bay. Grabbing the last of her books, she closed her locker door and made her way to history class. She was the last person to enter and took the only available seat at the back. Ignoring the snickers and the noises coming from people around her, she rested her head on her hand and took a deep breath.

Just one year to go and life would be simpler, easy. That's all she needed to do.

Listening to the teacher go on and on about the complications of wars and how they started throughout the years, Lucia rubbed at her side where she'd hit the locker. They were all under the impression that she didn't hurt because she had extra padding. The pain was there, and so were the bruises, but she wouldn't give in.

There would be something that would happen this year. A turning point. There *had* to be. She couldn't look back on her senior year with pain or hatred. Something had to give in her life, and she intended to make some damn good changes.

Feeling a little better, she found herself smiling as she sat up, taking notice of her lesson once again.

She would not be dragged down.

****

"I hate kids," Ms. Bertram said. She taught biology and was one of the sexiest teachers in the school.

At least that was what Jack Parker had overheard several of the students whispering. They loved it when they got her to bend over, as they could see right down her shirt. That was the kind of crap he had to listen to when they should be reading Shakespeare or a simple book on etiquette and talking to a woman. Not that he could complain. Most of his teenage years had been spent chasing women like Elizabeth Bertram.

He had been the ultimate bad boy and had fucked his way through all of the teaching staff before deciding to go after girls his own age. Anyway, that was another lifetime, when he didn't have to be responsible. Now he dealt with kids who could be complete assholes, like today.

Connor was a self-serving asshole who thought he was something special. Jack had grown up with kids like him, and for a time had been completely like the Connors of this world, but not anymore.

"Anyone tell you that hating kids is not in your profession?"

"Shoot, I knew I was in the wrong career."

He chuckled. "What can I do for you, Beth?"

"Well, I was wondering if you were doing anything Friday night?"

Jack paused with several of the homework sheets in his bag. "I'm not sure I follow."

"Look, I know you don't date people you work with, but we've known each other a couple of years now."

"I appreciate it, but not right now. The school year has started up. There's a bunch of kids I'm getting to know." This was the first time he'd taught seniors, and it was turning out to be quite the experience, not that he minded. This was the post he'd been wanting to fill since he qualified as a teacher several years ago.

Beth held her hands up. "It's fine. Honestly."

"I think you're really nice."

"Let's pretend I didn't ask. I feel so embarrassed."

Now he felt like shit. "How about we get a couple of other teachers together and go out? Have a meal, some drinks this Friday. Compare notes on a few of the kids."

"You know what, that sounds like the best plan ever." She clapped her hands with that usual excitement that she always seemed to have. He chuckled. "I'll do all the organizing. I'll be back tomorrow morning with all the details."

"Can't wait."

The moment he agreed, he couldn't help but wonder if he'd screwed up. Beth had been showing him attention ever since he got to Beyer Hill High School. Any normal time he'd have jumped at the chance to be with Beth. She was sexy, smart, cute, all the things that normally mattered to him, but he wanted to make this work. He loved his job, and teaching had been something he'd stumbled onto during some community service he was forced to do when he was a kid.

He watched her leave and finished packing up his stuff for the day. There were a lot of papers to grade and several lesson plans to go over. He intended to do all of that with a nice cool beer and a juicy burger.

Leaving the school grounds, he passed several other teachers, whom he stopped and talked to. Everyone had that beginning of the year excitement that he found utterly addictive. He listened to the school door close as he made his way toward his car, only to stop when he saw Lucia sitting on one of the benches near the parking lot.

She had earbuds in her ears and was clicking away at her phone.

"You okay, Miss Deen?" he asked.

She looked up, pushing some of her hair off her face. "Yes, Mr. Parker. Thank you."

"It's a bit late for you to be here still." Most of the students had already left for the day.

Lucia bit her lip and glared around her. "Yeah, I had a text from my dad. He was supposed to be picking me up. Clearly, he forgot." She rolled her eyes.

He didn't like the thought of leaving her alone. It wouldn't be long before it got dark, and some of the students traveled quite a way to get to this high school.

"Do you want to call him? I think it best you remind him to come and get you."

"Sure."

She clicked on her phone and placed it against her ear. He didn't like this. Was she accustomed to being left behind?

"Hey, Dad, yeah, it's me. Erm, where are you?"

There was silence, and he saw her cheeks start to heat. "You texted me. Told me to wait at the school. Oh … okay. No, it's fine. Totally fine."

He saw it was anything but fine.

"Bye." She clicked her phone and sighed. "He's not coming."

Already Jack didn't like this man. Whoever her dad was, clearly the man needed a lesson in how to deal with his daughter.

She grabbed her bag, climbing off the table.

"Is there anyone else you can call?"

"No. It's fine. I live about forty minutes from here. It's no big deal for me to walk."

"You don't have a car?" he asked.

"Nope. My parents don't think it's logical me having a car just yet. They want me to focus on my studies and, you know, walk."

Jack saw there was some other underlying reason, but he didn't say anything, or even ask. Teenage girls had a lot of drama in their lives, and he wasn't about to delve into that kind of sticky mess.

"I don't feel it would be good for you to walk home. I will take you."

"You really don't need to do that."

"Yeah, I really do. I don't like the thought of you walking home alone, and it's the least I can do."

She cringed. "Isn't that kind of wrong?"

"What?"

"A teacher offering a student a ride home?"

He chuckled. "I'm being a gentleman here, Lucia. You're perfectly safe with me. I promise nothing will happen. I just want to make sure you're safe. I'd do it for every single student. You're the one with all the power here, Lucia. You can make me lose my job by saying one bad word."

She wrinkled her nose. "I'd never do something like that."

"And I won't let anything happen to a student."

He saw she looked nervous, but she nodded her head.

"We all good?" he asked.

"Yes, perfectly good."

Urging her forward, he walked her toward his car. Pulling his key out, he opened it up and placed his bag in the trunk of the car. Climbing in the driver's side, the sudden hint of strawberries hit him.

Lucia had leaned to the side and strapped herself in. The large bag she carried was on the floor between her legs.

He liked the smell, and quickly opening a window, he turned over the ignition and pulled out of the parking lot. She kept tapping her fingers against the door. He found the sound oddly soothing as she kept up the same beat.

"So, how am I doing in English?" he asked. He'd never taught Lucia, not even when he was temping for the other English teacher who'd quit.

"You're doing really well," she said. "This is not your first class, is it?"

"No, it's not my first."

"Whatever you do, don't show that you're nervous. They will eat you up and spit you back out."

He burst out laughing. "I was a kid once, you know. I know what I'm doing."

"Yeah, I get that. It was a good lesson. I know several girls are already happy that you're teaching English this year."

He didn't like how uncomfortable that made him. Even in this past week he'd noticed a couple of the girls opening their shirts, exposing their bras. He wasn't interested in them, not even a little bit.

"So, what do you think of poetry?" he asked.

She groaned. "I'm not good with poetry. I find it a little boring."

"You think it's boring?"

"What good is it?"

"You don't think some poetry is romantic?"

"I guess," she said. "I mean, some of it is funny. You know the odd little rhyme and stuff, but it's not great. I don't think you can get great romance unless it's in a book."

"Books can be a little too long to help express your feelings, Lucia. Poetry provides a quick outlet for some of our rawer feelings. It delves deep into ourselves, to find those words that mean so much to us."

"You ever thought that past writers and authors just wrote something for the sheer hell of it?"

"Sure."

She chuckled. "I sometimes wonder if Shakespeare can see, you know, the whole heaven and hell thing. If there was one and Shakespeare was looking down on us all, and he'd just say, dude, it was a fucking play or a story. A lame-ass betrayal, or that sucks of a love story."

Jack couldn't help but be entertained by her views. "That is really good."

"I don't know," she said, shrugging. "I sometimes think we put more into stories than is actually there."

"We probably do. Stories speak to all of us in different ways. *Romeo and Juliet* is a tragedy and has so much to also do with families, the feuding of families as well."

"I love the Leo and Claire version better than the book," Lucia said. "I love to read, I really do, but the way they talk. It's, like, really off-putting." She wrinkled her nose. "I do love stories and words. I am a great believer in the pen being mightier or stronger."

"It's mightier," he said.

She gave him directions to her home, and as they were coming up ahead, he couldn't believe that it had already taken him thirty minutes by car. Talking with her had been a real pleasure.

"This your house?" he asked.

"Yeah, it's my parents'."

The house was huge, at least three floors, with a large driveway. "What do your parents do?" he asked.

"One is a research assistant in a laboratory, and the other is a partner in a law firm," she said. "Thank you so much for the ride, Mr. Parker."

She released her seatbelt, and the car smelled like strawberries once again. He watched her climb out and said goodbye.

Jack waited until she was safely in the house before turning around and going in the opposite direction.

He stopped by to grab that burger he wanted, making sure they wrapped it up to keep warm. Pulling up into his drive, he grabbed his food and his bag out of the trunk. Entering his home, he locked the door immediately behind him. Living and teaching in the city had taught him to always lock his door.

Taking a beer out of the fridge, he pulled the cap off and went straight to his backyard table. The evening was warm, and he didn't plan to be stuck inside all day. The stack of papers demanded his attention. Sipping at his beer in between bites of his juicy burger, he got through the stack of paperwork.

At the end of it, he sat back, resting his head in his locked fingers as he did. His thoughts returned to Lucia. Considering the home he'd just taken her to, she didn't seem like a spoiled little brat.

He'd spotted her when she first entered his classroom today. She carried that bag like a lifeline, her head always bowed, even when she'd been near her locker or walking up and down the halls. Her long hair cascaded down around her.

When Connor had said that nasty shit to her, he'd been pissed.

She'd merely taken it though, even all the giggles that had followed the nasty statement. Compared to the other girls, yes, she was bigger, but that didn't make her fat or ugly.

"It's not your problem, Jack. Just carry on doing what you do."

He picked up the empty beer bottle and work, heading back inside. The last thing he needed right now was to think about one of his students.

All students mattered to him.

When he realized he wanted to be a teacher, he'd given himself three rules. One, never ever fuck a student. Two, never ever fall for a student. Three, don't ever break any of the first two rules.

None of them would ever be broken, ever.

Chapter Two

Entering her quiet house, Lucia leaned against the door, hating the loneliness that always crept over her when she came home. She'd been a surprise baby to her parents, and they hadn't wanted a repeat of that nasty little surprise. Releasing a breath, she moved away from the door. She went straight to her bedroom, tossing her bag on the bed and collapsing.

"You're better than this." She gritted her teeth, running a hand across her face in an attempt to gain some sanity. Life wasn't supposed to be like this. She felt a little broken just thinking about the last week.

The same old crap, just a brand new day and week.

"Enough!" She wouldn't allow their mean words to get to her. For a long time, she'd lived with it.

Getting up from her bed, she took a quick shower, changing into a skirt and blouse. Her parents didn't like her boyish style for school. She didn't have many skirts and dresses. They were kept neatly folded at the back of her closet. Opening up her textbook, she went through several of the test papers that had been handed out for them to study, and to be prepared for in upcoming tests in class. When that was done, she checked her cell to see if there was anything from Marie. Nothing.

Just as she was about to watch a movie she heard her parents arriving home. She ventured out of her room to see them in the doorway talking. They carried a takeout bag from some kind of vegan restaurant, which meant she had tofu in some weird ass sauce for dinner. *Yay.*

"I got you your favorite," her mother said.
"Yum."

She left her parents to sit at the table, taking a bottle of water for each of them from the fridge. They didn't believe in drinking wine or soda like normal parents. They wouldn't do anything that could damage their brain cells.

"How was work?" she asked.

It wasn't long before they were talking about their jobs. Her father's latest case, her mother's latest research.

"I'm so sorry I wasn't there to pick you up," her father said. "It was so last-minute that it completely slipped my mind."

"Don't worry about it."

"She got home safely enough," her mother said. "Walking is good for her."

Lucia gritted her teeth and didn't tell them her teacher had brought her home because he was actually worried.

"How was school?" her mother asked.

"Fine. It was fine. I've got a couple of tests to get through."

"Tests? What kind?" This came from her father.

"Pretty standard stuff. I think it's just to help some of the new teachers see where we're at in our grades," she said.

"New teachers? Bill, do we know any new teachers that have moved here?"

"No."

Lucia tuned out as they started talking about the educational system and how flawed it all was. The tofu had way too much garlic and ginger. She hated it and pushed it around her plate, not wanting to take another bite.

"So, I was thinking about you joining a gym," her mother said.

"Pat, not now."

"We need to do something, and we all know sticking around the house is not healthy for her."

"You want me to join a gym now?" Lucia stared at her mother, and she couldn't think of a single thing to say.

"I'm just saying, honey, it will do you good. It'll get you out there. Maybe help you make friends."

"You do know I'm nearly eighteen, and I've got Marie."

"But all you girls do is watch movies. It's time you got out there and did something." Her mother leaned over and kissed her head. "I only want what's best for you."

Her weight was always a problem for her mother. For as long as she could remember, she'd been on some diet or other. From milkshakes, to controlled calorie meals, to everything. She'd even forced her to go to one of those weird psycho doctors that told you to hold the fruit. That didn't last long. The small satsuma that had been in her hand, she crushed with how angry she was.

"You know, I'm not very hungry right now. I'm going to go and head up. Do my homework."

"We're going away for the weekend," her dad said.

"I know." She got to her feet, kissing them both before disappearing to her room. Diving onto the bed, she quickly called Marie.

"What's up?"

"Parental problems, as always. What ya doing?"

"I am painting my nails blue. It seems like a garish color, and I know my mom hates it. I know, lame, but I don't care right now. Do you know she wants me to go to camp to help out?"

Lucia chuckled. "Mom wants me to join a gym,

which means she already has me signed up at one. Probably with a horrible instructor that is going to make me run. I don't know how I'm going to get out of it."

"Your mother's a bitch. Sorry, she is."

She sighed. "It's not that bad."

"You're about to be forced to work out. Isn't that, like, child abuse or something?"

"Or something? I don't know." She got up and looked at the mirror. "I guess I could work to lose a couple of pounds. I just don't want to do it in front of everyone. You know, I can't stand that. Ugh, this is so frustrating right now."

"I think you're totally fine. You have these huge boobs that I would kill for. I have to pad mine out, and if I get it wrong, I look stupid."

Lucia giggled. She remembered the first time Marie had done it. She couldn't stop laughing for days after. For a good few years now, Lucia didn't have to pad anything. Her tits were one hundred percent real. Turning to the side, she saw she wasn't slender.

Marie talked about some of her studies for a few more minutes and then screamed as her baby brother ran into the room. "I've got to go, Lucia, talk soon."

Before she could say anything, Marie hung up.

Throwing her cell phone on the bed, she turned this way and that. Her stomach grumbled, and she opened her door, about to head downstairs when she heard both of her parents in the kitchen. Sitting down, she pressed her hands together, listening, waiting.

"You need to lighten up with Lucia. She's perfectly fine the way she is."

"Bill, stop kidding yourself, okay? I get it. She's our little girl and we want to protect her forever, but that's not going to happen."

"Just … give her a break on her weight."

She heard her mother huff. "She doesn't date, Bill. Not once has a guy come around to ask to go out with her. She's not going to know what it's like to have that rush of a guy wanting to be with you. There's no way that isn't lonely."

"I don't want our little girl dating. Damn it, Pat, I've become our own fucking parents here."

"Language. Look, we were never meant to have Lucia," Pat said.

"But we did, okay? We did, and between the stupid fucking nannies and everything in between, I don't even know if I know our own daughter."

"We know our girl."

"No, we know her grades and, because you like to print it on the fridge, her BMI as well."

Resting her elbows on her knees, Lucia ran her fingers through her hair, resting, waiting, listening.

"I just want her to have everything a normal girl her age should be having. I don't want her to get diabetes or be laughed at. I wasn't like her in school, Bill. I was the popular girl. You know that, so even though we don't talk about it, we all know exactly what's happening to her. Boys are laughing at her, girls are pushing her. I don't want her to have that kind of senior year."

"She's nothing like us, Pat. I want you to lay off her. We've already missed so much, and we're missing more. We're going away to London, and we're leaving her here."

"She wouldn't like either of our conferences. It's boring, and she probably has something set up with Marie anyway. Lots of movies and bad food galore."

She'd listened to enough. Getting to her feet, she ignored her grumbling stomach and went back to her room, being careful to close the door. She'd never been close to her parents. In fact, for a long time, when she was a kid she'd thought her nanny was her mommy. She'd even called her nanny "Mommy" in front of them, and the next day a new nanny arrived.

Sitting on her bed, Lucia twiddled her thumbs before finally glancing up toward the mirror. Her mother hadn't liked her weight for so long that it was like a never-ending debate between them.

Her mother wanted her to be slim. She didn't really care about any of that. Her weight never felt like a problem to her, just to everyone else. Standing up once again, she stared at herself in the mirror. Her tits were too big, and so were her thighs, which jiggled and rubbed together. She couldn't pull off tight pants as they showed her extra pounds in a not so flattering way. Her ass curved out, as did her stomach, and she just wasn't the perfect size.

She was … fat.

Why did people treat her like it was a crime to be this way? She'd never hurt anyone or been mean. She always helped the elderly lady across the road, or the frazzled mother carry groceries to her car. Babies laughed when she pulled funny faces, and she worked damn hard at school.

So why was it such a fucking problem to be fat?

She gritted her teeth as she felt the never-ending tears begin to start in her eyes. This wasn't what she wanted.

Her senior year was supposed to be perfect.

When someone knocked on her door, she quickly sat on the edge of her bed and grabbed her chemistry book. Science was such a hard subject for her that she had to study twice as hard to get a decent grade.

"Come in," she said.

"Hey, honey. I just thought I'd check on you."

"Hey, Dad. What's up?"

"You didn't eat anything, and I know you don't like tofu." She didn't have to turn around as she saw him place a sandwich with a couple of snacks on a plate for her.

"Thank you."

He moved to sit beside her, and she tried to hide the tears from her eyes.

"You heard all of that?" her dad asked.

"What?"

"I know you were listening on the stairs."

She turned toward him and frowned. "What?"

"Your door. I heard you leave the room." He took her hand, and she sighed. "I think you're fine the way you are, Lucia."

It was a lie. They both knew it, but he was trying to be the nice parent, the better one.

"Thanks, Dad."

She could tell he wanted to say more, but he didn't speak another word. Instead, he kissed her temple, and she watched him leave her room, closing the door behind him. Her mother wouldn't take the trip. She never came to see her.

Grabbing the plate of food, she picked up the sandwich. Ham and cheese was her favorite. She took a bite just as her stomach grumbled. It tasted good. She chewed the food and stared at herself in the mirror. Her gaze landed on her mouth, her puffed-out cheeks, and she just knew something had to change.

Maybe if she started doing some brisk walking or maybe some running. She would do something just to show that she was dropping a few pounds, and then maybe her mother would leave her alone.

****

It was Friday, and the bell had just rung for end of class. Already students were filing out, and Jack needed to head to the library to return some of the books he'd used for his class. Listening to poetry helped to soothe him, and today he wasn't in any mood to be going out with most of the faculty. Beth certainly knew how to round people up, and there were a lot of people coming.

This is what you wanted.

He didn't want to date or to have anything on a personal level with any of the teachers. This was the perfect solution, and yet now he wished he'd just declined the invitation. Packing up the papers, he gathered the books and precariously balancing them, he headed toward the library.

When he got there, he didn't see anyone behind the desk, and figuring he knew where they were kept he made his way down toward the poetry section. As he rounded a bend, he didn't notice Lucia crouched down, and he ended up toppling her over, dropping several of the books around her and on the floor.

"Ouch," Lucia said, rubbing at her head.

"Shit, crap, sorry, bad language."

She gave a little chuckle. "I know you're a teacher, but I get that there's curse words in the world, believe me." She got up and rubbed at her head.

"I'm so sorry. I didn't see you, and I hope I didn't cut your head or anything." He put his bag on the floor and moved close to her. The strawberry scent was strong once again as he neared.

"It's fine, honestly."

"Let me check, please. I don't want to hurt you, and those books can hit pretty hard. I know."

"You had books fall on your head?"

"Yep. Back at my home. I believed in the strength of one of my shelves, and I just kept adding book after book to this one precariously-built shelf on the wall. One day, I was reading one book while replacing another, and it was the final book, if you will. The shelf caved, dropped all the books on me and around me, and the pain was immense."

"Now that sounds painful."

"It was pretty painful. Not a lot to do about it though."

"Did you rebuild the shelf?" she asked, bending down to grab his books.

"Yes. It's now a floor-to-ceiling one. All perfectly protected and no risk of it falling down."

She held the books and smiled. "And that's exactly how books should be."

"What are you doing here? Don't you have any plans? It's a Friday night, and I happen to know you've got one piece of homework to finish."

"Yes, I do. I kind of signed up to help in the library every Friday after school. You know, putting the books away, cleaning up. It sounded kind of fun for a girl like me."

He wondered what she meant, but then, recalling her quiet house, he kind of figured her home life was pretty lonely. He got that.

"Well, I better return these books."

"There's a lot there. Do you want a hand?" she asked.

"If you don't mind."

"Kind of my thing right now. Cleaning books, returning them."

They walked toward the poetry section, and he watched her. She'd pulled her hair back into a ponytail, and he'd only ever seen it down.

"Here we go," she said.

He watched and waited as she placed the books in the correct numerical order, and then got started on the ones he was holding.

"There's quite a few here. You can just put them down on the floor, and I'll finish them up."

"It's fine. I don't mind. I've not got much of anything to do later anyway."

"I heard Miss Bertram talking. You've got a hot date." She smiled, and he noticed the two dimples in her cheeks.

"Erm, it's more like a faculty thing."

"I don't know. I've heard a couple of girls talking, and they've been all over the whole Parker and Bertram thing." She closed her eyes and shook her head. "Ignore me. You speak so normally and without judgment I forget you're a teacher."

"It's fine, Lucia, and I do appreciate it. Honestly, I do."

She finished putting the books back on the shelves and sighed. "There, all done." She tilted her head to the side and turned to him. "Any exciting books to look forward to?"

"Still not a lover of poetry?"

"It has only been a week of school, sir. I can't exactly fall in love with something that fast."

"I don't know. You've got to learn to open your mind up to new things. They could surprise you."

She shrugged. "We'll see. Have a good weekend." She stepped away, and he didn't like the fact she was here late.

"How are you getting home?" he asked.

"What?"

"Home. You don't own a car." He recalled her telling him that.

She patted her thighs. "These trusty things are taking me home. Thank you, Mr. Parker."

He didn't like that.

"How long will you be?"

"Another hour, maybe, why?"

"I'll drive you home."

"You really don't need to do that."

"I don't like the thought of you walking alone. I saw those streets, and they're pretty scary, especially for a teenage girl."

"I'm very grown-up for my age."

"Where's your car?" he asked. She should have a car. If she did, he'd leave it alone. After years of growing up in the city, it was something he couldn't shake. Bad shit happened to women and girls walking alone.

"I don't have one. I'll be fine."

"That's what they all say. I'll stay and wait."

He moved toward one of the tables, sat down, and began marking some work. The librarian came over to him, and they talked about the night ahead. It didn't take Lucia long to finish her work, and when she was done, she pushed the empty stand toward the front of the desk. She smiled with the librarian, and he packed up, saying his goodbyes as well.

Leaving the library together, he noticed Lucia kept glancing toward him.

"You know this isn't supposed to happen," she said. "I don't want you to get a bad reputation or anything."

"I'm doing the gentlemanly thing right now. If you like, we could go and see the principal and I can tell him how your parents are leaving you alone to walk in the dark where it's dangerous."

"Not a lot of people really see it as a gentlemanly thing though." She paused near his car. "I don't want you to get in trouble."

"Taking you home will not get me in trouble. Nothing is happening here, Lucia. If I ever had a daughter and I couldn't be there for whatever reason, I like to think that a teacher would do the considerate thing, regardless. People need to stop seeing the negative sh-stuff in everything other people do."

"I know that." Her cheeks heated, and she looked a little upset.

Climbing into the car, he caught the scent of strawberries again, and he didn't ask.

Unlike the first car journey where they talked the whole way, they didn't even speak during this one. He parked up outside her house, waited for her to go inside before pulling away.

This time he didn't go home and instead headed straight toward the bar that Beth had told him to be at.

When he arrived, he saw several cars were already parked outside the bar. Climbing out, he made his way toward the doors. He'd already loosened his tie and removed his jacket. It was still warm as he made his way in. He spotted the table full of teachers but went to the bar to order himself a beer.

Making his way to the table, he listened as all of the teachers made the introductions. From the look of Beth, she was already two beers over her limit.

"I'm Derick Coleman," a large, muscular man said.

"Jack Parker. I teach English literature."

"I'm physical education and also sex ed now as well."

"Great."

"Yeah, ever since we had two seniors the previous year leave pregnant, Principal Dowed petitioned the parents, and it became part of the curriculum. Seeing as I'm the physical guy and sex is all about bumping and grinding, I got the job."

"I'm sure they're delighted by that." He hoped his sarcasm wasn't detected. He really didn't want to be here right now, and Derick seemed to want to sit with him.

"It's a pretty good job. You know. Getting kids to roll condoms on bananas and seeing them struggle. It is pretty funny. The punk-ass kids think they know so much. I had that Connor kid, can't remember his last name. He shouted out that a bitch wouldn't get pregnant if you did it standing up."

Again, Jack had no idea what to say to that. "Wow," he said.

"Yeah. Then of course he turned on Lucia and said she'd never have any problems getting knocked up unless she wore a bag over her head as no man would want to fuck her. Tried not to laugh but we all know the kid is right."

"You told him to shut his filthy mouth, didn't you?" Jack asked. He felt anger, rage, and something twisted in his gut that he didn't get right now.

"What? Of course. I told him to be more respectful in my classroom."

He remembered Lucia's complete lack of trust when he spoke to her after Connor said the shit that he said.

"You know what, I need some air."

Grabbing his beer, he left the heat of the bar and quickly breathed in the fresh air.

"What the fuck are you doing?" He closed his eyes and tried to cool down his raging temper. "No wonder she looks sad half the time." Especially if no teacher was taking the time to understand what was wrong with her. He was fucking pissed off and angry.

"Hey, handsome thing," Beth said. "You didn't have to leave so fast."

"It's fine."

"I heard what Derick said. I like Lucia. She always does her homework on time. She's a good kid."

He didn't say anything, as right now, he didn't trust himself.

"Her parents though, they really don't give a shit about her. They've forgotten parent-teacher night and they'd even booked every single teacher. Lucia sat there and finally after two hours of waiting for them, she just asked to put everything on a report card so she could take it home." Beth stood close to him, and her perfume seemed to be on thicker than normal. He felt like he was choking on the fumes. "I even heard a couple of kids say that the only reason she doesn't have a car is because she's too fat and her parents make her walk everywhere. I've seen her ride in with Marie."

This wasn't helping.

He'd seen Lucia around school plenty of times. This was the first year that he'd gotten the opportunity to teach her, but right now, he didn't trust himself to speak or to say anything.

Beth hiccupped and leaned in close. "I'm not wearing any panties, Jack. I'm a monster in bed. A man-eating monster. I could do things to your dick that you've only ever dreamed of. Ask Derick, I've taken him for a spin a time or two. I don't have a problem fucking, and you seem to need help lightening up." She ran her hand down his front, and he caught her wrist, holding her in place as she finally threw up the contents of her stomach.

It had missed his shoes, but the stench was awful.

"You bring your car?" he asked.

"Nope."

Picking her up, he carried her toward his car, opening up the backseat. The scent of strawberry was still heavy in the air, and he ignored it. He ignored everything. Putting her in the back, he headed inside and told them that Beth had thrown up, which just made everyone erupt in a fit of laughter about how Beth couldn't handle her beer.

Once he dropped her off at her house and avoided any more feeling up, he got back in his car and drove home.

Resting his head on the steering wheel, he took several calming breaths. His car stank, and not of the strawberry smell that he particularly liked.

One, never ever fuck a student. Two, never ever fall for a student. Three, don't ever break any of the first two rules.

"Get a grip, Parker. Get a fucking grip."

Chapter Three

"You're blowing me off to run?" Marie asked.

"I'm not blowing you off, okay? I'm just spending an hour to see how well I do. This is not blowing you off. Not at all. I'm going to be there, complete with all the bad food I can eat to help me feel better about myself."

"We're still doing a Brad Pitt marathon. I don't care what you say."

"Yes to Brad Pitt. Yes to a movie marathon and minimal homework." She'd done all of hers anyway and didn't need to even think about homework all weekend. Her parents had gone, leaving her a hundred dollars in case of emergencies. The fridge was full to bursting with all that good stuff. Fresh fruit, more tofu, and her mother had even purchased her a vegan cookbook, yay.

She tried to be thrilled, but the only thing good about this weekend was Marie, her best friend.

Getting to the park, Lucia felt nervous. It was already hot even though it was eight in the morning. She knew the park was mostly filled with runners, but she'd also gotten the park's satellite view from the internet last night, and she'd found herself a path that should have minimal chance of anyone seeing her run. She didn't want to be laughed at, and she was in running shorts that hey, still fit. That got a little victory from her this morning, and she wore a large shirt to cover everything. Her hair was pulled back, and she was ready. Running was supposed to be a good choice of fitness activity. She didn't know how true that was, but she was willing to give anything a try right now.

"I can do this."

She'd seen several ways of warming up, and she

gave them a try, also recalling what Mr. Coleman told them to do when they were forced to run track. After more time avoiding what she was going to attempt, she finally decided to just go for it.

Starting at a steady pace, she began to jog.

One foot in front of the other, and when she was happy, she gave a little sprint, and after about ten minutes, maybe not even that, she stopped.

Her fitness was really, really bad. Deciding to go at a steady jog, she kept on going, feeling the perspiration run down her back. She wiped her forehead, only to see her arm covered in more sweat.

This was why she avoided all things fitness. It was gross, and it didn't make her feel so good.

She was also panting.

Not attractive pants either.

These were fake, and as she rounded a corner, she hit smack dab in the middle of a very hard chest. She didn't go far, other than flat on her back, and she looked up only to find her English lit teacher staring down at her.

He wore running gear and had one of those timer things on his arms.

"Lucia," he said, pulling his earbuds out.

She was gawking up at him. This was the first time she'd seen him without a suit on.

"Mr. Parker," she said. "Funny seeing you here."

"Yes, it is funny, isn't it?" he asked. He held his hand up, and she hesitated a second to take it, but seeing no other reason not to, she held his hand as he helped her up.

She wondered if she felt heavy to him.

Biting her lip, she looked up at him. He was taller than she was by several inches, so that wasn't hard to do.

"How are you?" she asked.

"I'm doing great. You're running now?"

She looked down at her body and then at his, and it was kind of pitiful.

"I'm … attempting to."

"I'm sorry. I didn't mean to knock you over."

"It's fine. Perfectly fine." She waved her hand in the air and realized that they were actually alone. The large bushes and trees that surrounded the park stood in front of them. The area was a little secluded as well, and that was one of the reasons she'd opted for this path to run.

How … odd that Mr. Parker was there.

"Did you have a good time last night?" She just kept blurting these words out, and he was her teacher. "I'm so sorry, Mr. Parker. I didn't—"

"Jack."

"What?"

"I'm not in school, and 'Mr. Parker' sounds like my dad. So, outside of school grounds, I'm Jack."

"Jack." She tested his name and kind of liked the sound of it coming from her lips, which was so strange. "I'm sorry for interrupting your run."

"I'm the one who's apologizing. I shouldn't have bumped into you."

"It's fine. I'm perfectly fine. I have a pretty good landing pad." She rubbed her rear and winced. "I'm going to go now."

She nodded her head and moved past him. Widening her eyes, she mouthed the words, completely in shock about the way she'd acted.

"Get a grip, Lucia." Again, she still mouthed the words so he didn't hear.

"Music helps," Jack said.

She turned toward him. "Pardon?"

"When you're running on your own. Music helps,

and it makes it seem less of a chore."

"Thank you. I'll remember that."

"You're going to be running often?" he asked.

"I'm thinking about it. Maybe, I don't know. It depends how close to death I am after this one."

He chuckled. "I'll see you around, Lucia."

She watched him go. Her heart raced a little, her cheeks heated, and it was just totally ridiculous what had just happened. Picking up her pace, she finished her first initial jog of the route in the park and made it home in time to see Marie waiting on the front step for her.

"You look totally gross right now."

"I'll put more clothes on."

"Not that, stupid. I mean you're all sweaty, and it's gross." Marie put her finger over her nose and pinched. "You're taking a shower, pronto, while I get everything set up."

She didn't argue, leaving Marie alone as she went to her room.

Removing her clothes, she climbed into the shower and quickly rubbed some soap across her body. Grabbing the tube of shampoo, she washed her hair, conditioned it, and was done within minutes.

Wrapping her hair up, she quickly pulled on a dress, deciding that she wore jeans throughout the week, and today with her best friend, she'd allow herself the luxury.

Her thighs hurt, but she felt … good.

She knew she was going to suffer later, but that was okay. She could suffer a little. She didn't mind. As she brushed her hair, she thought about Mr. Parker; Jack. The small smile he gave her as he said he'd see her around. Biting her lip, she stared at her reflection in the mirror. Since he'd moved to the school, she'd thought he was a nice teacher, and he'd given her a ride home a couple of times.

She shook her head. It was completely ridiculous. Jack Parker wasn't ever going to see a girl like her. Not when he had Ms. Bertram and all the other girls at school who were prettier, slimmer, and just a better match.

Still, she liked talking to him, and he didn't treat her like a child, or like she possessed some kind of disease. She liked that, and after she finished combing her hair, she made her way downstairs.

"Well, don't you look all sexy," Marie said.

Her friend was in a summer dress, hands on her hips as she swung them from side to side.

"Stop it."

"I thought you burned all your dresses?"

"I didn't. I've got a couple. My parents don't like me dressing in jeans all the time." Also, her mother liked to buy her clothes that were always a dress or skirt of some kind. "I just don't wear them for school."

"You know Connor is a jerk. I bet he has a small dick, which is why he acts like a bigger one. It's compensating for being an asshole."

"I love you," she said, moving up to her friend and holding her close.

"Of course you do. Don't you get it, yet? I am totally awesome. The best friend a girl could ever have."

"That you are," she said, hugging Marie.

"Okay, you're starting to freak me out right now. What happened on your run?"

It was on the tip of her tongue to tell her about bumping into Jack, but she just shook her head. She didn't want her friend causing any problems, not that she would.

Jack Parker was a nice man, and she liked him.

He was good at his job, and he'd been nice to her, but that was it.

"It was just a good run."

"You do know I find that weird, right? The whole running thing?" Marie said, opening a bag of cheesy fries.

"You find a lot of things weird."

"I just don't get it. At least you don't have one of those weird running machines either. Now, I've got everything set up. Pizza is already ordered, and the DVD is in."

"What are we watching first?" she asked.

"*Sleepers*."

She groaned. "Isn't that a little ... dark?"

"Come on, it's a classic, and so good."

Seeing no point in arguing, Lucia sat down beside her friend, her own bag of cheese chips in her lap as they watched the movie unfold. Brad Pitt was barely even there at the start, or for most of the movie. They paused it halfway through as pizza arrived.

Marie demanded Brad Pitt marathons often, so Lucia didn't have to sit and watch them to know what was going to happen next. Her thoughts returned to her encounter with her teacher. She'd been thinking about him more and more over the past couple of days. Friday night had been a little awkward when he'd offered to take her home.

She hadn't meant for it to be so. When he'd said to her that he was just being a gentleman, she'd understood that.

Then she'd felt embarrassed at him believing even for a second, she meant something else by it. She knew that Jack would never do that.

Teachers and affairs, or relationships like that. It would never happen.

She hadn't known what to say to him, or how to make it better, so she'd stayed silent.

"You okay?" Marie asked.

"Yeah, I'm fine. Why?"

"You're just … tense."

"The run is making me ache is all."

She was a little uncomfortable with her own thoughts about her teacher. She didn't want to think about him or try to understand what was going on in her own head.

"Do you think students sleep with teachers?"

"All the time, why?"

"I don't know. It was just something I thought about."

"I guess it happens often. I don't know if anyone is doing it in our school. I doubt it would even be gossip-worthy, you know."

"I know. It's fine." She rested her head on her friend's shoulder.

"You're being weird, and coming from me, that means something."

She chuckled, glancing up at her friend. "How did you get cheesy chips in your hair?"

"It's a gift. I'll shower later. Remember, we're making a weekend of it."

"You don't want to go home?" Lucia asked.

"Nope. I like being here." Marie took her hand, and they continued to watch the movie.

Lucia would stop thinking about Jack Parker. He was her teacher, and that was how it was going to stay.

Even as she thought it and knew there was no chance of him ever looking at a girl like her, she wished that just once, maybe he would. Maybe he'd see past her flaws and maybe like what he saw.

Don't be so stupid, Lucia.

****

"Poetry brings emotions to real life without the

need for creating characters, or situations for them to be in. The author can be completely anonymous and no one could ever feel or even understand that true pain or that love. It's what sets poetry apart from prose," Jack said, looking around the classroom. He couldn't help but look at Lucia as he spoke. There was so much to be had with poetry, and he didn't think she understood the power it had. He didn't have long to teach about poetry, but he intended to make sure his students certainly didn't mock it, especially as it was part of their exams as well. He checked the time and saw it was nearly time for the bell to ring. "Right, for next Monday I want you all to write a poem. Yeah, yeah, yeah, I get it. I'm such a bad teacher."

The grumbling changed to laughter.

"What exactly do you want us to write about?" Rachel asked. She had *that* smile on her face, and he noticed she'd opened a couple of buttons of her shirt.

"I want you to write about your feelings. What makes you tick. How life affects you."

"That's easy. I'm fucking awesome," Connor said, slapping the hand of his friend beside him.

"What you love. What you hate. This is the point of poetry. It doesn't have to have any one theme. It can be a load of nonsense if you wish, or something deep. It depends on how seriously you guys take it, but as you're writing, think about it. Think about the past authors of poetry and what they had to do." The bell rang. "Right, I'll see you all in a couple of days."

They didn't all have English classes every single day, and he would be teaching another year soon.

He noticed that Lucia dawdled. She took her time putting stuff in her bag and she kept waiting for people to leave.

"You okay?" he asked.

Her gaze moved to him. "I'm fine. Just waiting.

It'll be easier to get to my locker."

"It's lunchtime."

"I know, but it will be easier." She smiled, and her dimples were once again in place.

"I expect you to take this assignment seriously," he said. "I know you don't like poetry."

She rolled her eyes. "I get it, Mr. Parker. I'll write a poem. You never know, I may even like it after."

He chuckled. "That's the aim." He held up the book, realizing he didn't want her to leave the room.

Bad.

Fucking bad.

"Are you set to make it home tonight?" he asked.

"Yeah, Marie, my friend, is taking me home. Thank you."

He stared at her, wanting to ask so many questions.

She licked her lips, and he quickly looked away.

"Please tell me we're still friends," Ms. Bertram said, coming toward his door.

Before he could say anything, Lucia left, and he turned his attention to Beth. It was lunch so he didn't have much planned. Just sitting and enjoying the sandwiches he'd made for himself.

"Of course, why wouldn't we be?"

"You know." She ran a hand down her face. "I can't believe I totally drank too much Friday night. I promise that rarely happens." She held her two fingers close together.

"It was fine. I took you home. Made sure you were safe."

"You're such a gentleman. There's not many men left like you in the world," she said, stepping closer into the room.

He didn't say anything, but his thoughts returned

to Lucia. Ever since he'd seen her at the park Saturday morning, he'd thought about her, and it was so fucking inappropriate of him.

"Thank you." He didn't feel comfortable right now talking to this woman. Fresh air was what he needed. Grabbing his keys and lunch, he looked toward the door. "I'm just going to step out for a bit."

"You're not coming to the staff room?"

"Not today, no. Maybe another time. I just need to clear my head. Get ready for another class." He locked the door, gave her a smile. "I'm pleased you're okay. Not too much of a hangover."

"It was awful, but I survived." She touched his arm, and he nodded his head.

"I better be going. Lunch time is ticking." He left her standing beside his door, and he walked out of the school building, heading toward a small, secluded place where he'd been able to go many times to clear his head. It was close to the bleachers that were outside overlooking the large football field.

He'd never played football in school.

Instead, he'd been one of the rebel kids who shouted back to teachers, and did whatever he wanted.

Pulling the small box over, he sat down and couldn't help but laugh at how he'd changed. There was a time he'd have been in that staff room and had every single woman eating out of the palm of his hand. It had been a long time since he'd been with a woman.

Moving to Beyer Hill High School, he'd made plans to change, to make sure he didn't screw this up. He liked the school, and they were one of those that started their academic year in mid-August.

Taking a bite of his sandwich, he closed his eyes.

"What are you going to do about the gym thing?"

"I don't know. She'll probably give me the card

today and make me go. I checked it out online, and they've got a pool. That could be cool." When he recognized Lucia's voice he looked up, and there she was, with a friend he guessed was Marie, eating lunch. She wasn't at the cafeteria.

There was no way they could see him either. Gritting his teeth, he chewed his food, and couldn't help but listen. He'd come here for privacy, away from all the talking of the teachers. Most of the time he could stand it, but today, he'd simply wanted peace.

"I think it's wrong. What kind of mother gives her daughter a gym membership?"

"The kind that thinks their daughter is fat and needs a helping hand. It's no different than not getting a car, Marie. You know that."

"Ugh, that still pisses me off."

Why wasn't she allowed a car?

"Walking can be fun."

"Yeah, and when it's dark and lone serial rapists are on the street and they hurt you, they're going to be wishing they got you a car."

He clenched his hands into fists, and then his gut twisted at Lucia's response. She laughed.

"There's no way a serial rapist will ever look twice at me."

"I hate it when you do that," Marie said. "You're not fat, and you're not ugly."

"I'd say you're one against most of the population of our class."

"They're idiots and clearly can't see."

He liked this Marie. She was a good friend.

Lucia chuckled. "I love you, and this is supposed to be our lunch. Not both of us arguing about my mom's gift to the gym to help me lose all the extra pounds."

"Yeah, well, your birthday is at the beginning of

October. I hate to think what they'll get you."

She would be eighteen. Officially an adult.

"I don't know, but I'm sure we'll both have something to say about it." He watched as Lucia nudged her friend. "Come on. Let's not argue about this."

"You've already said senior year is sucking in a big way."

"Yeah, well, it is. Everyone is the same. They're not grown up. They're total assholes, and I can hate this if I want."

He saw Marie hug her. "I want you to love this year. Come on, it's the last year of our lives before it gets really serious. Right now, it's only a little and we're supposed to have so much fun."

"What would you consider fun?"

"Skinny dipping."

"Yeah, good one," Lucia said.

"Making out with random guys."

"Ew. Think about what I could catch."

That's a good girl.

"Okay, how about having an affair with a teacher?"

"What?" Lucia asked. "That is not even possible."

"Why not? Rachel, the slut, keeps talking about how she's going to bag your English teacher. What's his name?"

"Mr. Parker?"

"Yeah. The only good-looking teacher around, I've been told."

He heard Lucia laugh. "You're so funny. There's no way in hell that I would ever have an affair with a teacher."

"Why not?" Marie asked.

"Because it's wrong."

"It's kinky. Think about it, he's, like, way old, and he looks hot, which means he knows a thing or two. What better way to lose your virginity than with a guy that literally knows it all."

"You're insane, okay? I think this lack of chocolate thing has gone completely to your head. What happened to you thinking he was old, or that most teachers are old and gross?"

He shouldn't be listening to this.

This conversation was for girls' diaries.

Not to be overheard in the bleachers.

He had to leave, but he couldn't force himself to stand up.

"I've thought about it, and you know what, high school guys are the stuff of a virgin girl's nightmares. But a very experienced older guy? The stuff of a virgin girl's dreams. Are you denying it because you think you're not pretty enough to catch his attention?"

"Can we drop this?" Lucia asked. "I don't want to talk about it. I'm not the kind of person who has affairs with teachers. I'm just me, and I want to finish lunch and head to my next lesson."

"Fine. Fine. I'll shut up."

They were silent for several minutes, and he finished his lunch.

"But if something was to happen, you'd tell me, right?"

"No," Lucia said with a giggle. "Okay, if I had this amazing, 'kinky' affair as you're calling it with Mr. Parker, I wouldn't tell a soul."

They stood up, and he listened to them walking away.

Once he was sure the coast was clear, he got up and made his way back to his classroom. He felt in a bit of a daze from what he'd heard.

Lucia was a charming young woman.

She wasn't a girl.

None of the kids he taught were girls anymore.

He remembered what it was like to be that age.

At fourteen he'd already lost his virginity and made it his personal mission to find out everything about pleasuring the opposite sex. If women fucked him or girls his own age did, he wanted them to be fucking amazed by how good he actually was.

It was also the best way of making them come back for more.

Pushing those thoughts to the back of his mind, he finished the rest of his day in a bit of a daze still and didn't linger to chat with the other teachers.

He went to his car, which was parked toward the end of the parking lot, and there was Lucia up ahead, playing with her phone once again as she walked away from the school. Climbing into his car, he drove toward her, pulling up beside her. At first, she didn't even notice someone was there.

Jack followed her, waiting until she spotted him.

When she did, she jumped and placed a hand across her chest.

"You scared me."

"Good. Get in."

"I'm good."

"You lied to me," he said.

"No, I didn't lie."

"Where's your friend?"

"She had to go and help her mom out. She *was* giving me a ride, I promise."

"Get in."

"You really don't need to take me home."

"I don't feel comfortable with you walking all that way home."

She rolled her eyes, but stepped toward the door, opening it.

"You know I could scream 'stranger danger,'" she said, climbing in.

"When I offer you candy or something like that, I expect you to scream it."

She burst out laughing. "I'm not much of a candy girl, but a big tub of strawberry cheesecake ice cream and I'll be putty in your hands."

He made a note to remember that.

"So, you don't think my homework is too hard?" he asked.

"Oh, it is. I'm going to completely suck at this. There's going to be a lot of laughs."

"I imagine there will be a lot of stupid poems. Stuff about being pretty. Being popular, sex, and all those kinds of things. It's supposed to be fun mixed with serious."

"How can it be serious?" she asked. "Especially if they're going to write 'stupid poems.'" She air quoted, which he found the cutest thing.

"Because even though it starts out being a joke, most people will sit back, think, and then it allows them to process their inner pain. Their thoughts that are completely secret. They become exposed, raw, and in need of someone to hear, to see. Writing, poetry, it is all part of that."

"Wow," she said. "I never really thought about it that way."

"Think about my homework. Don't mock it just yet."

She chuckled. "I won't mock it. Thank you for the ride, Mr. Parker."

Chapter Four

Lucia tore the piece of paper from her notebook, crumpled it up, and tossed it away to join the other fifteen pieces she'd filled with notes and small rhymes. This homework was next to impossible.

She couldn't think of a single thing to say.

There once was a girl called Lucia,
Who had a great big rear.

Again, she ran her pen across the page, hating it.

She didn't want the poem to be about herself or to even allow people the opportunity to laugh or mock.

With her pen poised above the paper, she couldn't think of a single thing to say. Jack's words had really struck a chord with her, and she couldn't do this piece of homework. The last thing she wanted to do was make a mockery of it, or not do it.

Sitting up, she made her way downstairs to grab herself a snack. Her dad was sitting at the table, doing calculations of some sort.

"Hey, Dad," she said. She'd not even heard him come home.

"Hey, honey. You okay?"

"Yeah, I'm just doing some homework. It sucks big time." She grabbed a bottle of water as they were not allowed soda. "Where's Mom?"

"At work, finishing a few things up." He looked up from his work. "You okay?"

"You ever write poetry?"

He chuckled. "Poetry?"

"Yeah."

"No, I can't say that I have. I rely on stuff that is already written. You know, in cards I get your mother for Valentine's Day."

She nodded. "I remember."

"Why? Is some kid sending you poetry? That's a sign of a crush."

"It's an English assignment, Dad."

"Oh, okay then. What do you have to do?"

"Write a poem. I'm finding it a lot harder than I thought. Not everyone can rhyme." She sipped at her drink.

"Not all poetry does, Lucia. Why don't you look online, read some of the poems, and you'll see?"

"Thank you."

She didn't bother him anymore and made her way back up to her bedroom. Sitting on the floor this time, her bottled water beside her, she grabbed her notebook and just wrote. She'd already done all of her research, and the poems she loved were the ones that seemed to have a flow. Almost as if you could sing them.

Life has a way of scaring you.
Igniting a path of pain and fear,
and scaring you whole.
Beauty, love, sex, it all is relevant right now.
To not fit in, you become the problem.

Wrinkling her nose, she didn't cross this one out, but decided to close her folder.

Making her way downstairs, she saw her father was still sitting at the table. "I'm going out for a walk. Clear my head."

"Do you need me to drive you anywhere?"

"It's okay. I like the walk."

She left her home just as her mother was pulling into the driveway.

"Where are you going?" her mother asked.

"I'm just going for a walk. I'll be back soon."

"Excellent. I've found this great vegan place that'll deliver. They've got cauliflower pizza on the menu."

"Great." That kind of pizza was disgusting. Lucia hated it. Instead of arguing though, she left her mother to gather her things as she made her way out of the house.

At first, she didn't know where she was going, and then suddenly realized she was heading toward the park.

She didn't detour and instead found a quiet bench all to herself. It was Friday night. There was a football game at the high school, and the odds were higher for their team. Following sports wasn't her thing, but there a few places to avoid when they were playing.

Sipping at her bottled water, she suddenly realized that poetry *was* making her think. It made her feel things that she didn't want to feel or to even acknowledge, but they were there, open, exposed, raw.

Only there wasn't a lot of love right now but hate, sadness.

They were feelings she wanted to avoid, and as she sat on top of bench with darkness already fallen, she allowed the tears she had long denied to finally fall too. Staring up at the sky, she felt sick to her stomach, panicked, nervous, and so many other things rolled into one.

She hated her parents for not being impressed by all that she'd accomplished. So she wasn't a star in school or popular, but she had good grades all the time, and teachers said nice things about her all the time. She didn't get into fights or cause trouble. She stayed to herself and with her friend Marie.

Wiping the tears away was useless as more just kept on coming, and they were not helping the way she felt.

Her parents were barely there.

Her peers treated her like a social leper because

she was fat, and it just hurt.

"Lucia, you okay?"

She gasped, turning to see Jack Parker standing there.

Quickly averting her head, she didn't want him to see her tears, to know that she was so broken inside. This was supposed to be *her* year. Senior year should change everything, and instead, she was more miserable than ever before.

The pain was unlike anything she could ever recall, and it made her angry.

She didn't kill people.

Why were people so adverse to someone who weighed more than they did? It wasn't like she was going to sit on them, squash them.

"Mr. Parker, what are you doing here?"

She sounded miserable even to herself.

"I needed to walk, to clear my head."

Staring down at the bottle of water, she hoped it had been dark enough that he didn't see how miserable she was.

"You shouldn't be out here so late," he said, moving to her side. She didn't know what to do with the warmth that suddenly flooded her at his closeness.

Why was it that he cared more than her parents? Not once had either of them told her to be safe.

"I'm okay." He smelled amazing, and she felt her arousal begin to build. She wasn't an idiot. Her parents had made sure at a young age that she knew about sex, arousal, peer pressure. Pretty much every single thing that could be explained scientifically, they had made her aware of. They got her to look at books, read biographies of struggling teenage mothers.

Yes, she had heard it all, so when it came to attraction, arousal, she knew exactly what to expect.

Jack was the first person she'd ever felt it toward, and that was insane. He was her teacher.

"Why are you sitting on a park bench after dark, crying?" he asked.

Those words set off the waterworks again, and she sniffled as she tried to hide it.

"I'm just a little cold," she said.

"That's not it." Even as he said it, he removed his jacket and placed it over her shoulders. "Tell me what's wrong, Lucia."

She turned to look at him, and she didn't know what came over her, but suddenly, not telling him seemed wrong. "It was your stupid homework."

He chuckled. "You found the power of the poem?"

"No. I can't write anything, and then when I started to think about it, I just … why?"

"Why what?" He reached out as if to touch her but suddenly stopped. "What do you mean?"

"Why is being fat such a huge crime?" she asked. "It's like I killed someone because my very presence offends, and I don't get it. I'm a nice person. I've always been nice, and I can't. I can't even believe I'm talking about this with you. You know you're on the popular girls' most wanted list because you are the hottest teacher in school, and why am I saying that?"

She covered her face, mortified that she'd just broken down, and Jack Parker, her teacher, had seen that.

Lucia expected him to laugh, or to do something. She didn't expect him to wrap his arms around her and hold her close. His fingers ran through her hair, stroking down her back.

The last thing she should do was hold him closer, but that was exactly what she did. She hugged him tightly as she let the tears begin to fall.

Neither of them spoke, and she was scared to. There was no way she'd ever be able to go back to school and face him again.

"You are a very beautiful young woman, Lucia."

She pulled away, snorting.

"No, I'm serious." He cupped her face, and she stared into his intense blue eyes. His black hair was messy this evening, like he'd been running his fingers through it repeatedly, and nothing would make it work. "You're not ugly, and I don't think you're fat. There are men out there who will love your curves and be happy with you the way you are. You're not a bad person, but you cannot let these people hurt you, Lucia. You can't let them get to you. You're stronger than them." He wiped the tears away, and she couldn't handle it.

Pulling away from him, she stood away from the bench, and stared at him. "I better get home."

Biting her lip, she went to walk past him, and he caught her wrist, stopping her.

Heat flooded her at his touch, and it shocked her.

Her feelings for him scared her, terrified her.

"You're a beautiful person, Lucia. They can't see it, but I do."

"I bet you were just like them in high school," she said. She could imagine him being the star student, the jock.

"I was the rebel, Lucia. I didn't conform to what they wanted. I spent most of my time chasing after girls. I didn't bully anyone. I simply fought those that stood in my way. Do not let them get to you. I mean it."

"Thank you, Mr. Parker." She stared down at her wrist, waiting for him to let her go. When he did, she missed his touch.

"I'm not telling you this stuff because I'm your teacher," he said.

She looked back at him, surprised. "You'd be in trouble."

"Yes, I would. You're a beautiful young woman, Lucia. You've got your entire world ahead of you, and I just know you're going to live an amazing life."

She wanted to say more, to ask him more, but right now she couldn't. This wasn't the time or the place. Instead, she walked back home, just in time for the vegan delivery. Even the smell made her stomach rebel.

Sitting at the dining room table, she listened to her parents talk, one about their special case at work, the other about research. They didn't even say a word as she dumped her food in the trash and made her way upstairs. Her notebook was still on the floor. Sitting near the words she'd written, she ran her fingers across the letters, thinking about her teacher.

Attraction wasn't something she was used to, but she was attracted to him. There's no way she could let him see, and she wasn't going to become *that* girl. The one that stayed after class just to have a few moments with him, or even sit in the front. She'd move toward the back, ignore him, and just forget everything.

She had to make senior year work for her, and that was what she was going to do.

****

Monday afternoon at the beginning of September
Entering the library, Jack noticed the librarian was absent. Deciding once again to put away the books that he'd used, he made his way over to the English section and paused as he found Lucia on the floor across the aisle. Three books were open. She had her earbuds in, and she was listening to some kind of music that he didn't recognize.

Every single person in class today had handed in their homework, and he'd been tempted to make them all read theirs out, but he didn't want that. Not when he saw how nervous Lucia looked. It was wrong of him to change his lesson for one student, but he just couldn't help it.

He should just turn around, ignore this pull she seemed to have, and go the other way.

Jack didn't. Instead, he began to put his books back on the shelf and waited to see if she noticed him.

"Mr. Parker," she said, after only a couple of seconds.

Before he could say anything, she'd already taken several books from his hands, and started to place them in the right order.

"You know you could just leave them at the front desk. We can put them away. You don't have to do this."

"It's fine. I don't mind doing the extra work," he said. "Are you working on an important project?"

"Studying for a test we've got on Wednesday while also working." She nibbled her lip. "Have you had time to look at the poems yet?" she asked.

"Not yet. I'll be going over them tonight."

"Okay. I hope that's not too bad for you."

He chuckled. "Wait until we get to telling a story, then it will be something different."

She smiled. "Great, another thing to look forward to." She tilted her head to the side, and some of her brown hair fell down her back, exposing her neck.

"Well, I better get going."

"Have a nice evening, Mr. Parker."

Nodding his head, he spun on his heel and walked away. Unable to resist, he looked back and saw her standing in the same spot, looking a little lost.

Don't do this.

Don't fucking do this.

He turned back toward her and stepped closer.

"Will you be running at the park any time this week?"

"Running?"

"You know, legs, walking, but at a fast pace."

"Oh, yeah, I mean, I hadn't really set out a routine."

"I don't like the thought of you running alone. If you're going, text this number. That way I'll know, and I'll be able to keep an eye on you." He pulled out his card and handed it to her. He did this for parents of students who needed a little extra help.

She stared at his number. "You know you don't have to do this."

"The world is not a safe place. Even in a small town, there are still dangers all around."

"Thank you, Mr. Parker."

Again, he wanted to say more, but this time, he walked away and didn't look back. Grabbing his briefcase from where he'd left it on the table, he shook his head.

Giving your number to students is fucking wrong.

But Lucia, she was … different.

So fucking different it drove him crazy.

He'd noticed that she had changed places that day in class.

When she entered his classroom, he'd been looking over a book report from his previous class, and when she didn't stop at the first row, but went right to the back, near the window, he'd not liked it.

She was the only student who really listened in that class, who took in everything that he said.

Seeing her all the way back there had hurt, and he didn't get it.

No student meant more to him than the next.

Lucia … she mattered.

He'd seen the pain in her eyes when Connor said

that shit to her, and he'd also witnessed her pain on that damn bench. She meant something to him, and she wasn't just another schoolgirl.

After talking to Principal Dowed, he'd read her reports, to see that she was in fact a bright student. All the teachers had nothing but polite things to say about her. She worked hard, had good grades, worked to the best of her ability, rarely took any time off.

Her parents, though, were always absent.

There was even a note from most of the teachers to make a report card for Lucia to take home for the parents to read.

She came from two workaholic parents who seemed to care more for their jobs than their daughter.

From what he'd heard under the bleachers, her own mother wanted her to lose weight. There was pressure all around her, and he found it heartbreaking to watch, but he also understood it.

He was the son of two lawyers himself. There was rarely a time he remembered having family dinners. They expected him to achieve, and even though he was one hell of a teacher, there was an air of disappointment in his lack of drive for a more prominent position. That was their view on the choices he'd made in his life.

Teaching was something that was in his blood. He loved it, thriving to see the joy in others' eyes as they learned something from him.

His parents saw it as a mediocre profession without much pay unless he went to the private schools.

He wasn't interested in teaching at private schools.

He'd never gone to private school, even though his parents had wanted him to. They'd placed him there for three months, and he caused so much trouble they were willing to let him go to whichever school he wanted.

Lucia wasn't a hard student to understand. Where he rebelled, she conformed.

Where he broke tradition and screwed around, she stayed trapped in this world, feeling constantly alone.

From her outburst, he knew she felt broken, like a criminal, for being who she was.

Arriving back home didn't help him to feel any better. He felt fucking torn when it came to her.

"Remember your fucking rules," he said.

Grabbing a beer, he twisted the cap off and leaned against his fridge, taking a long, hard swig of the drink. It was Monday night, but right now he needed to focus, and thinking about Lucia didn't help him.

She was his student, and he needed to remember his rules. *One, never ever fuck a student. Two, never ever fall for a student. Three, don't ever break any of the first two rules.*

Nodding his head, he felt calmer, ready to face whatever shit was thrown at him.

He made himself a quick sandwich in between swigs of beer and headed back out onto his porch. Taking a seat, he enjoyed the last embers of warmth, knowing soon it would be too cold to do this and that he'd be back inside.

Finally, he opened up his file and graded a couple of tests, making notes, and then also placed advice on where students needed extra help. After an hour of grading, he couldn't put it off anymore, so he pulled out the small pile of poems he'd asked them to write.

His beer was gone, as was his food, so he took his plate and empty bottle back into the house, taking another out of the fridge. Back outside, he got comfortable and began reading.

Part of being a teacher was making notes as he

went, and he did so, grading each paper based on grammar, correct use of words, and things like that. Some of the poems weren't too bad.

Then of course he had some of the ones that just weren't worth the paper or air time.

I've go a big dick. He made a note that it's "got" not "go".

And I'm a great big prick. He looked at the author and saw it was Connor and couldn't agree more.

I screw all the girls,
Cause that's how I roll.
And this assignment is sick!

That was it. Five lines that he probably wrote while getting his dick sucked.

Putting that to one side after marking it up, Jack moved onto the next one. That was pretty much the same, and he saw it was also a friend of Connor.

Over and over, he marked up poems, some good, some bad.

Flowers are the keys to the soul,
They grow all year long, but
Their beauty is always there.
Pure like a summer's day.

That wasn't too bad. Down the pile he went until he got to the last one.

I don't know how many syllables, lines or anything. I hope this is okay.

Broken, alone, feeling blue,
The feeling never ends.
There are times I can't breathe,
The darkness swirling all around.
Only beauty matters, not real feelings.
Cut to the core, no one's perfect.
We're all flawed in our own ways.
But if you can't see it, you're set free.

No one cares as long as you're the prettiest.
What happened to skin deep?
It's all lies!

Jack sat back, seeing that this was indeed Lucia's poem. She'd given his homework a try, and he was impressed with what she'd shown him. The poem wasn't anything great, not unless you knew the author, and she'd done exactly what he'd asked her to.

She had taken a long time to look deep within herself, to find the darkness, the embers, the pain.

He felt this pain inside her.

Putting her poem down, he stood up and paced the porch.

They were all flawed. Every single human being, and she spoke of being trapped, and he felt utterly helpless.

Sitting down, he read the poem again, marking where she went wrong, the grammar mistakes, then finally, he gave her two grades. A, for content and doing what he asked, along with a C, for the actual poem.

Gathering up his work, he replaced it in his file and headed inside. He needed to clear his head, but that wasn't going to happen on a Monday night.

"You can't do this," he said. "She's a fucking student. An *underage* student."

Running a hand down his face, all he could see was Lucia's smiling face and then the tears rolling down her face on Friday night.

So much emotion, so much strength.

She didn't see it yet, but he knew it was there.

He saw it inside her.

Closing up his home, he made his way upstairs to his room. His laptop sat on his bed, taunting him. Instead of opening it up and seeing what he wanted, he made his way into the bathroom.

He stood under the spray of the cold shower, but it did little to clear his head, or appease his need.

His cock was still rock-hard as he made his way back into the bedroom. Once again, his laptop called to him, begging for him to pick it up and take a look.

Finally, he gave in to temptation and opened up the laptop. Opening his social media page, which he kept quiet, he typed in her name, only to come up with a blank name. When his searches didn't find anything, he typed in her friend's name, and there Marie was. There was a picture of Marie, but nothing of Lucia.

Didn't she do social media?

The main picture was of Marie and Lucia. They were at a beach.

Her friend wore a bikini while Lucia wore a dress. They were both smiling, and he saw the love she clearly had for her friend.

This was fucking wrong.

He shouldn't be stalking a student or trying to find her online.

Logging out of his account, he pushed his laptop to the bed and ignored the call inside him. He wasn't about to become one of *those* teachers.

He'd worked too damn hard to be where he was right now, and falling for a student, caring about her, wanting her, that was not part of his plan.

Slapping his face, he stared up at his ceiling.

"Get a grip, Parker. This is not going to happen to you."

He slapped himself again for good measure, hoping that he'd finally put some sense into himself.

Chapter Five

Running through the park, Lucia checked the time and saw it was still a little before six. She'd woken up from a nightmare, and instead of trying to sleep, she'd just decided to head on out and get in a run.

The park, for some bizarre reason, called to her, so that was why at such an early time, she was running across the route she's seen on the maps online. Clenching her hands into fists, she ignored the pain in her thighs, or the tightening in her stomach. She wanted to just stop, bend over, and pant.

She ignored those pains, but slowed down so she could last just a bit longer.

Her dream always did this to her.

She was in a forest, surrounded by faceless people. They meant nothing to her, but whenever she was in the forest, she was always terrified. She knew that death was coming.

When the first person started to hit her, she screamed, only no sound came out. For as long as she could remember this dream had been a plague to her.

Each time she had the exact same dream, sleep always failed her. Normally, she got up and watched some television or read. This time, she'd thrown her running clothes on and left the house. It wasn't like her parents would be overly concerned for her leaving.

They wanted her to lose weight.

Clicking to the next song on her phone, she was so busy looking down at her hip that she collided into a rock-hard, heavy body.

One second she was running—or speed-walking could also be used to describe what she was doing—the next, she was on her back, staring up at the sky, then up at Jack. He pulled his earbuds out, and she realized she was bumping into him a lot lately.

Keep your crush in check.

Don't embarrass yourself.

"Mr. Parker," she said, pulling her own buds out of her ears. "Morning."

She smiled up at him, and he frowned. "You didn't text me to say you were out running today."

"It was spontaneous, and I didn't think you'd be awake this early."

She lifted up a little, and Jack held his hand out to her to take.

Biting her lip, which she seemed to be doing a lot lately around him, she gave a little yelp as he lifted her up.

He was a lot stronger than she thought he would be.

Also, he hadn't let go of her hand, and it felt really good for him to hold her. She didn't want him to let her go.

"I'm always up early. No matter what time or day it is, you text me, okay?" he asked.

She forced herself to look up at him, and nod. "Okay."

"Are you all right?"

"Yes, of course. It's not every single day you'll catch me out here running. This is kind of a new phenomenon for me."

"I read your poem."

This made her gasp, and she pulled her hand away from his, only to miss the contact the moment she did it. She cursed herself for feeling anything right now.

Her tits felt heavy, and her nipples puckered.

All that teaching about sex was paying off. It's too bad she couldn't go tell her parents.

"Hey, Mom, Dad, remember all that extra homework you made me do when I was twelve? You know, the one about all the teenage sex, hormones, arousal, that kind of thing. Yeah, totally paying off. I can now see that I'm highly aroused by my English teacher, and not just that, having sex with him is hitting high on my fucking list."

If she was cussing in her mind, she needed to get a grip and fast. She was losing the plot already, and she didn't have time for this.

"Oh," she said. She had kind of forgotten about the poem. "I didn't know the specifications. There seemed to be a lot from short to long."

"You did exactly as I asked. You looked deep inside yourself, and your poem was raw. Thank you, and I happen to agree with you."

"About what?" she asked.

"People are flawed. Every single one of them. There is no perfection out there, and the prettiest, even they have pain, Lucia."

"They don't need to deal with it though."

"They still have it. Pretty, ugly, no matter who you are, flaws are out there. You just got to learn to take hold of your own and make yourself fly."

She nodded and glanced down at the ground. "Thank you."

"You're not an ugly person, Lucia."

"You keep saying that. You really shouldn't."

"I know. I'm your teacher, and I can get in trouble."

"I won't tell anyone," she said. She shrugged. "I'm not a tattletale." She licked her suddenly dry lips, and his gaze focused on them.

Her heart started to race, and she liked this. She liked having his attention focused on her.

"Why are you not on any social media pages?" he asked, changing the subject.

"Huh?"

"Social media? You know the thing that allows you guys to stay connected. Like an active beehive only online."

"I deactivated my account, why?"

"Why did you do that?" he asked.

"There was a thing a year or so ago. I came to school in a skirt, and it got lifted up. The picture ended up online, circulated, laughed at. Made coming to school really fucking miserable actually. You know, fat thighs, rubbing together, lumps and bumps," she said.

"Is that why you don't wear skirts or dresses?"

"Unless I'm with my parents I don't wear any of those things. It's no big deal." Again, she shrugged her shoulders. Glancing down at her watch, she saw it was getting late. "I need to head back home," she said. "It was nice talking to you."

"You should wear dresses and skirts again," he said.

This made her pause and turn to look back at him. "Why?"

"To stop them from winning. Every single day you don't wear what you want, you're losing your fight and they are winning."

"It's not a battle I care to win," she said.

"It should be. Your style, it's who you are. Next time, report them to the principal, or better yet, come to me. I'll deal with it."

"You'll be my personal savior."

"I'll make sure you have a senior year to enjoy and not look back with regret."

"You do this for all your students?" she asked.

"No, it seems I do this for you."

Her heart started to pound.

"And any teacher who touches you or makes you feel uncomfortable, no matter who they are, you report them too. Don't let them get away with it. Put them in their place."

"Yes, sir."

She saw his eyes flare, and instead of questioning him, she made her way back toward her home.

As she walked up the steps to her house, she saw that she was smiling. She didn't linger, quickly taking a shower from her run, drying out her hair, and changing into a pair of jeans and a shirt.

Heading downstairs, she found her parents drinking coffee.

"Morning," she said.

She put a couple of slices of bread in the toaster. For the first time, she didn't listen to what her parents had to say, but thought about Jack Parker, her English teacher. What would he have done if she had looked at him and said he could touch her anytime?

Biting her lip, she grabbed the jam with no added sugar and slathered her bread thickly. Out of the corner of her eye, she saw her mother watching her. This time, she ignored her. She didn't give a shit what her parents thought right now. Her only care was for Jack, her teacher.

Finishing off her toast, she licked her fingers, washing up the dishes.

"See you later."

Before either of them could say anything, she was out of the house and gone, her bag slung over her shoulder as she made her way across town toward the high school. She always left home early, but this was even earlier than usual.

The school was already open, and she saw

teachers parked.

She even saw Jack Parker's car already in his spot. Ignoring the tightening in her gut, she kept on walking.

She went straight to the library and sat at one of the tables. Pulling out her books, she began to study.

"You're everywhere I go today," Jack said, taking a seat at her table. Half an hour had passed, and the bell would ring in ten minutes.

She looked up from her books as he took a seat. "I got here early. I wasn't in the mood for parent drama today."

"No?"

"No."

"Then do you want to help me get a few books for my class? I could use the extra hands."

"Sure." She quickly packed her stuff away, putting the bag on her shoulder and hiking it up high.

The librarian had supplied him with several copies of William Shakespeare's complete collection of poems.

Holding several copies, she followed Jack down the long hallway to his classroom. They passed several teachers, who nodded at him.

Once inside, she put them on his desk, placing her hand on top.

"Do you want me to put these out?" she asked.

"Yes."

She moved up and down the aisles putting books on each table, aware of Jack's eyes on her. This was wrong.

She knew it was wrong and that if anyone ever even suspected their conversations, they both could be in trouble.

Her parents would freak out.

She'd have no choice but to leave school.

Once she was done, she turned to see him still staring at her.

"I better go," she said.

She wasn't even eighteen yet, and this desire she felt for him, it scared her. She didn't want him to get in trouble, but she liked that he didn't see her as "the fat girl."

"Have a good day, Lucia," he said.

She paused at his door, getting the feeling that he wanted to say more.

"You too," she finally said.

Leaving the door open, she made her way out toward her locker, and began changing the books that she would need for first period.

"Well, well, well, if it's not little chunky. Already in school? Have you eaten the cafeteria out already?" Connor asked.

She ignored him, even as his friends who were near burst out laughing.

"The only thing you'll ever get in your mouth is fucking food. No guy would want to risk his dick going in that mouth. It probably wouldn't come out."

Every single time he decided to do this, she took his insults. She listened to their crudeness, and just accepted it.

Everyone is flawed.

She was tired of being everyone's punching bag.

Her mother.

Her father.

Classmates.

She was completely fucking done, and tired of it.

Spinning around, she smiled at him. "You jealous?" she asked.

"What?" Connor asked.

She had clearly surprised him.

"You seem so obsessed with what I stuff in my mouth." She stared down his body. "Don't worry, Connor, when you're a man you'll grow balls. But I'm allergic to peanuts, so there's no way you'll be in *my* mouth." Slamming her locker closed, she patted his chest and walked off.

There was no laughter, and she heard Connor sputtering.

She wasn't allergic to peanuts.

Far from it.

Her mother just stopped buying the good peanut butter and opted for that horrible, nasty stuff that didn't taste good.

It felt good to stand up for a change. She liked it, and knew she was going to do it more often. The only power people had over her was what she let them have. She was done giving anyone any power.

****

A couple of weeks later in mid-September

In between random visits to the library, and some bumps in the park, Jack made sure he wasn't alone with Lucia again. She wasn't a dangerous student, but he didn't trust himself. He watched her walk around high school. Most of the time she was with Marie.

She still hadn't worn any skirts or dresses, but again, he'd been determined not to notice that shit.

The principal had announced a parent-teacher night, and he'd gotten the note to say that Lucia's parents intended to attend but to write a report card, just in case they didn't show.

He was pissed off for her, but he kept reminding himself that he couldn't be. This was not his place to be pissed off.

Instead, he wrote out the report card, ready for the

night.

The evening was for a Friday, and most of the students had already left. He'd made his classroom presentable.

"It's that horrible night," Beth Bertram said, coming to his room. "I hate these nights. There are some parents who don't give a shit and are here for the free food and beverages. Then there are those that care too much and want to know why you're not giving their child special privileges."

"Every child is special in their own way."

"Oh, I know, just not in a good way either." Beth smiled at him. "We've not had a chance to talk for some time. How have you been?"

"Busy. I spend most nights grading, lesson planning, that whole thing."

"Yeah, me too. You've got to remember to take some time for yourself, Jack." She patted his chest, and he didn't like her touch, not one bit.

"I'm going to get myself a drink before this entire thing kicks off. You care to join me?"

"Certainly."

He didn't offer his arm, but she took it regardless. They made their way down the long corridor toward the main cafeteria. Entering the large room, he spotted Lucia up on the ladder. Marie, her friend, was holding it, while a couple of the men and boys were off to the side, displaying the table.

What the fuck was wrong with this picture?

He knew, and saw it, and he was pissed. Marie was in no way capable of holding that ladder steady.

"What the fuck is Lucia doing up there?" he asked.

"Oh, she does this every single year. She always helps out where she can."

"I'm going to go and help." He made his way toward Marie. "I'll hold this for her."

"You sure? I'm afraid of heights so I can't go up there."

"I've got it."

Holding the ladder, he watched as Lucia pinned the large banner to the wall.

"Right, I'm coming down."

She stepped down the ladder, and he held it.

Her ass came to his face, and the scent of strawberries was intense.

"Step away, Marie, I've got to step off."

"It's not Marie," he said.

She gasped and turned to see him. "Jack. I mean, Mr. Parker."

"What you just did was careless and irresponsible."

"I do this all the time. You've seen me do it before."

"I didn't know you then. You don't do this again," he said.

"I like to help."

"You can help, just do it where you're safe."

Her gaze moved past his shoulder. "Marie was holding the ladder."

"She wouldn't have been able to help you if you'd started to fall. Do not put yourself in danger again. You may not think people care, but believe me when I say there are people who do."

He didn't want to move away, but her body was like a flame to him, and he forced himself to step back.

The past few weeks, he'd been able to get his shit together, and now there was no fucking chance of that.

"Your parents are coming?" he asked.

"They said they would. I don't know if they'll

actually show up."

"They should show up. You're worth showing up for."

She smiled. "I appreciate that."

"Hey, sorry, but Mr. Parker said that he had that ladder," Marie said, coming to them. She held a soda out to Lucia.

"Thank you," she said. "It's fine. The banner is up, and everything is all set."

"I want to know why those boys were not the ones up the ladder."

"They never do it," Marie said. "A bunch of wimps if you ask me."

"It's fine. I don't mind doing it. I can handle putting up a banner."

He wanted to say more but the principal came in, and it was time for him to get back to his classroom as parents made their way inside.

The night went by rather fast; too fast as far as he was concerned.

He was putting away his notebook as Lucia knocked at his door.

"Sorry to bother you, I don't suppose you have a report card for me to take home, do you?" she asked.

He'd completely forgotten about Lucia's parents. "A no-show?"

"It's not exactly a surprise to me." She chuckled. "This was something the principal arranged so my help doesn't go unrewarded."

"They should be here, Lucia. You're important to them."

"I know. I know. It's just … I was the mistake," she said. "You know, they both have these amazing careers, and I shouldn't have been born."

"Do I look like I give a shit about that?" he asked.

"You're here now. They need to learn to care. To fucking be here for you."

He saw tears in her eyes. "Thank you for the report card."

She was leaving his classroom, and he was pissed off.

Closing up his room, he saw Beth waiting for him. "So, I was thinking we could go and get a drink."

"I can't. I've got things to do. Take Coleman. He'd love to go for a drink with you again." He'd had to sit beside Coleman several times and listen to how much of a catch she was. He was bored and tired of hearing of the same old shit.

He got it.

Beth was a total babe, and kinky as fuck in the sack. Again, he didn't care.

He had a lot of other things on his mind. Important things.

Leaving the school, he went to his car, and saw Lucia up ahead, walking.

She was always fucking walking.

It pissed him off.

She shouldn't be walking this late at night.

Just because it was a small town didn't mean she wasn't at risk of being hurt or worse.

Climbing into his car, he drove the short distance toward her. "Get in," he said.

"You really don't need to do this."

"Do I look like I'm fucking kidding right now? Get in." Yes, his anger was starting to get the better of him, and he needed, really needed, to control his shit right now.

She stared at the car then at him. "I'm perfectly fine."

"I swear, Lucia, do you want people to witness

me picking you up and dumping you in my car? Right now, I'd even put you in my trunk. Don't even get smart with me either." He saw the attitude coming from her. "You'd fit."

She glared. "It would be a tight fit."

"You'd fucking fit so don't start with me."

"It's not fitting for you to use that kind of language."

"Bite me. Get in the car. I'm not arguing. I will make you."

She rolled her eyes and moved toward his car. She opened the door and climbed inside. "There, happy?"

"Not completely, but for now it will do. Strap in."

"You've not got far to go."

"My car. My rules."

She strapped on her seatbelt, and as he tapped on his steering wheel, he had several choices. The right choice was to take her home, and not listen to this need calling inside him to do something.

He ignored that, and instead, he spun the car around, going in the opposite direction of her house.

"Where are we going?"

"I'm not taking you home just yet."

"Why not?"

"They should have come to your parent-teacher night. You shouldn't be returning cards for them to read through."

"They're really busy, Jack. They don't have time."

"Don't have time for their own kid? My parents were fucking useless at giving a shit. Their careers were the most important thing to them, and guess what, they still had time for me. They still went to my school and dealt with all my problems. That is bullshit."

She was silent, and he kept on driving.

He headed out of town.

It was a Friday, so a lot places were packed full. He knew a nice little diner and drive-thru that sold burgers and fries.

"Do you want to eat in or in the car?" he asked.

"Eat in."

He saw the challenge in her eyes. "More than fine to me."

Climbing out of the car, he took several steps toward the diner. "I don't want you to get in trouble."

Jack stopped and turned toward her. "We won't."

"I can eat in the car."

"We won't get into trouble. We're out of town. I've never seen anyone else even come here. We're both safe here. So long as you don't mind being seen with an old man, that is."

She smiled. "Then sure. Why not?"

Taking her hand, he made his way into the diner. He found the booth and slid the menu toward her.

"Pick something."

She opened it up and scanned the menu.

"You're sure?"

"I've brought you here. The house special is pretty amazing if I do say so myself."

"Then I'll have that."

He ordered for the both of them, and sat back in his seat, watching her. The scent of strawberry was still heavy in the air, and he loved the smell.

"You have two career-obsessed parents?"

"Yes, both of them are lawyers."

"And you're not."

"Much to their annoyance, yes. Law didn't appeal to me. I don't like it, never have. They assumed my passion for teaching was just some lame-ass excuse. It wasn't. I was very fucking serious."

"You do love teaching?"

"I do. I think education is important, and I'm not giving you some bullshit here either. I'm telling you the truth. We can learn a lot by learning, by understanding, by thinking. Some teachers are naturally gifted and can have every single student eating out of the palm of their hands, and others, they're useless. They can't even hold a classroom together."

"But you love it?"

"Yes, I love it. It's … magical. Especially when you find a student who is passionate or special. They have a talent for writing and telling stories. I'd love to find that person." He watched her and smiled. "You're not special at writing."

She burst out laughing. "I didn't think I was. That poem took me hours to write. It was so hard. I didn't want to just do something stupid."

He chuckled. "Well, we'll see if your story-telling is any better soon."

"I have no talent for writing. I know that."

"What do you want to be?" he asked. "Have you gotten a focus point? Do you see where your passion is?"

"I don't know. It has been a weird couple of weeks so far. Everything seemed to have tilted on its axis, and I've been stuck in a rut on what to do."

"And now?"

"And now, I'm still in the same place. It's just not as tilted, if that makes sense."

"It makes perfect sense."

"I had so many hopes and dreams for senior year. I imagined people would let go of pettiness."

"No one lets it go. It stays with you everywhere you go, Lucia. You've got to learn to fight those feelings."

"I'm getting that, which is why the other day I stood up to Connor. I insinuated he had tiny balls and dick. It was weird, but it felt really good. Who knew insulting someone could actually make me feel better." She winced. "Nope, it didn't. It was just nice to see him shocked that I stood up for myself for a change." She paused. "I don't ever stand up for myself."

"You should."

"What were you like in high school?" she asked.

He chuckled. He couldn't help it. "You really want to know?"

"I wouldn't ask."

"Be careful what you ask for. I was the rebel. The bad boy."

"You were?"

"Yes. I did what I wanted when I wanted it. I didn't care who stood in my way. All that mattered to me was getting what I wanted."

"Wow, really? That doesn't seem who you are now?"

"It's not. I'm different now. I know what I love."

"Teaching?"

"Yes. It is a passion of mine, and I never want to give it up."

"You're a pretty good teacher."

"Well, I have some pretty awesome students who listen."

She smiled, and those dimples were back again.

The food was brought to their table, and he watched her grab her burger and take a bite. "Oh, wow, you know, I didn't know I could miss actual food."

"What do you mean?"

"My mom has got me on a vegan diet right now. So falafel, cauliflower pizza, stuff like that; tofu, tahini. Yuck. I mean seriously. It's not real food."

"That does suck."

"Yeah, add into that I've got to join this gym that she keeps going on about."

"Why don't you say no?" he asked.

"It's kind of hard to say no to your mom."

"You're going away to college soon. What are you going to do then?"

"I don't know. I guess you're right, but it's just easier to do what she wants."

He wanted to say so much more, but he couldn't. His hands were tied on this one. Picking up his own burger, he took a large bite, relishing the taste as the juicy meat rolled over his tongue. It had been a long time since he'd come here, and it was one of his favorite places in the entire world.

"I suppose I could tell her I'm running," she said.

He glanced over at her, and her cheeks were flushed. "You are running."

"Not really. I try, but I get a stitch in my side."

"You'll get used to it."

She picked up a fry, taking a bite. "I like this."

"The food?"

"No, your company. Besides Marie, I think you're the first person to treat me like an actual person, and I do like that."

"You *are* a person, Lucia." *Just one with a few extra curves.*

He shouldn't have taken her to his diner. This was the place where he liked to come to in order to think.

Taking a student to dinner wasn't what he was supposed to fucking do.

Even as he was all over the place inside his head, he smiled so Lucia didn't realize that anything was up.

"I appreciate this," she said.

"What?"

"This, taking me out. I mean, not taking me out, out, but just, you know, giving me some company before I head home. It's nice."

"I'm sorry your parents were a no-show."

"Not your fault. You don't have to say sorry for them. I didn't even expect them to come. They never did any other time of the year, why now?"

"You're alone a lot?"

"They work a lot and travel."

"They do that together?" he asked.

"Most of the time. I told you, I was the mistake child. They weren't supposed to have me, and I think if they both believed in abortion I wouldn't be here."

He didn't like that one bit.

"Don't think like that. They're your parents. They love you."

This made her laugh. "No law says they're supposed to. Take care of me, yes. That's what any normal person is supposed to do. Love me, they don't have to."

He stared at her for a long time, not really sure what to make of her statement. "Do you think they don't love you?"

"Most of the time I don't know."

They finished their food, and he turned the conversation to safer topics, school, upcoming projects. He asked her about her science assignment, and a few other things. Time flew by so fast that it seemed within a blink of an eye he was already parked outside of her home. The lights were on, but the curtains were closed.

"They're home," she said.

"I can see that."

"Thank you for tonight. I really do appreciate it."

She opened the door and climbed out.

"I enjoyed it, Lucia."

She bent down, giving him a smile. "Me too, Jack."

He watched her close the door and waited until she was inside.

It was the first time he could ever recall not wanting a woman to leave his company. He'd never had a long-term relationship. He'd always found women particularly boring, and they weren't worth his time after a few fucks.

"You shouldn't have taken her to the diner. You shouldn't keep giving her lifts home."

There were a lot of things he shouldn't be doing, but he couldn't seem to stop himself from doing all of them. She called to him, and he knew that was wrong.

It was all wrong.

Every single part of it.

She was his student.

Underage.

Forbidden.

Wrong.

He shouldn't be anywhere near her.

The best thing he could do was ask for her to be transferred to another class.

Entering his home, Jack knew he couldn't do that.

There was a trust between them, and he didn't want to be someone else in her life that ruined that trust.

Fuck.

He couldn't hurt her.

He didn't want to.

He was screwed.

Chapter Six

"As I'm sure you're all aware, there was an attack outside of Beyer Hill High School Saturday night," Coach Coleman said.

Marie grabbed her hand, giving it a squeeze, and Lucia offered the same comfort back to her best friend. She'd heard the news. A woman had gotten a flat, parked at the school, and a guy had walked over, offering to help, and the next thing, she'd been screaming.

He was about to rape her when he heard the sirens of the approaching sheriff. It had been scary, and all over the town within a matter of hours. The woman was relatively fine, shaken, scared, as they all were.

Her father had wanted to give her the car, but her mother still forbade it and told her she was to run home. She didn't even argue.

Her gaze landed on Jack Parker. He'd been warning her about this.

It was Monday, and she'd heard that each year from junior up had been taken into the gym to be taught some self-defense.

She stood in her shorts and shirt with the school logo across her breast. He'd seen her in shorts before, but this felt more intimate. This emphasized that she was a high school girl, and she didn't want him to see that, or to think of her as a young girl.

"What are you staring at?" Marie asked.

"Nothing. I'm listening."

"So, with that in mind, the principal has asked me to conduct some self-defense lessons. Now, this attack was real. That poor woman is in the hospital recovering, and because of the severity of the attack, your partner has to be male. Same goes for the boys, pick a girl. Two minutes, I want you on the mat."

They both groaned. They were always each other's partner. No one was picking, so Coach Coleman took over, and teamed everyone up, and once he did that, there was no one else to argue with, and yes, of course, Lucia had to join with Connor.

She didn't look over at Jack.

Stop thinking of him as Jack.

The last thing she wanted to do was call him that and then have people, or Marie, question her.

Mr. Parker.

Mr. Parker.

She said his name over and over in her head, making sure she got his name right.

Mr. Parker.

"I wonder if I can even lift you up. Don't you weigh, like, a ton?"

"Wow, and here I thought you had a brain," she said. "Believe me, I don't want to be here with you."

They stood on the mats, facing each other.

She didn't like Connor, or his sneer.

"Right, ladies, turn your backs on your partner. We're going to deal if they come up behind you on the attack." Unwillingly, she turned her back, not wanting to do so to Connor.

"Nice ass, Deen."

She rolled her eyes.

"Now, put your hands on your partner's hips. This is not sex or copping a feel. We're being serious right now."

The moment Connor put his hands on her hips, she jumped back, not wanting his touch.

"Sir, I object," she said, feeling her cheeks heat as every single person in the room looked toward her.

She refused to look at Mr. Parker.

"What the hell for?" Coach Coleman asked.

"I just think this is a little … sexist. I mean, what's to say girls didn't attack the boys?" God, she felt so embarrassed right now. She wanted the ground to open up and swallow her whole.

Of course, it didn't. Like always, it completely ignored her.

Stupid ground.

"A woman was attacked."

"Yes."

"So we're doing this to help you."

"Come on, Deen, Scared that you can't defeat me?" Connor asked.

She looked toward Mr. Parker. He stood not too far away. His brow rose, but it was the look in his eye that told her she was safe. He wouldn't let anything happen to her, even though Connor was known for getting his father to get him out of trouble. Not once had he ever gotten in to trouble for anything. There had been many times she swore he was high on something. There were always rumors swirling around about his drug use.

"Sorry," she said. "My mistake."

Mr. Parker gave her a slight nod, and she forced herself to turn her back on Connor once again.

She averted her gaze from the teacher she was seriously struggling to control her feelings for and caught Marie's gaze.

"*What the fuck?*" She mouthed the words.

Lucia shrugged and flinched as Connor put his hands on her hips.

Coach Coleman wouldn't let them go any further, explaining how this simple touch could bring a woman down from a simple push, to a pull, to a stripping of her dignity.

She hated this, especially as they were told to

push.

Lucia lost her balance and fell onto the mat, and within seconds Connor was on top of her.

"I always knew you wanted me on you, Deen. You're practically begging for it. Fat chick like you should be lucky to have me."

Unable to resist, without any word of coaching from Coleman, she brought her knee up hard, slamming it against his dick. He released her, and with a quick turn, she straddled him, grabbing his arms, and pinning him down.

"You've got that wrong, asshole," she said.

Once again, she was aware that people were staring at her. She had just reacted, and she quickly released Connor's hands, sitting back, only to find that Connor was in fact hard beneath her. Grossed out, she quickly tried to move away, but Connor stopped her, holding her in place as Coach Coleman came over.

"What happened here?" he asked.

"She got the better of me," Connor said. "Not that it was hard. She weighs more than me."

Her cheeks were on fire as she stared up at Coleman. Mr. Parker approached, and she couldn't bring herself to look at him, not right now. Not sitting straddled across someone else, especially as that someone happened to be the guy who liked to bully her, to torment her, and he was fucking aroused by doing it, the asshole.

"Let her go, Connor," Mr. Parker said.

"But it's so nice having her here."

She slammed her hand against his chest and climbed off him.

"I demand a partner change," she said.

"Not happening. You two can be our demonstrators and the others can copy. You kneed him in the balls?" Coach Coleman asked.

"Self-defense."

"I don't care what it was. You did a good tackle there, Deen. Well done."

Coleman got her back into position, this one a standing position again. Using her and Connor as the demonstrators, he made them both work through each retaliation and each defense maneuver, and she did everything she could to avoid eye contact with Connor and Mr. Parker. She didn't want to think about how guilty she felt at straddling Connor's hips, or that he'd been hard while doing so.

She wasn't an idiot. She knew what arousal and sex were all about.

She just hadn't expected that reaction from Connor, and she didn't like it. He was a sick pervert.

By the end of the lesson, she'd had enough of touching Connor and having his hands on her.

They were sitting grouped together, and she sat with Marie.

"To be safe, you must be with someone. Have your cell phone on hand, and always keep your guard up. Until this son of a bitch is caught, I want to make sure all students are taken care of. Dismissed."

She got to her feet about to follow Marie into the changing room when she tripped on her shoelace, which had come undone.

"Shoot, go, I'll be there in a second." Bending down, she quickly tied her shoelace, and was heading back toward the changing rooms when she was suddenly pulled inside a cleaning closet.

She gasped and nearly screamed as a hand covered her mouth. The moment the light came on, she saw it was Mr. Parker, and any fight she had left her.

He'd pulled her into a closet?

Slowly, he released her, dropping his hand down from her face.

"Are you okay?" he asked.

"Yeah, I'm fine."

"I wanted to intervene."

"It's fine. There was nothing you could do. I was perfectly safe."

She knew she was. After her first tackle on Connor, Mr. Parker had stayed close, and it helped that Coach Coleman had used them to aid with the class, doing many demonstrations.

"I didn't like seeing his hands on you."

She couldn't help but smile, and she quickly looked down at the ground. "I didn't like them on me, if that helps."

She didn't know what to say or what to do.

They were on dangerous ground here. She wasn't a fool and knew what this could mean.

"It was an intense class," she said.

"No one will ever hurt you."

She placed her hand on his chest and quickly pulled away from him. This was wrong. She shouldn't be having feelings for him.

He loved his job, and there was no way in hell that she could ever, ever, do this to him.

"I … I can't. I've got to go," she said.

Mr. Parker didn't move away.

This was wrong.

Why did it feel so good? So right?

She brushed past him, leaving the cleaning closet even though all she wanted to do was find out exactly what he meant.

Making her way into the changing room, she saw Marie was already partly dressed.

"What took you so long?"

"Nothing. My lace was being a pain in the ass." It was a lie, but it wasn't like she could tell her the truth.

"So you're totally getting a lift home with me," Marie said. "Your mother is a first-class bitch. Your dad is fine though."

"I can walk."

"Not now. I couldn't handle anything happening to you."

"You're so sweet." She pulled her friend into a hug, kissing her cheek. "I love you, too."

"Yeah, yeah. Who else would I go to for my movie marathons?"

"That is completely true. You would be doomed to watch your Brad Pitt, Matt Damon, and every other guy that is flavor of the month for a long time."

She pulled her hair out of the ponytail that she'd placed it in.

Their class was the last one of the day. "I've still got to go to my locker," she said.

"I'll go warm up the car."

They went their separate ways, Marie heading out while she went to her locker. Once there, she quickly put in the code, and opened up the locker.

"Hey, Deen," Connor said, standing behind her.

She grabbed her books and tried to ignore him. He didn't walk away, nor did he trip her, or do anything else.

He just stood there, glaring at her. His eyes looked a little dilated.

With the last book out of the locker, she shoved it in her bag and turned toward him. He was still staring at her.

"What?" she asked.

"Good lesson."

"Okay." She went to move past him, but he

stepped closer, putting a hand on the locker behind her head. They were alone, and she didn't like this. "What are you doing?"

"You won't tell anyone what you felt. Not that anyone would believe you. There's no way in hell I could ever like a fat bitch like you," he said.

Her cheeks heated, and she shook her head. "Of course I won't. You think I want to remember that? Or that I even wanted to feel that? You're disgusting."

She shuddered.

Connor was about to say something else when they heard voices. Within seconds he was gone, and she was confused. Glancing down the hall, she saw Ms. Bertram with Mr. Parker, and pain sliced right through her.

The older woman placed a hand on his arm and laughed at something he said. There was also a smile on his face, and it just hurt. She shouldn't be feeling this way, not about Jack, not about anything.

He was her teacher, but seeing him with a woman of his own age, it seemed to drill into her that these feelings, they were one-sided.

She couldn't think that because they'd had a burger together that anything else would happen. Far from it.

Nothing was going to happen.

He was her damn teacher, and that didn't mean anything.

Pulling away from the locker, she caused it to make a noise, drawing their attention. She averted her gaze and quickly left the school. Marie was sitting in her car, music blaring.

"What took you so long?"

"Are you the time police?" she asked, forcing a smile.

"Ha-ha, come on, let's get you home, my little pretty."

Marie pulled out of the parking spot, looking behind her.

Lucia stared at the front and watched as Mr. Parker came out of the building. He was looking down the street, and as Marie began to turn, he caught sight of her.

Her heart pounded, but she ignored it. There was no way she could ever trust anything like this.

Marie drove down the street.

"You'd think your mother would have allowed you to get a car or something."

"It's my mom. She doesn't believe in cars or helping anyone out. You know that."

"She's a first-class bitch. I think you should come and have a sleepover."

"Maybe another night. I've got a ton of homework, and I want to get it finished."

"Sure, sure. We'd be talking all night long, so I get it."

She smiled at her friend, and it wasn't long before they were singing along to the songs that were blasting out as Marie took her home.

All too soon, she was home, and from the dark windows, no one else was home.

Yay.

"I'll pick you up tomorrow morning. Don't even start with me. Tell them that we're working on a super-secret project with each other," Marie said. "Or something. I don't care. I'm not leaving you to walk on your own."

"Thank you."

She hugged her friend and climbed out of the car. Marie didn't leave as she entered her home, flicking on the lights. She checked every single door and window to make sure she was safe.

She was acting like a crazy person, but that didn't stop the nerves.

Someone had been attacked outside of the high school, and it did scare her. It must have scared a lot of people because they wouldn't be forcing them to teach self-defense.

Once she checked the entire house, she made her way to the kitchen, putting herself together a quick sandwich, and of course the only spread that was available was one with damn tahini in it.

Making her way upstairs to her bedroom, she spread her homework out, and started working on each piece. Marie texted her to let her know she'd gotten home, and Lucia sighed in relief. She loved her friend. Marie was the closest she had to a sister.

She finished her sandwich, then her homework, and sat back, leaning against her bed. She dropped her head back looking up at the ceiling. Her thoughts returned to Mr. Parker. The man she couldn't have.

He was … different.

She'd never been drawn to a teacher before, but he was easy to look at, to be close with. It was all just hard right now to even process what the hell was going on.

He was older than she was, and he was her teacher.

Grabbing her laptop, she opened it up and stared at her internet search browser.

She didn't have parental control on her laptop or any part of her life.

Biting her lip, she hesitated for a split second before finally caving and typing in her search.

"What is sex like with an older guy?" She read it

out as she typed. She hovered over the enter button, and even though she regretted it, she pressed it.

Images, articles, and other items came up.

She clicked her way through, seeing some porn scenes and a few other things. Watching the porn movies, she watched as the older man drove his dick deep inside the younger woman. Moaning echoed around the room, and she felt her pulse race just thinking about Jack doing that to her.

What would it feel like to be in his arms?

To allow the forbidden?

This attraction she felt toward him wasn't going away, and it was only getting stronger. Closing the search down, and removing it from her history, she put her laptop on the floor beside her. She had to get a grip. This wasn't doing her any good, and she didn't want to deal with this.

Scared, terrified, panicked, aroused—she felt it all.

She was his student.

There's no way he'd ever consider looking at her.

She wondered if Rachel, the most popular girl in school, would take no for an answer.

"Get your head out of the gutter. It doesn't matter anymore. Not one tiny little bit." She got to her feet, grabbed her plate, and put it in the sink.

The house creaked a little as it warmed up, and for the first time, the noise worried her.

This was what happened when an attack happened in a small town. She started hearing things.

"It's just the house settling," she told herself.

Moving into the sitting room, she glanced out of the window, and thought she saw something in the garden. She was about to go and check it out when she heard her parents' car pull into the driveway. As she looked out, whatever it was had gone.

She frowned and moved away from the window, going to greet her mom and dad.

They were talking to themselves. They hugged her, kissing her forehead, but for the most part, completely ignored her.

She wasn't surprised by that either. They always seemed to be doing that.

****

Jack pushed himself just a little harder. It was already getting cooler as summer let go to fall. The leaves on the trees were already starting to change color and drop to the ground. Pushing himself up the mud-slicked hill, he listened to the blaring rock music, trying to focus on something else, not on the same scene going on and on inside his head.

Always the same.

Connor whispering something to Lucia as he moved between her thighs, the fire blazing in her eyes as she kneed him in the nuts and moved to straddle him. Something passed between the two, and Lucia had tried to get off him, but the kid held her in place, stopping her from moving.

When she was finally able to get to her feet, he'd seen the hard-on that Connor was trying to hide. He'd wanted to fucking hurt that kid, to teach him a lesson about touching what belonged to him.

He released a growl, running harder, pushing his body to the limit as those same thoughts, those memories, kept on circling around his head. Gritting his teeth, he tried to think of something else, but he couldn't.

Jack didn't have her number either, so he couldn't even call her to make sure she was okay. She'd seen him with Beth. The other teacher had propositioned him again, and he'd turned her down, not wanting to be with her.

She's a fucking student.
Lucia isn't mine.
She's underage.
Not for much longer.

Lucia wasn't like any normal seventeen-year-old. She didn't act like a spoiled brat or a girl.

Over and over, he kept on pushing, driving himself harder so that he could clear his mind, but the running wasn't helping. It was only making him angrier. She was such a beautiful, sweet young woman.

He adored her smile.

The laughter that he caused, and so much else.

It was easy to talk to her, to be with her.

When he was in her company, he could completely forget her age, and the fact that he was her damn teacher.

He rounded a large bush and knocked someone on their ass from the impact of his run.

Pulling his music from his ears, he saw the subject of his troubled thoughts was on the ground, touching her chest.

"Shit, we have got to stop doing this," he said.

"You need to work out a route so that I can avoid this one." She didn't take his hand and stood up on her own.

Her cheeks were flushed, and she wore a large shirt that covered all of her curves. The shorts she wore went to her knees, and he felt like a fucking voyeur taking what he could get.

She pushed some of the mud and fallen leaves from her back.

Jack just drank her in.

"You didn't text me," he said.

"What?"

"To let me know you're running."

"I was supposed to?"

She had an attitude, and he didn't like it.

"What's going on?" he asked.

"I came out here for a run. Nothing is going on. I need to know the route you run in because we keep doing this and my butt can't keep taking the fall."

She rubbed her ass, and he wanted to do that; to rub it better.

Too fucking young.

"It's not safe out here, not for you."

"Don't worry, I know how to knee them. I think I got the handle on that."

"Yeah, but you couldn't stop them from stopping you moving," he said. "Connor liked having you in place, didn't he?"

Her cheeks heated even more, and he felt like a total asshole for spitting it out.

"Then why don't you ask Ms. Bertram? I think she'd love to have you running."

She made to move past him, but he caught her hand. "It's not safe for you. When are you going to learn?"

Lucia pulled her hand away from him. "I am safe. I just needed a run to clear my head, okay? Is it so hard to understand?"

"You can run, but you're not doing it alone. Your parents may not give a shit, but I'm not them. You want to run to clear your head, that's fine. I'll stay a few feet behind you." He placed one of his earbuds in and stepped behind her.

"Are you serious right now?"

"You want to run, that's fine. I get it. Running helps me to clear my head as well. You're not doing it alone, and seeing as it's late, dark, and you're pissed, I'll make sure we're both safe."

He saw her hands clenched at her sides.

"Unless you want me to take you home."

"No. I don't want to go home. I want to run."

"Then fucking run, Lucia," he said, finally yelling the words.

She glared at him, and before he was ready for it, she took off.

Jack ran after her, keeping pace. It wasn't hard to as she kept on running, and he followed her.

He listened to his music as his blood pumped inside him.

Chasing her, running after her, wasn't part of the plan, but as he watched her, he couldn't help the fire building inside him.

He wanted to chase her, only he didn't want to take her home.

These feelings were fucking destroying him, and they weren't even through their first semester.

He was completely screwed.

She was his student.

There was no way he could have anything else.

Even as he thought it, an overwhelming sadness overcame him.

Lucia needed someone to take care of her. No one else took care of her. Marie did, but only to the point of a friend.

Her parents pushed her aside, forcing her to grow up.

He knew all about that and could relate to her. It was always hard to be forced to grow up, to have your parents constantly push you aside until you show that you have a great mind.

His own parents had done the same to him until he'd proven that he was an intelligent man.

Right now, that intelligence was the furthest thing he had.

He wasn't thinking straight.

Lucia was a student.

He shouldn't be running in a park with her, chasing after her, making sure she was safe.

This was wrong.

He knew it.

She knew it.

At any time, she could report his ass to the principal, but she hadn't. Instead, she looked pissed and sounded jealous because she'd seen him with Beth, even though seconds later he'd turned her down again.

Some women liked a challenge, and he'd become that for Beth.

After ten minutes, Lucia slowed down, and finally stopped, bending forward. Her hands went to her knees as she took several deep breaths. He watched her, unable to look away even if he wanted to.

"Meeting you for a run isn't right," she said, panting out each word.

"I don't care. You're not going to call anyone else to make sure you're all right."

"I don't need anyone to take care of me, Jack. I've been doing it fine for a long time."

He took a step toward her and forced himself to stop.

This wasn't right.

"Nothing happened between Beth and me."

"Beth?"

"Ms. Bertram."

She licked her lips and looked away. "You're my teacher."

"I know."

"Why is it so hard to just think of you as my

teacher?" she asked. "I've been doing fine. More than fine. I get up, go to school, do my lessons, and then I go home, stuff happens, I wake up. Do the entire thing again. Only now I like you taking me home. I like bumping into you running. I … you love teaching."

"Yes."

"And I'm only seventeen."

"Nothing is happening here," he said, lying completely.

She placed a hand to her head, and he watched as she checked the time. "I've got to go home."

"Let me walk you."

"It's not really safe for you to keep being seen with me. The wrong person sees and we're in the office explaining stuff."

"But nothing has happened, Lucia. It won't happen." He was stronger than that. She nodded her head.

"You're right."

He followed behind her as she walked all the way home. At her gate, she paused and glanced back. He saw so much in her eyes. The yearning, the need; so much, and all he wanted to do was fucking protect her.

That was something he couldn't do right now.

She ducked her head and made her way inside.

They couldn't have this.

He ran back to his place, taking a quick shower before changing into his suit. Grabbing his briefcase, he was in his car and heading toward the school.

This time he didn't stop at the library, nor did he check to see if she'd arrived safely. There had to be some distance created; there had to be.

Entering his classroom, he wrote on the white board what the start of class would be, then made his way toward the staff room. Derick and Beth were already there, sipping their coffee.

"You two okay?" he asked. "Looking really snuggly." He turned back to the coffee machine, rolling his eyes. *Snuggly?* What the fuck was that?

"Derick was just telling me about your self-defense class yesterday."

Jack nodded. "It went really well."

"You don't think it's a bit much teaching a bunch of kids to defend themselves?" Beth asked.

"Not at all. Someone was attacked. We need to make sure the students all know how to handle that situation. Speaking of, any news from the hospital?"

"Broken wrist and some bruises, but she'll make a full recovery. They don't have a clue who it was. He kept her eyes covered and didn't speak," Derick said.

"Anything on the security cameras?" Jack asked.

"Nothing. It was just a random attack. It may not have even been a local guy. Just some punk ass passing through."

Normally, he went back to his classroom, but right now he didn't want to be alone with his thoughts. After this morning's run, he needed to clear his head.

"Has this ever happened before?" he asked.

"Not that I know of. It's a pretty safe place. Not many people here who would attack someone else. I mean, if it was two kids then I'd have pointed the finger at them at school."

"Hey, did you see the boner on that kid yesterday, Connor?" Derick asked.

Jack gripped his cup. The last thing he wanted to think about right now was kids, boners, and Lucia.

"What?" Beth asked.

"Connor and that fat chick, what's her name?" He looked at Jack, but he shrugged his shoulders. There was no way he'd think of Lucia as "the fat chick." The thought alone was offensive to him. "Deen kid?"

"Lucia Deen?" Beth asked.

"That's the one. They were partnered up, and I don't know what happened but she got the better of him. Had him pinned to the mat and when she climbed off, kid's boner was showing. Fucking ridiculous."

"Lucia's not fat," Jack said, looking at the two of them.

"We know we're not supposed to say anything, but she is bigger than a lot of her peers."

"That doesn't make her fat. There are models out there that are bigger than others, but that doesn't make them fat."

"No, that makes them plus-size," Beth said. "What's the matter?"

"How do we expect our students to stop bullying when we can't even stop doing it?" Jack asked.

He glanced up at the clock, tired of the conversation.

"I've got to get to class."

He took his coffee with him, leaving the staff room.

"Jack, Jack, I'm sorry. I didn't know this was a touchy subject for you," Beth said, following him.

She put a hand on his arm, and he wasn't interested in her touch at all.

"Look, I don't like it, okay? I figure the girl gets enough from her peers. The least we could do is stop all the judgment."

"Lucia's a good kid," Beth said.

She's not a fucking kid.

"I've got to get to class."

"Okay, I'm sorry. Lunch?"

"Yes." He had no intention of sticking around for lunch. He'd probably eat a snack in his car or something.

Right now, he really wasn't the best company.

Rounding the corner, he stopped as he caught sight of Lucia at her locker. There were only a couple of students milling around. No one paid any attention to him, and he sipped at his coffee, watching her.

She had a book open in her locker. She'd placed the tip of her shoe on the floor and was waving it back and forth as if she was completely lost in a world of her own. Her hair was down once again, the brown locks seeming to have a natural wave. The jeans she wore molded to the curves of her ass, and instead of wearing a shirt three times too big, she actually wore one that seemed to accentuate her figure.

He watched as Connor made his way over to her.

His friends were watching, and Jack could see this wasn't a trick as they looked genuinely shocked by his sudden interest. Something else was going on though. Connor wasn't the kind of guy to turn like this, not without a reason.

He rested a hand above her locker, leaning in close. "Hello, baby."

She jerked up as if she'd been hit. Her gaze landed on Connor, and then she frowned. The book she'd been reading snapped shut, and Jack's heart sped up.

He recognized the front cover as one filled with poems. It was one of the books he'd taken back to the library and recommended to her.

"What do you want?" she asked.

Connor reached out to tuck some hair behind her ear, but she swatted his hand away.

"What the hell?"

"I'm only trying to help you out," Connor said. "After all, we made such good partners yesterday. Just want to make sure you understand the deal with it."

"Yeah, this is not happening, ever." She grabbed

her bag, stuffed her book inside, and slammed her locker.

"Come on, and here I thought you liked me. Here I am showing you attention. You could be nice to me and I'll make your life a lot easier."

"Are you insane?" she asked.

Jack didn't like the way this was going.

There was no way he could stand and watch. Rounding the corner, he made his way over as he saw the discussion getting heated.

"What's going on here?" Jack asked.

He kept his gaze on Connor, not trusting himself to look at Lucia.

"Nothing is going on here, teach. Just talking to a friend."

Connor went to put his arms around her, but she dodged his hold. "I've got to go to class."

She spun on her heel and quickly made her escape.

Connor watched her go, but he watched the kid.

"You don't get to treat a girl like crap for a long time and then expect a date," Jack said.

"Get over yourself. I don't want to fucking date the fat pig."

Jack stepped closer, staring at him. "You may have gotten a hard-on yesterday and realized that all this time you've been calling her fat, you didn't know what you were missing."

"Well, teach, you got a hard-on for a student now?"

"I'm looking out for all of my students, Connor, and I don't like the reputation you have. Your daddy may like to get certain allegations squashed or disappeared, but I know the truth. She doesn't want you, and you like that you make her uncomfortable."

Connor looked cocky as he walked away. "We'll

see. Every chick has a price. I just got to find out hers. I always have what I want."

Jack watched him go. The kid was clearly high.

He wasn't afraid of the Connors of this world. Never had been.

They were cocky sons of bitches who thought the people around them were their slaves, and the world their domain.

This was something he was going to have to keep an eye on. He didn't like the thought of Lucia being in any danger, and it would seem she was on more than his radar right now.

Making his way to class, he pushed those thoughts to one side and focused on his lesson.

He found a budding new student in freshman year who had a keen eye for poetry. He made a quick note in his books to keep an eye on the young man.

This was why teaching was so important to him. He didn't know who he was inspiring for the next generation, but he took everything he did seriously. This was his world, his life, and he had no intention of leading anyone astray.

At lunchtime, he made his way out toward his car with every intention of eating. Only, Lucia sat on a bench all by herself. Her hair fell over one shoulder, and she looked far ahead of her as if she wasn't even seeing anything.

"Why don't you ever eat in the cafeteria?" he asked.

"I pack my own lunch. You never know what they put in the food here," she said, holding out her tray. "Zucchini chip?"

"Zucchini chip? You're not a vegetarian."

"I know that, and my mom knows that, but she likes me to eat food that is full of vegetables and flavor."

She wrinkled her nose as she took one. "Marie had to leave early today, otherwise I'd have shared some of her food."

"Why do you put up with it?"

"It's not so bad. After you get over not liking zucchini you kind of get used to it." Again, she wrinkled her nose. "It's easier. At least with this attack I don't have to make excuses about not going to the gym, so yay." She held both of her thumbs up at him, and he chuckled, finding her utterly cute.

He glanced around the parking lot, spotting Connor's car in the corner. "I need you to be careful with boys like Connor."

"He's an asshole, but for the most part he's harmless."

"Connor's the kind of guy that doesn't take no for answer."

She snorted. "Please, for most of our life he's been calling me fat, cow, and all the names similar to it."

"Yeah, only the other day he finally got to feel what you're really like, and he knows you're not fat but curvy." He gritted his teeth, realizing what he'd just said.

"You think I'm curvy?" she asked.

"I know you are."

He stared at her again.

Everything fell away for him. She was the only person he was interested in.

Lucia was the first one to look away, and he kicked himself.

"I'm sorry about being angry with you this morning. I shouldn't have been angry."

"Apology accepted. Don't go out after dark or earlier. I don't want you to get hurt."

A wind blew, and her hair covered her face. She pushed it out of the way with a big smile.

"Okay. I may even text you when I do leave."

"You'd better. Is Marie coming back to school?"

"No. She has a dentist appointment, so she'll be sobbing on her sofa eating ice cream and using any excuse she can to have her mother wait on her." She smiled.

"I'll drive you home."

"You don't need to do that."

"I'll drive you. No questions."

"Yes, sir."

Chapter Seven

Friday, start of October

Lucia rolled over and stared up at the ceiling.

Eighteen.

She couldn't believe she'd made it.

Legally an adult now.

Eighteen years old.

Pushing her hair off her face, she kept her gaze on the ceiling, waiting to see what would happen. She felt a little different. It was kind of surreal and not easy for her to place what she was feeling exactly.

Getting older was a rite of passage.

Her parents had said it would bring a lot of changes, but she'd already been dealing with them when she was fifteen and they had their first convention abroad. It was the first time she was home all on her own. That had been a weird experience for her.

There was a knock at her door, and she sat up.

"Come in," she said.

Her parents had started knocking when her dad walked in on her to discover her completely naked and fighting with a bra. She'd then walked in on her parents making out in the bathroom, which was why an en-suite bathroom was installed for her, and knocking was a rule within the Deen household.

Both of her parents entered, and she smiled. They were still dressed in pajamas, which was strange for the two of them.

"Morning," she said, looking between the two of them.

"Happy Birthday, sweetheart," they said.

She squealed as they dived on the bed and began raining kisses all over her face and tickling her.

Neither of them had done this since she was a kid, and having it now seemed kind of strange to her.

She loved it though, laughing as they tickled her, until they all collapsed on the bed.

"Eighteen, wow, I feel old," her mother said.

She giggled. "It's not that old."

"I feel it right now. I never thought this day would come."

"Neither did I. I remember when you took your first steps, and said my name," her father said.

"Let's not forget blowing out the candles on her first cake, crawling, potty training."

"That is just gross now," Lucia said. "Yes, I've come a long way. I use the bathroom now. I call you both Mom and Dad, and I even walk to school and back on my own."

"Not now you don't," her father said.

"What?"

He held up the keys.

"You got me a car?"

"We wanted it to be a surprise for you. We felt you were too young to have a car," her mother said.

"Wait, I thought you didn't want me to have a car because of my weight?" Lucia sat up, taking the keys from her dad before he changed his mind.

"That was part of a reason I made up," Patricia said. "It wasn't entirely true." Her mother kissed her cheek. "I know we're not the best parents in the world. I only want what's best for you. We both do," she said.

"We'd talked about making the car your present for your eighteenth. You'll be going to college soon, and we wanted you to get used to having the car. You've proven to us more than once that you're a lot older than your years."

"Your report cards are excellent," Patricia said.

"We read them, and we are really sorry we didn't get to make it."

"It's fine."

"I hate it," Bill said. "Even your school doesn't expect us to turn up."

"I don't care, because right now I'm eighteen and I can drive." She climbed off the bed. She ran to her father, kissing his cheek, then to her mother. "Thank you. Thank you. Thank you."

"Tonight, we're going out. We're taking you to dinner," her father said.

She winced and looked at her mother.

"It's not a vegan place." She held her hands up. "I know. I cannot stand another vegetable. Burgers, greasy food, the works, I'm ready for it."

"Yes." Lucia smiled, and looked at her parents. "Can I get ready for school? I want to go and pick Marie up."

"Sure, sure," Bill said. He moved toward her, kissing her head. "Drive safe."

"I will."

Patricia pulled her in for a hug. "I don't like that you're growing up, but I know it's happening. You're a wonderful daughter."

She held her mother tightly against her. "I love you both as well."

Lucia waited for them both to go, and quickly changed into a pair of jeans, a shirt, and she even pulled her hair up into a bun, having it off the back of her neck.

Staring at her reflection in the mirror, she felt … amazing, strong.

"You're not going to be that sad, miserable person. Not again. It's your life, Lucia. Make of it what you will." She smiled, feeling a little silly that she was talking to herself.

Running downstairs, she grabbed a slice of toast, shouting bye to her parents. The car had a massive bow around it, and she loved it. It was a four-wheel drive, shiny, black, and just what she loved.

Climbing behind the wheel, she pulled out of the driveway and made her way toward Marie's home.

As she was driving, she realized there wasn't going to be a single excuse now for Jack to take her home. Rather than be delighted by that, she felt … sad.

Forcing those thoughts down, she parked outside Marie's home and honked the horn.

It didn't take long for Marie to come out.

Winding down her window, she struck a pose for her friend.

"What do you think?"

"I don't know, did you steal it?" Marie asked, laughing.

"My parents got it me for my birthday. Isn't that awesome? It's so pretty, Marie. Don't you think it's awesome?" She ran her hand down the side of her car door. It was still new, so no dirt was on the body of the car.

She was so fucking happy right now.

"I can't believe your parents finally caved," Marie said.

"I know. They surprised me with it this morning. Also, we're having dinner later as well. It's going to be awesome." Even as she spoke those words, she knew the chance of her parents remembering or even turning up was slim. They hadn't told her what the name of the restaurant that was booked or the time of their reservation. She knew next to nothing about that.

"I don't want to sadden you, Lucia."

"You won't. It's my day, and it's going to be awesome. I refuse to allow anything to get me down, but

I get it. You're just looking out for me."

Marie hugged her arm and placed a kiss on her cheek. "Happy birthday, how does it feel to be old?"

"Like I can tell you what to do for a change, so buckle up."

"Seriously?"

"This is my car, and I have my license, and I don't intend to lose it. Buckle up."

Marie chuckled as she pulled away from the curb. Lucia was on cloud nine, and there was no way anyone was going to drag her down.

"Have you had sex or something?" Marie asked.

Lucia burst out laughing. "Are you serious right now?"

"You seem different."

"I do? I feel a little different. I guess growing old has that effect on you. No, I've not had sex or anything. I can't even believe you'd ask that."

"You never know. It's not, like, the normal thing to wait for the right guy."

"I get that, and I'm not waiting for any guy, okay. Everyone is having sex now. I told you when my parents gave me *the talk* it was so embarrassing."

"My parents told me if I come home pregnant they'd kill me," Marie said. "Then of course my mom got all teary-eyed, and Dad caved."

"Your parents are awesome."

"Yours are as well."

"I guess we can agree to disagree on that. My parents are awesome, but at least yours turn up to parent-teacher night. Mine have a reputation for being no-shows."

"It could be worse," Marie said.

"How worse?"

"They could have put your ass in foster care."

"There is that." She shook her head. "I can't even believe we're talking about this right now. I don't want to hear another sad comment at all. Promise."

"Promise. I like this. You've got attitude."

Lucia laughed and turned on the music. The drive to school didn't last very long, but yelling out words to a song that she couldn't even remember the title of felt so good.

Parking her car in Marie's usual spot, she climbed out, beeping it shut.

"Wait, I have your present," Marie said.

Tucking some of her hair that had escaped, Lucia leaned against the car as Marie pulled out her present.

Opening it up, she smiled as soon as she saw the picture frame. It had the two of them at the beach, and it was one that she really loved. It had been a hard day at home, and rather than mope around, Marie had driven them to the nearest ocean to allow her to stand at the edge and the waves lap at her feet.

She'd loved it as they ate ice cream, and just relaxed.

"This is awesome, Marie, thank you."

"And this."

This was a smaller box. Handing the picture frame back to her friend, she opened it up. It was two severed hearts with the words *Best Friends*.

"This is beautiful."

Putting the picture frame in the car, she grabbed one necklace and slid it around Marie's neck, and then her friend did the same to her.

"Best friends forever and always," Marie said.

Hooking her arm into her friend's, they entered the school. They went to Marie's locker first.

"I'm thinking we need to do a Mark Ruffalo marathon," Marie said.

"You can pick whichever actor you want. You're the movie buff, not me."

"We've not done it, and I totally watched one of his movies the other night and it was fantastic."

"Then we'll do a marathon. Shall I come over to your place? My parents are home this weekend." She knew that Marie didn't get along with her mom. It always worked best to keep Pat and Marie away from one another.

"Sure, we can do it at my place."

"Excellent."

"What you got right now?" Lucia asked.

"I've got art class."

"That's opposite of my locker. I've got math. You go. I'll head to my locker and meet up with you for lunch."

"It's your birthday. We should have gone to your locker first."

Lucia laughed. "Stop being such an oddball. I'm fine to walk to my locker regardless of the day." She hugged her friend before heading back toward her own locker.

Hooking her bag over her shoulder, she pulled it around and opened it up. She took out the two English books, trading them for the math ones.

Lost in her own little world, she let out a gasp as a hand suddenly appeared near her locker.

"Well, hello there," Connor said.

This was, like, the fifth time in one week that he'd decided to be nasty and nice to her. She didn't buy any of it. It was like he wanted to use her or he thought she was an easy target to sleep with. She wasn't interested in anything to do with Connor. He creeped her out, even when he was trying to be nice.

Jack's warning also echoed around her head, and

she wasn't about to ignore him.

"What will it take for you to leave me alone?" she asked.

He placed a hand on her shoulder, stroking her cheek. "A little birdy told me it was your birthday today. Happy birthday, Lucia."

"Cut the crap, Connor. Seriously, right now. It's boring. You don't like me. You never have. I don't like you either. What's the joke?" she asked. Closing her locker, she placed her hands on her hips, glaring at him.

Being the butt of a joke wasn't a new thing for her.

It was quite an old and dated one, and she wasn't interested in that happening now, or ever again. Lifting her dress up was the last straw.

"No joke. I want you to go out with me. Like I said, you be nice to me, and I can make life easier for you. All you got to do is give in."

She couldn't help but laugh. "Yeah, you spent most of our school years from kindergarten to now making my life a misery. Not going to happen." She spun on her heel about to leave, but he was in front of her, stopping her from going. The look in his eye let her know the bad Connor was back.

"That was a mistake, fat bitch."

Tilting her head to the side, she stared at him. "Get out of my way, please," she said.

"Come on, we can have some fun together. Give me a shot and I'll let you pass." He leaned against the locker, and she went to walk around him, but he stopped her.

Licking her lips, she stared at him.

That twisted feeling in her gut wouldn't go away. She didn't like this, not one bit. For the most part she had always seen him as harmless, but right now he seemed anything but.

"Hey, Connor, I missed you," Rachel said, running her hands up the front of his chest. With him distracted by his on-again, off-again girlfriend, Lucia left them to it, not wanting to get involved with that drama.

Rachel didn't like her, just as she wasn't a big fan of hers either.

Instead of heading to math, she went to the toilet. Gripping the counter, she closed her eyes, and took several deep breaths.

She had never been nervous before. Her heart raced, and it wasn't a good feeling. Jack's warning echoed through her mind, and she couldn't help but wonder why now? Why was Connor taking an interest? She didn't want his interest, no matter what. He was the most popular guy in school, but she didn't like him.

"You better stay away from Connor," Rachel said, entering the bathroom.

Lucia looked up and stared at the queen bee in Beyer Hill High School. They had never gotten along.

"I have no intention of having anything to do with him."

"Really? You think I don't notice he's sniffing around you. I don't know why. Screwing you is like fucking a cow." Every now and then she'd sniffle and rub her nose.

"Wow," Lucia said. She wasn't going to be brought down by Rachel.

Her mood was too damn good right now to allow Rachel to affect her.

"Is that it? Warning me away from Connor?"

"I saw the way you looked at him. You wanted him, just like all the bitches and sluts here want him. He's mine."

"You mean in self-defense class? Are you real

right now? I didn't look at him like anything other than the disgusting pig that he is." She was tired of being pushed around. "No," she said, stepping closer to Rachel. "This is not happening. You are not spoiling today. I don't want your boyfriend, Rachel. He gives me the creeps. I've never wanted him, and if you think for a second that it's to get at you or to be part of your little crowd, you're very much mistaken. I've got my friend, and I'm happy to just have one because at least I know she's not stabbing me in the back."

She didn't even give Rachel time to respond as she left the bathroom. She made it just in time to math class, and she refused to think about her confrontations with both Connor and Rachel.

Moving from class to class on auto-pilot, she did her best to avoid going to her locker. Every time she was there, Connor found a reason to be there as well, and bumping into him was far down on her list of things to do today. He kept making her uncomfortable, either saying nasty stuff to her or trying to paw at her.

It was her birthday, and she didn't want to spoil it.

Marie made her laugh throughout lunch, and she was thankful to her best friend for doing it. She didn't know what she would have done without her.

She had science with Ms. Bertram after lunch, and her last lesson of the day was of course English.

The perfect end to a rather rocky day. She took a seat in the back as she really didn't want to seem like a suck-up, and with their encounters of late, she was nervous.

Mr. Parker was writing in his notebook as the class filtered in. When Rachel and Connor entered, she returned her gaze to her book, not wanting to be part of that drama. Rachel sat in the back on the opposite side of the classroom while Connor took the seat in front of her.

"Yo, teach, I think we should all offer Lucia a happy birthday."

"What are you doing?" she asked.

Her cheeks heated as every single student turned to look at them. This was the last thing she wanted from everyone. Connor was doing this on purpose. Was this his joke? Glancing across at Rachel, she saw the other girl glaring at her.

"It's your birthday, Lucia?" Mr. Parker asked.

"Yes, it is." She didn't look at him but offered a glare at Connor. He'd never done this, and her heart was racing right now.

"Happy Birthday," he said.

She looked up at him and smiled. "Thank you."

Connor did the same and made everyone else do it as well.

"Now you've got a good reason to eat cake."

Instead of rising to his bait, Lucia said her thanks to everyone else and was grateful that it was the end of it. She didn't want to do this again.

Mr. Parker got started on his lesson. They were comparing two different poems now, and of course it was about love.

Poems were always about love, at least the ones that were considered the greats were. He handed out books, placing them in front of each table. When he got to her desk, he held the book out and she took it, her thumb touching his.

She felt the heat, the warmth that flooded her.

This happened to her every single time she touched him or they were close. She couldn't look away, but they were in a classroom and she forced a smile before glancing back down at her notes.

He kept on talking, telling them to turn to a new

page.

She didn't want anyone else to see how much he affected her.

Taking notes, she made sure to put the titles of the two poems. This lesson flew by way too quickly as the bell seemed to ring the moment she got into the work. She sat for several seconds and watched as some of her peers rushed out. Opening up her bag, she took her time, aware of Connor in front of her. Rachel came over, and Lucia ignored the two of them until they both filtered out and only she was left.

Standing up, she held her keys in her hands and approached his desk.

Mr. Parker, Jack, smiled at her. "Happy Birthday," he said.

"Thank you. I don't even know why he's doing what he's doing." She pointed out the door, speaking of Connor.

"I had no idea it was your birthday."

"Yep, eighteen today, and look." She held up her car keys. "My parents finally got me a car. I brought Marie to school today."

He laughed. "Feel good?"

"Yeah, it felt really awesome, actually." She tilted her head to the side. "It was a good class today."

"Are you loving poetry yet?"

"I wouldn't say loving just yet, but I like it. So that's a step in a different direction for me."

"Good."

"Are you doing anything special tonight?" he asked.

"My parents are taking me out to dinner. No more zucchini chips tonight."

"I'm happy for you."

"This is if they'll show, you know. Their track

record is not the best at all when it comes to being a no-show."

"They should. You're their daughter."

"You always know what to say to me."

"If they knew what was good for them, they'd show up for everything. You're a good person, Lucia. Don't ever doubt that."

He stood up, and she watched as he moved toward the white board, using the board wiper to completely clear the ink marks he'd made.

It had been a good class, but right now, she didn't want to go. Marie would be waiting for her.

"Mr. Parker," she said. Her heart raced, and she couldn't even think straight as he turned around.

Just do it.

"What's up, Lucia?" he asked.

She didn't know what the hell came over her, but she stepped up to him, and before she could even think about all of the consequences, she pressed her lips against his.

Bold.

Scary.

Thrilling.

Exciting.

It was all of those emotions, and so many more all rolled up in one, and she didn't want it to stop.

Stepping back, she stared into his eyes, and then couldn't believe what she had just done. "I'm sorry."

She quickly turned on her heel and walked out of the room.

The first guy she'd just kissed was her teacher.

Jack Parker was a great deal of firsts for her, and now she'd gone and kissed him.

What were you thinking?

She *wasn't* thinking. Watching him wipe the

board clean, all of her feelings had come crashing all around her, and she'd just reacted.

It was insane.

Crazy.

She didn't regret it.

You've got to see him Monday.

Ignoring her locker, she made her way straight toward her car where Marie was already waiting. "It's about time you got here. It's really starting to turn cold. I heard on the radio that this was the coldest start to October in years," Marie said, bouncing from one foot to another.

"Sorry."

It was on the tip of her tongue to tell her what she'd just done, but she couldn't.

The kiss had to stay secret.

She wouldn't tell another soul.

Putting the key in the ignition, she started the car and headed toward Marie's house.

"Are you okay?" Marie asked.

"Yeah, sure, why?"

"You just seem … a little out of it."

"Oh, it's nothing. I'm fine. I promise. Just trying to process everything about the day."

"Are you sure?"

"Positive."

She forced a smile to her face as she looked at her friend. "It has been a really long day, and now it's that waiting game with my parents."

"Damn, I forgot about that."

"Yeah, no biggie. It's perfectly fine."

She parked outside Marie's house.

"You can stay with me. You can always tell your parents that you forgot. You know, be the first time you did that."

"That's not who I am, but thank you, bestie." She reached out and hugged her friend.

"Call me as soon as they get home."

"I will." She waited for her friend to get in her home before driving away.

Parking up in the driveway, she noticed there were no cars waiting, so her parents were not home yet.

"It's fine, Lucia. Perfectly fine." She climbed out of the car and let herself inside.

Making herself a coffee, she went around the house and closed some of the curtains as it had started to fall dark.

Sitting at the dining room table, her homework open, she kept an eye on the clock.

One hour passed.

Two hours went.

Three hours.

When it got to the fourth hour, she closed her last piece of homework and just sat at the table feeling overwhelmingly sad.

Just this morning, they'd both felt bad for being absent parents. Now, they were absent again.

Tears filled her eyes, and she grabbed her cell phone.

No notifications.

They were still at work, or knowing the two of them, had gone out with each other.

She scrolled through her contacts and came to a stop.

Jack Parker.

Her teacher.

The guy she had kissed.

Her first-ever kiss.

Licking her lips as the first tear started to fall, she knew she shouldn't press his name.

Shouldn't even consider him, and yet, she pressed on his name, and clicked text message.

He didn't have her number.

Once she did this, he'd be able to talk to her whenever he wanted.

What if he doesn't want to?

What if this is a complete mistake?

She started to type.

Lucia: **This is Lucia, just in case you don't know who it is. Parents are a no-show. What do you think I should order? Pizza or Chinese?**

She clicked on "send," and that was it. She'd done it.

Sent a text message to her teacher.

Even as her heart raced, her stomach fluttered.

She'd kissed him.

Now, she just had to wait.

****

Jack cursed as he received the text. He'd just opened his first beer and hadn't even taken a swig from the bottle.

On her damn birthday, her parents hadn't even bothered to show up. She'd looked nervous when she mentioned it that very afternoon.

Like she knew already that they wouldn't turn up, and it pissed him off more than anything.

Leaving his home, he climbed into his car and didn't think, just reacted. This could be a complete mistake, but he couldn't leave her alone for her birthday. Parking outside her home, he dimmed his lights and then typed a message back.

Jack: **You want some company? I'm waiting outside. No one should be alone for their birthday.**

He didn't have to wait long for an answer. Dressed as she had been at school, she came out of the house, locking it up behind her. She rushed toward his car, and within seconds she was in the passenger seat.

This young woman had completely shocked him with her kiss that very afternoon. Before he could even react, she'd bitten her lip and run out of the classroom.

She didn't mention the kiss, and he wasn't about to bring it up.

"Thank you," she said.

"Don't thank me. Right now, I want to go and find your parents and give them a piece of my mind."

She chuckled. "They wouldn't have a clue who you are."

"No, they wouldn't." He gripped the steering wheel tighter, not liking the rage pulsing through his veins.

Lucia was an amazing young woman.

They should be taking better care of her.

Instead, she spent most of her life on her own, and he hated that for her. He'd lived that himself, and knew firsthand what a lonely, miserable feeling that could be. It was one of the reasons he'd turned to sex.

Fucking his way through high school had helped him to deal with two workaholic parents.

"Where are we going?"

"Well, I can't promise you Chinese or pizza, but what I can do is promise you some pretty good food."

"We're going to the diner?"

"Yes, and you can order whatever you want, even cake. I think they even do a birthday special, so you can have that as well."

"Awesome. Thank you so much for coming over. I didn't know if you'd ignore my text."

"I wouldn't ignore you, Lucia." He had her number now, which was just another temptation he had to deal with.

She was also eighteen.

And she'd kissed him.

He'd not initiated the kiss.

She had.

Get your fucking head together, Jack. You're not some randy teenager.

"So, birthday girl, do you feel different?" he asked.

"I think so. It's really weird, but I do. I can't even describe it, but it's like today in the bathroom. Rachel followed me inside as I was just getting my bearings again. She warned me off Connor."

"He sniffing around you?"

"I don't think so. It's probably some kind of cruel joke. He's saying the same old usual stuff but trying to make me do what he wants. I'm not falling for it. They're good at mean jokes. She warned me off Connor, and it was like a switch went off inside my brain, and I felt like laughing. I mean, seriously, Connor? That guy has made my life a misery for as long as I can remember, and she thinks I'm interested in him."

"Is there a guy at school you *are* interested in?" he asked.

He didn't want to think about Connor right now.

When he'd announced in his classroom that it was Lucia's birthday, Jack had wanted to fucking hurt the kid, and that was showing him exactly why he shouldn't be driving Lucia to their place.

Fuck.

When had his diner become "their place" to eat?

Pushing all those thoughts out of his mind, he waited for Lucia to answer his question.

She didn't.

"What was it like for you when you were eighteen?" she asked instead.

He wanted to get her back on track, but he also didn't want to make her uncomfortable, so he left it alone. That was what he was good at, leaving things alone.

"The rebel, remember? That's what I was all about. Breaking laws, doing naughty things."

"You broke laws?"

"Only a few vows of marriage, but I didn't break them personally. I let the women break them."

"Wow, that's surprising. You ever been married yourself?"

"Nope. Never found the right woman. Besides, I'm a teacher. I don't want anyone to be tempted by someone like me."

She burst out laughing. "Some women don't always fall for the rebel, Jack, or the popular guy. Look at Connor. He's the most popular boy in school, and I can't stand him."

"Not even a little bit?"

"Not even that."

"What if he'd never bullied you?"

"Nope. He holds no interest for me. I guess I'm one of those, like, drones or something. I'm wired a different way than most. No desire to be popular or to have Connor in my life."

They pulled up to the diner, and it was a little busier than last time. He didn't recognize any of the patrons inside, but then he never did.

It was one of the reasons he came here often and enjoyed it.

The food was amazing, and he was left alone.

Pulling out of the car, he waited for Lucia to climb out of her side.

There was a chill in the air, and she rubbed her hands together.

Rushing her into the diner, they found a booth toward the back that was private. He liked that.

He didn't want to share Lucia with anyone. Once again, he slid the menu toward her.

"Order whatever you want, birthday girl."

"You can stop calling me that."

"I don't want to. I think it's fitting. Besides, you had to go to school for your birthday. That just sucked."

She laughed. "A lot of people have to go to school and work."

"Doesn't matter. Right now, we're talking about you."

"I'm not going to argue with that."

She bowed her head and looked over the menu.

"The special spaghetti sounds awesome, but it could be messy."

"Then be messy. Order whatever you want."

He gave her another couple of minutes to decide and when she was ready, he nodded for the waitress to come over. He listened to what Lucia wanted, and ordered the same.

"Have you tried that before?" she asked.

"There's not anything on that menu that I've not tried. You're going to love it."

"Awesome."

Pressing his elbows on the table, he leaned forward. "So, how are you liking your birthday now?" he asked.

"It has just improved a lot."

"A lot?"

"Yes, a whole lot." She smiled. "Thank you for coming for me. I mean that."

"I'll always come for you." He couldn't help but think of the dirty side of coming. "Have you been left alone a lot of birthdays?"

"Yeah, but they're not special ones, are they? Eighteen is a big one. For most places I'm an adult now."

"Very true."

"This morning they just sounded different. Kind of sucks to know that nothing has changed, not really. This's okay though. Being here with you, this is a million times better than what I could imagine."

She was sitting back in the booth, both of her hands locked together, resting on the edge of the table.

Don't.

Do.

This complete indecision was driving him fucking insane. Reaching across the table, he took her hand and rubbed his thumb across her knuckles.

"You can call me any time you want. Day or night. For you, Lucia, I will answer."

She licked her lips again, and he thought about that kiss she'd dropped on his lips. It wasn't overly sexual or desperate.

"Was I your first kiss?" he asked.

Her cheeks were on fire and she went to pull her hand away, but he held her a little tighter. He wouldn't let her pull away.

"Answer me, Lucia. I'm not going to hurt you."

"Yes," she said. "I didn't think that you'd bring it up."

"It was a pretty important kiss. I didn't really have much choice."

"I'm sorry."

"Don't ever be sorry for your kisses, Lucia. I liked it."

Her gaze moved up to his face. "You did?"

"Yes, I did." He continued to stroke her fingers, waiting to see what she'd do.

She nibbled her bottom lip, and he wanted to taste

her so badly. There was no time for him to do so as their food came out.

Reluctantly, he pulled his hand away, missing the touch as soon as it was gone.

You're a grownup.

Every single argument he had didn't seem to ring true inside his head. He couldn't find a single reason to *not* be sitting here with her.

She's your student.

They were all students at some point in their lives.

This was probably the biggest mistake of his entire life, but he couldn't walk away, not now.

She needed someone who'd stick around, who wouldn't back down.

Lucia didn't have that.

He watched her take the first mouthful of spaghetti, and she closed her eyes, and moaned.

"Oh, wow, that is good."

He knew it was. Incredibly tasty and cheesy, it was such a good combination of flavors, and he loved it. Watching her enjoyment filled him with pleasure.

Jack liked feeding her.

Seeing her smile.

And just being with her.

Grabbing his fork, he twirled the spaghetti around and took a large bite himself, loving the taste just as much as he did the first time.

"You didn't answer my question in the car."

The way her hand hovered over her food, he knew that she was aware of which question.

"I don't have my eye on anyone at all at school."

"Lucia?"

"What?"

"I don't want there to be any secrets between us,"

he said.

Again, she nibbled her lip, and he started to believe she did that when she was nervous.

"I like you," she said. "And only you."

She didn't look at him, and he leaned across the table. Cupping her chin, he tilted her head back so that she'd look at him.

"I know it's wrong," she said. "You're my teacher. I shouldn't have kissed you, and I shouldn't be here. I won't tell anyone though. You love teaching, and I won't do anything to jeopardize that. I also know it's one-sided."

"This is not one-sided, Lucia. This shouldn't be happening. Bringing you here the first time was wrong. This time, it's even more so. The kiss, I should have reported to Principal Dowed."

"You didn't?"

"No. I didn't. As far as I'm concerned that kiss belongs to you and me. I'm not going to report it."

"But?"

"No buts. I'm not. I liked it, and to report it means I wouldn't get the chance of tasting you again."

Her mouth dropped open, and she quickly closed it, glancing around the dinner.

This was wrong on so many levels.

"You're right though. I am your teacher. This is wrong. I'm the grownup and should know better. I do know better."

"But?"

"But I can't seem to stop myself. I don't want to stop myself."

"You don't?"

"No, and I know that's wrong."

"I'm not here out of fear or blackmail. I should have called Marie or even my parents to remind them."

"You didn't?"

"No. you're the first and only person I called."

He liked that.

She smiled, tilting her head to the side just a little. Her hair was still bound up, and the move exposed her neck. He wanted to kiss that tender flesh, to hear her moan as he drove her crazy with need.

"And you came for me," she said.

"I'll always come, Lucia."

"I know. I do."

Neither of them spoke for a long time, and he started eating his food.

Jack could label every single reason on why they shouldn't be here.

Why they shouldn't be enjoying her birthday meal.

From him being a teacher to the twelve-year age gap between them, but not one of those reasons was valid compared to the fact they both wanted to be here.

He wasn't using Lucia, nor was he blackmailing her.

They had this attraction that shouldn't be there, but it was.

Jack couldn't keep on fighting.

Lucia meant a great deal to him.

They finished their food, and he ordered her a slice of a cake with a candle, singing to her as she blew out the candle.

"I can't eat all of this," she said. "Share with me." She held out a fork filled with cake.

Taking a bite, he closed his eyes, enjoying it.

"Yum." He licked his lips.

"It's good."

"It's really good."

Once they were finished, he pulled out his wallet

and paid for the meal.

Leaving the diner, she shuddered, and he removed his jacket, placing it over her shoulders.

"It's fine. We're only moving to the car," she said. "I'll warm up there."

"I'm not having you cold. Just enjoy the jacket."

"Okay."

She pushed her arms through the jacket and wrapped it around herself. Going to the car, he moved toward her side, and he couldn't resist.

Gripping her shoulder, he spun her around and pressed her up against the car.

He held her hands, locking their fingers together. His gaze went to her lips, so plump and inviting.

"You kissed me earlier. Now it's my turn to kiss you."

Pressing his lips down on hers, he started out slow, taking his time, relishing the little gasp of surprise that left her.

Releasing her hands, he cupped her hips, holding her in place as he trailed his tongue across her bottom lip. She opened up, and he plundered inside, deepening the kiss. His cock hardened, and he wanted her so fucking badly.

He'd never wanted any other woman the way he wanted Lucia.

Her hands went to his shoulders, holding him tightly. Her nails dug into his flesh, and he loved it. He wanted her touch.

This was forbidden.

Wrong.

Yet so fucking good.

He couldn't bring himself to stop.

He didn't *want* to stop.

Pressing his cock against her stomach, he slid his

hand up her body, sinking into her hair, cupping the back of her head.

She met the stroke of his tongue, tasting him back.

The cold chilled his flesh, but he didn't care about the biting wind, only about the woman in his arms, and how she made him feel.

It was wrong.

A better man would step back, take her home, and report himself.

He couldn't do this.

Nor could he stop either.

Pulling away, he stared into her closed eyes.

Slowly they started to open.

She looked as shocked as he felt.

"That's how you kiss," he said.

Her tongue peeked out and licked her lips.

"I liked it."

He groaned. The action seemed so innocent.

"I've got to get you home," he said.

Moving her out of the way, he opened the car door.

His cock pressed against the zipper of his slacks, and it was so painful.

He'd not been this hard in quite some time.

Climbing behind the wheel, he felt her gaze on him as he started up the car, pulling out of the parking lot.

Glancing at her, he saw her swollen lips, which again made his dick twitch.

"We shouldn't do this," he said.

"I know."

"I need to take you home."

"I know."

"Have your parents left a message?" he asked.

She wriggled on the seat and pulled out her cell phone. "No, nothing."

He didn't drive toward her home where her parents were probably waiting.

He drove to his own home.

Parking up outside of his place, he felt tense.

This was the first time since he was a teenage boy that he'd broken any rules.

His record for teaching was impeccable.

"I texted my parents," she said, breaking through the silence. "I told them I was staying at a friend's."

There was the excuse.

The reason.

So innocently sent.

Most students were covering while they went to see a boyfriend, not a teacher.

He didn't say a word as he climbed out of the car.

The street was quiet, and he made his way to the front door. Flicking open the lock, he pushed the door and it swung open. Staring at her, he waited for her to enter. At any time, if she wanted to leave, he'd let her go.

She could walk away and he wouldn't be angry or sad.

Lucia stepped over the threshold, and he followed her inside.

Chapter Eight

Lucia tucked some of her fallen hair behind her ear. Jack closed the door, and the tension within the small hallway seemed to intensify. She was in his home. She'd already texted her parents that she was staying at a friend's and had turned her cell phone off.

No one knew where she was.

Not her parents.

Not Marie.

No one.

She was alone with Jack Parker, her English teacher.

"I'll take your jacket."

"Oh."

He helped her remove the jacket, the tips of his fingers grazing down her arm like a brand. Her body was on fire right now just from his presence alone.

Her mouth still tingled from his kiss.

She wanted to touch her lips but stopped herself at the last minute.

Jack took her hand and led her toward his sitting room.

His home was nice, rather modest.

"I thought you said you had lawyers for parents," she said.

"I do. They also provide me with an allowance that I don't use. This is what I pay for with my teaching salary."

"It's really nice."

"Not what you're used to."

"It's cozy. I like it. The big house that my parents got, it's not exactly cozy. Lot of open spaces, walls, and nothing."

"I know what you mean. My parents' house was bigger than yours. It had six levels. If they had important clients that they needed to keep an eye on, they brought them back home. I think it's why they had such a large space. They could live in a separate wing of the house from their client."

"Wing?"

"Yes, I also had a separate one."

"And here I thought I was special for getting an en-suite."

"I guess too much invasion of privacy?" he asked.

"Yeah, a little too much."

"My dad suggested I get a different wing when he caught me banging the nanny," Jack said.

She didn't like the twinge that twisted her gut.

His jaw seemed to clench. "I had a past, Lucia."

"I know. You can't get to being thirty without one."

"I won't hide anything from you. You see … a lot. This is…"

"I know, Jack. I know this is dangerous, and I don't want you to lose your job."

"I don't want you to go," he said. "This is not one-sided. I'm not being held here against my will. I know what I want. You can leave at any time though."

"I don't want to leave."

"Are you a virgin?" he asked.

She'd glanced down at the floor, but his question made her look back at him. "Yes." Her cheeks heated.

"Do you know anything about sex?"

"Yeah. My parents sat down with me, and we did the entire talk. You know the baby talk, the pregnancy talk. All the other kinds of talks in between. I think I was scarred for life. They even had pictures of STDs and STIs. It was really kind of graphic."

She loved seeing him smile.

The curtains in his front room were closed, and they stood in his sitting room.

He stepped toward her and cupped her face. Just that touch alone made her ache for more.

She wanted this so damn much.

Placing her hands on top of his, she stared into his eyes.

He leaned in close, and she didn't pull away. When his lips touched hers for the second time that night, everything fell away, all of her fears, panic, and insecurities, and she felt grounded in Jack's arms.

His tongue once again traced over her lips, and she moaned, opening her mouth, inviting him inside, and he took the invitation, plundering her.

Touching his tongue with her own, she melted against him. Running her hands up his arms, she gripped his shoulders.

He placed his thumbs beneath her chin, tilting her head back and moving her until she pressed against the wall.

Jack took hold of her hands, placing them above her head, holding her captive.

"This is so fucking wrong," he said, breaking from the kiss but trailing his lips down to her ear. He licked her earlobe, and she shivered from the touch, wanting some more. "But right now, I don't care, Lucia. You're the only one that I fucking want."

"I want you," she said, gasping as his lips moved down, going to her neck and sucking on the pulse.

Biting her lip, she tried to contain the pleasure from erupting, but it was getting harder for her to deny herself.

"Let go, Lucia. You don't have to control yourself in front of me. I'm so hard right now. I want to be inside you. To feel your virgin pussy give way to my cock. So fucking dirty, so sweet. I want to taste you, to show you the kinds of pleasure you've only read about."

He held her wrists now as he kissed the flesh just above her shirt.

Her nipples tightened, pressing against the fabric, showing him how aroused she really was.

She cried out, arching up, needing his lips on her everywhere.

Jack pulled away far enough so that only his hands were on her wrists.

His blue gaze ignited a fire inside her that wasn't going to be put out. She didn't *want* it to go out.

Then, slowly, he leaned forward, and she cried out as his mouth sucked on her nipple through her clothing. She wore a white lacy bra, and the shirt she wore wasn't overly thick. The pleasure went straight between her thighs, soaking her pussy with more arousal.

Jack didn't linger.

He moved on to her other breast, sucking on the bud exactly the same way.

Suddenly, he was gone, his touch no longer holding her in place.

He pulled on her shirt, tugging it up and over her head. He threw it across the room, and her first instinct was to hide.

To cover all of her extra bits.

He caught her hands and placed them against the wall, stopping her from trying to cover her body.

"When you're with me, Lucia, you don't hide."

"I…"

"Beautiful. That's all I see when I look at you. I think you're utterly ravishing, and I wouldn't have you any other way. Don't hide what now belongs to me, and it does, Lucia. Right now, in this moment, we do this, you become mine."

She loved that.

Those words were like magic inside her head.

"No other boys. No other crushes. You belong to me."

"Yes."

There was no one else. She didn't want or see anyone but him.

He stepped back, and she watched as he removed his shirt, throwing it to the floor to join hers. His heavily inked chest seemed to be the last layer that stood between them.

The teacher was gone.

She now had the man.

Their clothing caught her eye. It was just two shirts, but to her they seemed so intimate. Their clothing lying together on the floor, holding a secret. *Their* secret.

When she returned her gaze to Jack, he was staring at her, and she didn't understand his look, or even what he was thinking. She only knew that she couldn't back down, nor give this up. Within one afternoon her senior year had taken a dramatic turn, and she didn't want it to end.

Closing the distance between them, she walked into his arms, wrapping her own around his neck as she pulled his head down. His lips were on hers again, and she didn't want him to stop.

He sank his fingers into her hair, tugging on the length. She dropped her head back, moaning as his lips slid down to her neck. They didn't stop this time, his tongue tracing the edge of her bra. One of his hands ran down her back, flicking the catch of her bra.

It fell forward, and she wriggled out of it.

The tips of her nipples pressed against his chest, making her gasp.

This was real.

She stood partially naked in Jack Parker's home. His hand was in her hair, the other on the base of her back, and he was kissing down her body. This kind of stuff didn't happen to her.

Pushing all of her doubts and insecurities aside, she kissed him back with passion. She didn't know the first thing about kissing, so she hoped that she was doing this properly.

His lips moved down her chest and his hands followed, cupping her tits. They were large, and she usually tried to hide them. With the way he looked, and the feel of his tongue sliding across them, she no longer felt insecure about them.

She wanted his touch.

Jack pressed her tits together, his tongue stroking over each beaded nipple before taking one into his mouth and sucking hard.

She cried out as he bit down. The flash of pain shocked her, but he soothed it with a caress straight after.

"You're very sensitive," he said, releasing her tits.

"Yes."

His fingers teased the edge of her jeans. She wasn't wearing any belt.

"Are you afraid?"

"No."

"Do you want me to stop?"

"No. Never."

She was here because she wanted to be here.

He flicked the catch of her jeans, and she stared into his blue eyes. The echo of the zipper going down filled the room. She wasn't going to ask him to stop. This was what she wanted more than anything else.

"I should be arrested," he said.

"I'm legal, Jack. I'm here because I want to be. They can't arrest you." Even though her hands shook a little, she reached out, unbuckling his belt and working the button on his slacks. He took over, pushing his pants down, and as he did that, she did the same.

He was all rock-hard muscle while she had a few extra lumps and bumps. The running hadn't shown any changes to her body, not that she expected it to be an overnight thing.

No, this was going to take some time.

Jack wasn't put off though. He took her hand and pulled her close.

He ran his fingers through her hair, pushing it out of the way. "No hiding."

"No hiding." She repeated his words.

He cupped her cheek, his thumb running across her lips. When he pressed forward, she sucked his thumb into her mouth, and he groaned.

"Fuck, you have no idea what that does to me."

She'd seen the evidence of his arousal.

There was no way she wasn't aware of what was going on.

She turned him on, and that didn't terrify her. It delighted her. Jack Parker was her addiction, and she couldn't get enough of him.

Lucia gave out a little squeal as he suddenly picked her up,

"What are you doing?" She wrapped her arms around his neck, worried in case he dropped her.

"I'm taking you to a bed. For your first time, you shouldn't be fucked against a wall."

Her pussy clenched at the thought.

She was no stranger to porn, and his words ignited a fire inside her.

"You like that, don't you? You want me to fuck

you against you the wall?" He kicked open his bedroom door and placed her on the floor. With a slight shove, she was on the bed, leaning up her elbows as he knelt before her.

He pushed her thighs open and dragged her ass to the end of the bed. In one swift tug, her panties were gone, and she was spread open for him. "You didn't answer me, Lucia."

"Yes. I want that."

His hand cupped her pussy. One single finger slid through her slit, and she cried out, arching up as the pleasure bloomed deep inside her.

"Well, look at this pretty little pussy, you naughty girl. You're all wet for me. You want my dick inside you?"

"Yes," she said, crying out as he circled her clit.

Biting her lip, she couldn't believe the kind of pleasure he was creating.

She'd touched herself plenty of times, even bringing herself to orgasm, but nothing had ever felt like this.

With two fingers now, he stroked over her clit, sliding back and forth.

She arched up.

The pleasure was too intense, yet not enough.

"Such a sweet virgin pussy. Anyone else touched you?"

"No."

"This is all mine?"

"Yes!" She screamed the word, feeling a little hoarse.

She whimpered as he stopped.

"I want to taste you."

She didn't have long to wait as his lips latched onto her clit, sliding over and down to her entrance only to circle back up.

Back and forth, across, over, and he sucked in deep.

There was no stopping his tongue as it sent her higher and higher. She felt that peak that was so close, and she didn't want to lose it.

Right there, and he stopped, holding her at that pinnacle.

"I want you to come, but I know for your first time, this is going to be painful. I don't want you focusing on pain. I want you high on pleasure." As he spoke, his fingers teased the lips of her pussy. She felt swollen, and so in need. She couldn't form any coherent words.

Nothing made sense to her right now.

She only knew that she needed him more than anything else in her entire life.

****

Jack couldn't ever recall tasting something so good. Her pure, untouched pussy would soon belong to him, and he fucking relished that. Lucia had come out of nowhere and completely taken him by surprise.

The anger he felt.

The rage.

The jealousy.

He'd never been this affected by anyone else.

Connor showing an interest in her annoyed him. Cupping her pussy, Jack forced himself to pull away. Opening the drawer beside his bed, he pulled out a condom, and tearing into the packet, he rolled the latex over his dick.

"I want you to be safe," he said. "Are you on the pill?"

"No."

"I'll keep on using condoms." He moved her up

the bed until her hair was spread out across his pillows. She really was a tempting sight as far as he was concerned.

So beautiful.

So ripe.

And right now, she belonged to him.

Lucia was his.

Just as he was hers.

Spreading her legs wide, he gripped the base of his cock and ran the tip up and down her pussy, bumping across her clit. She released a gasp.

He'd not given her an orgasm yet for two reasons, one of them selfish, the other not so much.

The selfish reason was he wanted to feel her orgasm as he was balls deep inside her. The other, non-selfish reason, was this was going to hurt. Her first time would be painful, and as she was so close to orgasm the pleasure should wipe out any pain that she felt.

Staring into her pretty brown eyes, he was completely captivated by her.

Doing this.

Taking this next step.

It was complete and total madness.

A complete violation of all of his rules.

She was the forbidden.

His student.

But they'd crossed that line long before her kiss this afternoon.

Poised at her entrance, ready to take that leap, he wanted her, so he slammed to the hilt, tearing through her virginity. That tiny piece of flesh was now his own. She belonged to him.

He was her first, her only, and no one else would ever know the kind of pleasure to be had between her creamy thighs.

She released a scream, and she tried to push him away, to fight him.

He caught her hands, pressing them against the bed as he took possession of her lips. Plunging his tongue inside, he kissed her deeply, wanting her to forget everything else.

She broke from the kiss and cried out. "It hurts."

"I know it does." He kissed her neck. "I've got you."

When he took her lips once again, she relented this time.

Her entire body was tight. The tension cut him up, the cry of pain she'd released breaking a part of his soul.

He never wanted to hurt her.

This wasn't what he wanted for her at all.

He pulled back in time to see a single tear slide down her cheek, dripping onto his pillow.

Reaching between them, he felt her wince as his cock pulled out just a bit. With his dick still inside her, he stroked a finger over her pussy, teasing her clit.

"What?"

"I want you to come on my cock." She was so incredibly tight. Glancing down, he moaned at the sight of his cock spreading the lips of her pussy. There was some blood on his condom. He felt overcome with sadness that he'd hurt her, and there was the visible proof he had, but he was also fucking ecstatic. He'd taken Lucia.

She belonged to him now, and he was going to take care of her.

Stroking her clit, he slowly felt the tension ease out of her as he continued to tease her, his cock still hard and pulsing inside her. He could wait. This, right now, was all about her. He wanted her moaning and wriggling on his dick.

Within minutes she'd started to arch up, her pussy moving back and forth on his dick as he worked her toward an orgasm.

This time, he didn't deny her.

When her peak hit, he thrust her over the edge, savoring every pulse, squeeze, and clench of her cunt as she came. She did so, hard, his name echoing off the walls as she screamed it out.

He waited until she was ready, until her orgasm had subsided. Moving over her, he took her hands, pinning them above her head as he started to rock back and forth within her. She didn't wince or cry out in pain, so he pulled all of the way out until only the tip of his dick was inside her. Slamming in deep, he thrust to the hilt inside her again.

Her cries this time were filled with heat, with promise, and above all with pleasure.

Swallowing down the sounds, he kissed her as he fucked her hard. He built up a steady pace, slowing down, remembering this was her first time, and he didn't want to hurt her.

They had all the time in the world for what he wanted to do, and he wasn't in any rush to end this.

Taking his time, he made love to her, kissing her deeply, showing her with his body exactly how it was supposed to be.

Wrapping his arms around her, he drove in deep, feeling the tingle in his balls as he was so close to his own release. It had been so long, and with the feel of her rippling pussy around his length, he couldn't hold back.

He held her tightly as he came, thrusting every single inch of himself within her as he filled the condom with his cum, his release seeming to go on and on.

Opening his eyes, he stared into Lucia's brown

ones. There was a smile shining right back at him. Her hands were on his body, and he loved it.

He loved her hands, her touch, her everything.

"I didn't want to hurt you."

"It doesn't hurt now."

"I'm glad." He stroked her hair back, feeling connected with her, not wanting to let her go or pull away.

He didn't wish to create any distance between them.

"This is turning out to be the best birthday ever," she said. "Is that weird?"

Jack chuckled. "I don't think it's weird. Maybe a little. This wasn't supposed to be your present."

"It's a pretty good present though. Very hard to beat."

He kissed her again. He couldn't resist her lips. They were plump, inviting, and he couldn't stop tasting them. He didn't want to.

She was nibbling her lip again, a good sign that she was nervous.

"What's wrong?" he asked.

"I … is it … just this time?"

"You're sporting a very pretty little blush."

She groaned. Her hands going up to cover her face.

"That depends on you. Do you want it to be a one-time only deal?" he asked.

"No."

"Then it won't be a one-time only deal. Unless you're only using me for my body."

"I'm not using you," she said.

She reached out to touch him, only stopped.

Taking her hand, he placed it against his cheek. "You can touch me whenever you want to."

"I didn't like that other teacher touching you," she said. "Ms. Bertram."

"I don't like Connor showing an interest. He's bad news."

"Nothing is going to happen. I promise."

"Nothing will happen between me and Beth. You have my word." He couldn't even bring himself to touch another woman.

"This is … we're going to have to keep this a secret, aren't we?" she asked.

"Yes. I don't want you to be a secret, and if at any time you want to report me to the principal…"

"Why say that? I'm not going to report you. I know we're where we are right now."

"My dick is still balls deep inside your pussy."

"This wasn't you. I kissed you first. I wanted this. I still want this." Her hand moved down to his chest. "You have a lot of ink for a teacher."

He laughed. "I got it before I even went to college. Told you, I was the rebel."

She smiled, and he loved that look so much. "I don't mind us being a secret, Jack. Do you want me to swap English teachers?"

"I've already looked into that, and it can't be done. There's no room for the schedules to be changed or rearranged. I can do my job, and you won't be getting any special treatment from me. You'll do the work, and earn your grade." He kissed her lips. "And you shouldn't look so damn happy about that."

"I don't mind hard work. In fact, I love hard work so much."

"Good." He kissed her neck, breathing in her strawberry scent. "I've got to get you in the bath."

"Do I smell?"

"No, it's going to be painful for you." Easing out

of her, he stared down at his now flaccid cock. The condom he wore was slicked with her cream and virgin blood. "Stay."

"Yes, sir."

He winked at her as he made his way into the bathroom. Removing the condom, he tied it up and threw it in the trash. Next, he pushed the plug in and began to fill the water. Finding a bottle of relaxing bubble bath, he poured in a generous amount and made sure the water was nice and warm.

Entering his bedroom, he saw Lucia wasn't lying on the bed like he'd told her to. She stood in front of his mirror. She kept turning, looking this way and that. Her curves captured his attention. There was a slight jiggle to her ass that he loved. Her legs were full and rounded, as was her stomach.

To him, she looked beautiful, curvy, and every inch the woman he'd been craving.

"I thought I told you to stay on the bed."

"I couldn't help it. I've heard and read so many tales where people say you feel different or you look different. Do I look changed or different?"

He moved up behind her, placing a hand on her stomach. "You look every inch the well-fucked woman."

Again, her cheeks were a pretty shade of pink.

"I wonder if I can fuck the blush right out of you."

"I can't seem to help it," she said, pressing her hands to her cheeks.

"I don't mind. I like you blushing." He ran his hand up her body, cupping her tit. Staring at her in the mirror with his arm holding her, he felt possessive.

He didn't want anyone else touching her.

She belonged to him.

"Come on." He took her hand, leading her back to

the bathroom.

He helped her climb in. Kneeling beside the tub, he didn't let her go.

"You're not getting in?"

"No, this is for you."

"I can share."

He laughed. "I know you can share. I don't want to be tempted right now. You're going to be sore in the morning."

"Oh."

"Yes. Do you feel different?"

"I don't know. I don't think so. I feel the same." She bit her lip, and he saw the smile behind it.

"What?"

"I feel really happy. Like, on top of the world happy."

"Good. You should be." He pressed a kiss to her knuckles.

"Do you regret it?" she asked.

"What?"

"Me? You? This?"

"No. I don't regret this. It felt way too good to ever be a regret. Never think that. I don't want you to be in any kind of pain, and I wasn't … I was a little rough."

"Not too rough. I know. I've seen it."

"You've seen rough sex?"

"I'm not blind, and I can do searches," she said.

"Are you trying to tell me that you've watched porn?" he asked.

"Yes. Is it so hard to think that I could?"

"Not hard to think about but now I'm curious what you were thinking about while watching them?"

She sighed. "I don't want to tell you."

"So, it was about me?"

"Maybe."

"I know I've not done any sex porn tapes."

"I was … it was looking at older men with younger women."

"Ah, so the plot thickens. Have you been planning my seduction for a while, Miss Deen?"

She groaned. "No. In fact, I moved to the back of the class so it didn't look so totally obvious. I guess that didn't work."

"I was a little upset actually when you did that. I wondered what I'd done or said."

"It wasn't you. I liked talking to you, and I didn't want to make you feel uncomfortable."

"I'm a grown man, Lucia. It's going to take a lot to make me uncomfortable."

"I guess, but I was still your student and it was kind of embarrassing."

"Why?"

"Come on. You had to tell Connor to mind his language because of what he called me. I'm not like the Rachels of this world."

He sighed. "I'm going to have to spank you."

She chuckled. "That would be weird."

"I don't want the Rachels of this world. She's a spiteful little bitch, and I have no interest in her." He tucked a strand of hair behind her ear. "Don't listen to them. Not ever."

"You're going to be good for my ego," she said.

"I intend to be good to you. There is a lot of bad shit in this world, Lucia. I never want you to know it."

He cared about her a lot, and that alone scared the shit out of him.

Chapter Nine

Lucia rolled over and released a little wince as the pain clenched between her thighs, making her very aware of what she did last night. Opening one eye, she saw Jack lying beside her. He was also awake and smiling at her.

"You snore," he said.

She gasped. "What?"

"Just a little but it's so cute."

"That is so embarrassing. You shouldn't be laughing about that."

"Why not? It's cute as hell. It's not loud, and you didn't wake me up either."

She covered her face. "I snore?"

He took her hands, moving them away. "Hello, sleepyhead. I didn't think you'd ever wake up."

Jack kissed her hard, pushing her back onto the bed. Wrapping her arms around him, she moaned as the pleasure rushed through her body.

She was sore, but she loved his touch oh, so much.

Last night had been amazing.

The best birthday she could have ever asked for.

He pulled away. "How are you feeling today?" he asked.

"A little sore."

"I figured as much. No sexy time for you."

He held out her cell phone. "This has been buzzing for you most of the morning."

"You turned it on?"

"Yes. I think it's only fair that you talk to your parents."

"I told them I was at a friend's."

"Marie has also texted you. She asked if you still

want to do Mark Ruffalo day."

"Oh," she said, wincing. "I kind of forgot about that. Wait, you looked at my messages?"

"Yes, guilty as charged. I'm going to let you wake up. I'll make us both some breakfast. How do bacon and eggs sound?"

"That sounds amazing." Her mouth watered, and he chuckled.

Jack kissed her one final time. "I'll be waiting."

She nodded her head and watched him leave.

This was all a little surreal to her. Waking up in Jack Parker's home. Kissing him. Spending the night with him. He'd taken her virginity, and, apart from the pain, it had been amazing. *Oh, so amazing.*

Focus.

Glancing down at her cell phone, she checked her messages.

Ignoring the ones from her parents, she looked at Marie.

Marie: **Did they do dinner?**

Marie: **I take it from the no answer, they showed?**

Marie: **Kind of weird you not responding.**

Marie: **Still want to do Mark Ruffalo day? I'm kind of bored right now.**

Marie: **Love you.**

Lucia felt guilty for ignoring her friend.

There was no way for her to respond, not yet.

Checking her parents' messages, she felt disappointed, and an overwhelming sadness.

Dad: **I'm so sorry, honey. Work.**

It was always fucking work.

Every single reason.

Every single excuse.

Work.

Work.

Work.

She was tired of it.

Dad: **We'll make it up to you, honey. I'm so sorry.**

They'd make it up to her.

How?

By not going to work.

How could they have one moment of regret about being less than perfect parents, only to do the exact same thing on the same day?

Mom: **I'm so sorry, Lucia. Work got hectic and there was no leaving. I couldn't just walk out. You know that. I'll make it up to you, we'll make it up to you. I promise.**

Again, more promises.

Putting her phone down, she went to use the bathroom. She was sore, and she felt it with every step she took. It wasn't a bad ache, just a constant reminder that she'd had sex for the first time.

She'd lost her virginity, and she couldn't tell anyone.

One of Jack's shirts was on the bed, and she quickly pulled it on, the scent of bacon luring her to the kitchen.

He stood at the stove, only wearing a pair of sweatpants.

"Hey," she said.

"So, how are you feeling?"

"I've not responded to any messages."

"None of them?" he asked. "What about Marie?"

"I didn't know what to say. My parents would be home so I'd be going over to her place. You'd have to drop me off, but I don't want to ditch you. I don't know exactly how this is going to work. I don't want things to become awkward."

He put the spatula down and moved toward her.

Jack cupped her face and placed a kiss on her lips. "This is not going to be awkward. You've got your friends, and we can't make this public."

"I know."

"I don't want you to push your friend aside for me."

"I don't know if I can pretend today that something magical didn't happen last night."

She saw his smile soften.

"And if anyone would notice something different, it would be Marie. I swear it."

"You're not going?"

"Can I stay here? You know, for today? I can go home tomorrow." She hated asking, and it felt a little like begging right about now.

"You can stay with me, Lucia. You will always be welcome here. Do you want coffee or juice?"

"Coffee, please."

"Coming right up."

He kissed her again, and she took a seat at the counter.

She couldn't look away as he poured her some coffee.

"Why don't you let Marie know that you won't be available today?"

"Okay."

She left the kitchen, and, finding Marie's number, she clicked the "call" button.

"It's about time you got in touch with me, loser," Marie said after the third ring.

"Hey, sorry." She sat on the end of Jack's bed as she talked to her friend.

"How did it go last night?"

"My parents didn't make it home."

"They didn't? Those assholes."

"You already knew they wouldn't."

"I was hoping I was wrong."

"Nope, not wrong. I'm not really speaking to them right now."

"Do you want me to come over? I know your mom hates me and all, but I'd put up with her for you."

She hated lying to her friend. "I'm actually not feeling well at the moment. I'm sitting in bed, you know, trying to get well so I can be at school on Monday."

"Oh, I wonder if you've got that nasty bug going around."

"Yeah, I think I do. It's not too bad, but I don't want to let it spread. You know how it is."

"Say no more. Mark can wait. I've got him on DVD. Take care, and I'm going to let you get back to feeling better. Love you."

"Love you too." She ended the call, feeling awful for lying. Not once before had she lied to her friend.

"You okay?" Jack asked, drawing her attention to his presence.

"It's the first time I've ever lied to her." She stared down at her phone. making sure that she had in fact ended the call.

She had.

This was going to be new.

The lying.

The sneaking around.

"What about your parents?"

"I'm not ready to speak to them right now. They're probably at work or something. I don't know." Right now, she didn't care.

They had burst her happy bubble, and Jack had put it back together again.

"Are you hungry?" he asked.

"Starving."

"Come on, let's eat. Everything always feels better after food."

He took her hand, and she didn't fight him, willingly going with him as they entered the kitchen. The counter had been set up for breakfast, and in a small vase was a single rose.

"A rose for a pretty lady," he said, taking the rose and sniffing it.

He handed it to her, and she was careful until she realized he'd removed all the thorns for her. Sliding it in her hair, he smiled.

"How did you get a rose in October?" she asked.

"After Connor let it out that it was your birthday. I passed a florist on the way home. They had some and advised me to keep it warm and watered. I was going to take them to the park, go for a run in the hope of catching you."

"Wow," she said. "That is really romantic. The stuff from poetry."

"I did notice your sudden interest in poetry."

"I was intrigued. I wanted to see what you loved about it."

"And now?"

"It's still growing on me, but it's fun to read." She picked up her fork and dug into the bacon. It had been too long since she'd had any real bacon, and the taste was just ... she moaned. "I miss bacon."

"When you're here you can have all the bacon you want."

"Do you want a permanent resident?" she asked.

He laughed. "I never say never."

They didn't say anything more about it as they finished their breakfast. Afterward, Jack had some grading to do, and, seeing as she was staying with him, she sat on the sofa, her hair pulled back in a messy bun. She watched as he worked.

He read through every single sheet, marking each point, making notes. She couldn't stop herself from watching his hands. They had known how to touch her, what to do to make her moan, to make her ache just a little more.

She was still in his shirt, and she felt the heat flood her pussy at just the memory alone. Licking her dry lips, she tried to think of something else, but nothing helped.

His hands, his heavily inked arms already held a special place for her, and she didn't want to lose that.

"You're fidgeting," he said.

"I'm fine."

Her voice sounded a little thick. Pressing her thighs together, she watched as Jack put his paperwork down on the coffee table in front of him.

She squealed as he hauled her over him so that she straddled his waist.

"Now, I think we should have a few rules around here."

"You're the teacher. I'll let you make the rules."

He gripped her ass, squeezing her cheeks. She bit her lip in an attempt to contain her moan. She couldn't help it.

Even though she was sore, she wanted him again. Consequences be damned.

"And as my student, you will follow them."

He ran his hands down her thighs then back up again, cupping her ass. She never knew her ass could be so sensitive or that having him touch her would feel so damn good. She didn't want him to stop.

"Rule one, don't lie to me. Not once."

"That's easy."

"About anything. When I ask you a question, you answer it."

"That's going to be hard."

"When you want me to touch you because you're getting horny as fuck, you tell me."

He moved, and his hand cupped between her thighs. She wasn't wearing anything underneath the shirt, so it was very easy for him to touch. He stroked her tender flesh, and she gasped as he pressed a finger deep inside her. "Are you sore?"

"Yes, but I can take it."

"Such a brave girl, but this isn't about me today. This is about you."

He changed their position so she was now on her back, looking up at him. Within the next second, he had her shirt off and her legs spread wide open.

"Now that is a sight I've been wanting to see."

"What?"

"You spread out, open, ready for me."

He slid a finger between her slit and held it up. "You see that? That's how wet you are for me. You want me too."

"Yes."

"Good." He slammed his lips down on hers, and she gripped the back of his head. He pressed his body against hers, the hard ridge of his cock covered by his sweatpants. She whimpered because even though her body felt tense and a little sore, she wanted him. Jack didn't linger on her lips. His mouth trailed kisses down her body again. He took his time with each of her tits, licking and sucking at her nipples before moving down.

She cried out his name as he took one of her pussy lips and sucked it into his mouth, then did the same to the next before finally attacking her clit.

He flicked his tongue across the swollen bud, going back and forth, up and down. The pleasure was instant, and she felt herself becoming even wetter as he toyed with her clit.

"Watch us, Lucia."

Her head had been thrown back, relishing every lick, suck, and touch of his tongue.

Staring between her thighs, she watched him tease her clit before sliding down. She moaned as his tongue penetrated her pussy. His large hands pressed against her thighs, keeping them open, refusing to let them shut, not that she wanted to. She lapped up every single thing he was doing to her.

Jack kept bringing her to the edge of her release but not allowing her to push over, his expert tongue knowing what to do to drive her crazy. She wriggled, gasped, moaned, screamed, cried out, and still he didn't stop. He kept on going, driving her higher and higher until she practically wept with need.

He was the one in charge of her pleasure, her need, and he would be the one to decide when to let her push over the edge into bliss. He cupped her ass tightly, to the point that she knew she would have bruises on her flesh, but she didn't care. Not now, not ever.

She wanted his marks, craved his kind of possession, and knew she'd gladly come back for more as he threw her over the edge into a screaming orgasm that left her slightly shaken.

Jack wouldn't let her go.

He kept on stroking, drawing more of her orgasm from her until she went into a second. Only when she'd had her third climax did he release her.

Pressing a final kiss to her pussy, he moved up her body, pulling her into his arms. She tasted herself on his lips, but she didn't mind.

Turning to her side so that she could face him, she traced his lips with her finger. She liked when he got dirty, when he made a claim for her like this.

"I love listening to you come." He ran a hand down her body, reaching around to cup her ass. "I could get used to it."

"I rather like it myself." She snuggled up against him. "I don't want to go home."

She didn't know if she imagined it or not, but she was sure he tensed up.

"You've got to go home."

"I know. I didn't mean live here or anything. I know what's at stake. You don't have to worry about that."

"You're worth losing everything over."

She smiled and shook her head. "No, I'm not. You love your job, and you're pretty damn good at it as well. I wouldn't do that to you. I'm not selfish. It's just that … I like how I feel when I'm here."

"And how is that, besides being completely sated?"

"I feel like I'm not invisible. That I matter to you."

"You do."

He held her just a little tighter, and she loved it.

"When I'm at home I feel invisible. My parents, it's kind of hard to explain."

"You don't need to explain it to me. I get it. Believe me, I do." He pressed a kiss to her lips. "We'll make this work, and you're not invisible to me." He tucked a strand of hair behind her ear. "We can make this work."

She believed him.

Lucia spent the night with him, and on Sunday morning, she knew she didn't have a choice but to head home. She couldn't stay until the last minute, and Jack was already prepared to take her home.

He'd cleaned her clothes, but she didn't have any panties as he'd destroyed them. After she pulled her hair up into a bun, they drove toward the park where they ran. No one was around, and as they climbed out, Jack walked her as far as he could without raising any suspicion. He'd even changed into his running clothes so it looked like she'd bumped into him in the park. They left the park, walking the short distance toward a private walkway that would be a quick route to her home. When they got toward the edge close to the wall, and she was about to leave, he quickly grabbed her, kissing her passionately.

"Text me when you get home."

"I will."

"I'll be watching, but I want you to do that anyway."

"Another rule?"

"Keeping you safe, yes."

"I like it."

She kissed him again, and then all too reluctantly, she pulled away.

Blowing out a breath, she walked home. It was still light out, and she folded her arms, hugging herself.

When she got to her front door, both of her parents' cars were in the driveway. This was the first time she'd ever lied to them.

Just thinking about it made her feel a little sick.

Finally, unable to hold back any longer, she opened the door and entered her home.

Her parents were there.

"Where have you been?" her mother asked.

"We sent you messages. This is really irresponsible, Lucia," her father said.

"We get you a car, and this is how you treat us." This once again was from her mother. Already they were siding with each other.

She hadn't even turned around to look at them yet.

The past weekend had been the most glorious time of her life, and right now, both of them were spoiling it.

Gritting her teeth, she cleared her voice. "My car stayed in the driveway."

"And that is exactly where it *will* stay," her mother said.

She spun around, tears in her eyes. "Why am I not surprised by that?" She all but shouted at her mother. "Lucia didn't do exactly as you wanted. She didn't stay home when it was her birthday and her parents forgot."

Both of them seemed to pale and back down.

"We were sorry, Lucia, honey. It was work."

"It's always work. Don't you get that? Oh, my God, you really don't. I'm the only one that has the teachers write out report cards because you can't make it. Do you know how that feels? My eighteenth birthday you apologize for not being there and promise to go out. I wait. I do my damn homework for over four hours, and you guys forgot. You talk about *me* being irresponsible for going out and not keeping you updated on every single movement I do, but what about the two of you?" She was yelling now.

Eighteen years of being pushed aside.

Eighteen years of being invisible had brought her to this moment.

Not anymore. She wasn't about to end this weekend with them blaming her.

She'd experienced the most magical night of her life in Jack's arms, and they were not going to take that away from her.

"Lucia," her mother said.

"No. You are both responsible. I'm a good kid. Hell, I'm not even a kid anymore. I'm a full-grown adult. I spend most of my time alone. Before you tell me I'm irresponsible for having some time to myself then maybe you both should look in the mirror because you shouldn't have gone through with the pregnancy. You got me."

They were both pale, and now she was crying. Pushing past them, she ran up to her room.

"And I hate vegetarian food!" She yelled from her room and slammed the door. Flicking the lock into place, she rested her head against the door.

"You okay?" Jack asked, making her gasp.

She spun around to see the very man she was about to text resting against the wall.

"What are you doing here?" she asked, pushing some hair off her face, and wiping her tears away.

"I wanted to make sure you were okay. Then I saw the tree outside your room, and I guess my days of climbing through a girl's window are not completely over."

She laughed, moving toward him and hugging him tightly. "Did you hear that?"

"I did. I'm pleased you stood up for yourself." He cupped her chin and tilted her head back. After he dropped a kiss to her lips, she sighed. "I can't stay. I broke my own rule here."

"And what was that?"

"No climbing into a girl's window."

"I don't mind."

"I do." He kissed her again. "I better go."

She heard the footsteps outside her room.

"You okay?" he asked.

"Yes." She watched him climb out of her

window, and she was pleased her room wasn't near the front of the house for everyone to see. "Take care."

He was gone just as there was a knock on the door. Glancing around her bedroom, she brought her window partially down so that they didn't suspect anything.

Tears were still in her eyes but were no longer trailing down her face.

Batting them away, she took a deep breath and moved toward the door. "What do you want?"

"To talk," her father said.

It was always her father. Never her mother.

"I'm kind of tired right now. I'm going to shower. Get some sleep."

"Where were you, Lucia? I was so worried."

She licked her lips. "I was safe."

"You're wearing the same clothes that you went to school in."

Glancing down at her clothes, she didn't know what to say. "Goodnight, Dad."

He sighed, and she got the sense he wanted to say something more. "We do love you, Lucia."

She didn't respond. It didn't matter how much he loved her. It was just never enough. His love of his work and her mother came before her.

Stepping away from the door, she moved toward her bathroom. Stripping her clothes off, she glanced down and saw the finger marks of Jack's touch. They were on her hips, and a quick glance in the small mirror over the sink showed they were also on her ass. She wore the signs of his affection, and she couldn't help but smile.

This was real.

She hadn't spent the weekend imagining being in her teacher's bed.

She'd done it.

Had sex.

Been with Jack.

Only, it didn't feel like a dirty little secret.

Far from it.

This felt real.

It felt right.

She didn't want it to end.

Stepping beneath the shower, she closed her eyes, enjoying the warm spray. Her thoughts were still on Jack and then on how she was going to handle Marie.

****

Monday morning was always a busy and hectic time, especially for Jack as they were changing the topics they were learning about. He liked to mix it up, to help his students with their upcoming exams but to also make it fun.

He'd found it utterly boring growing up when it was nothing but work and exam-related. Still, it didn't matter as he walked into the building. Making his way toward his classroom, everything was different. He'd broken his three rules.

One, never ever fuck a student. Two, never ever fall for a student. Three, don't ever break any of the first two rules.

Over the weekend he'd broken those rules, but he didn't feel guilty. In fact, last night in bed, he'd missed her close to him. He'd even stroked the bed where she'd lain the night before.

Get your head out of your ass.

Running a hand down his face, he tried to clear the fog from his mind, but nothing helped.

"Hello, handsome," Beth said, knocking on his door.

"Morning," he said, without looking up.

Forcing himself to get his shit together, he pulled out his class schedule and tapped the lesson, which was the second one of the day that held Lucia's class. He needed to get his head in the game, as otherwise he'd be the one to completely blow this, and that was not what he wanted.

While he'd been so lost in thought, Beth entered his office, and it was only when she touched his back that he realized she'd not moved on.

Taking her wrists, he forced her to let him go.

"You seem a little tense today," she said.

"Just getting everything ready." He didn't want her in his classroom, but forcing her out wasn't going to help him. This was something he was going to have to deal with. He rubbed his chin.

"So, I wanted to stop by your place this weekend. I thought we could catch up."

"I was busy." He pulled out the marked sheets. Finding the correct folder for his first class of the day, he placed it on the desk.

"Oh, well, maybe some other time. I really liked going out with you."

"I hate to do this, but I've got to get ready, Beth. Can we talk another time?"

"You seem different, Jack."

"I'm not. Just focused. A lot of students to teach, you know." *And I fucked one this weekend. One I care about and you and me, it's never going to happen. Not in a million years.* "I've got to go."

"Of course."

Leaving the classroom, he closed the door, nodded at her, and headed toward the library. There were a few students in the hallway who greeted him, and he acknowledged them. They were all talking about the upcoming parties, one of which was the annual high school Halloween party. He'd already nominated himself to be part of it, and even had his costume ready. The zombie teacher.

It was lame and boring, but that was how he viewed high school parties. There was never any hard stuff unless one of the kids spiked the punch.

Entering the library, he gave a nod toward the librarian, who pointed toward the English section. "The books you requested are on the carriage, but I got sidetracked. They're all there."

He left her to it. She was on the phone, and he didn't know what pressing business she had, so he ignored it.

The library was empty, but as he saw the trolley that contained his own stack of books, he glanced across toward the science section and there she was. Lucia stood looking at a shelf. Her bottom lip was sucked into her mouth, her hair once again tied on top of her head, and she wore jeans and a shirt. Her bag rested precariously on her shoulder.

It had been all night, and he couldn't wait another second. Crossing toward her, he grabbed her arms and pinned her against the wall. She gasped but didn't fight him the moment that she saw it was him. The bag fell to the floor as he cupped her face, sinking his fingers into her hair.

Slamming his lips on hers, he knew this was dangerous, and he shouldn't do this, but he couldn't bring himself to stop. He had to taste her, to touch her, to consume that fire that was raging within him.

Her hands tightened on his shoulders and plundered her mouth as soon as she opened up. It wasn't enough, but then it would never be enough.

They had crossed that line, opened something up, and now they had to face the consequences.

Pulling away, he bit her lip and stared into her eyes.

"Not that I'm complaining, but I thought we had to keep this a secret," she said.

"We are." He forced himself to pull away even though he'd love nothing more than to push her to the floor and teach her something else that she could do. "How is your pussy?" he asked.

Her cheeks brightened once again. "It's fine."

"Good." He stroked her cheek. "I'll be thinking of you today."

Stepping away from her, he picked up her bag and placed it over her shoulder.

"How did it go with your family?"

"We didn't talk last night or this morning. They were still home, but that's no surprise. Not really. They don't like it when there's conflict at home. I guess it's why they don't stick around all that often."

He wanted to stay and talk about more, but the longer he was there, the higher the chance of him getting caught.

"They shouldn't have forgotten you."

"I can't complain. I had a really good birthday night."

"Good. How was Marie this morning?" he asked.

"Erm, she was good. She kept asking me a lot of questions, but she was just worried."

He saw the guilt on her face. "I'm sorry."

"You don't have to be sorry. I know we have to do this. I don't have to like it, though. She's my best friend."

"The one thing I've learned in this life, Lucia, is that everyone has secrets. Even our best friends."

She wrinkled her nose. "I don't know. She seems pretty open about everything. I did promise her that Mark

Ruffalo fest this weekend."

"Okay." He took her hand, kissing her knuckles. "I better get ready for class."

She nodded.

He didn't want to pull away, but he did. No one was around, and as he grabbed his books, he forced himself not to look back. He wanted to.

Fuck did he want to.

This was going to be torture for the two of them.

With the books in his hands, he gave a thumbs-up to the librarian as he made his way back to class. He'd set the books out where he needed them just as the bell rang. Students began to file into their respective rooms where they had registration, and he had his own class that he quickly dealt with. It was only fifteen minutes where the principal ran through a list of points for the upcoming week.

He listened with half an ear.

At the fifteen-minute point, the class left, and soon he had his own class that he had to teach. Pushing Lucia from his mind, he began to focus on his class, talking them through one of the more popular English plays.

He answered the questions, made his class laugh at some of his answers, and his assessments, and then before he knew it, the bell went again. He yelled out the homework with a warning that if they didn't do it, there would be consequences.

The first of his next class arrived. He'd already scrubbed at the board and was putting the next topic on.

"Morning, class," he said.

He felt when Lucia walked into the room. The scent of strawberries filled the air. He kept his back to the class, writing what they were learning. Love and hate. The fine line between the two. Connor swaggered in, and he didn't even need to look to know he'd taken a seat in front of Lucia. Rachel entered, and the look of hate on her face was so clear to see.

Jack didn't like this, not one bit.

Turning toward the room, he forced himself not to look, but like a moth to a fucking flame, he glanced toward Lucia's table. Connor leaned back in his chair, talking to her. From the look on Lucia's face, she wasn't interested in whatever the kid had to say.

Get your shit together.

"Poetry contains many different emotions and feelings, one of those being a love and hate relationship. Connor, stand up," he said.

He'd gladly have that kid as far from Lucia as possible.

"What up, teach?"

"Love and hate. Let me have it."

"There's a fine line between them."

"Is that all you've got for me? The same usual talk about how they're the same. Nothing that makes them better, worse?"

He'd never called on Connor to stand up in class. Now with every single person watching him, the cockiness wasn't there.

"Well, Connor, I'm waiting."

"What can I say, you love someone, you do. You hate someone, you beat them."

A few chuckles erupted around the classroom. "As always you provide a colorful interpretation but not one I'm interested in. Sit down."

He moved around the classroom, picking out select people to say what they thought of love and hate.

"What makes them the same is that they can be equal in passion," Lucia said, drawing his attention. "You love someone and you can hate someone the same way, but you also can combine the same two emotions for the same person."

"Well done. This is also subject to interpretation. Within stories and even within poems someone can hate with a passion, but everything they speak about can create love. It's like the opposite of each emotion." Placing a book on their desk, he made his way up and down the aisles, speaking as he did. When he got to Lucia's table, he waited for her to take the book. Her thumb stroked across his. He wanted nothing more than to kiss her, but this was something he had to keep to his fucking self.

Focus.

Ignoring Connor, he made his way to the front of the classroom, read out a single poem, and asked each of them to provide him with a point that the poem gave. He got the class flowing, and even though his gaze kept locking with Lucia's, he didn't draw any attention to her.

All too soon the bell went and the class started to filter out. He watched them leave. Connor moved past him.

"Good class today, teach."

"Maybe if you spend less time flirting and more time paying attention, you'll be able to answer my questions."

"I don't need to answer your questions, but I'll be careful. My dad would love any excuse to go after a teacher," Connor said.

"How manly you are. You get your dad for everything."

Connor had nothing to say, and he stared him down.

Lucia was the last to leave. "You shouldn't have done that."

"This is my classroom, and I will not have him

slacking on my time."

"It's not that. Connor's been known to get his dad involved. It's why for the most part the teachers are afraid of him."

"I'm not afraid of him, Lucia. I do a good job."

"I'd hate for you to lose your job over something he's said or done."

"Not going to happen. Remember what I've said though. Be careful around him."

"I have no intention of being alone with him." She licked her lips, but they couldn't say anything more. His next class came in, and she smiled at him, leaving him alone.

This was going to be fucking torture.

He got through the rest of the day, and he stayed in the staff room for his lunch. Beth and Coleman were there, flirting with each other.

Jack didn't know if she was trying to make him jealous as she kept on stealing little looks his way.

"Hey, did you hear?" Coleman asked.

"Hear what?"

"The attack on that woman. It was completely random. They found the guy, as he attacked two other women in different towns. He's a drifter, but they finally caught him."

"At least you taught the kids how to look after themselves," Beth said.

"Yeah, at least we did that."

The rest of the day went by without a hitch, but he didn't like the twisting feeling in his gut. Ever since they taught the kids self-defense, Connor had developed an interest in Lucia. One Jack didn't like, and with the way people talked about him, he didn't think it was healthy for her.

There was no one he could talk to.

When the bell went for the end of the day, he was relieved. Packing up his stuff, he made his way to the library, only to find that it had been closed. Returning the books to his classroom, he left the building. His car was one of the few that was left. No sign of Lucia or her car.

Driving home, he pulled up to his drive and got out.

He didn't go for a beer, and instead made himself a cup of coffee. Collapsing on the sofa, he saw Lucia. The way she'd looked spread-eagled, willing, open, fucking perfection as far as he was concerned.

His cell phone buzzed.

Lucia: **Did you get home safely?**

He smiled. Even though he was older than she was, he liked that she cared.

Jack: **Yeah. Lonely though. Missing you.**

Lucia: **Parents are home. I'm in my bedroom but they're cooking. I'm kind of scared.**

Jack: **Maybe they realized that they've been bad.**

Lucia: **I don't know. I think I'm used to them not caring.**

Jack: **Can't have it both ways.**

Lucia: **I wish I was with you.**

Jack: **You will be. Did Marie suspect anything?**

Lucia: **She kept asking what was different about me. I told her nothing and that she needed glasses. She should wear them but she refuses to. I don't like lying to her.**

He got that.

Lucia: **I enjoyed your class today but you really do need to be careful of Connor. Check him out online. You'll see.**

Jack: **I'm not afraid of him. I've done nothing wrong.**

Lucia: **Most teachers haven't done anything wrong but because they won't jump for him, he can get daddy involved.**

Jack: **Are you returning to social media?**

Lucia: **Nope. I learned my lesson. I'll keep my bullying to high school. I've got to go. Dinner is ready.**

He didn't like the thought of her getting bullied at all. Taking her advice, he did do a quick search and found Connor on his social media pages. The kid was an asshole and a bully. He'd seen some of the comments he'd left, but also, he checked out the one marked about one of the teachers.

"Sick bastard should have known not to mess with me," he'd written. "No teacher is safe."

This just proved to Jack that he didn't like the kid.

After running through the kid's social media pages, he still didn't like what he saw. Connor was a kid used to getting what he wanted or getting daddy to move them out of the way, which was fine. One quick glance, and Jack already knew who the dad was, and of course the weight he had to throw around.

This just made him smile.

Money equaled power.

He lived his life on a teacher's salary, but his family came from money. His parents made a lot being famous lawyers, but he'd also had his grandfather's inheritance. He'd taken that money and invested it.

A simple teaching life was all he lived, but he had a lot of wealth to his name as well. He simply didn't use it, much to his parents' annoyance.

Smiling, he closed the laptop just as there was a knock on the door.

Getting to his feet, he made his way over, and opened the door without checking who it was.

Lucia stood on the doorstep.

It was late, already past eight.

"What are you doing here?" he asked.

The smile on her lips died.

"I … erm … I…"

He pulled her into his home, pressing her up against the door. "The next time you're traveling over here, let me know. I don't want anything to happen to you. Do you understand?"

"I heard they caught that attacker guy," she said. "It's safe."

"It's never safe."

"Is this another of your rules?"

"Hell, yes."

She smiled. "Then as a very good student, I'll follow them, sir."

He loved her sass, her cheekiness, fucking everything. Slamming his lips down on hers, he felt her melt against him, moaning. He locked their fingers together, his dick already going hard at the feel of her pressed against him.

Jack groaned, wanting to be balls deep inside her.

"Am I too much for you?" he asked, kissing down her neck.

He was addicted to the scent of strawberries.

"I won't break, Jack. I want this. I want you."

"Do you even know what you're asking?" he asked. "There's so much I want to do to you. Fuck, I should be thrown in jail just for thinking about them."

She sank to her knees there in his doorway.

The front door was closed, and he flicked the lock in place just as she reached for the button on his jeans.

"I don't suppose this is one of the things on your mind."

"You wanting to suck my cock?" he asked.

"Yes." She eased the zipper down, and he hissed as the tension released and his cock sprang free. "You're my first, though, so you're going to need to tell me what you like."

That shouldn't be sexy, but he found it so. He wanted her, couldn't get her out of his mind.

"Wrap your fingers around my dick. That's it, now work it up and down to the base." The tip already had pre-cum leaking out, and he hissed at the pleasure.

Her touch was inexperienced but driving him crazy for more. This shouldn't be happening, but the forbidden certainly had its perks.

"Run your thumb across the tip. Now slide it down my cock."

She followed every instruction, tightening her hand, moving just a little faster.

When she leaned in close and pressed her tongue against the tip, he jumped from the touch.

"Sorry, I didn't mean to hurt you."

"You didn't. There's no pain."

"You're sure?"

"I'm sure. Lick me again."

Her tongue went against the tip of his dick and slid over the little hole that leaked his pre-cum. He watched her taste him.

Sliding his fingers in her hair, he wrapped it around his fist, groaning as her mouth covered the head.

"Don't use your teeth. You don't need to bite me, just suck." He sank inside her mouth until he hit the back of her throat, and the pleasure blew him away.

Pulling out, he slid back inside, and watched his cock, now coated in her saliva as she took him.

He never went too deep, not wanting her to gag.

Taking her hand, he placed it around the length she wasn't sucking on and showed her exactly how he liked it while also holding her in place so that he could fuck her mouth.

Her plump lips looked so good as they sucked on him.

It was all too much, and before he could stop himself, he came, flooding her mouth, and watched in amazement as she swallowed every last drop of his cum.

She stared up at him, the trust in her eyes bringing him to his knees as he held her close. Cupping her face, he stroked a thumb across her bottom lip where his cum lay, and she took him back into her mouth.

"You're fucking beautiful," he said.

"See, watching porn has its perks."

"You got all that from watching porn?"

"And reading. I do like to read, and the joy of having no parental control, I can do what I like." She looked empowered, strong, courageous.

Taking her lips, he tasted himself on her tongue, but he didn't care. Pulling her clothes off, he moved her back until they were on the stairs.

She was completely naked, and he spread her legs, sliding between her pussy, tasting her cunt.

She cried out his name, the sound echoing on the stairs, and he didn't care.

He wanted her to come, to flood his mouth with her cream.

When he plunged two fingers inside her, she rocked her hips back and forth as he licked her clit.

She was fire in his arms.

Her fingers held his head, moving her pussy against his face. He loved that she took as much as she gave.

When she gave, the sounds she made drove his arousal higher.

Even though he'd already come seconds before,

he needed her again. Pulling a condom from his pants, he tore into the packet, sliding it on.

He couldn't wait to take her upstairs to his bedroom. Pressing the tip of his cock to her entrance, he slid in deep.

"Fuck, Lucia, you feel so good."

Her tight cunt wrapped around his dick like a fist.

Pulling out of her heat, he looked down and watched as he thrust inside her. The lips of her pussy spread across his cock.

"Look at us, Lucia. Look at me deep inside you."

He pulled out and held his cock at her entrance.

They both moaned as he filled her, slamming in deep.

Kissing her hard, he drove inside her, taking what belonged to him. She was his woman, and he wasn't going to let her go. He couldn't.

They were meant to be together.

The age gap be damned.

The forbidden didn't matter as he filled her. Being inside her was a fucking dream. She was made for him. There was no other way to describe it.

Lucia was his.

Kissing down her neck, he sucked on each of her tits. Reaching between them, he stroked her clit, wanting her to come, to find her release before he did.

"Feels so good," she said, arching up.

Begging him for more.

Taking each and every thrust.

Driving up to meet him.

She was here because she wanted to be.

No one could take that away.

Lucia came hard on his cock, his name on her lips.

The pleasure of her tightening pussy set him off,

and he joined her, flooding the condom with his cum as he came.

Afterward they were both panting. As he looked at her, he saw the smile on her lips. Cupping her face, he smiled along with her.

"What?"

"I had no intention of doing any of that," she said.

This caused him to raise a brow. "You didn't?"

"No. I just wanted to see you, and I guess one thing led to another."

"Which led to another. I like seeing you, Lucia. I don't expect sex."

"Don't even think about being guilty." She sat up and cupped his face. "I was the one that went to my knees first. I initiated this. Actually, I'm starting to think I put in all the effort." She kissed him again.

He chuckled. "Well, I'm never one to be outdone, so I'll have to think of something else to make up for it."

"I like the sound of that."

Her kisses woke up his need once again, and her pussy tightened around his length.

"Can you stay?" he asked.

"I want to, but I can't."

"I know. It's fine." It wasn't fine. It was far from fine.

"We can make this work."

They didn't have much of a choice. Losing her was not an option for him.

Chapter Ten

One week later

Sneaking off had its perks. Lucia got to see Jack most nights of the week, but arriving home late and climbing the wall to get into her bedroom sucked. She also had to make sure she was quiet.

She locked her bedroom door every single night so her parents weren't able to barge in and see her gone. She'd also blown off Marie every single evening, apart from the movie marathon, even though she'd been tempted to cancel so that she could spend more time with Jack.

Heading downstairs, she'd left her hair down today, but stayed with her usual jeans and shirt.

Standing in the kitchen, she was making herself a coffee when her dad appeared.

Things had been stressful since the whole birthday incident. She tried to avoid them as much as possible, and had the excuse of homework, and checking out colleges.

"Morning, Dad," she said.

"Morning, honey." His arms were folded, and he had his serious face on, which only made her nervous.

"What's up?"

"What's going on with you?"

"I have no idea what you mean?"

"You're distant."

She stirred her coffee and noticed her mother was very absent. "I'm not distant."

"I know when my daughter is avoiding us."

"Don't you think it best that I do?"

"I don't get it, Lucia. Everything was going well."

She laughed. "On what universe was everything going well? I barely saw you. If either of you could make it to dinner it was to bring home that horrible takeout. Work is something you and Mom have in common."

"I get it, we're the bad guys. We've abandoned you, and you're punishing us."

"Wow, you really think that's what this is about? Me punishing you."

"How you're behaving now is like a child. We raised you better than that."

"You don't even know me," she said, the coffee forgotten. She turned to look at her dad. Her heart raced, and she didn't feel in the best of moods.

She was tired, and her period had started, and having this with him didn't work for her.

"We know you."

"No. You know I'm a good person. You know I'm a good kid. I have good grades. I work hard. But neither of you know *me*. Not once did either of you ask if I wanted to come to London."

"London? It was for a boring conference."

"That you love. You both have these careers that are your entire world, and you get each other, but I'm always the one left outside, not allowed to catch even a glimpse of it. You can call it 'the birthday incident' all you want, but it won't change anything. It won't stop you from forgetting me when something calls at work." She stepped away, looking around the kitchen. "I've got to get to school. I promised Marie I'd pick her up. Her car's in the shop."

She turned her back on her dad and made her way toward the front door.

"I know your mother and I make a lot of mistakes. We screw up when things should be natural. We love you, Lucia. Both me and your mother."

She nodded her head and smiled back at her dad. "I know."

Leaving the house, she climbed into the car, and without looking back she drove toward her friend's.

Every single day was getting colder, and as she waited for Marie, she wondered what the hell she was going to do. She couldn't keep arguing with her parents.

Wiping away the stupid tears, she tried to ignore the pain that twisted in her gut. This wasn't supposed to be that hard.

"What's wrong?" Marie asked, climbing into the car.

"Nothing."

"Don't tell me nothing. That's a lie. You're my best friend, Lucia. What's wrong?"

I'm a shitty friend.

I've been blowing you off for Mr. Parker.

I'm having hot-as-fuck sex, and I can't tell you about it.

"I just had an argument with my dad."

"Damn, I'm so sorry. Things are still not good between you."

"It's not. It will work out, I'm sure of it. I just wished it would happen. I know I need to get over whatever is wrong with me."

"You always do that," Marie said.

"What?"

"Assume everything is wrong with you. It's not always the case. Yes, your parents missed your birthday, and I think you should be pissed at it. In fact, I think you should have been pissed for a lot of birthdays they missed and forgot. Look at when you turned thirteen. They completely forgot that they didn't even get you a card or a present for over a week."

"I'm cared for though. A lot of other kids have it

a lot worse."

"So? I'm your best friend, so I'm going to take your side on everything. You've got to know that."

"You are a good friend."

"The very best and don't you forget it."

When they pulled up into the car park at the high school, Marie had to go. She was heading to the library to return some books. Lucia locked up her car, and was heading across the grounds toward the entrance where her locker room was when she was stopped.

Rachel and her little group of friends were standing there.

Even though it was cold, they still wore the shortest miniskirts that Lucia had ever seen.

Connor always sat in front of her table in English, and he always found a reason to be near her locker.

"What?" she asked.

"You do know he's only using you, right? He wants to fuck you and show everyone in school what a fat waste of space you are."

Her heart started to pound. Had she and Jack been caught? Wait, why would Jack do that?

"Connor thinks you're a joke, and this is a way for him to get his kicks."

Instantly, she felt relief and couldn't believe for a split second she'd thought Rachel was talking about Jack. Connor, on the other hand, didn't surprise her. She'd figured there was an ulterior motive. At least now she knew.

"I don't have to listen to this."

She made to go around them, but Rachel caught her arm, holding her tightly to the point of pain.

"I'm not done with your skank ass yet. That guy is mine. That fortune is mine. If Connor likes to play around, I really don't care. You, however, are a sham.

You're not fit for his interest."

"Let go of me."

"You're a fucking pig. So you will stay away from Connor."

"I don't want him. I have no idea what your crazy ideas are, but I don't. Let go of me. I mean it, otherwise you'll get to see what it's like to be punched by a fat girl, and believe me, we leave marks."

She hated confrontation, and this thing with Rachel was getting worse. She had some kind of design on Connor.

The gossip was they were going to marry and unite their two families, which meant more money, more everything.

Lucia didn't give a damn about Connor.

His attention left her uncomfortable, and she knew without a doubt that the only reason he showed any interest in her was because of their self-defense class, which she'd hated.

"You better watch your step," Rachel said.

The threat was there, but Lucia wasn't interested.

She went straight to her locker.

Her hands shock as she opened it up, and she stepped back as tissues spilled out; lots of wet, soaked tissues.

Gritting her teeth, she ignored the laughter.

It had been some time since she had the good old locker joke, but whatever.

"What the hell is this?" Jack asked.

No, it's Mr. Parker.

She didn't look up at him as she grabbed the trash can and pulled it closer to her. Whoever had done this would just love to watch her humiliation.

Rachel and her group of friends had followed her inside, and they stood, laughing into their hands.

Mr. Parker crouched down and started to help her.

"Don't," she said. "Don't help. You have to be the teacher." She kept her voice low so only he could hear.

She didn't dare look at him.

Between her confrontation with her dad, and now this, seeing Jack, Mr. Parker, she'd break down.

It was her time of the month, and her nerves were already on edge.

"Rachel, you find this funny? Come and clean it up."

"No, I don't clean shit up. Isn't that for the poor?"

"It's for everyone. Clean it up. You find it funny, and now as your teacher, you'll help a fellow student clean up the mess."

She didn't want Rachel helping her. This would just cause more problems, but she didn't argue with him. Instead, she kept on cleaning, and then Rachel was there, helping put the soaked toilet paper in the trash.

"What's the matter, Deen, piss your pants?"

"Congratulations, Rachel, you've just earned yourself a detention for the entire week."

"What the fuck?" Rachel asked.

"You want to keep starting with me, I'll make sure your ass doesn't even see prom, and I don't forget."

"My dad is going to hear about this."

"It sounds delightful. Why don't you invite him along when Connor's dad's due to see me? I'd like to have a nice, friendly chat with the two of them."

Lucia had not heard about Connor's dad coming to school.

She glanced up and saw Mr. Parker glaring at Rachel.

"He will!"

The toilet paper was cleaned up, and she looked inside her locker. Several of her books were soaking wet. They would be useless.

"Are you okay?" he asked.

She glanced up and down the corridor, but the fun seemed to be over.

"It's not the worst thing they've ever put in my locker."

"What's the worst?" he asked.

"Garbage. It stank, and they all laughed as I cleaned it out." She shrugged. "It took them some time. I'll have to change my locker code." She pushed some hair out of her face. "At least they only doused it with water. Anything else would have been really gross." She licked her lips. "You never mentioned anything about seeing Connor's dad."

"It's a recent development." He held a card up. "Wants to meet to talk."

"Jack, I mean, Mr. Parker—"

"Don't worry about it."

"How can I not?"

"Because it's not something for you to concern yourself with. I can handle them. It's my problem. Not yours."

"You'll tell me what happens?" she asked.

"You're coming around tonight?"

She couldn't resist looking around the corridor. There was a small distance between them, and she really wanted to close it.

"Yes, I'd like that."

"Then come."

"I've got to drop Marie off first."

"I'll be late as I'm dealing with this dad situation. I'll be there."

She nodded.

"Don't let them get to you, Lucia."

He went to touch her and she closed her locker, stepping back.

They couldn't do that, not here, not in front of people.

"Thank you, Mr. Parker."

"Miss Deen," he said.

She spun on her heel and made her way to class. Taking a seat in the back near the window, she rested her head in her hands, and hated the secrecy. She knew exactly why it had to happen, but that didn't make it any easier.

In fact, it made it harder.

Connor's dad was an asshole of the highest order.

He'd gotten teachers fired for making Connor look stupid. She didn't want anything to happen to Jack.

Her relationship with him meant a lot to her.

Tapping her pencil on the table, she zoned out in class, thinking about how good it felt to be in Jack's arms.

He made all the bad go away and stopped her from feeling like she didn't matter. He was the complete opposite and made her feel like she was seen and heard.

"Miss Deen?"

Her name being called brought her out of her thoughts.

Glancing to the front of the class, she saw the teacher looking at her.

"Are you done daydreaming and can you please answer the question?"

Several smirks echoed round the class, but she ignored them. Staring at the equation on the board, it reminded her of her mother's office, and she quickly worked it out. The teacher looked surprised, but he didn't say anything, instead moving onto the next question.

Stay focused, Lucia.

****

To Jack, Principal Dowed had seemed like a straight and narrow kind of guy. Getting the call this morning that he was wanting to be seen by a parent, he'd not thought anything of it. When Dowed then went on and on about how important this man was for the investment and donations, things had started to click together, and he knew instantly that Connor had run to Daddy.

He wasn't even a little bit surprised by this.

"Now, Mr. Mills, you know how the school likes to accommodate you, and we make every effort to ensure that Connor is well taken care of," Principal Dowed said.

Sitting back in his office chair, Jack watched the principal fawn all over him as if he was some spiritual creature.

The same went for Rachel James's mother.

Jack just sat there, waiting, expecting something better. They were both dressed up in their expensive designer suits. Their kids were spitting images of the two of them.

"And I pay for that privilege, Dowed, which is why I'm here today." Mr. Mills turned toward him. "You're Jack Parker?"

"The very one."

"I had heard good things about you, but Connor takes exception to a teacher that mocks him."

"Jack is very sorry about that—"

"How about I answer for myself because if you were going to speak for me, what was the point of me being here?" Jack said, interrupting Dowed. "I didn't mock Connor. He wasn't paying attention in my classroom. I got his attention. He was cocky, answered a question wrong. I told him so and moved on. I have no room in my class to stroke the ego of students who don't answer correctly. The same goes for girls who bully. Rachel deserved to help, and if she didn't like it, well, if you can't do the time, don't do the crime."

"It was some sodden toilet tissue. My girl is way too good for that. Tell him, Dowed."

"Mr. Parker, we have a certain agreement."

"I don't do agreements. I'm a teacher. You want them to throw money at you to kiss their students' ass, be my guest. I signed on to be a teacher, not to make a mockery of what I do. Connor and Rachel don't meet the grade, then as far as I'm concerned, they will not be fit for my class, and I will not be intimidated by money."

"I can have your job from you," Mr. Mills said.

"I'm Jack Parker, Mr. Mills. You can keep making your threats, but unless you wish for this special privilege to be made public, my job is secure. Cost me my job and I will take you to court."

"You can't afford it."

Jack smiled. "My parents are two of the best lawyers in the country. Not only can I afford it, but they never lose. Look them up, you'll see. You want to take this further, then I'm for it. I have never done anything wrong, and I'm happy for the world to know my teaching methods. Are you ready for them to know how you like to get teachers fired?" He looked toward Dowed. "Or that you allow yourself to be blackmailed by parents? It makes people wonder what you're willing to do to doctor exam results. That can be quite a handful." He stood up. "I'll let you guys figure this out." He patted Mr. Mills's arm. "Don't ever let a boy send you to do a man's job."

He left the classroom, and spotted Rachel and Connor. They had this evil look in their eye as if they expected him to look sad or worried.

"Connor, get in the car," his dad said.

"Rachel, now!"

"What the hell? You said you could handle it," Rachel said.

"Dad?"

"I don't want to hear from you."

Jack watched as the two kids left the building, but Mr. Mills stayed behind. They stood, staring at one another. He waited for the other man to speak.

"I'm aware of your parents' reputations," Mr. Mills said.

"I hold no ill will against you or your son. I grade correctly, and I do not ever believe in preferential treatment."

"Even though you're here because of your parents. We do what we can for our kids."

"As you saw, Principal Dowed didn't know who I was. Everything that I own and possess I earned on my own. Your boy, you keep cleaning up his messes there's going to come a point when you can't do that and he's going to have to answer on his own."

"That time won't come."

"For your sake I hope not. Don't threaten me, Mr. Mills. I don't take kindly to it."

They stared at each other, both of them masters in their own kingdom. If he'd allowed his parents to interfere, he'd be the head of this school, but he didn't want that. His grandfather had taught him that a man's worth was based on what he could do and achieve on his own.

Everything he had belonged to him, and no one was going to take that from him. Not now, not ever.

Parents like Mr. Mills and Mrs. James were not unheard of. He'd witnessed it in a couple of schools he'd taught at.

Teachers had crumpled in the face of all that power.

It was a power that he'd grown up with and recognized. When people said the name Parker in his parents' circle, it commanded respect. He learned to hold onto that power, and to only use it when absolutely necessary.

"Well, I think that went rather well," Principal Dowed said, coming to stand beside him.

Staring at the man, Jack no longer held any respect for him. "You're a disgrace to teachers, and have no right to wear the title," he said.

"Excuse me? You cannot speak to me like that."

"I can speak to you any way I like. You allow parents to bully you in order to look the other way. You have an entire school of students under your care, and you offer special treatment to two people that I know hurt others." He looked at Dowed. "You don't deserve to be principal."

He didn't linger.

The last thing he wanted to do was be in the company of a man that he now wanted to hit. How many teachers had been pushed aside because of this man? The very thought made him so fucking angry.

Climbing into his car, he drove out of the school. Turning up the music, he shouted to the rock song playing, not caring as he cleared his mind. This wasn't supposed to be so fucking hard, not now.

Life was supposed to be getting easier.

He didn't trust Dowed, and he wondered who else had a hand in Mills's pocket.

Arriving at his driveway, he spotted Lucia's car parked down the street. Climbing out, he watched her lock up and head his way. Opening the door, he let her inside. The moment the door was closed, he trapped her between the wall and his body, needing her strawberry scent and her taste to surround his senses.

"We keep doing this," she said.

"I can't help it. It's always too fucking long between touching you." He twirled a strand of hair around his finger, tugging a little on the length. "I missed you."

"Are you still a teacher?"

"It would be easier for the two of us if I wasn't."

"That wasn't what I was asking, and you know it."

"I'm still a teacher, so you're going to have to complete your homework assignment for me."

She chuckled. "How did you do that?"

"Quite easily, if I do say so myself. I fought fire with fire."

"You're the first teacher to not get burned by the wrath of Connor's dad."

"I'm sick and tired of hearing that boy's name tonight."

She pretended to lock her lips and throw away the key. "I'm more than happy to not talk about him again, like, ever."

"How long can you stay?" he asked.

"I changed my clothes. If you want, I can stay all night."

"I'd like that."

"But." She placed a finger against his lips.

"I don't like buts."

"We can't do anything. It's … erm … that time of the month. You know, being a woman and all."

He stroked her stomach. "How are you feeling?"

"I'm okay. I'm used to the cramps."

"Have you eaten?"

"No. I kind of left my parents' home. Told them I

was seeing a friend."

"You should text them. Let them know you're staying the night. I'll cook us up some food."

"Not vegetarian? Please tell me it's not."

He laughed. "Babe, I'm a grown-ass man. I don't do vegetables unless it's a little salad on the side of my plate. Call your parents or text them. I'll get started on some food."

Putting his briefcase on the table, he made his way into the kitchen. He'd purchased some steaks yesterday at the market. Preheating his oven, he opened up a bag of precut, precooked fries. Dumping them in the oven, he looked up as Lucia entered.

"They're not happy about it."

"No?" He didn't imagine they would be.

"I just need some space right now."

"Things will work out with you and your parents."

"You think so?"

"I know so. There's no way it can't."

"Did it work with you and your parents?" she asked.

"We're still on speaking terms, so I guess it did." He winked at her.

They both froze, however, when his doorbell rang.

"Are you expecting someone?"

"No." He moved away from the stove and made his way toward the front door. Closing his eyes, he wasn't interested in the woman on the other side. "It's Ms. Bertram."

"I better … hide."

"Yes."

He waited a few minutes for her to hide, and he didn't know where she was.

Opening the door, he forced a smile to his lips as he stared at Beth.

"Hey, Beth, what brought you here?"

"I hope you don't mind. Derick told me that you had an appointment this afternoon with Connor's dad, and I just wanted to make sure everything is okay. That you're fine."

"Yes, everything is fine," he said.

"It is." She bounced from one foot to another, and the last thing he wanted was for her to be in his home but the gentlemanly thing was to let her.

"Come on in."

This was his fucking time with Lucia. Closing the door behind her, he made his way down toward the kitchen.

No sign of Lucia at all.

"I'm just about to make me something to eat." He quickly put the steaks into the fridge so she didn't see he had two of them.

"Oh, I'm so sorry."

"It's fine. You were worried?"

"Well, the man does have a bit of a reputation."

"Yes, well, I'll be at work tomorrow, and we have an understanding. There's no need to worry." He faced her and didn't know what else to say to get her out of his home. "How did you know where I lived?"

"I may have taken a trip to the principal's office during lunch, and he was looking through your file. I wanted to tell him that I thought you were an outstanding teacher and didn't deserve to be put on the chopping block."

"It's not going to happen. Men like Mr. Mills just need to learn that money can't buy them anything."

"It just makes life easier."

"Is he known for bribing teachers and officials?"

he asked.

"It's not like that, Jack."

"Look, you clearly have a way of doing things in Beyer Hill, but I don't. I'm used to following the book, and that means no preferential treatment for any one student. I don't give a fuck if Connor's daddy is rich. That won't stop me from correcting him in my class or calling on him. I think it's best that you leave."

"Jack?"

"No, I would like to eat alone, and that was exactly what I'm going to do."

He saw she wanted to argue, but he really wasn't interested. There was no way he'd lose his job, and it was time Connor's little reign of terror ceased in the school.

Moving her toward the front door, he held it open, letting her know in no uncertain terms that she was no longer invited into his home.

"Jack, I'm really sorry."

"It was thoughtful of you for stopping by. I appreciate it, but I won't be blackmailed into giving a student a break or threatened because I refuse to. Goodnight, Ms. Bertram." He closed the door, locking it. Glancing through the peephole, he waited until she had gone before turning away from the door.

"You okay?" Lucia asked.

"Yeah, I'm fine. I had no idea she was coming over."

"I gathered with the way that whole conversation went down."

He moved up to her. "Are you okay?"

"Me, I'm fine. Starving."

He cupped her face, dropping another kiss to her full lips. "I put the steaks away so she didn't see them."

"Ah, you're not wanting to share your food with anyone else. I get it." She winked at him, which made him laugh.

"I want to feed *you*, Lucia."

Grabbing the steaks out of the fridge, he quickly checked the fries, and they were not burned. He finished them and then got started on cooking the rest of dinner.

"Who knew you could cook?" she said.

"I live on my own. It's not something I enjoy doing all that much, but I can whip something up for my girl."

He saw her smile, and he wanted to keep her that way. Placing the steaks on the hot grill, he started to toss a salad, and within fifteen minutes, dinner was served. They didn't eat outside as there was a chill in the air, but they sat at his dining room table.

It was a little surreal to him to be eating with her, or to be eating with anyone.

"This is really good," she said, pointing down at the food.

"Good."

Watching her eat and enjoying his own food, Jack felt a peace settle over him that he'd never felt before. He'd always been busy, driven to finding the next challenge to face in life, but with Lucia, she didn't make him want to go out looking for something else.

He loved her company.

He enjoyed being with her.

For the first time in his life, he was actually happy.

She sipped at her water, and he watched her swallow before going back for more food. He wanted to take care of her. For her to be in his life.

"You keep staring," she said.

"That's because I'm sitting with a very beautiful woman, enjoying some good food. I'd stare at you all day if I could."

"Do you struggle in class?"

"Class is the hardest, but I get through it, especially knowing I'm going to get to hold you at some point."

"I like your answer."

After they finished food, she helped with the dishes, and then they sat down to enjoy a movie. Lucia rested her head on his knee as she looked through the homework that he'd set and been handed in. Every now and then he'd pause, watch a bit of the movie, or merely stroke her hair. He loved the feel of the strands as they glided through his fingers.

All too soon it was late and time for bed.

Taking her up to his room, he watched as she slowly undressed, placing her clothes on the chair so that they didn't crease. She still wore a pair of panties, and he waited for her. Lifting the blanket, he was as naked as she was. He'd even put on a pair of boxers.

She climbed into bed, and he held her tightly against him, stroking her stomach.

"Does it hurt?"

"It's okay at the moment. Some times are worse than others." She covered her face and groaned. "I shouldn't be talking with you about this. It's personal."

He laughed, kissing her shoulder. "It's completely natural, and I don't want to see you in pain."

"I'm not in pain, I promise."

She rolled to her back, and he continued the gentle strokes of her stomach. "I was so worried today," she said.

"Why?"

"You're the first teacher to have a meeting with Connor's dad and make it back. I don't want you to leave Beyer Hill."

"I thought we discussed no more talk of that

boy."

"I know, but … I'd miss you. I want you to know that."

"I'd miss you as well." He leaned forward and dropped a kiss to her lips. "I'm not going anywhere."

"You promise?"

"I don't need to promise. I know. Get some sleep, Lucia." He kissed her lips, then wrapped his arms around her.

She was part of his world now, and he didn't like that feeling that swept through him at the thought of never seeing her again. It wasn't something he wanted to think about, and there's no way he could let it happen.

He held her just a little tighter.

Lucia meant a great deal to him.

This wasn't just a taste of the forbidden to him.

In fact, that held no appeal.

The only woman he wanted was Lucia.

He'd do everything he could to keep her, even though it killed him to keep her a secret.

She was worth shouting from the rooftops over, and he would. One day, he'd be able to.

Lucia was his.

Chapter Eleven

"What are you going as?" Lucia asked.

"I'm going as ... zombie teacher." Jack thrust his arms out and started to groan.

"Oh, come on, that is so lame. Seriously?"

"Halloween is lame," Jack said, dropping a kiss to her lips before stealing the carton of noodles from her hands. "What are you going as?" he asked.

"I don't know. I was thinking of not going."

"No, come on. You've got to go to the Halloween party. It's, like, the most awesome party in the entire world." He flicked his head back, and she rolled her eyes.

"You've got to stop doing that. It looks so you."

"I thought so. How do you think I'd look with long hair?"

"Like something out of the seventies."

"Hey, they were supposed to be good times."

"I'll take your word for it."

"I wasn't actually born then, loser," he said.

She giggled.

"In all seriousness now, and stop giggling. What are you going as?"

"I'm not going. It's ... boring."

"Everyone is going, and I think it could be fun for you. Marie's going."

"I know, but..."

"Come on. No buts."

"I don't know." She wrinkled her nose.

"Have you ever enjoyed Halloween?"

"Sure. I'm the one with the large bowl of candy feeding the kids. My parents are always the ones heading out to a party or something. I stay in and watch Halloween movies."

"That is just sad. I won't have you staying in while I'm having to make sure they spike the punch properly at the school."

"Seriously?"

"How do you think I get through a party like this? I have to spike something, as otherwise the alcohol is in short supply." She watched him slurp up some noodles. "And some of the kids can get their hands on some really good stuff."

She stood up and went to his liquor cabinet, pulling out a bottle of really strong whiskey. "You mean like this?" she asked.

"How do you know that's good stuff?"

"I have eyes, and this is pretty up there, pricewise."

"I have expensive taste."

"I always think whiskey tastes like mold anyway."

He laughed. "That just goes to show you've not got the taste for it." He grabbed a glass and took the bottle from her hand. Lifting it up, she watched him take a sniff before downing it in one. "You've got to be drinking the hard stuff from a good age."

"You've mentioned how you were a rebel. Did you cause some trouble as a kid?"

"I drove my parents up the wall with my behavior. I drank a lot, smoked at the time as well. I didn't do drugs though, not even a little. I just screwed around, a lot."

"Maybe that's what I need?" she asked, teasing him.

"What's that?"

"To screw around, to act rebellious."

He caught her hand and pulled her down onto his lap.

She gasped and then moaned as his hand moved between her thighs, cupping her pussy. She loved it when he touched her.

"This is mine, Lucia. You can screw around, but only with me. I'll give you everything you need."

"You will?"

"I know what I'm doing, and I'll take care of you."

He flicked the button of her jeans, and he used his legs to get her into a position that spread her open.

Arousal flooded her pussy, and she bit her lip, trying to contain her moans. His hand slid between her jeans, moving past her panties. He gave a little tut. "You need to start wearing skirts."

"I like you working for it." She leaned back, flicking his earlobe before sucking it.

He groaned, and then she cried out as he plunged a finger within her pussy.

"Now there's my dirty girl. All wet and desperate for my nice, hard cock."

Out of the corner of her eye, she watched him fill his glass once again. He didn't make a move to drink it.

"Take your shirt off," he said.

Her hands shook a little as she worked her shirt off, and then her bra at his instruction. Sitting with just her jeans on and his arm wrapped around her, and down her pants, it felt so fucking good, even wicked.

"Damn, I love how wet your pussy is. Especially as I know it's only my dick that has been inside you."

He drew his finger up, stroking her clit, making her shudder with the pleasure as he moved back down to tease her some more.

"Wriggle out of your jeans."

She started to, but he wouldn't let her go, so she had to do some weird shimmy to get her jeans down.

"I love to feel you move against me. Your cunt is tightening around my finger, Lucia. Do you want my dick?"

"Yes."

"Good."

He pulled his finger from her pants, and she watched as he sucked the digit into his mouth, tasting her on his tongue.

Jack tapped her thigh, and she got to her feet as he moved the coffee table out of the way.

She stood completely naked, desperate, excited, and she wanted more.

He removed pillows from his chairs and placed them on the floor. Then taking her hand, he eased her down on the floor.

"Lie back."

She lay back and was surprised by how comfortable it was.

"That's it. Now, spread those pretty thighs for me."

Even though she blushed, she did exactly as he asked, spreading her legs open for him to see. She wanted this, craved his touch, and what he did to her, she was addicted to. The porn she'd watched and the books she'd read had nothing on this man.

He was a force to be reckoned with, and she loved every second of it.

Not once did he humiliate her.

Jack was sweet, caring, loving, and sexy as hell.

He didn't just take, he gave, and he showed her how good it could be if only she allowed herself to relax in her own skin.

"Now, touch your pussy," he said.

Sliding a hand down her body, she cupped herself, giving a little gasp as she was so sensitive to her own touch.

"Slide a finger inside yourself and let me watch."

This time, he sipped his whiskey, and she found him fully dressed, the sleeves of his shirt rolled up, giving a hint at his inked arms, and the way his presence seemed to command attention, so sexy.

"Let me see how wet you are."

Removing her finger, she held it up. He left his place and took her wrist. With his blue gaze on her, he sucked her digit into his mouth, and she felt the pull deep within herself.

He released her hand and stepped back, taking his seat once again. "Again."

Thrusting a finger inside herself, she moaned as she lifted up, fucking her own fingers.

"Now that is a pretty sight. Enjoying my expensive whiskey, watching my woman finger-fuck herself. That is something that's priceless. Money cannot buy what you give me, Lucia." He sipped at his whiskey, and she continued to play with herself, loving every single second that he was watching her. "Now, pull your finger up, circle your clit. I want to see how you get yourself off."

She stroked across her clit, closing her eyes as the pleasure flooded her entire body. The ache began to build, and she didn't want it to stop, not for a second.

"I didn't tell you to close your eyes. I want your gaze on me, Lucia. No one else."

She stared at Jack, watching as he drank his whiskey. She glanced down his body and caught sight of his rock-hard cock pressing against the front of his pants.

He wasn't unaffected by this.

Lucia loved his cock.

He was always so hard and ready for anything.

"Slowly, you don't need to rush, Lucia. You need

to learn to take your time, to let your body build, to become aroused. That's it … yes. Feel how good that is. Slowly, oh baby, your tits are shaking. I fucking love your tits, so big. They call for me to suck on them. I thought about that the other day, you know. Watching as you were making your way down the corridor. You didn't know I was there, watching you. Every step you took there was a little bounce, and I knew you had on that silky little bra. The one that drives me crazy. I wanted to pull you into my classroom, spread you over my desk, drive my dick inside you, and tear that bra off."

"You can have them now," she said.

She didn't know that he thought of her during school.

Lucia knew she thought of him often. In fact, during class, she'd get aroused as she watched him write out their assignment having firsthand knowledge of just how good his hands were on her body.

"Oh, believe me, baby, I will."

The promise in his voice made her ache.

Stroking her pussy, she slowed her touch, relishing every pull of pleasure. She couldn't look away, nor did she want to.

"You feel it?" he asked. "Building?"

"Yes."

"Good. I want you to come for me, Lucia. Come screaming my name. Let me see."

She stroked her pussy, watching him as he stared at her. There was something hypnotic in his gaze as he held her captive.

The pleasure started to build, to drive her closer to the edge.

Her release was just there, and she cried out, hurtling over the edge of her peak.

The sound of his name echoed off the walls in

another sign of her orgasm.

She'd closed her eyes as she came, and now she opened them as Jack moved between her spread thighs. His pants were gone. His cock sprang out, the tip already slick and ready.

He pulled his shirt off, revealing his muscular chest with his tribal ink tats. She knew he'd gotten them when he was in high school. She'd spent a lot of time tracing the outlines. Each piece of ink had a story, a moment in his life when he felt like he was going off the rails, and she loved that he shared these stories with her.

She loved hearing everything about his life, not just the glamorous parts either, of where he went on vacation. Jack had made her aware of his wealth and who he was related to. She didn't care about that. Money didn't matter to her.

Jack wrapped his fingers around his length, and she watched him work from the base up to the tip then back down again.

He reached into his pants pocket and handed her the condom. "I think it's time you knew how to put these on me."

She tore into the packet as she'd seen him do so many times.

Slowly rolling the condom over his cock, she was careful not to break it, covering his cock in the thin layer of latex. The moment she was done, he sat back, gripping her knees. Sliding his hands up her thighs, he cupped her pussy, sliding a finger deep within her.

"Such a nice, tight pussy."

He withdrew his finger and grabbed the bottle of whiskey. "Now, there is only one thing that I can think of right now that would make this whiskey taste a little better."

He slowly tipped the bottle, spilling some of the

amber liquid over her tits.

She gasped as his mouth licked and sucked at her flesh, drinking up the whiskey.

"Now that is tasty."

He poured the bottle down her stomach, and he kissed again, licking a path up her body until he claimed her lips.

She tasted the whiskey and him, and she wasn't repulsed either but excited.

"You're the tastiest thing I've ever had, Lucia."

He kept on spilling his expensive liquor onto her body and licking it up. She moaned, his touch driving her crazy. She didn't want him to stop as the arousal flooded her.

Jack didn't fuck her straight away. He took his time, drawing her closer to another orgasm before he finally filled her with his cock.

This time when she came, she did so on his dick, and he fucked her harder. He held her down, and she watched as he drove his cock within her. She screamed his name, thrusting up to meet him, not wanting this to end or to stop.

"You're mine, Lucia. All fucking mine," he said, groaning out as he came.

Even with the condom between them, she felt every single pulse.

Wrapping her arms around him, she smiled. "And that makes you mine."

****

"Hello, earth to Lucia," Marie said, waving a hand in front of her face.

It was bitterly cold outside. There had been a freak snow shower, which had made eating outside impossible.

"Sorry, I kind of zoned out there," she said.

Her thoughts were remembering a wicked teacher and a bottle of whiskey. Every time she passed the whiskey bottle now, she thought of him, of the way he held her body as he licked the amber liquid from her skin.

"You're doing that a lot lately. Is everything okay?"

"It's fine." She twirled her fork in the spaghetti she had bought. It tasted like cardboard and grease, not very nice.

"So, Halloween party. I know every single year you turn it down, but it could be awesome and tonight I'm going to pick out an outfit, and I miss you, Lucia."

She laughed. "What do you mean you miss me? I'm right here."

"You know what I mean. I feel like I don't get to see you anymore. You're always so busy with helping out at the school, or arguing with your parents, or doing your homework. Other than around school, or if I demand a movie day, I don't get to see you."

Guilt flooded her.

She'd been blowing off her friend in favor of driving over to Jack's.

Biting her lip, she forced a smile. "I was actually going to ask you if you'd like to come and help me find a costume for this party?"

"You're really going?"

"Yes, I'm really going. Why not, right? It's our last year. We should do something amazing."

"I know you love Halloween and that you avoid celebrating it because of your parents."

"Let's not talk about them," she said.

"Still not good between them?"

"It's not bad. I guess I could go back to being blissfully ignorant. You know, where I didn't think they knew any better."

"But that wasn't a good place."

"It was better than the one we're at now where I know they love work and each other more than me." She waved her hand in the air. "Ignore me. Honestly, I don't want to talk about them anymore."

She also didn't want to risk tripping up to the fact she'd been telling her parents that she was staying at a friend's. She never said that she was staying at Marie's as she didn't want to add another lie on top of a lie.

"I don't mind, but you know you're more than welcome to come and stay at my place."

"I know." She reached over the table, gripping her friend's hand.

She had to be a better friend to Marie.

Marie deserved better.

"Angry bitch coming our way," Marie said.

Spinning in her chair, Lucia saw the threat in Rachel's eyes. Over the past couple of incidents since the whole locker drama, she'd successfully avoided the other girl. Now, that was not going to happen.

In fact, Rachel came up to her and pushed her hard.

"This is not your cafeteria. You do not get to sit here."

The push had shoved her off the bench, and Lucia landed on her back with a hard thud. Rachel had never liked her. In fact, one of the reasons she stopped eating in the cafeteria were Rachel's taunts about how she'd eat all the food, or that she should be banned as she made people want to vomit by looking at her ugly self.

She didn't have time to get the upper hand as Rachel straddled her, pulling on her hair so hard that she let out a scream as Rachel landed a punch to her face.

Lucia didn't know what was happening, and the

pain exploded behind her cheek.

"This is not your place. You're a fucking dog, you bitch."

"Fight!"

"Fight!"

"Fight!"

"Fight!"

The sound echoed around the room, and as Rachel landed another punch, Lucia couldn't handle it. Using all of her weight, she pushed Rachel off her, and seeing as she wasn't holding onto anything, Rachel tripped.

Getting to her feet, Lucia stared at Rachel. She saw that Rachel's friends were holding onto Marie.

"I thought I told you not to come to this cafeteria again."

"You don't own this place."

"People like you disgust me. Your fucking fat ass on display for everyone to see."

Her jeans were very much in place.

"What the hell is going on here?" Principal Dowed said, entering the dining room.

"She started it," Rachel said. "She just attacked me."

"You lying bitch," Lucia said.

"She didn't," Marie said. "Rachel started it."

No one else would come to her defense, and she saw the smirk on Rachel's face.

"You don't want me to phone my mom again, would you, Mr. Dowed?"

Lucia was all too aware of what happened, but she couldn't mention that. If she even let anyone know that she knew about Jack, it would raise suspicions. Her face hurt.

"Come with me, Lucia."

Stepping up to Rachel, she stared the popular girl down. "One day, you won't be able to hide behind Mommy."

She grabbed her bag and smiled at Marie.

Leaving the dining room hall, she followed Principal Dowed down the corridor.

"I will phone your parents," he said.

"Why waste your time? Just send me home with whatever you're going to do."

"Sit," he said.

She sat down on the seat outside his office, arms folded. Her cheek burned because of the punch. Using her chilly hands, she placed it against her cheek. She had been in her first fight, and she was the one that was going to pay the price and she'd not even started it.

"What the hell happened?" Jack said, rounding the corner and taking a seat beside her.

She glanced over at the receptionist, who was on the phone and not paying them any attention.

"I dared to eat in the cafeteria. Rachel took offense, and then she blamed me for starting the fight."

He reached out as if to touch her, and she pulled away, shaking her head.

"No." She mouthed the word, and she saw it was hard for him to ignore. His hand clenched.

"Where's Dowed?"

"Phoning my parents. Good luck to him. This will be the first time I've been … suspended."

"You won't be suspended."

"How did you know what happened?"

"I heard a couple of students talking about it. They didn't know I was listening."

The sound of footsteps drew her attention, and she was surprised to see her father heading her way.

She frowned. "Dad?"

"I came as soon as I got the call." He moved toward her, and she stood up. He cupped her chin. "We need to get some ice on that. You started a fight."

"No, I didn't. I was sitting in the cafeteria, eating and talking with Marie, when Rachel started it. I promise, Dad, I didn't."

"I heard a couple of students talking. Lucia didn't start anything," Jack said.

Her heart started to pound. This was her dad and … boyfriend? Lover? She didn't know what Jack was.

"Who are you?"

"This is Mr. Parker, Dad. He teaches English."

Her dad shook Jack's hand. "William Deen. Most people call me Bill."

"I'm going to go and have a word with Dowed. He needs to know what I heard."

Jack gave her a look, and she watched him knock on the door, and then leave.

Turning back to her father, she frowned. "What are you doing here?"

"I was working from home today. Your mother and I have been taking it in turns to be at home. You're right. We're not home enough, and it's really embarrassing that I think this is the first time I've even entered your high school."

"It is. You've not made it for any of the parent-teacher nights."

"Excuse me," he said, looking toward the receptionist. "Can I have an ice pack for my daughter?"

"Yes."

The receptionist left, and they took a seat.

It felt awkward, and she glanced at him, and looked away. Jack still hadn't come out, and she was nervous.

Did her dad suspect anything?

The receptionist returned, handing her an ice pack. Pressing it against her cheek, Lucia winced. "Do I look like a badass?"

"No, it's not funny."

"I'm not laughing, Dad. For a skinny chick she knows how to pack a punch." She was trying to make light of it to help settle her nerves.

Her father was in her school.

The man she'd been sleeping with was also in the school. The two had never met before or even passed in the same circles.

She was tense, scared, relieved, sad, and all other emotions in between. She didn't know what to do or what to say.

"I will get this matter resolved, Lucia. I promise."

"It's fine, Dad, honestly."

"No. If you didn't start that fight, I won't have you paying the price for it. You're a smart, considerate young woman. I believe you."

She felt tears fill her eyes, but she quickly pushed them down as Jack and Dowed came out of the office.

"I need to speak with your father alone. Mr. Parker has brought me up to speed with what he heard, and I will speak to a couple of students. You're not suspended, Lucia, but I think it is best that you go home for the remainder of the day."

She nodded.

"Wait for me," her father said.

The door closed, and she turned to Jack. "What did you say?"

"We had a few choice words. Nothing for you to worry about. So that's your dad?"

"Yeah."

"He's taller and bigger than I thought he would be."

She smiled. "I don't know if I should be thanking you for that."

"I guess I imagined a small man or something."

"No. Mom's tall as well."

The receptionist wasn't there anymore.

"How do I look?" she asked, removing the ice pack. "Can I join your zombie war?"

"It's swollen and already bruising."

"Yeah, I told Dad that Rachel packed a mean punch. She may have even been wearing rings."

He went to touch her again, and she shook her head.

"You can't. You shouldn't be here."

"I'm not going anywhere until I know you're okay. Class be damned."

"You love teaching."

"Don't care. I'm not running off. I'll wait until your dad is out, and then I'll return to class."

She liked that he cared so much about her. It meant a lot to her.

"So, zombie," he said. "You're coming to the Halloween party?"

"Marie already asked me to go shopping and with this and Marie, I won't be able to make it tonight."

She saw he didn't like it, but still he nodded. "If I have to share you with your family and friend, I will."

"I like how you said friend."

"Marie's a good friend. I heard she was yelling your defense and calling Rachel and the entire hall out on her bullshit."

"It's a shame that it doesn't matter now. Thank you for whatever it was you've said. I don't want to get suspended. It won't look good on college applications."

"That's something we've got to discuss," he said.

"I've been trying to talk to my parents about it,

but they want to talk to me about opportunities available. So far, they've been too busy."

It was something she'd put off as well. With spending more time with Jack, she was able to avoid a great deal of conversations. Applying to colleges was important to her. It just hadn't come up in conversation.

The door to the office opened.

Her father and Dowed were talking as they appeared.

When they finished, she noticed Dowed and Jack shared a look, before the other man left. She didn't know what that was about, and from the way they were looking at each other, she didn't *want* to know.

"Well, I think we should head on home for the day," her father said. "Thank you for staying with my daughter."

Jack and her father shook hands once again.

"It's a pleasure to meet you."

With her father's hand at her back, she followed him outside.

"I'll follow you home. You're good to drive?"

"Yes." She'd left the ice pack on the bench. Climbing into her car, she headed for home.

Her dad followed her, and as she climbed out of the car, he was doing the same.

Entering her home, she felt nervous.

"Do you have any homework?" he asked.

"Yes."

"You're free to join me at the table."

"What did you and Dowed talk about?" she asked, joining him.

"You and your exceptional record at school. I reminded him that you were not a troublemaker and this was your first 'offense.'"

"Right. Am I going to school tomorrow?"

"Yes."

"I had plans with Marie. Can I still go ahead with that?"

"I don't know if it's wise for you to go to that party."

"I'd really like to go," she said. Also, she wanted to see Jack as a zombie, which could be a lot of fun.

"I'm trying here, Lucia. You've got to give us a break sometime."

She glanced down at the table.

"I know we fucked up. I get it." This made her look up. Her father rarely cursed. "For so long we've been the ones our work has called on. We've worked our asses off to get where we are, and we know it has been at the expense of you and this, and everything. Something is going on with you. We both see it, Lucia. We're not blind."

"Nothing is going on." The lie rolled off her lips, and she hated it. She didn't like lying.

"You're lying. I know you are. Is it a boy?"

"Dad, I'm just … you've not been home all the time, and I've been doing other stuff. Nothing is going on."

"We trust you, Lucia, to make the right decisions."

"That fight today wasn't my fault."

"I know. I know. You can talk to us about anything. You know that, right?"

She sat back, arms folded, and looked at him. "I don't know what you want me to say."

"I'm sorry," her father said. "I had the restaurant booked, and I was even leaving the office when I got called back in. Your mother texted to let me know she was just running behind."

"I get it, Dad. I do."

"No, we wanted to be there for you. We want to be here for you. We know you're going through a lot right now. It's your senior year. We went through that as well. You're doing amazingly well. You're a good girl, and we want what's best for you. We've sucked. We get that."

"Then where is Mom?" she asked.

"I told you. Dividing our time between work and home. We're trying, Lucia. You've always told us, and we've always treated you as an adult. Adults would meet halfway. They wouldn't hold grudges or avoid the problem. They face it, head on. Stop acting like a child or we will impose a curfew and anymore sleepovers will cease. We are your parents, and we can do that."

She stared at him, seeing that he meant business.

Being mad at him was exhausting.

"I'm sorry," she said. "I'm not a child though."

He held his hand out, and she placed hers inside his. Her father was a large man, kind of scary to a lot of people, but she adored him.

She loved both of her parents, which was why it hurt a lot that they didn't seem to care about her all the time.

"Now, was that so hard?"

Lucia smiled but shook her head.

"See, we can make this work."

"You promise?" she asked.

"Yes. I'm a believer in conversation and talking through our troubles." He gave her hand a squeeze. "I know this has been hard for you, but we're here, and you won't be alone anymore."

"Okay."

"Now, get your homework done. I'll organize dinner."

She worked on her homework as her father

cooked. Her mother arrived before six o'clock, and Lucia was further surprised when her mother showed concern over her eye.

"Does it hurt?"

"It stings, but it'll go with my Halloween look. I'll scare off a few kids."

Her mother kissed her other cheek. "I hate seeing you hurt like this. I should call that girl's parents."

"They're not good people, Mom."

"I don't care. I'm not afraid. The only power people have, honey, is the power you give them. Don't ever let anyone scare you like that."

Then her mother shocked her again.

She pulled her into a hug and held her tightly.

Lucia couldn't remember the last time her mother hugged her or even showed any real concern for her. It was ... weird but good.

She held her mother, closing her eyes as she did so.

Maybe it was going to be all right.

Chapter Twelve

Seeing Lucia's bruised eye the next few days angered Jack. He especially didn't like that Rachel was still in school, but he made sure to keep an eye on her. With Lucia's parents at home, she'd also not been able to get away, nor had they been able to find a couple of spare minutes just to talk.

He missed her.

Staring at his reflection in the mirror, he was more than ready to play chaperone to the school. His hair was a mess, makeup on his face, and his clothes were torn with fake blood at some of the tears.

He hated Halloween. People dressing up bored him, and as he arrived at the school, he wasn't impressed. The cafeteria and several of the classrooms had been decorated for the party. Several cars were already parked, and he wasn't interested. As he entered the main hallway, music blasted all around, and he went straight to the main gym where the dance was already in full swing.

"Hey, Jack," Beth said.

She hadn't been as much of a pest since he'd called her out on her bullshit. This thing with Connor and Rachel had really pushed his limits of acceptance right now.

He was more than aware of power-hungry parents after growing up with a couple himself.

"Hey," he said.

"They did such a bang-up job of this. It's amazing."

Glancing across the hall, he saw several seniors already spiking the punch. He was about to head over there when a figure in white caught his attention.

Lucia stood at the entrance looking like an angel.

Her friend, Marie, was dressed as the devil. The dress Lucia wore was more revealing than anything he'd ever seen her in. The skirt of the dress was tight to her thighs, going to her knee, but it was good, and droplets of blood coated the bottom, fake blood obviously.

Her hair cascaded in ringlets down her body, and her face had makeup on as well. She hadn't covered up the bruise, but it only helped emphasize the outfit. She looked like a fallen angel.

She didn't need the makeup. To Jack, she always looked beautiful.

Beth had already left, and as Marie made her way toward the drinks, Lucia walked toward him.

"Hey, Mr. Zombie Teacher," she said.

"Not too bad, fallen angel."

She smiled. "All that was left at the store was dirty maid, or something else. This seemed pretty cool, but right now I'm not so sure."

"You look beautiful."

"Thank you," she said. "I've missed you."

"I've missed you, too. How are things with your parents?"

"They're … okay, I guess. Not a lot to say really. We're working through everything if you can call it that. I've been wanting to get over to see you, but they've been everywhere. Mom has even dropped me off at school."

"Nothing has happened between you and Rachel?" he asked.

"No. Nothing. My parents had a sit-down with hers, and they told me not to worry by the end of it, so…"

"Hey, Mr. Parker," Marie said, letting her presence be known.

He forced a smile. "Marie, lovely to see you."

"Well, I'm sure Mr. Parker can wait for whatever homework question you have. Come on, I promised you a good time." Marie pulled her away, and he smiled as he saw Lucia mouth the words, "I'm sorry."

This was his curse, to always watch her walk away.

He went toward the punch bowl where several kids were adding a bottle of vodka. Dipping his cup into the bowl, he stared at them and gave it a taste.

"Don't use shit vodka. You're going to spike the punch, do so with some quality shit."

He hated Halloween.

Moving around the dance floor he watched as Marie and Lucia laughed as they moved to the beat of the music.

He was happy she seemed to be having fun.

Leaving the dance floor, he went from room to room, keeping an eye on everything. Seeing kids make out was not on his list of things to enjoy.

"Hello, Mr. Parker."

Rachel ran her hands up his back.

He turned toward her and stared at her outfit.

"Do you like it? I'm a naughty little witch, and I can make every single one of your dreams come true."

"Right." He spotted Derick Coleman. "Excuse me."

She placed her hands on his hips. "I can make every single fantasy you've had come true."

"Can you disappear? I'd love that."

"If you don't give me what I want, I'll scream. Tell everyone that you raped me."

He stared into her eyes. "Do it, Rachel. I've done nothing wrong, and from what I've been made aware, you have a history of getting what you want. You're only as strong as your parents. See if they would be willing to take me on. Now grow the fuck up and accept that I don't want you."

Leaving Rachel in shock, he went to stand with Derick. Clearly, Rachel was used to scaring people into submitting. Wow, it had been a long time since he'd been so immersed in student bullshit.

"You okay there, buddy?" Derick asked.

"I'm tired of spoiled brats thinking they can boss me around."

"Yeah, I heard about the whole Connor thing. You okay?"

"I'm fine."

"I just steer clear of that bullshit, to be honest. Don't have the time or the energy to work on that. These kids, they think they're entitled to everything. They want everything but earn nothing, always going to their parents to keep them out of trouble. Half of them are on drugs. Can't prove it though."

"Not on my watch. They'll earn their grades with hard work. Excuse me, I better mingle." He didn't need Derick to tell him about the drugs.

Time was passing, and with it, he was getting pissed. Entering the gym once again, he saw Marie dancing on her own, but Lucia caught his eye. She stood on the edge of the dance floor looking so beautiful. He just couldn't stand it another moment.

He moved toward her, stepping close. "Follow me."

Without waiting to see if she even heard him, he began to make his way back down the long corridor, away from the party. He heard the clicking of heels as Lucia followed. Unlocking the doors that led to his classroom, he closed and locked it behind him. Once he was at his door, he stepped back, giving her room to enter.

"What's wrong?" she asked.

It had only been a few days, but to him it had felt more like fucking weeks since he'd last felt her lips on his.

Pressing her up against the wall, he captured her hands, slamming his lips down on hers. "I can't fucking resist you. That's the problem."

He had a good track record until Lucia. No student had ever tempted him. None of them had made him even think of breaking his own moral code.

Then Lucia came with her big as fuck brown eyes, her full lips, and a smile that melted his heart, and he couldn't say no. He didn't *want* to say no. She belonged to him, was his.

Dropping his hands from hers, he sank his fingers into her hair, the silky strands sliding through his fingers.

"I've missed you," he said.

"I've missed you too. I've wanted to get away. I freaked out a little at you meeting my dad."

"It was nice to see him, actually. At least I now know that he cares for you in his own way."

She smiled. "I guess he does."

"How is your face?"

"Bruised, but it doesn't hurt anymore."

Her hands rested on his shoulders.

"I wanted to hurt her," Jack said.

"No, she's not worth it. Nothing is worth losing your job over."

"You're worth it."

"No, I'm not. You're an amazing teacher."

"Do you want this to stop?" he asked.

She shook her head. "No, of course not. I love being with you. I just … I don't want to take anything away."

He frowned. "What is it?" he asked, sensing

something within her. "I can tell something is bothering you."

"Tonight, I overheard my parents talking about something, but it doesn't matter."

"Whatever bothers you, talk to me, Lucia. Don't lock me out." He wanted to help her in any way that he could.

"I heard them talking about a possible move next year. I don't know if it's something they're just considering or definite. I don't know, but it scares me."

"Where?" he asked.

"To London. That's what they were talking about."

He slammed his lips down on hers.

If they moved to London, he'd never see her again. Just the thought of it tore him apart. She could come to college in the States, but he didn't see any parents wanting their kid to be so far away, not even Lucia's parents.

"We'll deal with that when the time comes. It could just be something they're talking about." He kissed her, hoping that it wasn't a relocation.

This thing he had with Lucia, it was the real fucking deal.

All of his life he'd moved from woman to woman, never having a serious relationship, never knowing what it was like to fall for a woman.

He was falling for her.

This wasn't an attraction to the forbidden.

This was an attraction to Lucia.

"Please," she said. "I need you." She ran her hand down his chest, cupping his arousal.

He was already hard as rock.

Moving her toward his desk, he lifted her up and pushed her dress up to her waist. Next, he spread her legs wide and stepped between them. Tearing off her panties, he shoved them in his pocket and cupped her wet, naked flesh.

"Every time I sit at this desk I'm going to remember how you felt against me. The taste of you on my tongue." He sat down in his chair, gripping her ass. He pulled her up to his face, and licked from her entrance up to her clit, circling her bud before sliding down, plunging inside her. "Don't let me hear you scream."

"Jack!" She said his name on a groan as he teased her body, driving her wild.

Pressing two fingers inside her pussy, he drew them out only to push them back in. She took him, thrusting down on his fingers, whimpering as he licked and sucked at her clit.

She tasted exquisite. His cock pressed against his pants, desperate for release, which wouldn't come.

"Please, Jack, please." Her begging thrilled him, and as he held her in place, he controlled her orgasm. Bringing her to the edge of pleasure, he waited, prolonging her need, and finally pushing her over the edge as she came on his face.

Before she had even finished, he pulled away from her tight heat, found a condom in his wallet, and quickly rolled it on.

Jack moved her, bending her over the desk, kicking her legs apart as he spread the cheeks of her ass.

He found her entrance and slid in deep. The tight walls of her cunt clenched around him, letting him know how much she was loving this.

Pulling out, he slammed to the hilt inside her, over and over. He watched his cock in the dark room, able to make out his glistening shaft from the light cast by the moon.

Gripping hold of her hips, he pounded inside her.

Lucia held onto the desk, pushing back, driving onto his cock with so much force that it rocked him into his own release.

He drove in deep as wave upon wave of his cum released into the condom. Wrapping his arms around her tightly, he kissed her neck.

"That was incredible," Lucia said. "We've got a problem though."

"What?"

"How am I going to be able to pay attention to you now? I know how bad you can be, Mr. Parker."

He chuckled. "You and I both know that you're more than capable of doing whatever you set your mind to."

He eased out of her, pressing a kiss to her ass cheek. Using some tissues, he pulled the condom off his dick and wrapped it up. He grabbed some tissue that he left in his desk, wrapped it up tight, and placed it back in his pocket.

Jack pushed her skirt down over her ass.

"What about my panties?" she asked.

"They're my treat."

"We've got to make it back without being seen."

"Easily done. Trust me?" He held his hand out for her to take.

"Of course." She rested her hand inside his and something twisted inside him. His heart seemed to pound, and as he looked at her, everything was clear. "Are you okay?"

"I'm fine. More than fine." He gave her hand a gentle squeeze, refusing to think about the possible chance of Lucia moving away. That could all wait as far as he was concerned.

****

The days passed, and still Lucia's parents avoided

any topic of conversation that included college and moving. She knew they were talking about it though. Every time she entered a room, they would change the subject, which made her nervous.

They were no longer keeping her on a tight schedule, so she was able to visit Jack after school, but she made sure to be home before eight at night. It sucked big time because all she wanted to do was spend the night with him.

At night, lying in bed, she'd text him, and often fall asleep with her cell phone in her hand, wishing more than anything that she was with him and his arms were wrapped around her. She missed him so much.

Marie no longer had any suspicions either. The days she wasn't with Jack, she spent with Marie catching up. Time was going by so fast, or at least it felt like it was going by quickly, and it wasn't long before Thanksgiving was upon them. She'd already seen her parents off as they had another conference to go to that had already been booked months in advance.

They had wanted her to go, but she declined.

She found it a little suspicious that they were going to another conference in London and especially as they'd been talking a lot about it.

Lucia had intended to go and visit Jack, but he'd also been away to his parents' place for Thanksgiving and Marie went to see her grandparents, so she was in fact alone, which wasn't a problem. She'd rather be alone at home than have to sit in a foreign country alone while her parents attended multiple conferences. They had offered to take her, and even tried to get her to go, but she'd not been interested.

Sitting on the sofa, she felt lethargic, and her stomach seemed to be twisting and turning. It was quiet, and she had the television on watching some old black and white movie.

Her cell phone rang, and she smiled, then winced as her stomach gave another turn.

"Hello," she said.

"Hey, beautiful. I thought I'd check in."

Jack's voice made her close her eyes and lie back on the sofa. "How are you?" she asked.

"Oh, you know, fine. My folks have a bunch of people here. It's boring as fuck. It doesn't help that they've made sure there are plenty of available women here as well."

Jealousy struck her hard. "Oh."

"Don't get like that. I'm not interested in them. Remember who you belong to."

"I remember. Do you?" she asked, rubbing her stomach. The sick feeling wasn't going away, and she closed her eyes, feeling dizzy as well. She let out a breath, trying to help the sick feeling.

Nothing seemed to be helping. In fact, everything was only getting worse.

"I remember who I belong to, Lucia. Are you okay? You're doing some serious panting."

"Yeah, I'm fine."

She was going to be sick.

Rolling over, she got to her feet, ignoring the dizzy feeling.

They didn't have a bathroom downstairs, so she quickly ran into her own. Dropping her cell phone on the floor, she grabbed the toilet, and threw up everything that she'd eaten. Over and over, she vomited, aware that Jack could hear her.

She kept trying to stop, but her body had other ideas. Resting her head against the toilet, she reached for her cell phone.

"I'm going to have to go."

"Lucia, who is there?"

"What?"

"Your parents are away, aren't they?"

"Yes."

"Marie?"

"Away with her family. They went to go and see her grandmother in Texas, I think she said, or something like that. I don't even know."

"Shit. You're there all alone."

"I'm fine. It's just a sickness bug. I really have to go."

She hung up her cell, leaning over the toilet to throw up again.

Her body was so cold, and yet she knew it was hot at the same time.

Flushing the toilet, she did her best to clean up the mess. Running herself a bath, she went through the motions, making sure she took care of herself.

Climbing out of the bath, she wrapped a towel around herself. She felt another dizzy spell, which turned her stomach. Collapsing on the floor, she pressed her cheek to the ground, suddenly too hot to be in anything.

For the first time all day, she was comfortable.

There was no reason to move.

She was perfectly content here on the bathroom floor.

She'd get up in a minute.

Closing her eyes, her body slumped, and sleep claimed her.

****

Lucia wasn't answering the door, and Jack was pissed. He'd gotten on the fastest plane, paying a ridiculous amount to get on the last-minute flight. His parents weren't impressed that he'd walked out on them during Thanksgiving, but he really didn't give a fuck.

Lucia was sick, and there wasn't anyone to take care of her.

He rushed around to the side of the building and began to climb. Her window was partially open, and as he got to her room, he didn't see any sign of her, but there was light coming from the bathroom.

Lifting up the window, he noticed how cold it was.

Closing the window, he made his way toward the bathroom where he saw Lucia, shaking on the floor. Her face was pressed to the linoleum.

"Shit, Lucia."

She was sleeping, and he placed a hand to her cheek, which was burning up. The towel only partially covered her, and he grabbed a robe, wrapping it around her. Lifting her up in his arms, he carried her to her bed.

He pushed the blankets up, and kicking off his shoes, he climbed between the sheets with her.

She gave a little moan. Using his body heat to warm her, he ran his hands up and down her body.

"Jack?" Her voice was croaky.

"I'm here, Lucia. I'm here."

"You're not."

He chuckled. "I'm here, lovely. I'm going to take care of you."

Listening to her vomit last night, he'd never felt so helpless in all of his life. She was alone, and he was determined to take care of her by any means possible.

There had been no hesitation. He'd grabbed his stuff and gotten to the airport immediately.

She sighed. "I missed you."

She fell to sleep, and he stayed with her another few minutes before wrapping her up in the blanket.

Tucking some of her hair back, he watched her sleep, making sure she was okay.

Next, he sprang into action.

Cleaning up her bathroom, he saw a few spatters of vomit on the floor, which he took care of. Once her bathroom was sparkling, he took her clothes and found his way around her parents' home. The washing machine was full, so he moved that to the dryer, then put another load of wash in.

After that, he stood in the kitchen.

He found all the makings for his old nanny's chicken soup. She'd sworn by it as a cure for all ills from hangovers to sickness.

Pulling out all the ingredients, he checked the time, and quickly looked in on Lucia again. She was still fast asleep.

He walked back downstairs and began making the soup. He roasted up the chicken after sprinkling some salt, pepper, and poultry seasoning on it. While that was cooking away, he prepared all the vegetables, carrots, celery, leeks, onions, potatoes, rosemary. Once all those were done, he began to assemble it all.

When the chicken came out of the oven, he let it rest on the stove, going to check on her again.

When he saw she was still asleep, he finished the last of the soup, using the pan drippings to add to the soup without the grease. He poured the excess off, then chopped up the chicken. Once everything was together in the stock pot bubbling away, he changed a load of wash, and couldn't help but smile to himself. This felt very domesticated.

Helping a sick woman was last on his priorities, but he'd come to see that Lucia wasn't just any woman.

She meant a great deal to him.

After five hours' worth of sleep, he decided it was time to wake her up. He didn't know how long it was since she last ate.

Spooning out some of the precious soup, he made her a medicinal drink and carried them up on a tray he found. Placing them on her desk, he sat on the edge of her bed, and began to stroke her hair back from her face.

"Morning, sleeping beauty," he said.

It was far from morning.

Slowly, she began to come around.

She opened her eyes and frowned. "Jack?"

"At least I can rule out concussion."

She sat up, frowning as she looked around the room. "You're at your parents'."

"I was. I decided to cut that trip short. I'm here." He took her hand, pressing a kiss to her knuckles.

"Wait? You came all the way here?"

"You don't think I'd listen to you vomit and hearing how sick you are, leave you? Ignore you?"

"I ... I don't know. I don't know what to think."

"I've been accused of many things in my time, Lucia Deen, but heartless isn't one of them." He'd never been put in a position where he had to care about anyone but himself.

"But ... your family?"

"They understand."

"You told them?"

"No, I didn't tell them about us. I think my dad would have a fit if he knew right now." He winked at her.

"I'm so confused." She ran a hand down her face.

"That's fine. You can ask any question you want, but I have soup." He got up, picking up the bowl, and came back to sit on the bed, holding the bowl. "I'm going to feed you now."

"I can feed myself, Jack."

"I imagine you can. From what I know about you, Lucia, you're capable of taking care of yourself. Right now, you don't have to. I'm here to take care of you, and I will. Don't even think to argue with me." He dipped the spoon into the liquid.

She opened her mouth, and he heard her little moan. "Oh, wow, that is good."

"It really is. It's a top secret, not-so-secret recipe that one of my nannies shared with me eons ago."

He fed her a few more spoonsful, and he caught the smile on her lips.

Lucia liked being taken care of, and he loved taking care of her.

When she'd eaten half of the bowl, she held her hand up.

Whatever color she had, was gone.

Completely butt naked, she ran to the bathroom and threw everything up. Wrapping her hair around his fist, he rubbed her back, wincing at the vomiting sounds. She was so poorly.

"It's okay. I'm here."

When she finished, he helped her to brush her teeth, and then put her back to bed.

"I'm so sorry," Lucia said. "The soup was lovely."

"Don't you worry. I've got plenty more, and clearly it's too early for some awesome food." He tucked her back up in bed, sitting on the edge.

"Thank you," she said.

"What for?"

"For coming to check on me, for taking care of me. It's … really nice."

He leaned forward and kissed her head. "It's worth it. You're worth it."

"But what about your Thanksgiving?"

"I don't mind. I'd rather spend it with you, knowing you're getting better. Now, rest."

He left her alone to rest, carrying the tray downstairs to the kitchen.

Gripping the edge of the counter, he closed his eyes, trying to focus, trying not to think of all the reasons why he'd boarded that plane, why he'd come back here. He'd gone to his parents', trying to get his thoughts back in check, to put his life back into perspective, but there was no fucking way in the world that was going to happen with how he felt about Lucia.

She wasn't just some girl from the school where he taught.

This was so much more than that.

He wasn't using her.

Nor was it the taste of the forbidden.

When he was with her ... everything felt clear.

He had a purpose, and it was taking care of her.

Look at where she was now. Alone on Thanksgiving. Collapsed, and she could have died.

Fucking died!

Just the thought made him to want kill her parents.

He got it. He did. Their work came first, and their work would always come first, but he didn't accept that.

Lucia was an amazing young woman, strong, funny, passionate, loyal, everything he could ever want, wrapped in one curvy as fuck package.

He'd been running away. Not forever but to be around two people who he loved and hated with an equal measure. When he was around his parents, it was like he completely zoned out, and it allowed him to think.

After everything he'd experienced with Lucia, and especially Halloween, he'd been desperate to clear his head, to do something that would help him.

His feelings for her were not disappearing or wilting in any way. They were fucking growing.

Listening to her vomit on the phone, knowing she was all alone, had completely destroyed him inside. There's no way he could just hang up and ignore her. That kind of shit wasn't in his DNA. It could be in her parents to just leave their very capable daughter alone, but that wasn't in his.

"You got to get your shit together, Jack." There was no out for him, not with Lucia.

She meant too much, and he'd been running from that.

She was a senior in high school. Their time was limited.

He wasn't a fool.

He knew it more than anything else.

They were on borrowed time.

She'd be making decisions about college, about how to move on with her life, and he'd have to live with that. To watch her graduate, move on, and to end this.

What alternative was there?

He'd have to let her go.

That's what a good man would do.

The gentleman.

He'd let her go.

There's no way it would be easy. He wasn't a fool. This would be one of the hardest fucking decisions of his life, to watch her walk away.

Could he do it?

The telephone rang in the background, and he hoped it didn't wake Lucia up. He'd not seen an extension for one in her bedroom, and as he moved toward it to answer, he hesitated. Lucia wasn't supposed to have a boy over, let alone a man.

When he was poised above the damn thing it finally clicked off, and he listened to the message.

"Hey, honey, how are you doing? London is

awesome. We miss you, and we hope you're having a lot of fun. Love you, honey, take care. We'll catch you later."

The message ended, and he clenched his hand into a fist.

This wasn't what he was interested in listening to.

Stepping away from the machine, he finished cleaning away all of his stuff, and focused on keeping his shit together right now. Lucia needed him, not some man who didn't know what he wanted.

Putting away all the dishes and keeping the soup on a really gentle simmer, he glanced around her home, changing loads of wash, closing doors and windows, taking care of the house.

When he couldn't put it off any longer, he made his way upstairs and found Lucia coming out of the bathroom. She'd pulled on a nightshirt, and she smiled at him.

"At least I know I didn't hallucinate," she said.

"How are you feeling?" he asked.

"Like I've been run over by a bus and they've gone back and forth over my head repeatedly."

He winced. "Ouch."

"Yes."

She eased back into the bed. Rather than sit on the bed, he pulled up a chair and lowered himself in it beside her.

"You came all the way back from your parents'?"

"Yes."

"Why?"

"I heard you vomit on the phone."

"Oh."

"I guess a lot of things are a little fuzzy to you."

"Yeah, I don't … you fed me soup?"

"I fed you soup, and I cleaned up the bathroom."

"Ew, I'm so sorry."

He chuckled. "You don't have to be sorry. Your parents called as well. They left a message." He liked taking care of her. Her parents didn't deserve her, not one bit. She was precious, and he wanted to give her everything her heart desired.

"You didn't answer it?"

"Of course not. I don't think they'd be all that happy with their daughter having a man in the home."

"Ah, you're right." She chuckled. "I just can't believe that you came here when you could have been with your parents."

"I hate to break this to you, Lucia. My parents are not the best people."

"They're not?"

"Well, they're not *bad* people. They want to see me settle down, and I only went there to try to clear my head."

"Is that because of us? What we have?"

"Yes."

She nodded.

He didn't elaborate further, and she didn't ask for more.

"How long had you been sick before I arrived?"

"I was literally sick on the phone. I'd started to feel a little lightheaded, and then before I knew what was happening, I knew I was going to be sick." She reached out, and he took her hand, locking their fingers together like he'd done so many times. This, to him, felt right. This wasn't wrong.

He wanted to take care of her.

He craved her touch at every single turn and knew without a shadow of a doubt that he couldn't lose her. She was perfect.

"Thank you so much for taking care of me."

"I'm not going."

"What?"

"You're still sick. I'm staying here to make sure you feel better, much better."

She smiled.

"I wasn't sending you away, Jack. I like you here. I don't want you to go. I want you to stay."

He knew all about that, but he couldn't say anything else.

Smiling, he didn't beg her to stay, to give him a chance after graduation. He kept his mouth shut.

Chapter Thirteen

Lucia stared at Jack in the mirror, watching as he brushed her hair. It seemed like a simple thing, brushing hair, but watching him do it felt intimate. His fingers ran through the long brown strands, and he was so focused on his job that a little crease had appeared between his brows.

"What's wrong?" she asked, unable to contain her chuckle.

"Nothing, trying not to hurt you."

"I've thought about cutting my hair a couple of times."

"Don't you dare. I happen to love your hair just the way it is."

Every time he said the word "love" she got this little fluttering inside her chest that she found harder to ignore. They were not directed her. He'd not come out and said that he loved her, not that she expected him to.

Still, she often found herself fantasizing about what would happen if it ever did just spill out as a confession.

Not that it would.

She had to be realistic here.

There's no chance of there ever being more than what they had. He was a teacher, and she a student. This … what they had, it was as good as it got.

There was going to come a day soon when she was going to have to leave. That her graduation would push her to the next step.

Leaving him though, it made her feel sick inside. It devastated her.

Still, she couldn't bring herself to talk about it, not yet. Neither of them really knew what was going on with each other.

"Then I won't get it all cut off."

"It's lovely."

She watched as he ran his fingers through it before wrapping it around his fist, giving it a gentle tug.

"See, it has its uses." He pulled her head back, and she moaned as he pressed a kiss to her lips.

"Then the hair stays."

"Good, and you're not using me for sex. You're not completely well just yet."

"I feel fine, and I've not vomited for an entire day."

"Don't care. We're going down to have some toast, and you're sticking to water as well. I don't like you being ill, and I'm the one in charge of taking care of you. I get the deciding vote." He dropped a kiss to her lips. "Care to argue?"

"No, sir." She gave him a weird salute and then burst out laughing. "So, have you talked to your parents yet?"

"Nope, and I don't plan on it either. Not yet anyway."

"Why not?"

"Because I know exactly how that conversation will go. We'll start with the usual pain in the ass reprimand. That nothing was more important than finishing dinner. How they worked hard all year to see me and that they hated me just walking out. Then it will move to topics about the women they'd decided to invite. So more boring stuff."

"None of them appealed to you?" she asked, nibbling on her lip.

"None of them. Why would I want anyone else when I have perfection right here?"

"Perfection, huh?"

"My own little virgin canvas."

Again, his lips felt so utterly good, and she didn't want his touch to end. She felt driven toward him, like a moth to a flame.

"Okay, so lots of ladies."

"Yeah, how I'm getting older. That I need to settle down. Find a decent wife that they accept, and think is good to have the Parker genes mixed with. Then we'd move to teaching. How they don't approve of it."

"They don't?"

"My family is rich, Lucia. I told you that. They have a fortune and are two of the top lawyers in the country. My family has also dealt with stocks and shares, which was what my grandfather did. They made a fortune, so they have certain expectations."

"You don't live up to them?"

"If I was in a prestigious, elitist school, yes. Where I'm working, they think I'm doing it to make a mockery of them."

"I hate to say this, Jack. Your parents don't sound all that great. You're a fantastic teacher."

"I love it. I kept it a secret from them for a long time."

"What do you mean?"

"In college. I didn't tell them that was the path I wanted to go. They were hoping I'd get over my silly nonsense and just go to law school."

She wrinkled her nose.

"I think what you're doing is really pretty great."

He was still brushing her hair, and he looked at her in the mirror. "Thank you. It's something you've got to learn to do. People will walk all over you in this life if they think they have a shot at it. Don't live a life that others want you to, Lucia. Be the woman *you* want to be. Have the career you want."

"I don't know what it is I want."

"You will when you're ready. There's nothing wrong with having this indecision."

"My parents wouldn't think that. They are always telling me how they wanted to be a lawyer and research scientist most of my life. How life is way too short to be taking one's time in deciding your fate."

Jack finished combing her hair. His hands landed on her shoulders. "It's still your life, Lucia. That's what they can't change."

"Is that what you finally decided? That you were the master of your life?"

"Yes. You need to see it as well." He leaned down again, kissing her cheek.

He was about to say something more, but the phone began to ring again.

"I have a feeling that is your parents."

"I'll go and answer it."

As she moved away from the desk, she missed his touch so much, but forced herself to keep on walking. Grabbing the phone, she lifted it to her ear.

She clearly wasn't well because she felt exhausted.

"Hello," she said.

"Honey," her mother said.

"Hey, Mom, what's up?"

"Why have you not been answering the phone? Your father and I have been so worried."

"I've actually been pretty sick. I've spent the past couple of days in bed. I've not been able to come to the phone."

She watched Jack roll his eyes and shake his head.

Pressing her lips together, she tried not to smile, but that didn't seem to work. It wasn't funny, and yet it was at the same time. *Weird.*

"Oh, no, what was wrong?" she asked.

Lucia told her what had happened, leaving out the collapsing in the bathroom, and instead told her about landing in bed, and just not leaving apart from to vomit.

"I cleaned everything up though. I'm feeling better now. I've kept down a little soup."

"We need to come home. We'll cut this trip short and be right there."

"No," Lucia said. She didn't want this to end with Jack. He was at her home, taking care of her, and she loved his company so much.

"Lucia?"

"No, you really don't need to do that. I'm perfectly fine, honestly. Stay for the rest of your trip. You've still got a few more days, and I bet you're loving London."

"It is amazing here, Lucia. We've not stayed in London though. We've actually been traveling."

Her stomach twisted. "You have?"

"Yes, we've gone through some little towns and villages that are just the most delightful thing."

Her parents rarely traveled.

"You'd love it here, Lucia. It's so beautiful."

"Oh."

"Here's your father."

She heard her mother quickly speak, updating him on the fact she'd been ill.

Licking her lips, she gripped the edge of the kitchen counter as Jack got to work on the toast and tea. He'd said water, but she was going to try to convince him to at least let her have tea. Her mother had some English brand from her last trip, and she'd taken an instant liking to it.

"Hey, honey."

They were always calling her honey.

It never ceased to make her smile, especially as she hated honey. The stuff tasted vile to her.

"Hey, Dad. Mom said that you're having a blast."

"We really are. We've gotten the time to explore. In the U.K. they don't celebrate Thanksgiving so we're not dealing with any traffic or closed shops. It's been amazing for traveling, cold but not unreasonable."

"It's snowed here a few times. You'd have loved it."

"Are you feeling better?" he asked.

"Yes, I am. Much better. In fact, I'm gonna go. Toast and stuff."

"Okay, well take care and we love you."

"Love you too."

She hung up the phone, resting her chin on top of it.

"What's wrong?" Jack asked.

She looked up at him and frowned. "Sorry?"

"You look worried. Did they suspect anything?"

"No, they never would suspect anything."

"What's wrong then?" he asked, turning to her, hand on hip.

For just a few short seconds she could imagine that they were living on their own like any other normal couple. That she'd not called her parents and lied about taking care of herself.

This was all normal.

"Nothing really. I'm ... they've been going to London and the U.K. for some time now, but in the past year, their visits have increased and I'm just worried."

"You think they're planning on moving?"

"I know they're wanting to move. I even saw the information from the real estate agent to sell this place."

"They're still undecided?"

"I don't know. They've not said a word about it to me. They're keeping it from me."

"And that bothers you?"

"Yes, it does. I don't want to move." She looked past his shoulder. "This has been my home for a long time. I don't want to move or relocate."

Jack stepped toward her, pulling her into his arms.

She closed her eyes, resting her head against his chest.

"You're ill. I don't want you worrying about anything right now."

She held onto his back, breathing in his warm scent.

"We can worry about everything else some other time."

He rubbed her back and moved away. They sat together at the dining room table. He sipped his coffee, and she stared at her water.

"Can't I have a cup of tea? Pretty please?"

He was reading the paper and looked so sexy with his inked arms on display. He wore a short-sleeved shirt that did wonders for his muscular arms.

"It's got milk in it. I don't want you to have anything that will turn your stomach. Be happy that you've got butter on your toast."

She giggled. "I want something warm." She batted her eyelashes, and he rolled his eyes.

"And if you're sick?"

"We'll know that I'm really poorly and it was my bad. Please, pretty please."

She wasn't too embarrassed to beg him.

He sighed but got to his feet.

She watched him walk into the kitchen and make a cup of tea.

"You know how to make it?"

"Yes. I've visited London a couple of times. It's not a strange thing, tea."

She laughed, and he came back, cup in hand.

"I hope you're not sick." He kissed her head and took his seat again at the table. She blew over the surface of the liquid and watched him.

He was concentrating on the words in front of him, and she couldn't look away. This felt … amazing. Like it was a glimpse into a future that she could possibly have.

Could it be possible?

Could she have a life with him?

It seemed almost too good to even be true.

She sipped her tea, nibbled her toast, and instead of ruining the mood, she watched him, basking in every single second.

Once he was done with the paper, he drank the last of his coffee. When he got to his feet, he stroked her shoulder then took her empty plate into the kitchen.

It was the little things, like the touches, the tenderness, the sweetness that he showed her. She craved him so much.

Jack hadn't forced her into anything.

Far from it.

She'd been with him every single step of the way and then more so.

"How are you feeling?" he asked, coming to her side, pressing a hand to her head.

"I'm fine. You need to stop worrying."

"It seems when it comes to you, I'm always going to worry."

She took his hand and smiled. "I'm okay for now."

"Come on." He led her into the sitting room. He

sat down on the sofa, and she lay down beside him.

Jack wrapped a blanket around her, then took control of the remote, flicking through the channels. He settled onto a movie about dancing.

"You know I've never danced before," she said.

"I watched you dancing with Marie."

"No, I mean with a guy who's not my dad. I've never danced with a guy before."

He sighed. "That is easily rectified." He changed the channel to a music one, and she watched as he moved the coffee table out of the way.

Within the next second, his hand was inside hers, and his other at her back as he held her in the middle of the sitting room.

"Dancing is easy."

"You took dancing lessons?"

"No. But all it takes is to hold one another, and move to the beat of the music, or not. Just do what comes naturally to you."

He held her hand against his chest, and they moved slowly from side to side.

"Do you want to get married?" she asked.

"Sorry?"

"You mentioned about your parents trying to set you up. Do you see marriage? Kids? That kind of thing in your future?"

"I don't know. I guess one day I will. There hasn't been a woman that has made me want to take that next step."

His words both delighted and gutted her.

She didn't let it show though.

"What about you?"

"One day, I imagine I will. I want a family. That I do know. Maybe a son or daughter. Being an only child sucks big time."

"I agree."

"We're in the only children club," she said. "My parents didn't even plan on one child, let alone a second."

"What do you want? If you ever settled down and had kids?"

"I'd love both. A boy and girl. To be honest, I don't care. It's not like I can order one of each. I'd just take whatever was on offer. Consequences be damned and all that."

"You'd be an amazing mom."

"You think so?" she asked.

"I know so. Everything you do, Lucia, you do to the best of your ability."

"That's the teacher in you."

"Yep. I just can't seem to help it."

"Well, Mr. Parker, do you grade me in all areas?"

"Nope, but if I did, you'd get an A plus."

She giggled. "I would?"

"Yes."

She tried to ignore the yawn, but Jack caught it.

"It's time for you to rest."

"I don't want to rest. Can't we just dance until the end of this song?"

"Yes, we can."

She rested her head against his chest, closing her eyes, not wanting to move. It felt good to be in his arms.

All of her worries drifted away as he held her.

He'd take care of her, she knew that. What they shared was more than just a bit of fun. It was the real deal, and no one could take that away from them.

****

Thanksgiving break was almost over, and Lucia was better. She wasn't completely well but the worst was finished with, and she was on the road to recovery. Jack didn't want it to end. For the first time in his thirty years, he'd played pretend.

Instead of seeing it as her parents' home, he'd imagined it being his own. That they weren't sneaking around and trying not to get caught. He'd slept in her bed with Lucia in his arms, watching her sleep. Every night he held her tightly, and in the morning, she was still there in his arms.

He'd never gone to bed with a woman or been there the next morning to tell the tale.

He wasn't the kind of guy to do something like this.

Yes, he'd fucked his fair share of women, and gotten a reputation as being the love 'em and leave 'em kind of guy. With Lucia, he couldn't bring himself to walk away. He craved her smile, relished every laugh, and wanted her touch every single fucking day. She'd gotten under his skin, and he didn't want to shake her.

She was inside his head.

He stared down at her, and she looked so peaceful in sleep. Teasing a strand of her brown hair back off her face, he smiled. She was so precious to him, beautiful.

Her eyes opened, and she sighed. "Morning."

"Morning, beautiful."

She covered her mouth with her hand. "I've got morning breath."

"It's fine. I've got morning breath too."

She giggled. "How long have you been watching me sleep?"

"Enough to know that you don't snore all the time."

She gasped. "I can't believe you'd bring that up."

"I can't help it. You bring the worst out in me. Besides, you need to know what you're getting yourself into. You know, if you ever date."

The smile slipped a little, and he wanted to kick himself. He didn't want to hurt her. It was the last thing on his fucking mind.

"You're right, but who would want to date someone who snored?" she asked. "I'm confused. It is way too early to be talking about snoring and dating. Another time, maybe."

"Yeah, another time. You don't have to date though. You've got me, and I don't mind your little snores. I find them so very cute." He dropped a kiss to her lips, and she cupped his face, doing that little moan that he loved.

"I've loved this Thanksgiving," she said.

"Really? Vomiting, being sick, ill, and pretty much passed out with exhaustion has been your best week?"

She tapped his shoulder. "You know what I mean. That part sucked, but I loved being with you. Having this. It has been a dream. Honestly."

He was about to say something when the sound of doors slamming and voices could be heard.

Lucia gasped. "My parents. What the hell are they doing back?"

She quickly jumped over him, running toward the window. She opened the curtain and gasped. "Shit, it is them."

Getting to his feet, she rushed toward the door, closing it.

"You're going to have to be quiet," she said.

"Do they ever storm into your room?" he asked.

The front door opened.

"No. Just … crap. I'll be calm. Is anything of yours downstairs?"

"No." He quickly pulled on his pants and buckled them up. "Go, slow them down."

She grabbed a robe, rushed to his side, and cupped his face. "I'll call you as soon as I can."

He sank his fingers into her hair, not wanting to let her go but knowing he didn't have a choice.

The harsh reality of their situation had come crashing down around them, and there was no hiding from it.

She pulled away, and he had no choice but to watch her go. She closed the door behind her, and he quickly pulled on his boots.

It had been a long time since he'd had to sneak out of a girl's window.

You shouldn't have been here in the first place.

Everything would have been okay if you'd just ignored this.

He couldn't ignore it though.

Lucia, she was everything to him.

"Mom, Dad, you're back early," he heard Lucia say. Moving toward the window, he saw Lucia's dad at the trunk of the car. Even though her room wasn't at the front where they'd parked, he saw clearly down to the front of the house toward the garage.

Once his shoes were on, he pulled on his jacket and moved to the other window that dropped down out of the back of the house.

He was slow, not wanting to draw attention to the patter of feet, and as he got to the ground, Lucia was at the kitchen window, watching him.

She blew him a kiss, and he quickly left her alone, making his escape.

On one of the days that Lucia had been feeling better, he'd driven his car back to his place and taken a cab back so it didn't raise suspicion her having a car in the driveway that wasn't her parents'.

The walk back home took him close to an hour,

but he didn't mind.

He had to clear his head some way.

Lucia: **I'm so sorry.**

Jack: **It's fine. How are you feeling?**

Lucia: **Much better, but I didn't want you to leave.**

Jack: **Any news about London? Your relocation?**

Lucia: **Nothing. They're just talking about the conference. Really boring. I don't know if I'll be able to get to you before school starts.**

Jack: **Get well. I don't expect you to visit me.**

He entered his home and quickly put the heat on.

Dropping his cell phone onto the kitchen counter, he pressed his palms to the granite surface and tried to count to ten in his head. To calm his nerves.

His home was silent, deathly silent.

The knowledge that his home didn't have Lucia or a family never used to bother him. Now that he'd lived for just a few days of waking up with her in his arms, hearing her laugh, it fucking cut him to be here.

His place was cold, silent, empty.

Opening the fridge, he grabbed a beer from inside, slamming it closed. It was still early, but he didn't give a fuck. Right now, he needed to drink, to numb this pain that was gripping him. He wanted Lucia, and it was becoming more than that, he *needed* her. Walking away every single day was getting harder. It was killing him inside to leave her. Looking around his space, he didn't see anything that fucking marked the place as his.

This was … just a place to crash.

He didn't have any pictures on the wall, no artwork.

There were books, so many books.

Reading had been something he'd loved for so

long. Even when he'd rebelled, he'd often hide books in his locker, or hidden away for a couple of hours. He'd been too embarrassed to let anyone know his love of books.

Staring at his bookshelves, he remembered Lucia sitting in front of them, legs crossed, a book spread open on her lap, tucking some hair behind her ear, smiling.

They had made some memories here.

Rubbing at his eyes, he tried to think, to clear his head.

His cell phone buzzed, and he glanced down to see a message from Lucia.

Lucia: **I miss you.**

He missed her, too, so fucking much. Dropping down onto his sofa, he finished his beer, and placed the bottle on the table in front of him. His whiskey was on the table beside him with a few glasses.

Pouring himself a stiff drink, he sat down, taking the whiskey back to his throat.

All of this past week, he'd not once touched her. He'd taken care of her, nursed her back to health. Sex had been the last thing on his mind.

He'd wanted to get her well, and he'd loved how she trusted him. How they stood in the shower and she held her arms up above her head as he soaped her body. She'd giggled as he'd stroked over her arms, finding spots that tickled her.

She had the sweetest laugh.

In fact, he couldn't find a single fault with her.

Running a hand down his face, he sat back, and stared at his television.

She'd become his entire world, and there was no way he could let her go. He was royally fucked.

Chapter Fourteen

"You know you've been a lot weirder than normal, and you don't talk as much either," Marie said.

Lucia looked up from the book she was studying to see her best friend standing over her. Thanksgiving had been a bust when it came to studying, so she was catching up, using all of her spare time at the library to try to get all of her assignments done.

"Wow, your manners need a lot of work. Does your mother know you just go around school calling your BFF weird?" she asked.

Marie chuckled. "There's the girl I know and love." She pulled out a chair and sat down on it.

Every time she was with Marie, Lucia found it a little exhausting. The guilt weighed heavy on her, and she couldn't make it stop. She wanted to scream the truth, but she couldn't. This was between her and Jack. She wouldn't do anything to hurt him, even though her best friend wouldn't tell a soul.

"So I totally heard a rumor around school that Rachel wants to smash your face in."

This made her pause, looking up at her friend. "Really?" She'd not had an incident with Rachel, or with Connor for that matter.

Years of being bullied by them had meant she had perfected the art of staying out of their way.

"Yep, I take it that you didn't know?"

"No. I wonder what I did now." She'd avoided the cafeteria because as much fun as it was having her father stick up for her, she didn't like the bruise that decorated her face afterward.

"Does it really matter? It's Rachel."

"Yeah, well, I'm not exactly thrilled to be

watching my back either. I don't get what her problem is."

"You don't?" Marie rested her head on her hand.

"What's that supposed to mean?" Her pen was poised on her notebook.

"Look, I hate to be the one to break it to you, but have you seen the way Connor looks at you lately? He's always around you, and again the rumor mill—"

"I'm getting tired of this rumor mill, okay? Connor is just an asshole who takes a great deal of enjoyment in humiliating me. Not only that, no one has heard what he says to me. Sure, he plays up to the whole drama, but he's a piece of shit and mean. Now when it comes to Rachel, again, cruelty. I'm sick and tired of all this crap." She slammed her book closed, feeling her anger rise.

"Wow," Marie said. "That has really pissed you off."

"I'm sorry, but I'm tired of all this bullshit." Lucia rubbed her temples. It had been a couple of weeks since Thanksgiving had ended, and her parents were home more and more. She'd heard them talking about London, relocation, and it was starting to freak her out. Then of course she hadn't been able to get away to go and see Jack. Between the weather, school, her parents, everything had been working against her.

She missed him more than anything.

Marie held her hands up in surrender. "Sorry. Don't kill the messenger and all. What is with you lately?"

"What do you mean?"

"We rarely have a movie day. You don't come over as much as you used to. Something has got to be bugging you."

"Nothing is bugging me." She had to lie all the

time, and the easiest way of not doing it was avoiding everyone.

Her life had become one big mess of avoiding.

"I've … got to go and ask Mr. Parker a question," she said, pushing all of her books into her bag.

"Seriously? You're blowing me off for a teacher?"

"I was ill over Thanksgiving, Marie. I'm behind on a lot of things, and you know what my parents are like if my grades start to drop. I can't … I've got to go and see him." She winced at the desperation she heard in her tone.

She had to keep her voice down and stop letting all of this get to her. She was better than this.

With her bag hiked high on her shoulder, she left the library and headed toward Jack's classroom.

Everything seemed to be going to shit, and she hated that.

Standing outside of his classroom, she saw Beth in the room, and she leaned against the wall, hating that jealousy that suddenly gripped her at the sight of him with another woman.

"So, I was thinking that we could all go out again. I know for a fact that Derick would just love it."

"I'm not interested, Beth. I've got a lot to do, and I don't have time to keep going out."

Was that because of her?

Had she caused him to be behind with his work?

No matter what she seemed to do today, she was a complete and utter fuck-up.

Just wait.

"Come on, Jack. It's really not that hard. A couple of hours. I'll make it worth your while. I certainly know a thing or two that will keep you entertained. I do this really wicked thing, and I can swallow your cock whole."

Oh, my God, that is just... She was going to move away from the wall, and leave them to it, but one of her books fell out of her bag, and she winced, bending down to pick it up.

She hoped neither of them realized how hot her cheeks were or that she'd been leaning against the wall listening.

Could a woman really swallow a cock without dying?

Lack of breath and all that?

Picking up her book, she stood in the doorway. "Erm, I was wondering if I could have a word with Mr. Parker? There's an assignment that I have to … complete." She didn't look at Ms. Bertram. Right now, she didn't think she could stomach being near the other woman.

"Sure, if you'll excuse me, Ms. Bertram, I have to help Lucia."

"Think about it."

Wow, could women really be that forward without coming across as being a slut?

He didn't say anything, but he gave a nod as if he'd consider it.

Tapping her fingers against her thigh, she stepped into the room and forced herself to smile at Ms. Bertram.

She didn't have any way of warning the other woman. She just had to accept that, and she hated it.

There was no way she could claim Jack for herself.

"Miss Deen, how can I help?"

She approached his desk, and words failed her. He stood in front of it, but her gaze was caught on the cuffs of his shirt. The ink wrapped around his wrists, peeking through.

"I, erm, is she like that all the time with you?"

"Yes, it would appear that Beth doesn't like to take no for an answer."

She sighed. He reached out, and his fingers grazed her hip, sliding down to cup her hand.

It was dangerous.

If they were caught, it would be a nightmare for them both. She didn't want to be the one responsible for getting him fired.

"I don't like it," she said, feeling tears fill her eyes. "I don't like not being able to say something to her. Like leave him alone, he's…"

She didn't finish. She couldn't.

"Like I'm yours?" he asked. "I know what you're feeling, Lucia. You don't think I experience it every single time I see Connor sitting in front of you? How I want to pound the fucking face of my student? Or when I see him near you when you're in your locker. There's a lot of things I don't like, but I have to deal with them. Beth, she's not a problem. Not even in the slightest. She holds no appeal for me." He kissed her knuckles. "Now, did you need me to help you with homework or did you have something else in mind?"

"I miss you … so much."

"Yes. I'd been hoping that you'd come to see me."

"I think something is going on with London. I don't know what, but they could be relocating there."

"Lucia, if they relocate, there's a chance you'll be going with them."

She shook her head. This was all just too much.

Prior to starting school at the end of the summer, she'd have been all for a move, but now, it risked everything. The one person she loved seeing, that filled her with enjoyment, was this man right here, and if … if she moved that would all go.

"I don't want to go."

He held her hand just a little tighter, and she felt that need within him as well. "We all have to do things we don't like, Lucia. That is unfortunate, but it's also life."

She nodded. "I didn't need to see you about any homework. I just wanted to come and see you."

He cupped her face, tilting her head back. "Don't for a second think that you're the only one affected by this. You're not. I miss you all the time, Lucia."

"The gym," she said, suddenly.

"What about it?"

"Mom, she reminded me this morning that she'd paid for me to go."

"So? I don't see how going to a gym is important."

"It gives me a reason to leave the house. I can say I'm going to the gym, and drive to see you."

"I love that idea, Lucia, but when they see you're not losing weight they'll get suspicious."

"You could help me. You run. We could do some warm-up exercises or something. It's a shot." She felt hope bloom, and when he smiled, she knew she got him.

"Lucia Deen, you are a temptation I cannot seem to hide or to shake, and you know what, I don't want to either."

With her head tilted back, he stepped forward, and she smiled up at him. All of her troubles melted away, and the only person that mattered to her was right here, in this very room. His lips brushed across hers, and she moaned, gripping his shoulders a little tighter, not wanting to let him go even for a second.

His tongue traced across her lips, and her eyes closed. When she opened her mouth, he plundered inside, and she tasted him, relishing every second as he stroked his tongue with hers.

She held his arms, not wanting to let him go.

This moment was what she'd been wanting.

That sweet little dance together that promised so much more.

She couldn't lose this.

It was the only thing in her life right now that made any sense. Nothing else ever made sense to her.

As his fingers sank into her hair, and the kiss deepened, he pressed his body against hers, and she felt the hard ridge of his length that she wanted so badly to be fucking her hard. There were no sweet or easy words for the touch that she craved. All she wanted was him, all around her, inside her, fucking her raw as she screamed his name.

Within a second that was taken away as a gasp filled the air, seeming to echo off the walls with the fierceness of it.

Jack tensed at the same time as she did.

Pulling away from him, she turned around, and there in the doorway stood her friend. Marie looked shocked, angered, scared, and the worst of all, betrayed.

"You left this," Marie said, holding up her cell phone.

Her friend's face was bright red, and guilt swamped her as she stared at Marie.

Before she could take the phone or say anything, Marie turned on her heel and ran out of the room.

"I'll fix this," Lucia said, spinning around to look at Jack. "She won't ever forgive me."

"If she's your friend, she will."

"I've got to go." She didn't kiss him again like she wanted to. She spun around, racing across the school. Marie was already walking away from the parking lot.

Lucia had been the one to drive them into school that day. Rushing to Marie's side, she caught her arm.

"Please, stop," Lucia said.

"All this time, I thought something was going on with you, and I was right, so fucking right. He's a teacher, Lucia. An old teacher."

"Marie, please, I am begging you, keep your voice down." There were not many students around, but she didn't want to draw attention to this.

"Do you even have a clue what you're doing? What he's doing? You need to report him for abuse or rape or whatever the hell it is."

"It's not rape or abuse."

"He's your teacher, Lucia. He's older than you, and there's a code."

"I'm eighteen," she said.

"What about when it all started, huh? I bet he's brainwashing you, is that it? Pick the vulnerable girl to get your kicks out of. Is that what this is all about? Is that why you're suddenly not available?"

"It's not like that, I promise."

"I don't get it, Lucia. I really don't. You're … you're better than this."

"Let's talk, okay? I can stay over at your house, and we can talk."

Marie shook her head. "I'm confused."

"Then let me make it up to you. I promise. You and me, and we'll talk all night, I promise."

"You said that twice."

"Let me drive you home."

Marie stared at her. "Tonight, and then if what you have to say is total crap, we're reporting his ass tomorrow."

Lucia nodded. There was no way she'd report him. Nothing that was going on between them was wrong. Okay, the student-teacher element was wrong, so fucking wrong, but that wasn't a problem, at least not to her.

"Fine. Please."

"Yes, but I keep this until afterward," Marie said, holding onto the phone.

"Marie?"

"No, you owe me this. You've been lying to me, and I can't … I need to make sure you're okay. Your parents don't even know?"

"Of course not."

"Then I'm going to be the one looking out for you. No questions asked," Marie said.

She always knew her best friend was overprotective. "Deal."

They walked toward her car in silence. She didn't know what to say, but the guilt ate away at her.

Lucia drove to her own home, seeing two cars parked in the driveway. Her parents were home.

Her heart raced as Marie climbed out of the car, and she stopped. "Please, don't tell them."

"Lucia, we have a deal. I won't break that, no matter what."

Entering her home, she paused as she heard her parents talking.

"She could go to university there. I've already spoken to the Dean. He's looked over Lucia's work—"

She turned to Marie, whose eyes had just gotten wide.

"Mom, Dad, I'm home," she said, moving toward the dining room. Right now, she didn't want to think of her future. It was getting clearer that a relocation to London was on the cards, but she just didn't know when it was happening.

She had to fix her other problem before she

started to try to deal with this one.

Her parents closed whatever file they'd been looking at and smiled over at her. "Lucia, honey, you're home early. I thought you were studying."

"I was, but Marie and I feel the need for a girls' night. I'm just grabbing some clothes."

"Marie, it's good to see you," her father said.

"Yep, you two too. So, university. Isn't that like a British way of saying college?"

"I'm going to go and grab some clothes." She left Marie to her parents, not feeling even the slightest bit of guilt about it.

Her life was unraveling in ways that she couldn't control. Her parents hadn't even asked her what she thought of a relocation, and now this crazy shit with Marie over Jack. Everything was a nightmare.

Shoving some clothes into a bag, she made her way downstairs to see Marie's arms folded. She looked pissed.

"I'll see you guys tomorrow," Lucia said.

She didn't linger and was back in the car within a minute.

Marie fastened her seatbelt.

"You do know what that is all about, don't you?" Marie asked.

"I have a hunch."

"Lucia, they're planning a big move right now, and you've not even told me."

Lucia winced, pulling out of the drive. "I don't even know, okay? They've not said a word to me. In fact, they keep changing the subject, and I didn't want to talk about it."

"When did you become the avoider of all things? Weren't you the one that said in order to deal with this life you've got to hit things head-on?" Marie asked.

"A lot of things are going on in my life right now and moving is in the cards, and I don't want to know. I'm not trying to do this to be awkward. It's happening. I know that. I just ... I want to not think about it."

"You can't keep doing that," Marie said.

"For *now* I don't want to think about it. The longer they keep it to themselves, the better I feel. They've not even found a buyer for their house yet, so I've got a bit of time."

"Wow, Lucia, buyers can be found within days. He has really messed with your head."

"No, he hasn't."

"I mean it. If he's hurt you or put you in a position that makes me uncomfortable then I'm going to make sure you do the right thing."

"*I* kissed *him*," Lucia said. "I was the one that started it, Marie. He didn't."

"What?"

"On my eighteenth birthday, after class, I kissed him, and then I ran away as if I had been fucking burned, okay?"

"Is that all it's been? A kiss?"

"No."

"What do you mean?"

"After my parents were a no-show on my birthday, I texted him, and then I went over to his house."

She paused, not wanting to say anything more, but Marie wouldn't let her.

"And?"

"And we had sex. There. Are you happy? We had sex, and it was the best experience of my life, and he was amazing. We've been seeing each other since, and no, he's not after just sex. He's taken care of me. Over Thanksgiving I was so sick that I passed out on my bathroom floor. I'd left a window open, and I could be dead right now if it wasn't for him. So, before you judge him harshly or think we need to ruin his life, *I'm* the one that pursued *him*, Marie. I'm the one that wanted this to happen. Even if it is just sex for him, I don't care, because I've loved every single second and wouldn't trade it."

"It sounds like you love him," Marie said. "The way you look ... just everything. You're in love with him."

She pulled into Marie's driveway, feeling the tears flood her eyes. The emotion seemed to completely floor her. Resting her head on the steering wheel, she let everything come out as she sobbed into her hands.

Marie's rubbed her back, not saying a word, as she unleashed everything. Every single tear as she was overcome with fear, panic, happiness, sadness, and pleasure.

"Come on, let's go inside before my mom comes out. You know I'm a terrible liar."

"You're an awesome liar."

"I know, but come on."

They made their way inside, and when Marie's mom stopped them, her best friend showed how expert she was.

"Yeah, the Connor dude I was telling you about in school, he's been saying awful things, and Lucia's been doing the whole running thing so it completely knocked her confidence."

"Lucia, honey, do not listen to those boys. You want to find a man who'll appreciate those curves, and believe me, there's one out there for you."

"We're going to go and study, Mom."

Following Marie upstairs, they entered her room, and Lucia slumped down on the bed, feeling completely exhausted. "Not a good liar?" Lucia asked.

"Yeah, well, it takes one to know one," Marie said, arms folded, leaning against the door.

"I wanted to tell you every single day."

"Why didn't you?"

"It's not just my secret, Marie. This is Jack's life, and regardless of our relationship, he's an excellent teacher."

"Look, I get that he's been able to face off with Connor and Rachel's parents. I was even hoping that we'd get to see a parent showdown, but that didn't happen. Still, he's older than you."

"I know."

"And that rings a lot of alarm bells inside my head, so you're going to have to start at the beginning with all this."

"Afterward if I've convinced you nothing is wrong and that it's all perfectly safe?"

"Then I won't force you to go and report his ass. Believe me, Lucia, you've got to convince me."

Lucia started at the beginning, from their innocent car rides up to the kiss, then to the birthday sexathon, and beyond that. What happened on Halloween night, even down to the Thanksgiving where nothing happened between them but he took care of her.

"You love him?"

"Yes."

"Does he know?"

She shook her head.

"Wow, that is … pretty intense," Marie said.

"I wanted to tell you. I hated lying to you, but I didn't see any other way."

"I get it. I don't like it. I don't like that you even felt you had to lie, but I do get it." Marie looked down at the cell phone, and then held it out. "Here you go."

"You're not going to … report this?"

"No. I'm not going to report your salacious relationship with our teacher. It doesn't sound the least bit dirty or disturbing at all. In fact, I think he could love you too."

"You think so?"

"He's taken care of you. Held your head as you've been sick, cleaned up after you. If this was just about the dirty, hot sex, he wouldn't have flown all the way home to take care of you. No offense."

"None taken."

"No, I think it's safe to say that Mr. Parker is in love with you."

"I don't know if it goes that far."

Marie chuckled. "You were always the negative one. Since we're sharing, I'm going to tell you that I lost my V-card over Thanksgiving."

Lucia gasped. "What? You did?"

"Yep, to a ranch hand. You know my Grandma owns a big ranch down in Texas. Well, he was there to help out his father, and one thing led to another, and we did it outside in one of the barns. Not quite that romantic, but it was a lot of fun."

"Have you heard from him since?"

"He texts from time to time, but he also moves around a lot with his dad so I don't see anything coming from it. It made Thanksgiving a lot of fun though."

"And you didn't tell me."

"Let's not argue about who told each other what. If I'd not seen your cell phone, I wouldn't know either."

"I know, and I'm sorry."

"I'm sorry too," Marie said. "Who would have thought it though? Lucia Deen, one of the sweetest girls in high school, screwing the English teacher. It's kind of sordid."

"Stop it."

"It would make a wicked porn film."

"Now you're being gross. I did watch them though," Lucia said, lying back on the floor like Marie had done. They stared up at her ceiling.

"What?"

"Watched porn. I wanted to see if it was different being with an older guy."

"And is it?" Marie asked.

Lucia burst out laughing. "I have no idea. I've got nothing to compare it to, not that I want to or anything. I love being with Jack."

"Oh, Jack."

"Shut up," Lucia turned her head, looking at Marie. "Do you forgive me?"

"Always. You know I can't stay mad at you." They held hands, and Lucia smiled. It would be okay. She had her best friend still, so everything would be more than fine.

"Psst," Marie said.

"What?"

"You're into old dudes."

Lucia laughed. "And you think I'm the weird one."

Chapter Fifteen

Several days later

"Lucia, darling, we know you're heading out to see Marie, but we want to talk to you," her father said.

Since the revelation about her relationship with Marie, their friendship was now back on track. Marie had even offered to be the cover that she needed so that she could keep up her affair. She did spend some extra time with Jack, but even he agreed that it was only right she spent time with Marie.

He'd been nervous as hell when she finally called him to say that everything was fine. She told him everything, including the threat Marie had made about reporting him, and how she wasn't going to do it. Once she made him realize that everything was going to be okay, he'd calmed down.

It was just another area of their relationship that made it a lot less than perfect. The secrecy was staring to wear a little thin, and she felt that it was also affecting Jack. He didn't like sneaking around.

"Sure, what's up?" she said, moving toward the table.

The file that she'd seen her parents hiding whenever she was around was now on the table, between them.

Sitting down in the chair, she stared at their smiling faces, and knew without a doubt that they were going to turn her world upside down.

"So, your mother and I have been talking about this for some time. We think it's the best decision, and I'm sure you've had your suspicions about our plans." This all started with her father.

"So, there's a new research development started

in London, and they've reached out to me and want to me to head the department. It means more funding, more time, and a chance of finally going to the next level with my research." This came from her mother.

"Also, I've been looking at offices in London. There's a company there that really wants my area of expertise in family law," her father said.

"What does all this mean?" Lucia asked.

"It means that we're going to be moving to London, but we've also been looking into several prestigious universities there. We're going to stay here until you graduate next year. It will mean a gap year for you to decide, but we figured that year could give you a chance to explore your options. We're aware that you're undecided about what you want to study, but with some time and guidance, we think this would be the best fit for you," her mother said.

"It'll mean a fresh start for all of us."

Lucia stared down at the folder, which they opened and were showing off the new house that they'd already put a down payment on, and were working at having it redecorated so that everything was ready for when they moved in.

"So instead of being alone in a country and a town I know, I get to be alone in a foreign country." Lucia got to her feet. "I've got to go."

"Lucia Deen, this is a great opportunity."

For you!

She wanted to scream the words, but instead, she just smiled.

"I know it is. It'll be a wonderful opportunity." She didn't stay. Getting into her car, she drove to Jack's home. She parked a few yards down so as not to raise suspicion. Grabbing her bag, she walked toward Jack's front door, knocking. Everything seemed to be working on autopilot.

When he opened, his smile was the only thing that lifted her heart. That quickly turned to a frown when he stared at her. "Lucia, what is it?" he asked.

"My parents."

He pulled her into his home, closing the door and taking her to the sitting room. Jack took her into his lap, his arms wrapping around her, protecting her, loving her.

No words of love had been spoken between them, but she felt it. This deep connection to him that couldn't be taken from either of them.

"What's going on?"

"They're moving," she said.

"What?"

"We're moving to London. They've got everything organized." She laughed. "They didn't even ask me what my thoughts were. They want a fresh start, and they think it will be great for me."

"Start at the beginning."

Lucia told him everything that was said. He sat and listened intently, not once interrupting, and she hated that.

"This could be a fresh start for you, Lucia," Jack said. "London is a wonderful place. It'll be a chance for you to start seeing the world."

Tears filled her eyes once again, and she looked at Jack, her heart breaking at his words. "But … what about us?" He averted his gaze, and she felt a little sick. "Do you want us … to end?"

Silence met her question, and she tried to pull off his lap, but he wouldn't let her. "No!"

He held her tightly.

"No, Lucia, I don't want us to end."

"But you said it could be for the best."

"I'm trying to be the good guy here. The good

guy wouldn't tell you that the thought of not seeing you again tears him up inside. The good guy tells you what a great opportunity it is. How you'll love every single second of your time away. That you'll meet new people that will bring enjoyment and love into your life. How you'll find a man your own age, fall in love, and be so deliriously happy that you'll forget all about me."

She couldn't look away.

The fire.

The passion blazed within his eyes.

"I'm not a good man, Lucia. I'm not wired that way, and I don't want to lose you. Not to this, not ever. We'll figure something out. You're a grownup. You don't have to follow them." He pushed some hair off her face. "I'll take care of you."

"I'm not after your money."

"I'm very much aware of that. I know you only want me for my very wicked and tempting body."

Before she could say anything else, he pulled her down, and his lips were on hers. She gripped his shoulders, not wanting to pull away, never wanting to do that.

Jack took control, moving her so that she straddled his lap. He ran his hand down her back, gripping her ass.

It felt like it had been way too long since they'd been together. She couldn't control herself.

When he pushed her jacket of her shoulders, she attacked his shirt, pulling it open so that buttons scattered everywhere. She gasped as he tugged her shirt up over her head, and then pulled the straps of her bra down so her tits swung free. Within the next second his lips were on her, licking, sucking, biting at her nipples.

Lucia stared down at him, watching as he took charge of her body, doing with it exactly as he wanted without a care in the world.

Sinking her fingers into his hair, she watched his tongue as it lapped across each hard nipple, flicking the tender, sensitive tips. Each touch seemed to go straight between her thighs, the temptation of his mouth too great for her to stop.

"I love your body, Lucia. Fucking love it." His hands moved up from her ass to press her tits together. "Your body was made for fucking."

His thumb stroked across her beaded buds and then glided down. He moved her so that she stood and he could pull her jeans down.

Jack was fast losing his patience. She saw it and relished it. He pulled her back onto his lap where he'd already pulled out his cock.

The condom packet was already out of his pocket and open. He held the latex out for her.

"Care to do the honors?" he said.

Taking the latex from him, she slid it over his rock-hard cock, being careful as she did so that she didn't hurt him. He'd shown her how to do it, but unless he was hard, like he was now, she found it incredibly difficult to do.

It was something she was more than happy to take practice on.

Once the condom was in place, he lifted her up so that the tip was poised at her entrance.

"Watch us," he said.

Glancing down between them, she watched as his cock began to sink inside her body. Not only did it look good from her vantage point, but she got to see how good it looked at as it sank within her body, each inch stretching her.

It felt like an eternity since he'd been inside her, and she couldn't stand him not being within her.

Holding onto his shoulders, she slammed down on him, gasping as he filled her to the hilt, verging on pain.

The pleasure was also there as her clit rubbed against her pelvis.

She didn't have to wait long for Jack to take over. He started to stroke her clit.

"That's it, baby, ride me. Ride my cock. Show me how you love it."

She moved up and down, rocking her pelvis as she took him inside her. The feel of his fingers against her clit drove her need for him higher. She didn't want to stop. As she moved against him, he stroked her closer to orgasm. With his other hand, he either gripped her hip, guiding her over him, or slid it up to cup her tit, holding it out so that he could play with her nipple.

Every single touch just heightened her need for him.

When she came, she did so crying his name, fucking him harder, taking him just a little deeper.

The moment her orgasm slowed, Jack changed angles, pushing her to the sofa, lifting her hips so that he could get the depth that would drive her wild.

Wrapping her legs around his waist, his name spilling from her lips, she was desperate for more, aching for more, needing it.

"You feel so fucking good, Lucia. So good."

He pounded inside her body, taking what he wanted, and she was merely the vessel for his pleasure.

She watched his face, completely enraptured by the pleasure she saw in his blue eyes. So sexy, so beautiful, and all hers. This man, he was hers in every single way that counted, and she loved that.

These moments with him were precious to her, and she didn't want to lose them, not for a single second.

Over and over, he fucked her, bringing her to yet another screaming orgasm before he threw himself over the edge, and she watched him come. His cock pulsed inside her as wave upon wave of cum released.

She smiled, wrapping her arms around his back, stroking his body.

His lips crashed down on hers, his tongue sliding across hers lips until she opened up, and he plundered inside.

She moaned and then giggled as he sucked on her lip.

"That wasn't supposed to happen," he said.

Both of his hands rested on either side of her head.

"What *was* supposed to happen, Jack?"

"We were going to talk and solve this problem."

"We did. I don't have to go with them, problem solved."

"You and I both know it's not going to be that easy. You're their only daughter, and as much as they don't spend time with them now, another country, they've not even suggested it."

She sighed. "I know."

"I don't want you to go."

That sent a thrill down her spine hearing him say that.

"I know I'm going to have to."

Now that kind of sucked.

"It's an amazing opportunity for you, Lucia."

"And if I don't want to go?"

"You've got to make the decision that doesn't include me or us."

It was hard to keep her emotions in check, but she did it, just. She didn't want him to know how heartbreaking that was.

"I see how sad that is making you, Lucia. Think about it. I don't want you to regret this."

"What do you mean?"

"Your parents are moving to another country. It's a chance for you to see the world, and if you stick around because of me, it means that you could regret it. I'd hate for you to regret being with me, for any reason."

If he worried that she'd regret it, didn't that mean he saw them being together a lot longer than school, graduation?

Right now, she didn't care. She'd take it.

"Can we worry about this another time? I don't want to spoil our time together." She stroked his muscular, inked arms.

"We can." He dropped a kiss to her lips. "I love it when you come over."

"Me too."

He pulled out of her and she sat up, watching him as he stared down at the condom. "What is it?" she asked.

He had a frown on his face. "The condom broke."

"What?"

"It's nothing."

"Doesn't that, like, have a risk though?"

"It can happen." He glanced over at her.

"I could get pregnant?" she asked.

"You could."

This wasn't something she had anticipated. She leaned forward and then glanced over at him.

"We'll take care of it," he said. He pulled her into his arms, and she struggled against him.

"What does that even mean?" she asked, trying not to panic but totally failing as the realization of what a broken condom could mean sank in.

Could he lose his job?

What would people say?

No, she didn't want him to lose his job. He loved his work, and the thought of it being because of her, filled her with pain. No, whatever happened, no one could know, not for some time.

"Do you mean abortion?" she asked.

"Hell, no. What I meant was, I'd take care of you, Lucia. I'd take care of you and our baby. It's not a big deal."

"It is though. I know you love your job."

"Is that what has you freaking out right now? My job?"

"I know you love it, and I'll never let you lose it because of me."

"You're amazing, you know that, right?"

"What do you mean?"

"Some women would be going batshit crazy at just the risk of being pregnant. Not you. You're more worried about my job. Lucia, I love my job, I really do. Teaching is what I love, but if I have to, I can find other ways of making a living. Besides, I'm quite well off."

"No, I don't want to do that to you. You say that you don't want me to live with regrets, well I don't want you to either. This has to be an equal thing."

"How about we stop trying to write our future when we don't know what has happened yet? Now, I can either get a pregnancy test kit or we can wait a few weeks and see."

"We're going to have to wait a couple of weeks. Why don't we wait for the month and see what happens?" she asked.

"That's fine with me." He cupped her face, tilting her head back. "You've got to stop worrying about everything."

"I—"

"Don't even argue with me right now. I won't let you be upset by this."

"Okay."

"You're sure."

"Yes."

"Then let's go and get washed up. I'll order us some food, and we can talk about other things that won't stress you out."

"Okay."

He pressed a kiss to her lips. "How are you feeling now?"

"Good."

"Good." He kissed her again, and she chuckled.

"This was what got us into trouble in the first place."

"It has been too long since I last kissed that I need to know those lips are perfectly fine."

As he kept kissing her, Lucia's fears melted away.

She'd worry about everything else when she had to. For now, she cared about Jack and being with him.

****

Carols played all around the mall, and people in all different kinds of moods continued to shop. Jack tuned them all out.

Christmas was that time of year that both annoyed and excited him. As a kid he'd always be excited, hoping that Santa would bring him something special that year. Then of course he had the big reveal year that showed him no such miracle ever existed. Still, he loved the feeling that Christmas seemed to bring him.

Even though he was a grown-ass man, he still decorated his home, which he intended to do when he got back.

He still had the decorations from his first

apartment, and last year he'd even bought a few outside lights to enjoy the festive season. Perfecting the art of Christmas dinner still failed him, but that would mean a two-hour phone call with his parents' cook.

That was another thing that annoyed him this time of year, he'd have to avoid his parents' many phone calls and demands.

They'd already tried to get him to come over for their annual Christmas party.

That wasn't going to happen. He made that mistake a few years ago when he had no fewer than five prospective females that they had both said were right for him.

He should just go and be done with it, only he stood outside of a jeweler's, caught between a gold ring, a bracelet, or a necklace. Each would look amazing on Lucia. He'd stroked her neck, thinking how sexy it would be to have her only wearing a necklace and nothing else.

Her body was made to be worshipped.

"Hello, Mr. Parker," Marie said, catching him by surprise.

Turning his head, he saw Lucia's best friend laden down with several packages.

"Marie, would you like me to take any of those for you?" he asked.

"Nope. I'm good. I'm trying to cram all of my shopping in at once. I hate this time of year."

"Oh."

"No, I love it, I do, but shopping is the suck part of it. Especially the people. They seem to turn into mad, hungry beasts, and it doesn't make for the best shopping experience. What are you doing?"

"I'm attempting to pick something out for…" He stopped. Even though Lucia told him everything was fine between her and Marie, this didn't feel comfortable.

"Lucia? You're looking for something for her?"

"Yes."

"You don't have to be uncomfortable. I get it. Well, I don't because you're, like, old, but Lucia likes you." Marie stared at him. "You do like her, don't you?"

"I don't make a habit of starting a relationship with a student. No, I … Lucia's different." He couldn't even start putting into words exactly how he felt, only that she completely lighted up his entire world.

"Wow, you know, I didn't … I thought you were … using my friend."

"I can understand that." He watched Marie smile, and it didn't affect him. Being near Lucia, even when she walked into a room, she captured his attention, and there was no way for him to not look at her. She was so beautiful, so perfect, and he adored her. "I care about Lucia. I'd never hurt her."

"I get that. I can see that, and it makes keeping this secret between the two of you a lot easier knowing you feel the same way."

"Thank you."

"Lucia never needs expensive gifts. Even though she tries to hide it, she craves affection. Her parents are not big on that score, so she's never been comfortable saying it. Sometimes she just needs a hug."

"Thank you." He'd already noticed that she seemed more content when he held her tightly, keeping his arms wrapped around her.

"I better go. Enjoy shopping, Mr. Parker."

"Are you sure you don't need my help with anything?" he said.

"No, I've got it."

She gave him a little wave, and then she was gone. He watched her leave then headed into the jewelry store. The man behind the counter was wiping its surface.

The moment Jack entered, the cloth was gone, and the man's beaming smile landed on him.

"How can I help you?"

"I'm looking for something special for the lady in my life."

"Oh, are we thinking a Christmas engagement?" the man asked.

Jack paused. He hadn't been thinking about an engagement. In the back of his mind he'd always put a limit on their relationship. With Lucia's parents moving, and college being considered in England, he didn't really know how long their time together would last.

"Maybe not?"

Glancing past the man's shoulder, he saw in his reflection how devastated he looked. Just the thought of losing Lucia, it twisted him up inside.

"Erm, show me them anyway," he said. "I'd like to see what you've got."

For the next half hour, he looked at different kinds of engagement rings.

He saw a delicate gold band with a single diamond in the center. The band itself, looking like rose stems, was so beautiful. It took his breath away. Before he could even stop himself, he'd purchased the ring as well as a necklace for Lucia.

Leaving the store, he didn't linger anywhere else, and instead went straight to his car.

Pulling the small velvet box from the bag, he lifted the lid and stared at the ring.

This was a symbol of love, of a lifetime together. This wasn't just for a gift for something as trivial as Christmas. Marriage, as far as he was concerned, was for life. Closing the box, he sat back in his seat and took a deep breath.

Even if after she graduated and they were

together, there would be problems. His reputation would be in ruins.

Running fingers through his hair, he placed the ring back inside the bag and started his car. As he drove out of the busy mall, his cell phone started ringing. Clicking on the device, he answered the call from his dad.

"What's up?" he asked.

"Is that any way to treat your father?"

"It's Christmas. You've been talking about the same old thing, and I don't imagine you're calling to find out if I'm fine or asking about work."

"You've always been difficult, Jack."

"It's my charm."

"You'd have been so much easier to deal with if you'd been a girl."

Jack burst out laughing. "So you could have married me off to a man of your choice. Get real. You didn't have a daughter. You had a son." This was the same conversation they'd had multiple times. His father wished for a daughter so that he'd be able to control her better. He laughed and mocked the idea. They moved on, same old, same old.

"Your mother and I want you to come to Christmas dinner," he said.

"Not happening this year."

"Jack."

"Daddy," he said, speaking just a little louder.

"It's time you settled down."

"And I will when I've found the woman of my dreams."

Speaking of the woman of his dreams, Lucia hadn't told him yet if she'd gotten her monthly cycle. Since the condom broke he'd been noticing not just babies and families, but everything to do with a baby.

He'd even been caught in the baby section of the supermarket where he saw the perfect stroller.

Pushing all thoughts of a pregnant Lucia out of his mind, he focused on his father.

"Woman of your dreams doesn't exist. You always did have these fairy tale ideals, and none of them make sense. The world doesn't have room for such romanticism."

"Says the bitter old man. Didn't you once love Mom? Couldn't imagine being without her?" Jack asked, already knowing the answer.

"Yes, I love her, and I love you."

"You know what, I've got to go. I've got to decorate my house and make it look ghastly. Maybe you should come over sometime. I cook a mean steak."

"That is just ridiculous, Jack. You're always doing this. Always running away—"

"Bye, Dad."

He cut off the conversation and breathed a little easier. Arriving back at his home, he climbed out of the car and rushed inside his home. Making his way up to his room, he opened up the drawer and pulled back his boxer briefs where he stored the velvet box. The necklace he'd gotten gift-wrapped, so he took that back downstairs.

Not wasting a moment, he went up into his loft and began to pull down the decorations. Rubbing his hands together, he was about to assemble his fake tree when there was a knock at the door.

Jack checked through the peephole and saw Lucia on his doorstep.

Opening the door, he pulled her into his home and pressed her against the door.

"You know, we've got to stop doing this."

"I can't help it." He slammed his lips down on hers, overcome with a wave of emotion that he couldn't deny.

"I'm not pregnant," Lucia said, speaking up as he was sucking on her neck.

He pulled away.

"You're not?" Why did his stomach tighten and disappointment flood him?

"I … I took a test last night, but my period came this morning. We can't … do anything."

"I've already said that I don't care about that." He dropped a hand to her stomach. "You okay? Any pain?"

"None right now. Well, the usual, but they're bearable pains."

He stroked her stomach, not liking her in any kind of pain.

"Care to help me put the tree up?" he asked, taking her hand and leading her into the main sitting room where his box of treats waited for him.

"You like Christmas?"

"I love it. When I was a kid it was probably the best time of the year. The cook always had cookies baking and treats all around." He opened the box and pulled out his fake tree.

"You have a fake tree?"

"Yes."

"What about a real tree?" she asked.

"I can't keep them alive."

Lucia chuckled. "You can't?"

"No. The last one I had was already dead before Christmas. It sucked when I had to dump it out on the day. Not very festive. So, I decided that I love this time of year way too much to risk anything going wrong."

"You like to plan everything?" she asked.

"Within reason I like to plan." He started opening up the branches on the tree as Lucia rummaged through his box of goodies. "I bumped into Marie at the store."

"She told me you did," Lucia said.

"I was buying a present for you," he said.

"You were?"

Glancing over at her, he saw the smile across her lips.

"Yes, and I'll be putting it beneath the tree."

"My parents are going to be home this year."

"That's fine. We'll have a day that we can call our own."

"I got you a gift as well."

He moved toward her, wrapping his arms around her waist and pulling her close. "I look forward to opening my present."

They finished putting up his decorations, and as he finished on the outside, when he walked in to the scent of cinnamon cookies, he felt flooded with warmth.

Pulling Lucia into his arms, he pressed a kiss to her lips.

She wasn't pregnant.

Decorating the house, he'd been able to distract himself from the disappointment of knowing that she wasn't pregnant.

"Are you okay?" Lucia asked.

"I'm fine. Are you happy?"

"Yes. If you're thinking about the baby and pregnancy, we weren't ready, Jack."

"I know." He kissed the top of her head. "I know we're not ready."

It didn't mean that he couldn't want, and he did. He wanted so much.

Chapter Sixteen

The last days of school went by in a blur for Lucia. She was still avoiding Connor, but she was also trying to do the same when it came to her parents. Now that their plans were out in the open, they were talking about it all the time.

"You know, considering you're getting hot sex, like, most days of the week, you'd think you'd look happier," Marie said, coming to lean against her locker.

"Keep your voice down." Lucia glanced around the main hall.

"Oh, please, it's not like anyone ever paid us attention before and they're not going to now. Seriously, what's up?" Marie asked.

Lucia sighed, putting one of her books back inside her locker. "It has been a long couple of days."

"It's Christmas. We're on our last day, and you're miserable. Please tell me what is wrong with this picture."

"Moving to London," Lucia said. She turned to her friend, and Marie's mouth formed a perfect O. "We're moving, and I'm not even looking at colleges closer, and everything is moving so fast. They have this plan, and I don't know how to stop it."

"Start looking at colleges, Lucia. It doesn't have to be this hard."

"Why do you make everything sound so simple?" Lucia asked.

"Because life is. It's only the very weird and stubborn people that make it a hell of a lot harder than it actually needs to be." Marie sighed. "You know after Christmas I turn eighteen."

"Any news on your ranch hand guy?" She knew

that Marie had been keeping in touch with him.

"Nope. Last I heard he was traveling across Europe. It sounds very exotic, right? Europe. He enters rodeos, takes odd jobs, that kind of thing."

"I guess. Only if you want to go there and you can't. Then it seems very exotic, but it doesn't mean that it is," Lucia said, closing her locker. She didn't move away.

"I feel all blue and miserable," Marie said. "My aunt and uncle are coming this year for Christmas, and I've been moved into my brother's room. The loser farts, like, every single time I'm near him."

Lucia chuckled. "It's going to be one smelly Christmas for you."

"How are you and Mr. Parker going to go?"

Again, she looked around.

"Get over yourself. We're the unpopular ones, remember? We're the lame-os that no one cares about."

As Lucia held onto her chemistry book, they started walking down the hall. "I don't know what we're going to do. We're thinking of having a day before the big one."

"Your parents are not working this year?"

"Nope. They've even planned to have a turkey. It's our last Christmas there."

"Wow, I bet that sucks. You're not wanting to move, and now they're emphasizing everything by being home," Marie said.

"Yep, that's pretty much it."

"You know for senior year, it sucks big time."

Lucia was about to say something else when an arm landing across her shoulders made her pause.

"Hello, fatty," Connor said.

Pulling out from under his arm, she tried to ignore him.

"So, what are you doing this year?" Connor asked. "My parents have a yacht, and we're heading down to the Italian coast. Spending time there this Christmas."

"You know, we were talking here," Marie said, glaring at Connor.

"Buzz it," Connor said.

Marie went to open her mouth, and Lucia stepped in front of her friend. "Leave her alone. No! I don't know what the hell is going on with you or with this, but it stops now. I'm not interested in sleeping with you or being part of your games. I'm done. I don't like you touching me, just stop! There's no way I'll ever, ever fall for your crap or your games."

Quickly grabbing Marie's arm, she pulled her along, moving out of earshot. She saw Jack as she passed his classroom, and even though she wanted to stop to talk to him, she couldn't do it. This was just another painful aspect of their relationship. No one could know that they're together.

"Holy crap, you just totally handed Connor his ass. That guy gives me the creeps," Marie said, shuddering.

"You and me both."

"You know I've heard a lot of rumors about that guy."

"They don't surprise me. He's always hiding behind his daddy."

"You've walked me to my class," Marie said. "You're the other side of the building."

"I know, but I needed to get away and walking you to your class is the best thing that I could do." She waited outside of Marie's classroom.

Her friend hugged her, and Lucia left, but she didn't go to class. Instead, she made her way toward the main field. She sat beneath the bleachers on one of the chairs. Even though she was cold, she didn't make her way inside school.

She just seemed to be so fucking tense.

No matter what she did … everything seemed to be crumbling all around her.

"You know, skipping school is not the answer," Jack said, startling her.

"Shouldn't you be teaching a class?"

"Shouldn't you be actually attending one?"

Lucia gripped the edge of her book. "I just needed some fresh air."

"I saw what happened between you and Connor. You okay?"

"Yeah, I'm okay. I was just bored with all the crap that he had going on." She rubbed at her eyes. "Sorry, I don't seem to be the best company."

He crouched down beside her, his hand resting on her knee. "What's wrong? It's the last day of school, and you should be happy."

"It's just … I don't want to talk about it. I just really don't want to be here."

"Did you drop Marie off today?" he asked.

"No."

He pulled his keys from his pocket. "Go to my place. Take a bath, relax. I'll find Marie, let her know that you're not feeling well."

"You shouldn't be encouraging me to take time off." She smiled.

"I know, but you need it." He gripped her hand. "I'll be there after school."

She took the keys from him and watched him go. Holding the keys, she left the school, made her way across the parking lot, and climbed into her car.

Without a backward glance, she made her way

toward Jack's home.

She parked down the street and made her way inside his home.

Closing the door, she leaned against it, recalling every single moment that he'd pressed her against the door and kissed her.

Touching her lips, she closed her eyes, and peace finally settled on her. She didn't feel so tense being in his home. Dropping her bag into the sitting room, she smiled at the tree that was decorated in twinkling lights.

She'd loved every second of helping him prepare that tree.

Running fingers through her hair, she blew out a breath, and made her way upstairs to his bedroom. She entered his room and smiled as she saw his neatly-made bed.

This was her teacher's bed.

Moving across the room, she made her way toward the en-suite bathroom, and she started to run herself a bath.

Stripping out of her clothes, she paused as she caught sight of her reflection. Staring at her face, she took a deep breath. "I'm in love with Jack Parker," she said. "I'm in love with him, and I want to spend the rest of my life with him, but..." She stopped, feeling her tears well up.

There was no happy ending for them.

No way of either of them could make this work.

He was her teacher.

This was forbidden.

Stepping away from the mirror, she climbed into the hot water and leaned back, staring up at the ceiling.

There was no future for either of them.

That hurt her. She couldn't see a possible future for them.

Blowing out a breath, she rested her elbow against the inside of the tub. She couldn't even tell him how she felt. It was too selfish of her.

Her parents were planning to move.

Everything was in motion, and her life was spinning out of control with absolutely no way of stopping it.

Kissing Jack a few months ago had seemed like the craziest thing she'd ever done. Texting him, making love to him, fucking him, it had all been building to something. She didn't want it to be where she walked away. But how could it be any different? Their relationship had to remain a secret. There was no future for them.

After she washed herself, she quickly pulled on one of his robes and made her way downstairs.

Making herself a cup of coffee, she sat in his sitting room, feet curled up beneath her, staring at the tree. It was such a beautiful tree.

Her cell phone pinged. Reaching out for it, she flicked it open to see Marie texting.

Marie: **You okay?**

Lucia: **I'm fine.**

Marie: **Skipping class does not make it fine.**

Lucia: **Just having a rough day.**

Marie: **Tell me.**

Lucia: **Just thinking about me and Jack. You know. What's going to happen next year?**

Marie: **Ah, I get it. You just realizing that this entire thing could blow over?**

Lucia: **I love him.**

She jumped as her cell phone started to ring.

"Holy shit, you love him? Like honest to God have feelings for this guy? I thought you weren't serious before."

"Yes."

"Wow, that is really serious, Lucia. That's … a lot."

"I know."

"What are you going to do?"

"I don't know. I can't tell him."

"Why not?" Marie asked.

Lucia bit her lip.

"I don't know. I just can't."

"That's so fucking lame."

"What if he doesn't love me? What is the point of saying something else or making this worse?"

"How can you make it worse?"

"Because I love him, and you and I both know nothing else could ever come of it. How can we be together? It won't work out."

"Look, just because everything looks weird right now, it doesn't mean that it won't work out."

"I think this is wrong."

"No, Lucia. You love him, and you can't ignore that."

"I can't tell him. At least, not yet. It just … it's wrong."

"Running and hiding is not the answer, but I won't blow your secrets to your very hot teacher boyfriend."

"Hey!"

"What? It's true. I've just pulled up onto my drive. Yay, Christmas is about to begin, and my family is all here. Aunt and Uncle. My life is about to go to shit."

"Ah, smelly Christmas."

"Yep. If you're needing me to cover for you, give me a call and I will do my best. Think about it though, Lucia. Time is ticking, and you're both on limited time."

Staring down at her cell phone, Lucia released a

breath.

They *were* both on borrowed time.

Finishing off her coffee, she moved toward the tree. Sitting in front of it she saw the large square box that was wrapped.

"To Lucia, every time you look at this, I hope you think of me. Merry Christmas. Love, Jack." She ran her thumb across his name.

When had her life gotten so messed up?

Thinking back, she recalled that first-ever kiss. The way she'd stepped toward him, pressed her lips against his, and then instantly pulled away, afraid yet excited. She'd never for a second imagined herself on his sitting room floor in front of a Christmas tree, scared of the future.

A few minutes later she heard his front door opening. She didn't move but glanced up at him as he rounded the corner.

"Hey," she said.

"Hey. What's wrong?"

"Nothing, just admiring the view. You did a fantastic job."

Jack dropped his briefcase on the floor beside the chair, removing his scarf and jacket before taking a seat behind her. He put his legs on either side of hers and wrapped his arms around her.

"Are you trying to open your presents early?"

"You're sad," he said.

"I'm not sad. Just thinking."

"What did I tell you about thinking?" he asked, pressing a kiss to her cheek.

"Do you want this to end?" she asked. "At the end of graduation?"

Silence met her question. She went to pull away, but he held her close, refusing to let her go.

"Let me go," she said.

"Will you just sit still and listen? Stop having a temper tantrum."

"You didn't answer."

"That's because it's hard for me to."

"How can it be hard? It's a simple yes-and-no answer."

"No!" He yelled, which made her pause. They were both panting, and she glanced over her shoulder, watching him. "No, I don't want this to be the end when it comes to graduation. If you want me to be honest, Lucia, I don't see an end in sight. I've not got a clock ticking on this relationship. I never did."

"Then ... why?"

"Because we do have a clock ticking, don't we? Only it's not one we've set ourselves. I ... I want to be selfish. I want to beg you to stay here. To go to college close and that we can make this work. In time people will forget and then we can do the whole fake meet-up thing and then we have so much in common or something. People wouldn't even guess that we've been together fucking years." He stood up, and she watched him pull away.

"Jack?"

"I've never ... this has never happened to me before, Lucia. I don't want to ruin your life by making you not do things."

"I know you wouldn't do that."

"This isn't about me though, Lucia. This is about you and your needs. I can't be selfish with you." He stepped up toward her, tilting her head back. "I will do whatever it needs to make this work, that I promise you." He pressed a kiss to her lips. "I don't see this as a bit of fun. The whole forbidden shit. I see *you*, Lucia. I see an amazing, beautiful, kind woman that I love being around." He stroked her cheek. "We'll make it work."

"How do you know?"

"Because we have to. Because I don't want to think of not having you in my life, so I'll do whatever it takes to make it work." He rested his head against hers, and she closed her eyes.

They would make it work.

She had to believe in that.

****

Christmas came and went. Jack couldn't recall the time ever flying by so fast. His parents sent him a gift, a brand-new car, and also some new stocks and shares they thought he'd be interested in. He'd checked the market and for now used the money to invest. The car, however, was a bit of a pain as he loved his own car. The one that he'd purchased on a second-hand lot.

Lucia had been surprised by it when she finally stole a few hours while her parents were talking with the realtor about the house.

Other than a few odd hours spent with Lucia, most of his Christmas was spent alone grading papers or watching some reality show on television.

He loved the quiet and peace of Christmas. He caught up on all of his work and was able to spend some time planning for the return of school.

While he was alone, he also took some time checking out some of the schools in England. Yes, he was considering a move to England just in case.

He didn't want to be selfish, but he also didn't want to be without Lucia. When she wasn't around, he missed her.

Their time together was some of the happiest of his life. He even found himself planning a future with her, seeing them together, possibly a family. Yes, he was smitten.

By the time school was back in session, he was more than ready for it.

Arriving at school, he noticed several groups of students gathered together, talking. He made his way toward the classroom, feeling like something had changed, and he didn't quite know what it was.

He was opening up the blinds when Lucia and Marie appeared in his classroom.

"Did you hear?" Marie asked.

"Hear what?" he asked.

"About Principal Dowed?"

Lucia shrugged her shoulders. "She's only just told me."

"What about him?"

"He was removed from the school. I'm surprised you've not heard anything. It's been all around school. Someone reported him for taking bribes and money to help doctor students' grades. Apparently, he's been investigated for months, and they finally caught him on camera making a deal. He kept a record of it, or someone did. Anyway, not only did they remove him from office but also Connor was arrested over Christmas as well."

Now this did perk him up a bit. He'd not gotten the information.

"What happened?" Jack asked.

"He got caught on possession charges, and he was with Rachel, who was also high. Seriously, how did you two not hear this?" Marie asked.

"Grading papers," he said, holding up the stack of paperwork.

"My parents are going through all of their stuff. They're not moving everything with them, and they've started shipping some things to the U.K. They've got someone there who'll take it to the home they've purchased," Lucia said.

This was news to him.

"I didn't know that," he said.

"Oh, I feel I need to move out of the way of this argument. Let's face it though, we all knew Connor and Rachel were using. That's all I'm going to say," Marie said, holding up her hands and disappearing out of the room.

Jack didn't pay her any attention. His focus was on Lucia.

"It has only just happened in the past couple of days. They've found a buyer for the house, and they don't need it until the summer. Agreements and contracts are underway, and we're going through everything."

This became more real now.

"Tick-tock, I guess. That ticking clock that neither of us hears but are very much aware of."

He didn't want to think about that stupid, damn ticking clock.

"Mr. Parker," Ms. Bertram said, interrupting him.

They were at school and shouldn't be having this conversation in the open.

"Ms. Bertram," he said. "We'll talk about whatever you need during class, Lucia."

He turned his back on her and listened as she left his classroom.

"I'd be careful around that one," Beth said.

"Excuse me?"

"Surely you know girls that age have a crush. Lucia is spending a lot of time around your classroom. The last thing you'd want to do is give her the wrong impression."

"Lucia's a smart girl."

"Yeah, and I see the adoration in her eyes. Just because she's young—I remember being eighteen and so full of hormones. I'd have done anything to bang a teacher as well."

"You know what, I don't want to talk about this right now. What do you want, Beth?"

"Surely you've heard that Dowed's indiscretions have come to light. Taking bribes to change grades to help his students."

"Yes, I heard."

"We have a new principal, and she's waiting in her office. Her name's Helen Brandt."

"Okay, then," he said, leaving his classroom.

Heading down the long corridor, he heard snippets of gossip.

"I heard she was sucking him off and he was snorting when the cops got to them..."

"He raped someone."

"She's a terrorist."

"He's part of the mafia."

"Drugs and orgies."

Each one more elaborate than the next.

Entering the main reception area, he saw Dowed's name had been replaced with Brandt's. "A new day," he said to himself.

Knocking on the door, he waited to be called to enter.

"Come in," Brandt said.

As he entered the office, a brown-haired woman with glasses looked at him over the desk. "Ah, I take it you're Mr. Parker."

"The very one."

"That will be all, Ms. Bertram."

He nodded at Beth, then took a seat opposite the new principal's desk. "I've only been made aware of this sudden change. I'd have come and introduced myself before I made my way to the class."

"It was such a quick turnaround. No one wanted

Beyer Hill to be without a head teacher, and seeing as Dowed's doctored grades, every student's report sheet is being investigated. We want everything to run as smooth as possible. To help with that transition I'm just inviting everyone here so that we can say a quick hello and move on. I'm Helen Brandt. I will be here temporarily, unless, of course, they don't find a replacement." She sat behind her desk and sighed. "I've got to ask, were you aware of this situation?"

"I was aware something was going on. One of my students, Connor."

"Connor Mills, yes, I've been made aware of his indiscretions."

"I called on him in class. He answered a question wrong, he didn't like it, and I was pulled into the office. My job was called into question. It seems the boy's father has a history of removing teachers that caused a problem for his son."

"That is exactly where the complaint came from. It would seem Mills got one too many teachers fired, and because of it, this investigation opened up, which found Dowed's guilt. I, myself, am deeply shocked by what I discovered. Covering up students' drug problems, being paid to make sure students have the right grade to suit the parents. This is a damn school, not some political circus or television drama. How did you keep your job? Everyone else got tossed out on their asses?"

"I happen to have two of the best lawyers in the country as parents."

"Ah, you're one of *those* Parkers?"

"You heard of my parents?"

"I've heard of the Parkers. They don't only take the big, expensive cases for famous people, they do pro bono work as well. A few years ago, they helped me and another colleague out of a sexual harassment case. A female student had tried to blackmail one of the teachers. It was a very messy business. He wouldn't give her the grade she wanted and so she accused him of being inappropriate. They are tigers in their fields. It's damn good to know their son is here in this school." She stood and offered him her hand. "It's a pleasure to meet you, and I look forward to us all getting this school back on track."

He shook her hand, pleased that Dowed was gone. He didn't like that the principal could be manipulated, and his gut told him that Brandt would be a damn good replacement for that son of a bitch.

The entire day was filled with students talking about Dowed, Connor, and Rachel. It seemed a little surreal to have all three of his problems dealt with. Still, Dowed's firing had nothing to do with Connor and Rachel, as they had been done for possession charges. There was no way their parents could get them out of that sticky situation, and he did recall warning them that there would come a point when no one would be able to help them.

Knowing Lucia wasn't at risk of being hurt, he felt calmer. She'd be safe to walk the halls, and he wouldn't have to worry about her being accosted by that fucker or beaten by that bitch.

Finishing off the day, he felt positive for the future.

He was gathering his things when Marie knocked on the door, surprising him.

"Marie, how can I help you?" he asked.

"I wanted to talk to you about something."

"Okay." He nodded for her to close the door. "What is it? Is it to do with English?" He didn't have Marie. She was taught by the other professor, Kingsley.

"No, it doesn't have anything to do with school,

to be honest."

He leaned against the edge of his desk, seeing that she was nervous. "What's wrong, Marie?"

Lucia loved her friend, and he found himself feeling protective of anyone that Lucia cared about.

"I don't know. I'm kind of torn right now. I shouldn't be here, but I know that Lucia won't say anything."

"This has something to do with Lucia? Is she hurt?"

Marie shook her head. "She's not hurt, but it is about her feelings. Crap. You know what, if this makes me an awful friend, so be it. She's in love with you."

Jack stared at her, not really sure what the problem was.

"Lucia loves you, but she's too afraid to tell you because … she knows you love your job, and with everything changing in a few months, I know it's tearing her apart, but she's scared."

"Why is she scared?"

"Of losing you and of you not feeling the same way. I … I love my friend very much, and I know she loves you. I don't—how will you even make this work? You're her teacher, and she's moving away, which I hate so much, but I don't know what to do."

"Now I'm confused. Are you telling me that she loves me? Or that she's moving away?"

"Both. She loves you, and she's trying not to be selfish with you. She won't tell you, but I think you have a right to know, and also, do you love her?"

He stared at her, knowing the answer to that.

Marie stared at him.

"You're sure she loves me?"

"Yes. She told me." She pulled her cell phone out and handed it to him. "See."

He stared down at the words and smiled. She loved him. Neither of them had said the words of love. He'd been hesitant to express his feelings for her.

This was not how he anticipated his life to go.

"I don't want to make things awkward for you, but I also know she can be so stubborn. She loves you, Mr. Parker. I care about her, and I want to see her happy."

"I would never do anything to hurt her."

"I believe that, I really do."

"But?"

"She's going to leave. What are you doing to do then?"

He ran a hand down his face, no longer sure anymore what Marie was trying to say or do.

"Are you wanting me to end it with her?"

"No, of course not. I don't know why I came here, just that I needed to tell you. Don't tell Lucia that I told you, please."

"I won't." He was now so confused.

Lucia loved him. He'd seen that text, and he knew he loved her.

Their future together was so uncertain. She was leaving the country with her family, and he didn't know if he had a right to stop it, let alone if he should.

Everything was fucked up right now.

When he was younger, he thought he had all the fucking answers, but now?

Now he didn't have a clue what to do.

Chapter Seventeen

Time passed, and between studying, dealing with her parents, and just trying not to panic, Lucia found herself staring into her locker to see the single red rose lying on a card. Lifting it up, she pressed her nose to the petals and breathed it in.

"Oh, you got a little Valentine's Day gift?" Marie asked.

"It's Valentine's Day?"

"February fourteenth, the very day to celebrate love or to celebrate being completely single and alone."

Lucia put the rose down and lifted up the card. Sliding it out, she saw two bears snuggled together. When she opened it up, she found a small message from Jack.

"You wondered why I wanted your locker number, and this was the reason. Happy Valentine's Day, my love. I hope you have a wonderful day. Also, I've left you a little package at my house. Get dressed for me. I'm taking you to dinner. Love, Jack."

"Taking you out to dinner? Isn't that a bit risky?"

"I don't know. He always has something up his sleeve." She lifted the rose and pressed it against Marie's nose. "Sniff."

"Ew, gross. No, thank you. It's probably got some weird, shitty chemicals all over it."

"You're showing off your jealous side."

"I'm totally not jealous, but does this mean you need a super sexy cover?" Marie asked.

"Yes. Can I say I'm staying with you?" she asked.

"Yes, you can. Of course, you can." Marie winked at her. "Who am I to get in the way of true love?"

"You think it's true love?"

"When I look at you, I know it is. You have that mystical glow about you." Marie did some weird hand thing. "I've got to get to class. Catch you later?"

"Yes."

The rest of the day went by quickly. She didn't have a class with Jack, nor did she see him at any point during the day. She was tempted to stop by his classroom, but he'd warned her that Ms. Bertram was watching and how she had advised him to be careful.

She didn't much care for Ms. Bertram after that, but she didn't say anything, instead, keeping to herself and being careful not to seek him out.

After school she dropped off Marie and sent her parents a text to say she was spending some time with her friend. They didn't respond, so she drove to Jack's home. The car his parents had sent was still in the driveway, and she smiled. She had caught him several times staring at the large vehicle as if it had some kind of disease or something.

Parking up, she made her way into his home, which she now had a spare key for. Making her way upstairs, she found the package that he referred to. Opening it up, she found a deep blue dress. Unable to resist, she quickly removed her clothes and pulled the fabric over her body.

It fit her figure snugly. She'd started out the school year as a size eighteen, and with the running she'd been doing, she'd gotten down to a sixteen.

She ran her hands over the dress, and she started to pin her hair up just as Jack entered the bedroom.

"How do I look?" she asked.

"Stunning. It's exactly how I imagined you'd be."

"So, you imagined me like this?"

"Yes." He stepped up behind her, his hands going

to her hips. "You're perfect."

"Are we staying in for dinner?"

"No. We're going out."

"Jack?"

"Don't. I know what I'm doing, and I've found a restaurant that's quiet. Yes, it's expensive, but I'm taking you out to dinner."

"I forgot Valentine's Day," she said, feeling guilty. "I forgot."

"I don't care. I want to take you out. Now, will you let me?"

"Yes." She didn't even hesitate. He pressed a kiss to her knuckles.

"I'm going to get ready."

As he entered the bathroom, she pulled on a pair of heels. They were only a couple of inches high, so she didn't feel like she was going to tumble over in them.

Jack came out of the bathroom minutes later, dressed, looking sexy as hell in a tuxedo.

"Now, my lady, are you ready?"

Putting her arm through his, she followed him downstairs, and they left his home. He stopped at his car, opening the door, and giving her the chance to climb in.

"Your parents' car?"

"No, this is my car that my parents bought for me. I have no other use for it so I may as well use it for something good." He put the seatbelt around her before climbing behind the wheel.

Her heart pounded as they pulled away. This was the first time they'd left his home together, as a couple, heading out for dinner.

"Marie's covering for me in case my parents call."

"Do they call?" Jack asked.

"Never, but just in case. They seem to be all over

the place now. You know, bouncing from one job to the next around the house."

"How is everything looking?"

"Well, they've sent over a lot of artwork and photographs, along with books, and a few other things. Furniture they're keeping here. The buyer doesn't mind either having a yard sale, donating it, or even using it."

She didn't want to be talking about the future that didn't hold him.

"Let's not talk about that though. How about you? How was your day?"

"It's going good. Principal Brandt has her hands full right now with going through past student records."

"Was Dowed really that much of a problem?"

"Seems so. Even Derick has been suspended until further notice, and Bertram too. They both took bribes to hike their students' grades."

"Wow, that's ... what, three teachers now," Lucia said. It was quite the scandal, considering it had been over a month since it all happened. She liked Principal Brandt. She had been called into the office for questioning over the lunchroom event.

Much to her surprise, she'd been given an official apology over the incident. Whatever had happened, it had taken the school by storm.

"Yep. It would seem Mills pissed off one too many teachers. I don't blame them. I had every intention of notifying them of the situation."

"Why didn't you?" she asked, curious.

"Kind of got myself into a certain pickle. Started falling for a student and fighting it."

"Ah, that's just an excuse."

He took her hand, locking their fingers together. "It's a damn good excuse."

Her stomach fluttered, and she smiled, pleased

with his words.

"So, this restaurant."

"It's a French place. It's nice, and you'll enjoy it. Well, I hope you like it."

"I'm sure I will. Have you brought other dates here?"

"No. This is the one I tend to reserve for myself when I want to celebrate."

They drove out of town for nearly two hours before he pulled up in front of a very expensive place. A valet waited to take his car.

The man opened her door, offering her a hand. She didn't feel comfortable taking his hand, but Jack was there, offering his.

"I'll do the honors, thank you," Jack said, handing the keys over to the valet.

"Jack, this is a really posh place."

"I know. See why I knew we could come here."

"I feel a little out of place."

"Don't be. Hold your head high and ignore everyone around you. You'll fit right in."

She couldn't help but laugh.

Jack moved up to the maître d' and gave his name. They were escorted through the restaurant toward a private table. Jack pulled out her seat, tucking it underneath her.

"We'll have a bottle of your best red," Jack said.

"Wine?" Lucia asked.

"At least one glass, to toast your upcoming success. I know you're going to do remarkably well."

"I adore your confidence in me, but I've still got exams to take."

"Please, I've looked over your reports. You're a star pupil, Lucia. You've got this."

The waiter brought back their wine, and she

smiled at him before turning her attention to Jack.

He handed her a menu, and as she flicked it open she saw there were no prices on hers.

"I don't know how much anything costs."

"Lucia, this is my treat. You are my valentine. Let me do this."

She nodded, glancing down at the menu. She settled on a dish that had pasta and mussels, letting Jack know what she wanted. He went for the steak with herbed butter and potatoes.

Glancing around the restaurant, she was pleased that she didn't recognize anyone here.

"You're nervous," he said, pouring them both a glass of wine. She also noticed he'd gotten some water as well and was doing the same in a second glass.

"This is my first-ever real date. Water?"

"Yes, it suddenly occurred to me that I don't want to ply you with wine. It's there for you to taste, but I know you love water."

He smiled at her while taking a sip of the wine.

Lifting the glass to her lips, she took a sip of the dark red liquid. It was nice, fruity, but it also had a burn to it that she didn't like. "It's very nice."

He chuckled. "You hate it."

"I'm sorry."

He reached over the table, taking her hand. "Don't keep saying sorry, Lucia."

"This is ... it's an expensive place. I guess I still have you as the teacher in my head."

"I am still the teacher. I'm just someone who can afford a little more luxury when the need calls for it." He sipped at his wine, holding her hand. "I'm still me, Lucia. Nothing has changed."

"This is beautiful, thank you."

"Anything for you," he said.

The waiter brought them their first course. She'd opted for a salad that had grilled fruit and chicken while Jack had a soup. They talked about small things, neither of them wanting to ruin their date. She spoke about one of the classes she was finding difficult, and he mentioned a couple of students that concerned him. They never named people, but she liked that he could be open and honest with her. There was trust between them.

As their main course came out, she was about to tell him how she felt when someone stood next to their table, clearing their throat.

Glancing up, she saw an older couple. The woman was dressed in a floor-length black gown, and the man looked like an older version of Jack.

"Son, you've not been answering my calls," he said.

She turned her attention to Jack and saw his jaw clench.

"Hello, Dad," Jack said. "Lucia, I'd like you to meet my parents, Nancy and George Parker."

"Nice to meet you," she said.

"And you are?" Nancy Parker asked.

"Erm, I'm Lucia Deen."

"How old are you, honey?" George asked.

She glanced over at Jack, and she didn't know what was going on. Wasn't it rude to ask someone their age?

"She's eighteen, Dad."

"Jack!" Nancy said.

Looking behind them, she saw they were gathering a couple of curious looks.

"Dad, I'm having a dinner with my date."

"We need to talk about this. We're staying here. I expect you to come to our room before you leave."

Jack didn't say anything. He watched them leave,

and all the time, Lucia felt so nervous. This was the first meeting with his parents, and it didn't go well.

As she twirled the fork in her pasta, the thought of food actually made her feel sick.

"I'm sorry about that."

"Jack, that was your parents."

"Yes, they were. They always come here for their anniversary as it was where they first met."

She bit her lip, her nerves getting the better of her.

"Please, Lucia, enjoy your food."

"You've got to go and talk to them."

"I can talk to them anytime. Please, let me just … I want to enjoy this meal. Can we do that?"

She nodded her head. "Of course."

It was just another crash down to earth once again.

****

Jack didn't go and see his parents straight away. After their strained meal, all thanks to his parents, he took her back to his place, where he made love to her all night. He knew why she was panicking as he felt it too.

The ticking of that invisible clock. Everyone around them that seemed to want to tear them apart was happily making it tick away.

He wasn't ready.

Not yet.

There would come a point soon, so very soon, when he'd have to let her go, but right now, he couldn't think about it. There was no way he'd be able to live without her. He didn't *want* to have to live without her.

This wasn't about him though.

He shouldn't have fallen for her.

The line had been crossed, and it was up to him to be the one that fucking dealt with it.

The following day as Lucia was with Marie, he took the two-hour trek to the restaurant that also served as a hotel. He handed the valet his car keys once again and made his way toward the hotel reception, letting them know his name.

They gave him access to the elevator, and he stood inside it, staring at his reflection. He looked … troubled.

Releasing a breath, he waited for the elevator to stop before making his way toward his parents' room, which they always booked in advance to be sure they got to stay in the same one.

Valentine's Day was always a big deal for them as that was the day they first met. Going on a blind date all those years ago in college, he believed they said. The rest was history. No one else would do for either of them, apart from their precious careers.

He did have loving parents who were power-hungry as well.

His father opened the door first. "You kept us waiting long enough."

"I have a life as well. It's not about catering to your demands." Stepping over the threshold, he saw his mother on her cell phone, doing whatever kind of business. Following his father to the sitting room, he sat down just as there was another knock at the door.

Rubbing at his head, he drowned out the noises they were making until his father held a coffee beneath his nose.

"Drink it," he said.

George wasn't asking but demanding.

Taking the coffee, Jack gave it a sip just as his mother came into the room. "Did I miss anything?"

"No, honey. We're not starting without you."

"Is this going to be the moment where you all

gang up on me?" Jack asked. "Tell me that I've been bad."

"We're not blind, Jack. You never come this far away from that little school that you teach at. We may have been a lot of things growing up, but we know when you're trying to hide something."

"I wasn't trying to hide Lucia."

"No, but you were trying to hide from the people who'd have spotted you, weren't you?" Nancy took a coffee for herself, taking a seat on the chair opposite.

They always had to have luxury on Valentine's Day. It was the one day a year that they indulged. Rarely took any business calls.

"You never work on Valentine's Day or the day after. Who were you talking to?"

"I was actually talking to the dean of a private school."

"Why? I'm a little old to be forced into boarding school."

"To teach, Jack. I swear, thirty years old you may be, but you certainly like to test me at every single turn," Nancy said.

"This relationship with your student cannot go on. We will not have the Parker name dragged through the mud if this is ever found out," George said.

"So, we found a solution for you. End your relationship and move jobs. That way you don't have to be near temptation. You can start fresh, problem solved. We know you love teaching so much."

"You hate that I teach," he said.

His parents always had this way about them that made him feel so fucking small. He was a thirty-year-old man, not a child. There's no way he was going to let them bulldoze into his life as if it didn't matter.

"No, we hated you teaching if you were doing it

to get back at us. We're aware that is not the case and have in fact been made aware of exactly how good you are."

"Wait? What?"

"Look, we're not blind that we weren't the best parents," George said. "We wanted the best for you, and you wanted to do the complete opposite. Neither of us wanted you to throw your life away doing something you hated. When we saw and heard that not only were you damn good, but we saw your passion, we knew that it was what *you* wanted."

"But it's not what you guys wanted."

"Wrong, we wanted you to be happy," Nancy said.

"I need a drink," Jack said.

"You have one." George pointed at the coffee in his hand.

"I need a stiff one. This is too early in the morning to be having this conversation." He ran a hand down his face, not exactly sure what the hell was going on. His parents had always disapproved of his life as a teacher, of his passion. Now they were saying they accepted it?

"Grow up, Jack, we're being serious here. This is your future. This passing fancy of screwing one of your students must stop," Nancy said.

"This is not a passing fancy." Jack stared straight ahead, not looking at either of his parents. "I love her. I love Lucia more than anything else in the world. This is not some game where I'm trying to ruin your reputation. This has nothing to do with the two of you. This is actually about me."

It felt good to finally speak his feelings. He'd been keeping them under lock and key, even when Marie had told him how Lucia felt. His woman hadn't mentioned how she felt.

Neither of them had spoken about their feelings, but he'd noticed the way she looked at him. The softness, the love shining in her eyes. This wasn't for a bit of fun and hadn't ever been.

What future could you possibly have?

He didn't want to think of all of the other difficulties right now.

There had to be a way to make this work.

Turning the watch on his wrist, he glanced down and saw her smiling face in the memory they had shared of Christmas. He'd given her a necklace, which she didn't take off, and she'd given him a watch to always remember her by as well as the time.

"Jack, honey, this is … it's not going to work out." Nancy placed a hand on his arm.

"You don't know that." He glanced between his parents, seeing that they were communicating something between each other. "What? Don't give me that look or each other that look that I know you both love to share."

"Jack, there is no good ending to this, son. You've got to cut her out of your life."

Nancy leaned forward and scribbled something on a piece of paper. "This is the dean's number."

Jack took the number and laughed. "Wow, an all-boys school. You really are pushing me away." He got to his feet and walked toward the door, aware of them looking at his back. "You know she has parents exactly like the two of you. They push her away. They didn't want kids, but she was their mistake. They kept her though, raised a beautiful, intelligent daughter they rarely see. I bet if I asked them to describe their daughter or what she even liked, they wouldn't be able to list five things."

"What are you getting at, Jack?"

"I know she hates vegetarian food. In fact, she hates zucchini, and finds tahini too sticky. She loves peanut butter and spaghetti. She has a ticklish spot near the base of her back, and if you touch it just right, she giggles for hours. When there's an old lady needing assistance at the supermarket, she'll help her across the street, and even bag her groceries for her. She's self-conscious about her weight, and that's why she rarely wears anything but damn jeans. She doesn't have the first clue how to put on makeup. It's why she doesn't like it. Cream cheese bagels are her favorite. She snores ever so lightly when she's in deep sleep. Her best friend is like a sister to her." He stopped, realizing he could go on and on. "You don't like that I'm in a relationship with my student, I get that. You think I haven't driven myself crazy with knowing I broke my own rules? This isn't just about ethics. I love Lucia Deen. I care about her. There were times she's been alone that I've been so worried I couldn't even think straight. I get it. I'm a failure. A fuck-up. I'm a good teacher, but I love that woman more than anything."

He couldn't stay a moment longer.

Turning on his heel, he left his parents' hotel room.

Once he climbed inside his car, he threw the folded piece of paper with the dean's number into the glove compartment. The journey between his parents' hotel room and the car was a bit of a blur. He didn't recall making it.

Pulling out of the parking lot, he began the journey home.

Tapping his fingers on the steering wheel, he turned up the radio, but he couldn't find any decent music. Either love songs, which he really didn't want to listen to right now, or a bunch of people talking about their feelings.

He didn't want to talk about his feelings.

He was pissed off.

Angry.

Even before he arrived at their hotel he'd known they were going to be their judgmental selves. They didn't even ask him what the hell was going on. They simply assumed that he was being naughty, or doing something that he really shouldn't, and he was so fucking pissed off.

He focused on the road, trying his best not to think about everything that had happened in his life in the past year.

Meeting Lucia, watching her walk into his class for the first time.

"Am I in the right place?" Lucia asked. Her hair was pulled over one shoulder, looking a little out of place.

She was biting her lip.

"What's your name?" he asked, moving toward his student list.

"Lucia Deen."

He ran his finger down the page, spotting her name. "Yep, you're in the right place. Welcome to English Lit, one-oh-one."

She smiled. "Thanks."

She had been the first student to arrive, and as he began to write on the board, the scent of strawberries had filled the classroom.

He loved strawberries so damn much.

Jack had ignored her.

That first class, he'd introduced himself to everyone. He taught more than senior classes, and he liked to have at least one day at the beginning of school where he learned everyone's name, but also spotted the hard-working students from the assholes.

Connor had been the asshole.

"I'm Connor. You all fucking know who I am, so you can suck my large dick."

"Colorful." He looked around the room and landed on Lucia. "Well, introduce yourself."

"We already know the pig in the class, sir," Rachel said. "Don't forget to hide your lunchbox."

He was about to say something when she spoke up.

"Lucia Deen, sir. Not much else to tell."

She'd been so quiet. Her gaze wasn't even on him as she spoke but on her notes.

"You shouldn't have given her a ride." He could spend all day listing everything that he'd done wrong when it came to Lucia Deen, but what twisted his gut wasn't that he'd done them. No, it was at the thought, for even a second, that he did something wrong.

She needed someone to care for her. When everyone else seemed to be pushing her aside, he'd been the one to give a shit. To care.

There was nothing wrong with caring. With being worried about her.

He knew he'd crossed the line. He'd been the one to break the rules, and now he had to deal with them.

She was going away.

Her parents were taking her somewhere, and knowing that was tearing him up inside.

There was no way for him to stop it. It's not like he could ask her to marry him. Her father knew who he was and had seen him, and it wouldn't be hard to figure out that they'd been together for some time.

Time was ticking away.

Arriving at his home, he sat in his car, staring up at his home. So much had changed in his life. The school had gotten a new principal. Beth, Derick, and a couple of other teachers had been suspended or fired during their investigation. Connor and Rachel, two students who concerned him with the way they treated Lucia, were gone due to a drug bust, which didn't surprise him.

He'd stumbled onto their little problem, but he'd been so consumed with his own he'd not even given it a thought other than to demand that they didn't do that shit on school property.

Running fingers through his hair, he climbed out of his car, smiled at one of his neighbors, and entered his home.

He went to his fridge, pulled out a beer, snapped the lid off, and took a long pull on the liquid inside.

Resting his hand against the counter, he closed his eyes, gritted his teeth, and tried to fucking focus on all the shit that seemed to be going wrong in his life right now.

She's going to leave.
You'll be here.
She's going.
She's younger than you.
She deserves a life of her own.

"I know. I know. I fucking know." He finished his beer, tossed it into recycling, and grabbed another.

Right now, the only way for him to deal with anything was to get drunk. Really fucking, mind-numbingly drunk.

He grabbed a couple more beers and headed upstairs, intent on taking a shower, but he didn't go straight to his shower. Instead, he went to the drawer where the engagement ring still lay.

Lucia hadn't found it. She didn't rummage through his stuff.

In fact, she tended to give him privacy. His stuff

wasn't hers.

His home wasn't hers.

Nothing was hers, and yet whenever she was with him, in his home, he fucking relished every single second of her.

This *was* her home, and that was how he'd come to see it.

What was his belonged to her.

In his heart, he already belonged to her just as she belonged to him.

There was nothing he could do, so he drank his beer and tried to numb the pain that was building.

****

"So, his parents caught you two?" Marie asked.

Lucia nodded, taking the soda that her friend offered. "It wasn't bad or anything. I didn't say I was his student, but you could see that they knew. They looked really disappointed in him."

Marie winced. "Parents have that way about them. Don't they? Without even trying they can look at you, and they have that, 'you've been naughty, and we're going to look all disappointed,' and there's nothing you can really do about it."

Lucia burst out laughing as Marie kept trying to pull the same face that their parents were notorious for being able to do without any effort.

"Please, stop. You look more constipated right now." She sipped from her drink, and Marie's face relaxed.

"I imagine when we have kids it's like a natural occurrence."

"From all the sleepless nights."

"Let's not forget the cock-blocking," Marie said in between sips of her own drink.

"Cock-blocking?"

"Yeah, think about it. You've been screwing away quite happily. Then this little being comes along. They have no bladder control. Need love, feeding, changing, nursing, all of that stuff. Cock-blocking any chance for you to have any real fun."

"Wow, you sound so morbid."

"What you'd call me is realistic. Speaking of kids and all that stuff, is that something you guys have spoken about?"

"We've not talked about the future. In fact, Jack has said moving to the U.K. sounds like an amazing opportunity." She deepened her voice, adding in a splash of sarcasm as she did.

"Ouch. I take it that hurt."

"Yeah, no, I don't know. I feel like we're moving forward, and that this separation is going to be … it's going to hurt."

"You love him," Marie said.

It wasn't a question, and she didn't answer it.

"I don't know if he loves me," Lucia said. "It's not something that comes up all that much."

"You're seriously going to doubt that man loves you?"

Lucia shrugged.

"You know, I think you've been taken over by aliens or something." Marie leaned forward and began lifting up hair and looking behind her ears. "Have you been probed?"

"Get off. Stop being a crazy person right now."

"The only person who sounds even remotely crazy is you. How can you even doubt that Jack Parker, our very sexy Lit teacher, loves you?"

Lucia didn't know what to say.

"Oh, come on, Lucia. Don't you get it? He's not doing this for kicks or anything, or even to cross it off his bucket list. I've seen the way he looks at you. He loves you. You're just too blind to see it."

"I … I don't know."

"Ugh, I swear I'm going to have to spank you for you to see the truth. I mean, seriously. He smiles as you enter a room. His eyes are always on you. It's kind of scary. Imagine a scary horror movie meets, like, the teacher from the nicest of television shows."

Lucia started to giggle and collapsed onto the floor, resting her head against Marie's. They were spread out in her room, and she stared up at the ceiling, wondering what the hell was going to happen.

"What are you thinking right now?" Marie asked.

"That it would be the best thing in the world if he loves me."

"You know, I don't even have to question it. He loves you. Has those big cuddly feelings for you."

"What about your guy?"

"My ranch hand guy?"

"Yes."

"He's having fun making this big-ass name for himself. I think our thing was fleeting, but that was okay. I enjoyed it while it lasted."

"You still talk to him though."

"I probably won't stop. I like hearing the stories he tells me." Marie sighed. "You know, who would have thought it? I would lose my virginity to a dirty-talking ranch hand, and you'd lose it to a teacher."

"Senior year is supposed to be crazy."

"Yeah, but not for those reasons."

"I'm not going to complain," Lucia said. "It has been one amazing year."

"Did you know that the woman who got attacked pressed charges?"

Lucia turned her head. "She did?"

"Yep."

"How do you find out these things?"

"Mom made me take a big batch of cookies to the guys at the sheriff's office. It wasn't that hard to listen in to conversations. It turns out in three different towns this guy had attacked women. Random things."

"Jack took me home," Lucia said.

"What?"

"I was walking home. I didn't have a car, and he didn't like me walking the streets, so he took me home."

"And you're worried that he doesn't love you."

"That's how we both started, really. I had this crush on him, and I was so scared that I'd say something or do something that would be so embarrassing."

"Did the man ever fart?" Marie asked.

"You're gross."

"You didn't have to spend Christmas with your brother permanently releasing gas. I'm sure he ate chili regularly just so it was like poison to be in the same room as him. Disgusting." Marie took her hand. "Everything is going to be okay, Lucia. It'll work out in the end."

"Is this your unending belief in romance?" Lucia asked.

"No, it's knowing that when you love someone and they love you back, it doesn't matter what the world throws at you. So long as you're together and you have best awesome friends named Marie on your side, it'll all work out."

Lucia chuckled. "You are the most awesome best friend in the entire world."

"And don't you forget it either."

Her cell phone buzzed. Her heart leaped and she quickly grabbed it, wondering if it was from Jack.

It wasn't

Dad: **Hey, honey, we need help. Will you come home?**

"Is that Jack?" Marie asked.

"Nope. My parents. They need help."

"They're probably wondering what's important, your study books, or theirs?"

Lucia chuckled. "I'm going to have to head on over there."

"Okay. Leave me. I get it."

She giggled but got to her feet.

"Let me know if Jack calls or lets you know what is going on, or anything that is really fun and important."

"You just want all the gossip," Lucia said.

"Hell, yeah."

Leaving Marie, she made her way to her car. She was tempted to blow her parents off, go to Jack's place, and just wait. Instead, she went home. She couldn't keep blowing her family off, and right now she didn't want to see Jack.

Everything seemed to be going up all around them, and it was scaring her.

Arriving at home, she saw a large moving van was there.

They were one step closer to moving.

One step to her not seeing Jack again.

Climbing out of the car, she found her dad, lifting boxes. "What's going on?" she asked.

"Ah, honey. We need you to work on some of your stuff in your room. We're taking this in via boat. It'll take a few weeks to get there, but it will all be set up by the time we arrive."

She licked her lips, seeing her home slowly diminishing to just a carcass. The television, stereo had all gone. The furniture was staying, but all the throws and added personal touches had gone.

Leaving her father to lift the large, heavy box, she made her way toward her bedroom. It was the only room that had barely been touched. Sitting on the edge of the bed, she stared around the room that had been hers for as long as she could remember. This was her place.

"Hey, honey, what's wrong?" her mother asked, entering her room.

"I got your text."

"Yes. We know that you hate change, but we really need you to get a move on. We have to put this on one of the moving vans soon." Her mother entered the room and touched her dressing table. "This stuff can easily be packed away."

The necklace Jack had given her was around her neck. She rarely took it off, and she was careful that her parents didn't see it, just in case it was one of the few things that they noticed on her.

Her mother was about to say something else, but Bill shouted her name.

"Sorry, honey, I'd help, but I really need to get a move on with this."

She watched her mother leave, and stood up, moving from one space to another, picking stuff up, and boxing it away. Each item she placed away, that ticking clock in the back of her mind started ringing harder than ever before.

Checking her cell phone to see if Jack had called, or she'd missed something, she found her cell empty. No alerts. No messages. Nothing.

Putting it away, she finished packing up her room and carried it out to the loading van. Her parents were talking to the men.

Laughing.

Joking.

Happy about their life and the change that was

about to be made.

She wasn't happy.

They were turning her life upside down, and they didn't even see it.

"I can't wait. It's going to be so good. I can feel it. A fresh start," her mother said. "Look at this, Lucia. This is our home."

Her mother's cell phone was thrust beneath her face, and she had to force a smile as she was shown each new picture and image. The bedrooms, bathrooms, kitchen, garden, utilities. Each room looking more and more like her parents' place.

This home had started out being theirs, but she'd taken it over. She'd been the one to add the throws, the pillows, to turn it into a home. They hadn't even noticed it.

"Oh, dinner has arrived. Go and set the table, Lucia. We'll be in in a moment."

She went through the motions, going to the kitchen, grabbing utensils to eat with, heading to the table, then back to get drinks.

Her parents came in carrying a large box of Chinese food. They were talking animatedly to each other, completely oblivious to her struggle.

She listened as they talked about what was going to happen. The changes to their lives. How the English live. Nothing that Lucia cared about.

"What if I want to go to college here?" Lucia asked.

Compared to her parents', her voice sounded dead.

"What?" her father asked.

"What if I want to go college here and not move away?"

"Lucia, you're our daughter. England has some

amazing colleges."

"Yeah, and what if I want to stay with Marie, or go to college here, or stay in this house?"

Her parents stared at each other as if she'd lost her mind.

"Lucia, this is a great opportunity," her mother said.

"For the two of you. Like always. This benefits you. You're both happy about it because it is a decision the two of you have made. This is not my decision. You didn't ask me. You *told* me we were moving."

Silence met her words.

Lucia stared at the two of them. "Did you even consider what this would mean for me?"

"It's a chance for us all to have a fresh start. To travel the world, to see new things."

"I see. I was the last thing on your mind, right? You were both approached with these amazing job offers, and so you took it." Lucia took a deep breath.

"We're going to make this work."

"I know."

"I'm not … I'm not very hungry." She got to her feet and made her way toward her bedroom.

Her parents were silent until she got to the stairs when their conversation picked up.

"She'll see this is a good place for her, Bill."

"Really? Again, we're doing what we want and we're taking her along for the ride."

"We love our daughter. We're not bad people."

"No, we just don't listen."

"Do you remember Lucia saying she was going to the gym?" her mother asked. This made Lucia freeze.

"What? That is changing the fucking subject, Pat."

"I'm being serious right now. Did she ever say

that she was going to the gym?"

"I don't fucking know. What the hell has the gym got to do with our daughter?"

"I called them today to change the cancellation date. They informed me it hadn't been used in all the time I got it."

"What?"

"Lucia wasn't going to the gym, Bill."

"I can't even remember if she said she was going. Don't turn this around. Don't cause a problem right now."

Lucia didn't linger to see what else was said. She was very much aware of what she'd been doing, and she'd do it all again. Sitting on the end of her bed, she glanced down at her cell phone, hoping to see something from Jack. There was nothing there.

When her cell phone started to ring, her hope picked up.

It was Marie calling.

"Hey," she said, answering.

"Wow, don't sound so excited to hear from me."

"I am, I promise."

"Yeah, it totally sounds like it," Marie said, laughing. Slowly, the sound stopped. "You're upset."

"Just trying to deal with everything right now. I had to pack up my stuff, and I finally asked them why they didn't come to me asking me what I thought."

"We're talking about your parents right now?"

"Yes. They didn't have an answer."

"I don't know why you'd think they'd say something different, Lucia. Your parents are a little selfish. You always knew that."

"It doesn't make this easier though."

"It's never going to be easy." Marie sighed. "I … I don't want you to leave. It's why I try not to talk about it."

Lucia's eyes filled with tears.

"We've been best friends for as long as I can remember. We had plans, you know. A future together, college, a family."

She remembered all of their plans. How they were going to get pregnant, share babysitting duties.

"Now you're leaving and I'm not going to be able to do that, so I get it." She heard Marie sniffle.

Leaning back on her bed, she wiped the tears from her own eyes, trying not to sob. "It'll be okay."

"Is this where you try and tell me everything is going to be okay? My eternal partner of doom?" Marie asked.

"Yeah, it will all work out in the end. You have to have hope." Lucia burst out laughing. "It sounds so crazy, right?"

"Let's talk about something else. Have you heard from him? Mr. Parker?"

"No. I haven't. I'm a little worried about him."

"Do you think something might have happened?" Marie asked.

"I don't know. He doesn't really talk much about his parents." She sniffled. "If I get a chance I'll go over there. I don't think that will happen before school though. I don't know."

"It'll work out," Marie said.

This made Lucia laugh. "Listen to the two of us. We're making drama."

"I know, but it makes a change to be the two of us."

Chapter Eighteen

"They want you to end it?" Lucia asked him a week later.

For an entire week he'd been avoiding her, but now, on a Saturday morning, he didn't have any choice but to face her. To tell her the truth that after talking to his parents, he'd drunk himself into a stupor, and he was completely lost about what to do.

She'd tried to talk to him during high school hours, but again, he'd blown her off, working his way through lunch breaks, doing everything he could to avoid the problem at hand.

"It's for the best. At least they think it is."

"Oh," she said.

They stood in his kitchen, and he felt sick to his stomach. He kept looking everywhere but at her.

"What do you want to do?"

"I don't know, Lucia. I … don't … this is not easy for me."

"I know that."

"Yeah, well, it's hard. You're leaving soon." He ran a hand down his face. Upstairs in his drawer beneath his underwear was proof that he didn't want her to go, but could he be that selfish? Could he allow himself to hope for a future? "Look, I know if you want to report this—"

"Will you stop?" She yelled at him. "I'm not reporting you. This wasn't one-sided. I get that. I'm not going to ruin your entire career because you want to end this. Just come out, and say it, Jack. Say that you want to end it. Tell me to leave. To leave you the fuck alone."

He stared at her chest, seeing her pant.

What to do?

She's going.
You can't keep running from this forever.
You've got to make a choice.
Be the grownup.
I don't want to lose her.
We can make this work.
How?

"It's over," he said.

The words cut him to the core, especially as he heard her sudden intake of breath. She covered her mouth, and tears filled her eyes.

"We can't ... I can't keep doing this. It was a mistake, Lucia. This. You and me. We have got to stop this."

She nodded her head, but it was tearing him apart.

"Okay." She paused, tears streaming down her cheeks. "I've got to ... I've got to go."

She didn't linger, and as she brushed past him, he closed his eyes, flinching as his door closed.

It didn't slam shut.

She closed it quietly.

He listened to her car door close, and she pulled out of his driveway.

Jack didn't know how long he stood in his kitchen, ten, fifteen minutes? An hour.

He finally moved from his kitchen and sat down in his chair.

His home was no longer a safe haven to him.

It was a nightmare now.

Everywhere he turned, images, memories, sounds filled his head, reminding him of how happy he'd been.

Lucia giggling as she unwrapped her present.

He'd felt so ... happy.

Getting drunk, thinking about what his parents had said, it had all weighed heavily on his mind. He didn't know what to do or what to say.

In the end, he'd known he couldn't keep her to himself.

Instead of being the selfish bastard that he was, he'd let her go.

Closing his eyes, he counted to ten, trying to concentrate on the evenness of his breaths. He tried to think of everything that would take him away from the pain that was currently filling him.

He'd hurt her, and now he had to pay the price.

He didn't know if it was going to be a price worth paying.

****

Hugging her bear to her, Lucia stared at her best friend. She'd called Marie and begged her to come over to help her deal with the pain that was exploding inside her. She hadn't been able to stop crying.

At least she'd been able to avoid her parents, who were out doing some shopping.

"He ended it?"

"Yeah. He's right to," Lucia said. "It was wrong all along. It was never supposed to happen. I get that."

"You're miserable."

"It … it hurts so much, Marie. I don't … I can't seem to stop crying."

Marie moved toward her, holding her close, hugging her tightly. "You think it's something his parents said?"

"Could be," she said, in between sobs. "I don't know. He just ended it, but he was different, Marie. He didn't even open his arms or kiss me." She sniffled. The instant she'd entered his home, she'd sensed a difference.

Whenever he opened the door to her, he'd pull her inside and kiss her as if his life depended on it. That hadn't happened.

"I'm so sorry, Lucia."

"It's not your fault. It just … it hurts. He's been avoiding me all week. I should have known something was up."

"Do you want me to go over there and kick him in the balls? I totally will."

"It won't help."

"It'll make me feel better."

She chuckled. "No, it won't. It's not … he's right."

"No, he's not."

"He is. Think about it, Marie. Even if we stay together we're going to have to plan this elaborate scheme to be together. It's not supposed to be that hard. Love is supposed to be easy."

"And it is easy between the two of you. Believe me, Lucia. I've seen the way you two stare at each other. I bet he's a mess right now, exactly like you."

"He seemed okay."

"The key word being *seemed*. He's not. I can guarantee it."

She wiped her face, trying her best to clear the tears up, but more just kept on coming. "It's probably a good thing he's done it now."

"No, Lucia. It's not a good thing. There's no way that this can ever be a good thing." Marie tucked some hair behind her ear. "You have a right to be upset. What are you going to do when you go back to school? You've still got to sit in his class."

"I'll sit in the same place, keep my head down, study, do everything I can. It's too late in the year to change classes, and Jack is a damn good teacher." Her lip wobbled, and tears spilled. "I just wish I knew what I'd done wrong."

"You've not done anything wrong," Marie said.

"I'll be with you every single step of the way. You've got to get this crying under control though. Walking into his class and bursting into tears is not going to help you."

"I know." She heard her parents return, and she hugged Marie a little tighter. "Don't go just yet."

"I'm here."

Marie stayed for dinner, and with some help Lucia didn't look like she'd been sobbing her heart out as they once again ate Chinese. Marie dominated the conversation, talking to her parents, giving Lucia the break she needed to get to grips with everything that was going on.

She felt completely heartbroken, torn apart, and wrecked. She never knew she could feel this devastated in all of her life.

By the time Monday arrived, she finally had herself under control. She parked her car and said goodbye to Marie as her friend was once again on the opposite end of the building. Going through the motions, she got her bag full of books, making her way down to the library to cram in some study time.

Working through her lessons, she felt a sense of dread as they were getting closer to her English class.

Finally, with no chance of running away, she entered the classroom, and Jack was standing at the board. No one else was inside, and she ignored him, about to pass him as he stopped her.

She pulled her hand away and forced a smile to her lips.

"What's up, Mr. Parker?"

At least she hadn't gotten out of the habit of calling him that.

"Lucia, please," he said.

He had more than a day's growth of beard, and he looked a mess.

"I've got no questions for you now, so I'm going to go and take a seat."

"I miss you."

She ignored him and moved away.

Other students started filing in.

Ignoring the man that had broken her heart, she got to writing notes, listening as he worked through one of the tough exam questions from a previous exam year. She didn't try to think about the pain inside her chest, or the twisting of her gut. She ignored all of that, and wrote down her notes, being meticulous of every little detail.

At the end of class she was out the door, rushing away, not wanting a chance at being alone with him.

Marie was waiting for her at lunch, and she was thankful that it was getting warmer so they could eat outside, not that food had any appeal right now.

"You look a little pale," Marie said.

"I'm fine."

"No crying fest?"

"None."

"I saw him. He looked like crap."

"I know. I had a class with him today."

"You can't pretend to not be affected by this, Lucia."

"I'm not." She paused, licking her lips. The banana she'd been trying to eat felt like it was stuck in her throat. "I'm … I'm trying to get through. Bursting into tears in his classroom will cause problems, Marie."

"You don't want to ruin his reputation."

"He's a good teacher, and I love him. I don't want him to lose the one thing he loves the most."

"Lucia, he loves you."

"No, Marie. He doesn't. If he loved me … he wouldn't have ended it. We were never meant to be, and it didn't last."

They finished their lunch, and Marie didn't say another word. Instead, she talked about her ranch hand, who was currently in Spain. Lucia listened with half an ear, but it wasn't long before everything was silent as she moved between classes.

For so long it had always been just her and Marie. She'd never been the kind of person to make friends easily, not that she minded.

Marie was her closest and dear friend.

By the end of the day, Lucia was exhausted.

Eating was a chore.

Sleeping was always broken.

During the day, she was taking extra care not to remind her mother about the gym she didn't attend.

Maybe this was all for the best.

She stopped by her locker, and Marie joined her.

Her friend was talking about one of the classes when Marie went silent.

Closing her locker, Lucia turned, and there was Jack.

"Miss Deen," he said.

Marie looked concerned, and she didn't want her friend to worry.

"I've got to get home," she said.

Not giving him the chance to stop her, she herded Marie out of the school, practically forcing her into her car when they got there.

"That was really rude. He wanted to talk to you."

"I don't want to draw attention, Marie. He's being reckless. This was a mistake, and I can't have him ruining his job. I just can't."

"But what if he wants to ruin it? What if he wants you rather than his career?"

She shook her head, driving Marie home. "It doesn't matter anymore. It's over."

"You're both so stubborn. It has been a weekend, and look at the state of the two of you. Seriously, one of you needs to be a grownup."

"Marie, I love you, I really do, but he's right." She pulled up outside Marie's home. "We'll talk later, okay?"

"Sure, sure. Yes, so long as you're not sobbing on the phone."

She made sure Marie was inside before driving to her own place. Arriving at her home, she saw there were no cars in the driveway.

Breathing a sigh of relief that she didn't have to fake being happy, or fake being anything, she climbed out of the car, and made her way in. Dumping her bag on the floor beside the door, she entered her very vacant home.

No artwork remained on the walls.

Pictures were all gone.

She didn't think they had that many, but glancing around, she actually saw they'd had quite a few.

Her life was all different now.

So many changes.

Too many changes and there was nothing she could do about any of it.

With her arms folded across her body, she walked from room to room, noticing the changes. They were not subtle either. In the kitchen, her gaze was drawn to the calendar.

Lifting up the months that remained, she saw the date they were moving circled with a giant red tick in the center.

There was no going back.

Only moving forward.

This was what she needed to focus on.

Not her feelings for Jack or what had happened

between them in the past few months.

The future.

Without Jack.

Tapping her fingers against her thigh, she took a deep breath.

"You can do this, Lucia," she said.

The sound of the doorbell made her jump. She wondered who it could be, and without checking the peephole, she opened the door.

Jack stood on the other side.

She gasped, and for a few seconds, neither of them said anything.

"Can I come in?"

"What are you doing here?"

"I have to see you."

"Jack, this is a very bad idea."

"I don't care, okay? I've done a lot of bad stuff, but you know what, I'm not a bad person."

She frowned. "I know you're not a bad person."

"I don't mind having this conversation in the doorway or your neighbors knowing, Lucia. I'm not going anywhere, please."

She gritted her teeth. It was on the tip of her tongue to tell him to get lost, but she couldn't do it. She couldn't bring herself to throw him out.

"Come in," she said.

Tucking some hair behind her ear, she moved away from the door, heading toward the kitchen.

It seemed the only safe place to be.

Filling up the kettle, she placed it on the stove to heat up.

Pulling out two cups, she tried to keep her hands busy, and she hoped he didn't see that her hands were shaking.

She'd been making his coffee for some time now

and knew what he liked. Cream and sugar unless it's first thing in the morning, and then he preferred it black, no sweetener. It was strange how she recalled this little detail right now, and yet at the time, it hadn't felt like such a big deal.

"Lucia?" He spoke her name, and she closed her eyes.

This wasn't easy.

She didn't want to turn and face him, and yet that was exactly what she did.

"You shouldn't have come here, Jack."

"I had to see you."

"Why?"

"Because…"

"Because what?"

"I shouldn't have left it like that."

She glanced over his shoulder, not knowing what to think. "I have no idea what you're saying."

"I didn't *want* to end it."

"You avoided me for a week before doing it."

"Look, my parents are difficult."

"And you think mine are easy?"

"You're not in the wrong though, Lucia."

She frowned. "What?"

"I'm a teacher. I'm a thirty-year-old man, and I'm panting after a girl twelve years my junior."

"Wow, you're going to do this."

"I'm older than you. I should know better."

"I don't care, Jack. I didn't care, and I still don't. Nothing happened that I didn't want. I'm eighteen years old. I know what I was doing. I knew my own mind and that when I kissed you that day, I wanted to. You didn't do anything wrong." She turned away from him, closing her eyes. "I … I think you should go."

"One, never ever fuck a student. Two, never ever

339

fall for a student. Three, don't ever break any of the first two rules."

She turned toward him.

"Those were my rules. What I promised myself. I never wanted to fall in love with a student, Lucia. I never intended for this to be more, but you were always there. If not in the library being yourself and smiling, then at the side of the road. Talking to you, you didn't feel like a student to me. I've never felt this way for another person, never, not at all."

"What do you mean?"

"I'm in love with you, Lucia Deen."

She stared at him, shocked.

Had she heard him right?

"You're in love with me?"

"Yes, I'm in love with you, and I have been for some time. Being with you, knowing that you're going to go away, my parents, the reality of our situation, all of it—it's like a fucking bomb went off inside my head and I couldn't make it stop."

"And now?"

"Now, I don't want it to stop, Lucia. I love you. What I said to you on Saturday was fucking wrong, and stupid. I don't want to end this. I never wanted to end this. I love you, and I know you've got to go away, but I'd rather be with you than not. I can't look at you and know that I won't be able to hold you. I love you, Lucia, so much."

She couldn't resist it.

Running into his arms, she threw herself at him, holding him tight. "I love you too." She laughed and told him again as his arms tightened around her. She couldn't believe what was happening.

He gripped the back of her head, kissing her hard.

She moaned his name, never wanting him to stop.

"I made a mistake," he said.

"I forgive you." She cupped his cheek and stared into his blue eyes. "We can make this work."

"It's going to take some time."

"I don't care. I know we can do this. We can make this work."

He sunk his fingers into her hair, his other hand going to her ass, gripping her tightly.

She felt on cloud nine.

Jack loved her, and she adored him.

His tongue traced across her lip, and she opened up, moaning as he plunged inside. Feeling him, holding him, Lucia was completely lost in anything that wasn't Jack Parker.

"What is the meaning of this?"

They both jumped apart as Lucia gasped. Her parents were standing in the kitchen. Her father's face was pure red as he stared at her, and then at Jack.

"You're my daughter's teacher. What the hell are you doing in my house? Kissing my daughter?"

"Dad, it's not—"

"I'll deal with you in a minute."

She couldn't recall ever seeing her father so angry. When she glanced from his face to Jack's the rage was apparent. She didn't know what to do. She'd never seen him like this. It was like he was a different person.

"You think I don't know what I just saw? Men like you, perverts, should be fucking castrated."

"Sir … I love your daughter." Jack held his hands up, but that didn't help.

Lucia cried out as she watched her father throw the first punch.

"Dad, stop it!" She yelled, screamed, and her mother held her back.

"No, Lucia, he needs to handle this."

341

"He's wrong. He's got this all wrong."

"That man is a predator."

"No, he's not. Stop him, Mom, please, stop him." Considering her mother was so thin, she was surprisingly strong as she kept her away from the two men fighting.

Jack wasn't fighting back, and she screamed.

They moved out of sight.

She heard a lot of shouting and fighting, and then the door slammed shut.

"I know how to deal with scum like that," her father said.

Finally, her mother let her go, and Lucia rushed toward the door. Her father was standing there and wouldn't let her go past.

"What are you doing?" she asked.

"I'm making sure he doesn't go near young children again. He's already touched my daughter—"

"No!" She grabbed the phone out of his hand. "I was the one to pursue him."

"Lucia, he has you brainwashed—"

"I kissed him." Tears fell down her cheeks, but whatever her dad was going to do, she had to stop him, now, before he did something that would hurt the man she loved.

"Excuse me?"

"Jack, Mr. Parker, has been nothing but the perfect gentleman. He made sure I got home safely, and he took care of me. I … was the one that kissed him. I wanted to be with him. I love him, Dad."

"You're eighteen years old. You don't have a clue what love is. He's your teacher."

"And he cared about me more than you and Mom did!" She cried out the words, seeing her father pause. "Jack … he never touched me until I turned eighteen. I went to him when you and Mom failed to remember me.

He's the only one who cared."

"Lucia—"

"No!" She held her hand up and stared at her dad. "I love him. I know you don't believe that, but I do. He loves me too. I want to be with him. He's a good man. A good teacher, and I swear to you, nothing happened that I wasn't begging for."

She gasped as he slapped her face.

"Bill!" Her mother yelled.

Flicking her hair over her shoulder, Lucia stared up at her father. "He's a good man."

"You say you love him, that you've not been brainwashed by him."

She nodded. "Please, don't do anything to hurt him. He doesn't deserve that." She held the phone in her grip.

"Bill," her mother said.

"We're leaving immediately," he said.

"What?"

"You say that he's not a threat, and I believe you, but you're coming to England with us. You will not have any contact with this man. Do you understand me? If I find as so much as a phone call or a text, or even an email, I will make sure that his career is in ruins. I know who his parents are. I know who he is, Lucia. I will not have my daughter carrying on like this. You will prove to me that you mean every single word. Do you understand me?"

She nodded her head, sobbing.

To protect Jack, she was going to have to let him go.

Chapter Nineteen

Jack winced as he placed a cold compress on his split lip. This had gone disastrous. He shouldn't have kissed her, nor should he have gone around to her place. *Fuck!* One day he'd been without her, and he couldn't even handle that. Seeing her around school, knowing that he'd broken her, it had fucking cut him up inside.

He hadn't felt much better.

Working didn't help.

The heartache had been real.

He couldn't think of a single thing to do other than go and win the woman he loved.

Now she was having to deal with her father, and he didn't know what to fucking do. He didn't punch him back or beat down on him, even though he wanted to. He wanted to hurt the fucker and get answers to his questions.

Everything had moved so fast, he didn't know what to do.

His first instinct had been to protect Lucia.

No matter what, he needed to make sure she was safe.

A knock at his door made him wonder if Bill Deen had decided to go straight to the school and report him. He didn't mind.

He deserved it.

Opening his door, expecting some inspector from the school, he was a little shocked to see Marie on his doorstep.

"I'm so sorry. Lucia … she asked me to come."

He stared at Marie, seeing the young girl had tears in her eyes. "Is Lucia okay?"

"She's fine. She's fine. Erm, she told me what

happened. That you both got caught."

He nodded.

"She ... she's fine. They're moving immediately, and Lucia told me to come to you, to say that she's making it right. That she's really sorry for everything that happened, and that this was all her fault."

"What do you mean they're moving?"

"She's gone. Lucia called me, and I went over there. They were in the car, driving toward the airport. She's gone. She texted me everything." Marie held her cell phone out, and he took it.

Marie: **Why are you crying?**

Lucia: **Dad knows everything. He knows about Jack. About me. He's ... angry.**

Marie: **Holy shit. Are you okay?**

Lucia: **He was going to report him but I told him it was all me. That Jack didn't pursue me but he said that the only way to prove it was to go with him. We're heading to England now. I ... tell Jack I love him. I love him and I'm so sorry. I can't talk to him. I'm not allowed. Dad will report him and I know he loves teaching, I just, love him so much. Please, make sure he keeps on teaching. He's too good to give it up.**

The next few texts were his address.

Stumbling back into his house, Marie caught her cell phone just as he collapsed in a heap on the ground.

"Do I need to call an ambulance?" Marie asked.

"No, I'm fine. I'm just ... I'm processing. I need to go to her."

"Don't do it, Mr. Parker," she said.

"I love her more than anything, and I know she loves me. I can live without teaching." He had plenty of income and more means that meant they would never go without.

Marie stepped over the threshold and crouched

down to stare at him. "I've known Lucia a lot longer than you, Mr. Parker. She doesn't want you to give up what you love."

"But I love her more."

"I know you do. I know to a lot of *grownups*," she air quoted the last part, "we don't know what we're doing and that we don't understand people or whatnot. That's bullshit. We know a lot that you guys take for granted. Right now, you can give it up, but what about ten years, twenty years? You love teaching. I know because Lucia told me. She's doing this for you, and even though I'd love for you to go bring her back, I know her dad. Mr. Deen stays true to his word, okay? He will ruin you."

He ran a hand down his face, wincing. "I can't believe I'm being given advice by an eighteen-year-old."

"I intend to be a counselor one day. I think it's only fitting that I start getting in some practice." She held out her hand. "Come on, Mr. Parker."

She helped him to his feet.

"Do you feel any better?"

"No."

"She can't talk to you though."

"You'll tell me everything that is going on in her world?" Jack asked.

"Yes. I'll stop by your class when I know more. I better head back home. Mom needs me to take care of my brother. Bye, Mr. Parker."

He watched her leave and stood in his doorway, feeling incredibly lost. Grabbing his keys, he jumped into his car and headed out of town toward the city.

At first, he didn't have the first clue of where he was going or what he was doing. He just got in his car and drove. The past few hours echoed around his head.

"You better get the fuck out of my house before I

kill you. "

He accepted her father's anger, relished it even. He deserved it.

"This is what you get for breaking the rules," he said.

All of his life he'd been a rebel. Bending rules, breaking them, not giving a shit who he hurt in the process.

Lucia was different.

She was worth every second of breaking those rules.

He somehow found himself parked outside his parents' main city building. They had several homes around the country, and even around the world, that they used for special occasions. For work, they didn't live that far from where he'd decided to settle down. Jack couldn't even remember the last time he'd been here, or what he'd been doing. This was a lifetime ago.

So long ago that he couldn't even think straight.

Rubbing at his eyes, he climbed out, not caring if he got a ticket or if his car ended up crushed. It was the car his parents had purchased for him as if he was just a boy.

Entering the main reception, he ignored the woman at the front who called out to him.

There were only two people he wanted to see right now.

He clicked the code that accessed the lift to their main floors. With his parents being two of the biggest lawyers in the country, everyone had to have an appointment, and only a select few knew the codes to their floor. They never changed it either. He should probably warn them about that.

Standing in the elevator, he recalled being in this exact same elevator with his grandfather.

"They don't like me," Jack at age five had said.

"Oh, son, they love you. So much. They just don't know how to show it."

Clearly, Lucia's father had hit him a lot harder than he originally thought if he was already having flashbacks over his life right now.

The elevator doors pinged open, and he saw their secretary and several case analysts leaning over a computer.

"Mr. Parker, we need to let them know you're here."

He didn't say a word. Instead, he went to his father's office and opened the door.

His father was on the phone, but one look at him and he put it down. "I've got to go."

"Jack, what is it? What's wrong?" George Parker got up from behind his chair and moved toward him. "Get Nancy, now!" His father gripped his shoulders. "Son, what is it?"

"She's gone," Jack said. Tears filling his eyes as he spoke. "She's gone." He repeated the same words. "I had … I had nowhere else to go."

"George, what is going on?" Nancy Parker said, coming into the room. "Jack, what is it? Why does he look like he's been in a fight?"

The door to the office was closed, and he realized he'd come to his parents. Even though he'd never been able to rely on them in the past, this was where he'd come. "She's gone."

"That's all he keeps saying," George said.

"Lucia?"

Jack nodded.

"Why don't we start at the very beginning and we can see if we can help you in any way."

Jack didn't fight them as they led him over toward the sofa. Sitting back, he wiped the tears from his eyes, finding it all a little surreal that he'd gone to his parents.

His father started first, asking questions. His mother came next.

He told them everything about what happened, and he knew that even though he'd told them, there wasn't a single thing that could be done about it.

****

Five months later

Lucia stared down at the book in front of her, not really seeing anything. Today had been a long day. She'd spoken to Marie last night, who'd given her an update on Jack. He still worked at Beyer Hill High School, and no one was any the wiser.

Her father had kept his side of the bargain, and she had kept hers as well. There hadn't been any contact in five months.

Five lonely months in which she had felt so lost and alone.

England was … nice. It had a lot of people with different accents, people drove on the wrong side of the road, and the city was busy all the time. She rarely found a place near where her parents lived that wasn't busy.

The parks were always full to bursting, and she couldn't seem to find a spare minute to be herself.

Life had changed, and she didn't think it was for the better. What she found the strangest was that her mother had become the voice of reason while her father refused to budge on anything.

"You're not from around these parts," a guy said, drawing her attention.

"I'm sorry."

"Ah, American, right? The name's Ben." He held his hand out for her to take, and Lucia simply stared at it. "The polite thing to do is to take my hand and shake it."

She forced a smile to her lips, and then placed her hand within his. "Lucia."

"Pleasure to meet you. I noticed that you kept sitting in the same spot, on the same days."

She pulled away, and the smile dropped from her face.

"Oh, now I just sound like a stalker. I'm so sorry. I'm currently studying for a degree in psychology, and since taking the courses I find myself watching people in a completely non-axe-murdering kind of way."

"It's fine. Though the whole 'you're new around here' is a bit off," she said.

"Very true. Are you here to study, work, or for pleasure? I have to say sitting in the library every Friday evening is not exactly a fun way to spend your holiday."

"I'm here to live and work." She'd volunteered at one of the local campuses that helped with anything from class schedules to organizing trips, lectures, and stuff.

Since moving to England, she'd taken a gap year, and with her parents' help she was getting her visa changed so that she could work there as well.

She'd already graduated high school. Her parents had put in for one of the local high schools to transfer her studies, and she'd done a quick crash course, and now here she was. Graduated, volunteering, living with her parents, being completely away from everything she'd known.

Now she was talking to a guy named Ben.
Yay.

"Ah, so you're sticking around for a bit." Ben took a seat opposite. "I don't mean to blow my own horn, but I'm an excellent guide. I can take you wherever you need to go. You say a place, and I'll make it happen. You want to see the sights, we'll go."

This Ben sounded sweet and he was charming,

but he also wasn't Jack.

"I appreciate that, but I really don't … I'm not interested in anything right now."

"Oh," he said.

"I'm getting over a bad breakup, and I kind of just want … to be left alone."

"Say no more."

Before she could stop him or even try to say anything else, his hands were up in the air, and she watched as he moved on to the next woman.

She felt kind of bad for whoever took him up on his offer.

Closing her books, she made her way toward the shelves, and placed them back. Running her hand across the spines, she felt so empty.

Ever since she'd moved here, nothing had been right to her.

Pulling away from the books, she tried to ignore this desolate feeling, but it was dragging her down.

Leaving the library, she gave a wave to one of the women at the front desk before heading out into the busy city life. People were still coming and going.

Considering it was nearing the end of summer, the weather was miserable, but she'd come to see that was the case for every single thing in England.

It was either miserable or not.

Wrapping her arms around herself, she hiked her bag high up on her shoulder, and began the long walk back home.

Her parents had already gotten into the swing of things here. They were so happy and she tried not to put a downer on everything, but it was impossible to do.

She could have stayed in the States, but her father's threat of ruining Jack was what kept her home with her parents.

Entering their home, she grabbed a towel from the radiator and began to dry her soaking hair.

"I'm back," she said.

Her mother entered. "Sweetie, you're soaked."

"It's raining."

"I made you your favorite."

"What?"

"Spaghetti. I remember how much you love it."

"Thank you."

She put the towel back on the radiator, kicked off her shoes, dropped her bag, and followed her mother into the other room.

Her father was sitting at the table.

Like so many other occasions, she ignored him.

Grabbing some water, she filled it up and took a sip.

"Did you have a good day at the library?" her mother asked.

"Yes."

"What did you do?"

"I read."

"Oh."

She noticed her mother looking between the two of them, nibbling her lip.

Lucia finished her water. "I met a guy today."

"That sounds pleasing."

"Yeah, he came over, talking to me, and when I told him I wasn't interested, I watched him move on to another girl."

The smile that had been on Patricia's face dropped.

"Lucia, I know this is hard—"

"Stop pandering to the girl. She wants to be behave like a child, leave her to it."

Anger boiled up inside her as her father turned

the page on his newspaper. It had been like this since they moved. He was disappointed in her. He'd told her many times that he couldn't believe she'd do something so stupid. How he had faith in her to be the better person. She'd let him down, and their friendship, that trust, had shattered. Instead of blasting out and acting like a child, she left the kitchen.

"Your food," Patricia said. "I made your favorite."

"I'm not hungry."

"You know what, I've had enough of this."

Lucia kept on walking toward the stairs.

She heard her father slam his paper down, his hand smacking against the surface and then his feet padding toward the hallway.

"Lucia, enough is enough," he said. "Don't you dare walk away from me."

She stopped on the stairs and turned toward her parents.

Her father had his hands on his hips, looking really pissed off while her mother looked nervous. She stood in the doorway, hugging the wall, or at least from where she was standing it looked like that.

"What?" she asked.

"You're behaving like a child."

"No, I'm not."

"You won't eat. You won't give this a chance. Your behavior is…"

"What?" Lucia asked. "My behavior is what? You didn't give me the chance to explain. You threatened him. Dragged me here to a foreign country just to keep an eye on me. You don't care about me. You tell me repeatedly what a letdown I am, and how I disappointed you. What more do you want me to do?"

"I'm tired of your moods, Lucia. Grow up."

"I have been grown up," she yelled. "I'm sick and tired of you telling me I'm behaving like a child or you're sick because of the way I acted. Do you even know what a real temper tantrum is, or are you just assuming that any child or person that doesn't do what you want is acting out?" She glared at her father, refusing to back down.

Over the past five months he'd treated her like a child. It was like he'd forgotten all the years of her being left alone, of fending for herself. When they had a conference to go to, she was left cash or a card to deal with it. She'd never been a fucking child, and yet, he treated her as if that was all she'd ever been.

"That's enough."

"Yes, of course it's enough. Whenever something doesn't go your way, it's enough." She gave a little bow. "I'll be down for dinner after I get out of my clothes."

"I said I would believe you, Lucia, but everything you're showing me right now, your behavior, you make me believe he brainwashed you. That you weren't old enough to have the choice in this relationship."

She stared at her father, seeing he believed what he said. "I get it, I do, but, Dad, I love him. Being away from him, it hurts, and behaving like nothing is different, isn't the easiest thing to do. I'm not cold. I can't pretend I wasn't in love. He didn't brainwash me. Jack isn't a sexual predator. He's a gentleman, and one hell of a teacher. I'd be with him now if I wasn't scared that you'd ruin his life."

Without another glance at her parents, she stormed up to her room, sitting down on her bed as she pulled her socks off.

She needed to find some that were waterproof or something because her feet were soaking wet.

Padding over to her computer, she saw a message

from Marie.

Marie: **How is today? Still working your ass off or are you studying? Have you figured out what you want to be?**

From previous conversations, she knew Marie was undecided about going to college or not. Her ranch hand friend had asked if she wanted to come and see him, to spend some time traveling across Europe.

She sat down at her desk, her fingers poised over the keyboard.

With every passing day, she was growing less tolerant of all the changes.

This gap year was becoming one of the longest of her life.

Lucia: **It's another day in a long line of days. Nothing much has changed. Just had an argument with my dad. What's really new about that? Nope, don't have a clue what I'm studying when I do go to college. I like working though. Everyone speaks weird here, but that's okay. Have you decided on what you're doing to do?**

She clicked Enter and saw her message appear in the talk box.

After a few seconds she saw the three magic dots appear beside Marie's name. She had never lost contact with Marie.

Her father had wanted Lucia to stop all contact with everyone from her past life, but she'd gotten angry. Her mother had finally talked him down, and Lucia was able to keep in touch with Marie.

It was the only link she had to her old life, and she didn't want to lose it.

Marie was the only one willing to talk about him.

Marie: **I don't know. We've kept in touch but we've also agreed that we're not waiting for each** other. What if I get to wherever he is, and he's with someone else, and I've misread all the signs? Also, I have met someone else. I always wanted to travel, and I could do that after college. I miss you.

Lucia: **True, you can do everything you want after college. Who is the guy you're dating?**

Marie: **His name's Sean and he goes to the local college. He's sweet and funny. You'd like him.**

Lucia frowned as she read the last message.

Lucia: **Local college?**

Marie: **I'm undecided. My BFF is in England and these conversations can be a pain in the ass. I love talking to you but I miss talking to you in person. This fucking sucks, and you know I've always hated typing.**

Lucia missed her friend so much.

Lucia: **I wish I was home with you. We'd be able to help each other solve our problems, and we wouldn't have to rely on someone else. I haven't got a clue what to do. My parents want me to get over whatever misery I feel. I'm just … all alone.**

Marie: **I know. He's not doing much better, just so you know. Of course, he's still a kickass teacher but it's not the same. He misses you.**

Lucia sat back, pressing a hand to her mouth. She couldn't help it. Suddenly overcome with raw emotion, she closed her eyes, and tried to stay focused.

Lucia: **I miss him so much. I never realized just how much until now. I … I don't want to lose him. I don't know how much more of this that I can take. Dad's unreasonable.**

Marie: **Try to come around and see it from his point. You're his little girl and he was your teacher. I'm so sorry. I've got to go. Chat soon.**

She saw that Marie had left, and she was once

again alone.

For a few moments she was able to think of Marie's voice, pretend to be listening to her.

Staring at her computer screen, she nibbled her lip and wondered what to do.

There was a soft knock on the door, and she turned around to see it was her mother.

"Dinner's nearly done," she said.

"Okay."

She left the computer, not caring that her mother would probably read it.

Pulling her shirt over her head, she entered the bathroom, throwing it into the laundry room. Removing her jeans, she wriggled out of them before going into her room. She had her own en-suite bathroom still.

Her mother was sitting at the desk, scrolling through her conversation.

"No one said that I couldn't talk about him," Lucia said.

She grabbed a large shirt and some sweatpants, pulling them on.

"I know this is hard for you," Patricia said. "I think it would have been difficult for me as well."

"Try to imagine being in love with Dad only for your parents to decide that they know what's best for you at every single turn. You can't see him. Talk to him, and you're forced to attempt to live a happy life, and you'll understand what I'm feeling."

Patricia sighed. "It was never supposed to be this way. We'd hoped that you'd love it here, and that we could be the family that we always wanted to be."

Lucia sat on the edge of the bed, staring at her mother. There was a sad smile on her face.

"You loved him," Patricia asked.

"Yes." Tears filled her eyes. "I know you and

Dad think it was gross and seedy, and wrong. The only thing that was wrong was that he was my teacher, Mom. Jack…" Even his name was hard to say. She closed her eyes, trying not to cry. She was tired of shedding tears. "He was always there for me. When we were together, he stopped being my teacher and became something more. Something perfect. He always knew what to say to make me smile." She frowned. "I don't know what to say about it, to be honest. Dad hates me."

"Your father doesn't hate you, Lucia. He's worried about you. We both are. You've lost some weight in the past five months."

"Yay, that's always what you wanted." Eating made her feel sick, so she nibbled when she could.

Her mother's face lost the smile. "I never wanted you to be unhappy. I remember what it was like in high school being a nerd. The way they bullied everyone. I'm not the best mother. In fact, I'd say I'm probably an awful one, but I do love you, Lucia. Very much."

Neither of them said anything more as her mother got to her feet and the conversation was terminated.

There was nothing that either of them could do.

Chapter Twenty

Two months later

It was Lucia's birthday today. Beginning of October. Jack stared out his classroom window. All of his students were long gone for the day. A few stood around their cars, chatting, waiting for their boyfriends or girlfriends to be done with football practice. He stared up at the trees. The leaves had already started to change color. The year was nearly over with once again.

Closing his eyes, he tried not to think about all that had happened in the past year. He saw the kiss that Lucia had placed on his lips. It was like a movie in his mind that he got to watch, seeing her look so scared and then her lips had been on his.

So sure, so scared, so everything, and he'd held her in his arms, and told her it would all be okay.

Running a hand down his face, he opened his eyes once again and stared up at the trees.

No one had mentioned a word to him about Lucia's leaving. Principal Brandt had said that her parents made the quick decision and that she wasn't surprised. All the information on Lucia Deen was that her parents tended to make quick decisions and rarely turned up for their daughter's parent-teacher conferences.

He didn't completely understand what kind of files they had on the kids, but Brandt liked to keep detailed documents for her files.

Not for the first time he wondered if Lucia was happy.

If she missed him.

He missed her so fucking much.

In fact, he'd even put his house on the market and was looking for a new place. One that didn't have so many memories. He was also looking at a change of schools. Walking the halls was a nightmare for him. When he was near her locker, it was like he saw her, smelled her.

He hadn't been able to eat a fucking strawberry all through the damn summer, and that pissed him off.

A lot of things annoyed him of late. Even his parents, who had shown an interest in his life. They'd sent him at least five applications for different schools around the country, and not any of them actually appealed to him, mainly because it was his parents' friends, and he didn't want them doing him any favors.

Turning away from the window, he made his way toward the desk. The same desk that held more memories of a time when he'd been a lot happier.

The ring he'd bought for her still remained in the same place. The engagement ring that made a mockery of all of his plans.

There were moments that it actually felt like she'd died. He'd even drive past her house a couple of times a week, just to see, but a new family was there now, and he couldn't keep living in the past.

Lucia Deen was gone.

She'd gone to protect him, and he hated that he couldn't have done the same thing for her.

"Hey," Marie said, surprising him.

"You do realize you don't go here anymore," he said.

"Shoot, you could have fooled me." She clicked her fingers and smiled. "I knew I was in the wrong place."

"What can I do for you?"

"I wanted to come and check on you."

"You're not a high school student."

"I know, but I am a college student." She turned

around, showing him the sweater she wore with the local college logo on it.

"Very good."

Marie visited him often since Lucia left, mostly to give him updates on how her friend was doing.

"I thought I'd come say hi. You know, being what day it is."

"Lucia's birthday."

"Yes, she's now nineteen." Marie entered the classroom. She leaned against one of the student desks, arms folded. "I always imagined her being here, you know? Even when her parents were moving and everything was changing. I always thought it wouldn't happen. That she'd stay here for a long time, and that we'd move on."

He didn't interrupt her. Talking about Lucia was the only thing he had of her right now. That, and a few pictures that he struggled to look at anymore. The constant reminder of everything that he'd lost.

"I wanted to apologize to you," Jack said. "I ... I didn't think, and I've not thought how this has affected you."

"Talking to you, Jack, is not a problem. I loved Lucia. Still do. She was like a sister to me, and it hasn't been right her not being here. I can't believe her parents did what they did."

"Why not? *You* wanted to report us. It's the natural thing."

"Okay, so I screwed up. I didn't realize that this was the real deal to you. You're a teacher, and Lucia was a student. I didn't for a second think that you could have been in love with her until I saw it with my own eyes. I didn't report you because I knew Lucia loved you."

"I do love her."

"I can see that. You look like crap, just so you

know. Lucia doesn't look much better."

"What?"

"We did a video chat thing. I don't think she's doing all that well. She looks tired, and she doesn't smile. Isn't there any way for you to talk to her parents? Resolve this?"

"I don't know. I don't want to risk Lucia being in trouble, and now we've got a whole ocean between us," he said.

He wanted to see her, needed to.

"Look, Lucia wanted me to give this to you." Marie held out an envelope. "She mailed it to me, but because of where she lives now, it took forever to get to me. She had to do it in secret."

He took the envelope, holding it against his nose.

The scent of strawberries still lingered on the card. "Thank you, Marie. When you talk to her, tell her Happy Birthday, and that I'm thinking about her."

"I will, Mr. Parker."

"I think it's more than okay for you to call me Jack."

"I know, but it just seems weird to me. I'll try it, Jack." She chuckled, turned on her heel, and left.

He didn't watch her go.

Staring at the letter in his hand, he was tempted to open it up then and there, but instead, he packed away his things and left the school.

Heading to his car, he waved at some of his students, but once he was behind the wheel, he had one focus, getting home.

He did so without making any stops. The sign in his front lawn didn't calm him that day. The realtor wasn't happy that he didn't want to be present for any of the viewings. He didn't want to see anyone who would be buying his property.

Entering his home, he grabbed a beer and made his way outside to his table on the porch. There was a chill in the air, but tonight, he didn't feel it as he stared at her envelope. It was the first one he'd received, and he wanted to savor every single moment.

Turning it over, he opened up the envelope and pulled out the paper. Opening it up, he smiled at her handwriting. So neat, sure, and he ran his fingers across it.

You're a grown-ass man loving some handwritten work.

Get over yourself.

Releasing a breath, he focused on the words.

Dear Jack, Mr. Parker,

I don't know why I didn't think to actually write to you, and send it. It's the strangest thing, but I was watching a woman the other day in the park. She was sitting down, and she had this large coat. Her hair was swishing all around her, but she held this letter in one hand, clearly open, and in the other, pieces of paper with writing. My parents said I couldn't have any contact with you at all. Being the total modern-day girl that I am, I didn't even think of writing. I know you can't write back. I don't want you to get in trouble, and Dad's still being an ass.

My birthday is fast approaching, and I still can't stop thinking about you. The days here are so long. They're miserable as well. The weather is not the best. It's never the best to be honest, and I know I shouldn't complain, but there it is. It's my letter lol. See what I did there. I can still say lol.

Anyway, I feel happier just knowing that I'm writing to you.

I wanted to say how sorry I am about everything that has happened. That day on my birthday nearly a year ago now, I never for a second thought about what would happen. I had developed this crush on you. It was so big, which was why I went and sat in the back of the room. You know the spot. I didn't want you to think less of me for actually having feelings for you. I know, I'm weird, but I've accepted that. Kissing you was the best thing I ever did. Falling in love with you, I can't be upset about that.

Jack, I love you. More than anything else in the world, and this time apart, it is killing me. However, I have hope. I know it's not right of me to ask this, but ... will you wait for me? My parents can't keep this up forever, I just know it. I love you, and I want to be with you. I'm going to find a way. Somehow.

If you don't want to take that chance, I understand.

Please let Marie know what you want to do, and I will accept it either way. What we had shouldn't have happened. It was forbidden, wrong, but when you actually think about it, only you being my teacher was wrong. That was all.

Everything else is what people write books about, make movies for.

I love you, Jack Parker, and I will be yours always.

Lucia

Jack smiled as he read the letter a second and third time.

Being with Lucia, no matter the age difference or whether they should have done it or not, it was the greatest thing that ever happened to him. He didn't realize that he could have fallen in love or have these feelings at all.

Love was something he'd never known for most of his life.

It seemed rather fitting that the rebel in him would fall in love with a student.

"I'll wait for you, Lucia. Forever if I have to." He pressed a kiss to the letter, feeling some hope after so much darkness.

****

Lucia chewed on her cereal as her father entered the kitchen. She didn't say anything to him. It was her birthday, and her mother had already wished her a good day, kissed her head, and left for work.

To Lucia it was just another day.

"Happy Birthday," her father said.

"Thank you."

She didn't turn to look at him.

Their relationship had been strained for a long time. It was kind of funny actually. She and her mother had always struggled to see eye to eye, and yet it was her father that was difficult to talk to.

Every single night her mother came to see her now, to make sure she was happy.

"What are you doing today?" her father asked.

She chewed her food, staring at him. "Seeing the sights."

The university admin office had to let her go over the summer as they had no need for volunteers.

She was still looking for work and waiting on her visa change. Until then, her parents had said for her not to worry.

"How long are you going to stay mad at me?" he finally asked.

Lucia stared at him and wondered what to say.

Forever?

Until you let me go back to him.

"How do you feel about Mom?" she asked instead.

"What do you mean?"

"How do you feel about her? I know you met each other when you were young and you both knew what you wanted out of life. Neither of you wanted a kid. Yes, I know, you love me. I'm just curious though. Did you love her?"

"Of course I loved her. We both knew what we wanted out of life. We both were in love and had these plans. Why?"

"I was just curious."

"Why?"

"Because … I wanted to know. It's my birthday after all. I don't want to fight with you." She took another mouthful of food and stared at him. She didn't actually taste anything, but cereal seemed to be the only food that she could actually stomach right now. "What would you have done if you were kept apart?"

"Lucia?"

"I'm just curious."

"Your mother and I, we didn't do anything wrong."

"And yet Jack and I did." She watched her father's hands clench into fists.

"He was your teacher."

She smiled. "All my life I was the good girl. The perfect daughter you could have. I never made waves. I didn't stop you from going to your conferences, or your late-night work. Today is my birthday, and a year ago, you both presented me with a car and a promise. A promise that you wouldn't forget my birthday." She glanced down at her watch. "In about ten hours, a year ago, work took priority over me."

"Why do you keep bringing this up?"

"Because I want you to realize that you're not perfect. That I wasn't perfect. That I was happy. I fell in love with Jack Parker, and even though you didn't agree with it, it doesn't mean it was wrong. He's not my teacher anymore. I love him, and I'm not going to keep on letting you do this." She tapped the paper and pushed it over to him. "Once I find a job, and I can be on my own two feet, I'm out of here. I'm done being this person, Dad. I'm done behaving as if I've done something wrong. I'm a good person. I'm not going to keep being bullied or protected by you anymore."

She got to her feet, and without a backward glance made her way out of the house. The weather was once again miserable, but with an umbrella in hand, she felt like she had a chance.

There was going to come a point when her father's threat wouldn't stand. He wouldn't be able to keep her in check.

She didn't know what happened to her the other day as she'd stood in the park looking into the small lake. People were laughing, joking, arguing, and activity was everywhere.

As she stood there, she realized that she could write to Jack. She couldn't receive anything from him, but also that as the years passed, her father's threat would cease to matter.

A twenty-year-old, twenty-five–year-old, who would care if she dated a teacher? There was a way for them. She just had to wait and see if Jack felt the same.

****

"What are you going to do?" Patricia asked.

Bill looked dejected. Even though they'd both tried to put a brave face on it, the truth was, they were fast losing that fight. She'd always been the one that was at loggerheads with her little girl, and it was Bill who acted like a go-between. Now, their roles were reversed, and she knew it was tearing her husband apart, but also damaging their little girl.

"What do you want me to do?"

"Fix it."

"How?"

"You know how, but you're being too damn stubborn for your own good."

Bill sighed. "You really want me to do this?"

"It's our daughter, Bill."

"He had no right."

"They're in love."

"And if it doesn't last?" he asked.

"That's not our fault. We did our bit. I don't want to be one of these moms that have regrets. I already have them from missing the day she first walked to her words, to now. She fell in love and had sex, and that is something a mother and daughter are supposed to know. I've listened to other parents at work, and they know. They know their kids through and through. My girl was having sex and a relationship, and I didn't know. I couldn't see a damn difference, Bill. This is not perfect, I get that, but … we can't come between them. We can't."

She stared at her husband, knowing that he felt the same way.

"And if he's moved on?" He dropped his head into his hands. "Then it's my fault. I took her away."

"Then we did everything we could, but I don't think he would. Bill, he didn't even fight you when you attacked him." She'd never seen her husband attack anyone before. It had been a shock to see that kind of violence in her best friend, her love, and the man that was her life.

"You know you are a good mother," he said, getting to his feet.

"You don't have to lie to me."

"You're a good mother, because you know when

you're at fault. You recognize it." He moved toward her, kissing her head.

"Does this mean you'll do it?"

"It means I'll do something. I don't like him."

"I don't expect you to like him. Our parents didn't exactly get on, but they abided each other to help us be together. Why can't we do the same for our girl?"

He released a breath, but it was in that way she'd come to know. It meant he was going to do as she asked.

Patricia didn't know if she was doing the right thing or not, only that she had to do something. Seeing her daughter so unhappy didn't help.

She wanted to see that radiant smile she'd seen so many times before. The sadness hung over her like a dark cloud, and Patricia wanted rid of it for good.

****

Lucia whistled as she stared out of the window. It was pouring down with rain like it had been doing so many times in the past few weeks. She'd seen the news report of the recent floods that had been happening up and down the country.

"Your father should be arriving any minute," her mother said, sipping some of her wine.

"Okay."

"You could at least show some excitement at seeing him again."

Her father had been gone a week.

While he'd been away, Patricia had been present constantly. They had even spent the day touring the local sights, stopping by in a few museums, and doing some mother-daughter bonding.

It was kind of surreal to be getting along with her mother. Removing the peas from their pods, Lucia stole a couple as she worked. The tender green balls were really sweet. They'd gone to the farmers' market, and her mother had this big giant feast planned for when he arrived home.

She didn't get it, and it did seem strange to her that her dad would just leave for something work-related without taking her mom.

"I will. I do miss him."

"You do?" Patricia asked.

"Of course. I know we're not on the best terms right now, but I still love you guys."

Patricia bit her lip, and Lucia realized that was exactly where she got her lip biting from, her mother. "You're sure, even though we're bad parents?"

Lucia giggled. "You're not bad parents. I get why you did what you did," she said.

"You do?"

Her mother was saying those two words a lot.

Yes, there had been another moment of clarity for Lucia while watching the news where a girl had been killed after running away with an older man.

She'd watched the news bulletin and listened to the story. Then of course, she thought about her own situation, and realized for the past few months she'd been behaving like a spoiled brat.

Her parents loved her very much. They were worried about her, and rather than seeing this from their perspective, she'd only seen it from hers, which was they'd taken her away from the man she loved.

"Yeah. You both love and care for me. Jack and I, we made a few mistakes with our relationship, but I know you guys love me. You both want the best for me, and I want to say sorry to Dad when he gets home." She sighed and turned to her mother. "I'm so sorry for making your life hard, for making this somewhat unbearable. I didn't want to do that, but I ended up doing it anyway. I am sorry."

"Oh, honey." Patricia pulled her into her arms. "I love you so much, and I'm so sorry for being a pain in the ass and a nag. God, I wouldn't be able to handle anything happening to you. I know you're growing up and you're an adult now. You can make your own choices, but just know that I love you so much. So, so much."

She held Patricia tightly to her.

"How have you been without Dad? This is your first time apart?"

"We talk constantly. He lets me know how he's doing."

"Where did he go again? You never said why he had to leave."

She opened up another pod, shucking out the peas before turning her gaze back to Patricia. She saw the frown on her face.

"What? What is it?"

"It's nothing. I'm just surprised at how grown up you've gotten." Patricia stroked her cheek.

The ringing of the doorbell pulled her away. Patricia jumped, looking nervous.

"Mom, what's the matter? You're kind of scaring me right now."

"It's nothing. Just continue doing those peas. I'll go and answer it."

Shrugging her shoulders, Lucia continued to open up the pods, watching the peas fall into the bowl.

She'd never have thought Patricia was acting weird, but there was a first time for everything.

Since sending her letter to Jack, talking with her dad, the news bulletin, life, for the first time, she felt … okay. She wasn't pulled down by misery, but she could see more clearly and understand.

She'd already made the decision that when her

father arrived, she wanted to apologize to him. To say how sorry she was for the way she'd been behaving. Her relationship with her parents was not the best, but it was still there. One day she hoped to go back to Jack, but fear of what her father would do stopped her from immediately jumping on a plane and going to him. She didn't want to lose herself, and also her talks with Marie helped a lot.

Marie finally decided to cut her losses with the traveling ranch hand and was already enrolled in college, taking classes, and knew exactly what she wanted to be

Unlike Marie, Lucia was still trying to figure out what she wanted to study.

Lucia frowned.

They were taking a long time.

Shucking the last pod, she looked up and froze. There in the reflection of the glass was Jack.

She didn't know what to do or what to say. He was right there, in the kitchen doorway, staring at her.

Closing her eyes, she counted to three, and opened them again.

"I'm still here," Jack said. "I have days like that when I think I've seen you. You're not there though."

She spun around, and it was him. He stood in the kitchen doorway.

"It's cold out."

"Your mom hung my jacket up."

"She knows you're here?" she asked.

Panic, fear, happiness, excitement, all other kinds of emotions swamped her, and she didn't know what to do.

"We both know he's here," Bill said, drawing her attention to the side of Jack. Patricia was snuggled into Bill's side.

"Dad?"

"Look … you're my little girl. You will always be my little girl. I don't claim to be a good dad, but I reacted and I didn't think. I've only known anger these past few months. I, I was in shock, seeing my little girl, and I just blew. I was worried, but I decided that even though I don't agree on how you both conducted yourselves, or what happened, I know for a fact that you both love each other. Now, love, I understand. I've never loved anyone more than your mother. I won't come in between the two of you, and I don't want any more lies or sneaking around. We're going to give you a few moments to talk."

Tears filled her eyes, and she didn't know what to say or what to do.

When she turned to Jack, he opened his arms, and she ran into them.

The instant his arms were around her, holding her close, everything felt right in the world. This was her man, in her home, holding her. Everything was how it was supposed to be.

"Strawberries. I've missed this smell. I've missed you. Fuck, how I've missed you."

Tilting her head back, she smiled up at him, but he took possession of her mouth, and she was lost. His kiss drove her need higher, she wanted his lips more than her next breath. He slid his tongue across her mouth, and she opened up, and he plunged inside.

"I've missed you so much," she said as he pulled away from the kiss. "I don't … what happened? You're here."

"I'm here."

"Dad went and got you?"

"Yes."

She listened as Jack told her everything.

****

Three days earlier

Jack finally had a buyer for his home, and as he wrapped up one of the few pictures he possessed, he couldn't help but feel the velvet box in his pocket. Over eight months had passed since he last saw the love of his life, and a few weeks since he'd gotten that letter.

He was filled with hope, but he didn't know what to do.

Lucia wanted him to have his dream, but while teaching was great, it wasn't the same as being with her.

He'd already told his parents of his decision and the possible repercussions of what he was going to do. They of course advised him against going and finding the woman he loved. He didn't need to teach.

The inheritance and money he earned from that, along with his stocks and shares, made him a very comfortable man. Besides, there were other career avenues. Teaching was just one part.

He was only thirty-one years old. He could do anything he wanted.

The only thing he couldn't live without was Lucia.

Marie had stopped by to visit him, and he'd told her of his plan. She was all for it. She wanted her friend happy once again.

He'd just finished packing his third box of books when his doorbell had rung. It wasn't often he had guests. His parents never visited him, and there weren't many people besides Marie that he'd call his friends.

When Jack opened his door, Bill Deen was the last person he expected to see.

Glancing behind him, he saw that he was also alone.

"I'm not here to start a fight or to cause problems," Bill said.

"What are you here for?"

"I want to talk."

"You want to finally talk to me?"

"I don't think I've got much of a choice, do I?"

Rubbing the back of his head, Jack stepped away from the door and allowed the other man to enter.

"You're moving?" Bill asked.

"Yep. End of next week." He intended to put most of his stuff into storage until he knew what was happening.

"You're just going to leave?"

Jack sighed and glanced up at the other man. "I'm done."

"What?"

"You can report my ass. Accuse me of whatever you want. I no longer care. Lucia … I know you're pissed, and in your shoes, I'd feel the same way. I shouldn't have touched her or had a relationship with her. But it wasn't just about all of that. I fell in love with her. I can't live without her anymore, and if she would be willing to have me, then I want to marry her."

"What about your teaching? You love it."

"I do. Teaching is something I enjoy. I won't deny that, but it's not worth it without her." He smiled. "I never thought I'd fall so hard for a woman, but Lucia has that way about her. The moment she got inside my head there was no letting her go. I love your daughter, Mr. Deen." He pulled out the velvet box. "And I'm going to ask her to marry me."

Jack was done hiding. He was done with it all.

"You got her a ring?"

"Before last Christmas I got it for her. I saw it and knew it would fit perfectly on her." Jack ran a hand down his face. "I'm sorry. You're here at my house. I'm being rude. What can I do to help you?"

"I was wrong."

"Sorry?"

"I was wrong about you and Lucia. She's my daughter, and I will always worry about her. The past months, they've been hard. Lucia didn't take the move too well nor any contact with you. I can't say that I am going to agree to this, but will you come back home with me? My wife and I, we want to try and make this work."

"You want me to come to your home."

"Yes. Lucia's mother and I, our parents didn't always see eye to eye. We had to put up with a great deal to be together. I promised myself that if I ever had a chance to be different, I'd do it. Yet, I acted the same way as my father did. We always do crazy things for the people we love. I can see that you love my daughter, and I will give this a chance between the two of you. To make it work. Providing Lucia would have you, of course."

"Of course." Jack laughed. "Thank you. Thank you." He held his hand out for Bill to take. There had been a few seconds of pause, but finally, Bill held his hand out.

****

"He helped me pack up my home and now I'm here, with you." Jack stroked her cheek, retelling her most of what happened, leaving out the engagement ring part.

"You're here." She smiled. "Sorry, I can't see my dad helping you pack or actually being nice to you."

"It happened," Jack said. "He's a pretty good guy."

"I'm a very good guy and lenient. Get to the next part," Bill said, shouting to be heard.

On the way over here, he'd been driving him insane, worrying.

****

Two hours earlier

"I've never asked a woman to marry me before," Jack said.

"It's quite easy."

"You're on the wrong side of the road."

"We're in England. This is the right side of the road."

Jack tensed as they passed a large truck. "Crazy, crazy people."

"So, you've never proposed to anyone?"

"Years ago, I promised to marry my dog before she died." He'd never told anyone that before. "Just pretend I didn't mention that. I was six, and I didn't know any better."

"You're panicking and acting out."

"How did you do it?"

"I took Patricia out and asked her. I don't have much more experience at these things than you, Jack. I've only ever asked one woman. It's not like you can train for these things."

"What if she hates the ring?"

"She'll love the ring."

"What if she says no?"

"I went across the ocean to come and get you because my daughter told me in no uncertain terms that she was unwilling to live without you. She's going to say yes. It's a foregone conclusion."

"What do I say?"

"'Lucia, I know your parents are the best in the world and it's going to cost them a great deal to let me take you, but, as your father has said, I have his total blessing. I promise to love you every single day, to be completely faithful otherwise your father has also promised to sever a certain appendage and tie it around my neck, and to make you happier than you ever thought possible. If I fail all of these requirements, I forfeit my right to life, and will gladly die at your father's hand.'"

Jack remained silent, staring over at Bill. "You're kind of scary right now."

"That was a similar talk I had with Patricia's dad. I was so scared after that. For weeks, I kept checking where I walked just in case he was breathing down my neck. If I saw Patricia frown, I'd do something crazy like cluck like a chicken. It made her laugh every single time, until she realized what I was doing."

Jack winced. "Wow."

"I'm a pretty good father-in-law to have."

"I'm seeing that right now."

"All I ask is that you love my girl. To never do anything to hurt her, and possibly consider a move to England. It's a pretty good place to be."

"I could teach in London. It'll be a huge pain in the ass, but I'll do it for her."

"It's something to look into."

"You're happy with me being here?" Jack asked.

Bill was silent for a few moments. "I'm not angry you're here, and I don't want to kill you. I'd consider that progress. Besides, you're supposed to be focusing on how you're going to propose to my girl."

"Right."

****

Present

Bending down on one knee, feeling like this was his biggest moment, Jack reached into his pocket, feeling the velvet box.

"Jack, what are you doing?"

"I know you're young and we've been apart the last nine months. There is no one else. There hasn't been anyone else. I love you more than anything in the world,

Lucia Deen. You're the light of my life, and you have the best parents in the world." She laughed. "I did rehearse this."

"I approved," Bill said.

"Jack—"

"Please, let me finish. I've always rebelled. I've never followed the rules, and I even broke my three rules for you, but I never expected to find the perfect woman in you. The love of my life. I'm screwing this up."

"Keep going," Bill shouted again. Jack actually believed they could be friends. In the past few days they'd discovered they had a lot in common. They both loved books, poetry, life, the law, and of course Lucia.

"My home is with you. My love is with you. I don't care about teaching if I'm not with you. It's not important to me unless you're there with me. Lucia Deen, would you do me the honor of becoming my wife? I will try to be a good husband to you. To give you whatever your heart desires. You'll want for—"

Lucia silenced him with a kiss. She went to her knees, arms wrapped around his neck, and her lips on his.

He held her close, kissing her back with a passion.

The time apart melted away.

"What's your answer?" Bill asked.

Lucia pulled away, smiling. "Yes. Of course, yes."

"You're going to marry me?"

"Yes, I want to marry you, Jack. I want to be yours."

When he got to his feet, Bill and Patricia were there, hugging him.

"So, this was why you wanted to do the big feast?" Lucia asked.

"It was a feast to celebrate," Patricia said.

"We were the only two convinced you'd say yes," Bill said. "You were both so nervous."

Stepping into Jack's arms, he saw her father falter for a second, and knew it would take him time, but at least he'd given them both this, and he was so thankful for it. He'd never intended to fall in love, but Lucia had entered his world and turned it upside down. In time, they would no longer be the teacher and the student, but Jack and Lucia, or husband and wife.

Epilogue One

Ten months later

"Why did you decide to have your wedding in the height of summer?" Marie asked, fussing all around Lucia as she pulled a crease out of the dress.

"Because it's beautiful outside, flowers are in full bloom, and I wanted my wedding day to be just perfect. I'm only going to get one day."

"Not if it doesn't work out, sweetie. You could have six or seven big days."

"If that happens, you're going to complain about every single one," Lucia said. "You're always going to be my maid of honor."

"You've got that right." Marie winked at her.

She couldn't have anyone else but Marie at her side for her wedding.

"I never realized how much the two of you argue," Patricia said.

"Smile for me, dear, I want to make sure the pictures will look perfect with no food between your teeth," Nancy Parker said.

She had Marie, her mother, and Jack's mother all in the church waiting room. She and Jack were getting married in England, and it was one of the rare days that was in fact sunny, with no rain forecast.

After today, she and Jack were flying to his family villa in Italy to spend two weeks on a honeymoon, and she was excited about having him all to herself. In ten months, he'd found a place to live near her parents and a job at one of the local colleges. She got to see him every single day, and of course, he'd become good friends with her father. It had been difficult, as moving overseas does create complications, but seeing as Jack's parents were the best lawyers in the country, it wasn't hard for them to work through all the checks and paperwork.

Staring at her reflection, she saw Marie, Patricia, and Nancy looking at her. Some of her brown hair was held up with flowery pins, while ringlets cascaded around her. She wore a white dress that molded to her breasts and waist but flared out from her hips down to her feet, where she wore a pair of flat shoes.

She had yet to perfect the art of walking in heels.

"How do I look?" she asked.

"Pretty as a picture."

She turned to see her father standing in the doorway. "We're all about ready to start. Are you all ready for this?"

Lucia nodded.

She watched her mother, future mother-in-law, and best friend leave the room, and she turned to face her father.

"Did you ever think you'd see this day?" she asked, stepping toward him.

"No, I didn't. I knew it would come, but letting you go, I didn't think it would be as hard as this."

"I'll always be your girl, Dad," she said.

"I know." She saw the tears well up in his eyes. Throwing her arms around him, she held him close. "I love you, Lucia."

"I love you too, Dad." She had apologized, and over the past ten months they'd been able to work out their differences.

She'd been so happy to do that. She didn't realize how empty her life had been without not only Jack but also her father.

"Jack's a good man. I was wrong about him, and I know he will do everything in his power to take care of you."

She nodded. "I know."

Her love for him had only grown in the past ten months.

Sneaking around, their secret relationship couldn't touch the way they were with each other now. They could go anywhere, be seen together, hold hands, kiss. There were no secrets, no lies, and because of that, they were stronger together.

"I'm nervous."

"He is as well."

"He is? Do you think he's getting cold feet?" She nibbled her lip as she placed her arm inside her father's.

"No. It's weddings. They make people do crazy things."

The wedding march came on, and as she stood outside of the church, she saw the people, her parents' friends as well as Jack's, waiting.

Her heart started to pound.

"Dad?"

"Yeah."

"Thank you."

They walked down the long aisle, and the moment she saw Jack, everything else faded away. He stood near the priest, wearing a tuxedo that seemed to emphasize his maleness if that was even possible. His thick, bulging arms strained the fabric, and he looked perfect. So perfect, and all hers.

The moment she was at the altar, he came down and took her hand from her father's.

"Take care of her."

"Always."

They made their way up to the priest, and she released a breath. "I love you," he said, mouthing the words.

"I love you too."

There, before the priest, their family, and friends, they made promises and vows of love, of friendship, of a life together.

As she spoke her vows and listened to Jack's she recalled that moment when she'd taken a leap of faith and stepped close to him. She'd pressed her lips against his and she didn't realize it at the time, but she did right now, right this second. The kiss had just been the beginning. The moment she'd pressed her lips to his had sealed their fate.

"You may kiss the bride."

This time, Jack stepped to her. He cupped her cheek, and his lips were on hers. Her teacher, her lover, her husband, her soul mate. Forever.

Epilogue Two

Five years later

"You see, my darling little bump, your mother doesn't appreciate good, honest poetry. She never, ever did," Jack said. He ran his hand across Lucia's bump, and marveled as his little girl kicked.

Their first baby.

They'd been married for five years. Five blissful years, and now as she lay on her back and he read from his favorite poetry book, he couldn't quite contain his happiness.

His wife didn't know they were having a little girl. She'd opted not to know, but as she'd been gathering her things, he'd wanted to know.

He couldn't wait to see her face after she gave birth.

Her parents already knew what she was having as well. Yes, he couldn't keep a secret it would seem. He'd nearly slipped a few times with Lucia.

At the last minute, he'd been able to keep it under wraps that he knew what they were having.

"You cannot hold that stuff against me. I forbid it."

"You can't forbid everything," Jack said, pressing a kiss to her stomach. They were enjoying some of the summer sun while it lasted. "Your mother couldn't handle poetry class. She did okay though."

Lucia chuckled. "Do you think it can hear you?"

"I wish you wouldn't call he-it it."

"You do know that I know that you know," Lucia said.

"What do I know?" he asked, closing the book and avoiding eye contact. Grabbing the large bowl of strawberries and the heavy cream from the grass beside them, he dipped one in the cream, and as she was about to speak, he placed it in her mouth. "We've got to keep you both strong."

She rolled her eyes but chewed the fruit.

"You know the sex of the baby."

"I do not."

"You do. You've told my parents, your parents, and even Marie."

He didn't say a word. Marie was really excited and couldn't wait to be a godmother. Lucia's best friend had remained in their life, and he adored her. She was a nice woman and had even married a young businessman who had a keen eye on technology as the future. Listening to them talk was a headache in itself. Science, math, and everything in between. His own wife had chosen her career path in counseling for young people whereas Marie opted to counsel adults. Lucia had required a degree in psychology, which had been rather stressful as she used him to experiment on and ask him to be part of all of these chats.

When she graduated a year ago, he'd never seen her so happy.

Of course, they had wanted to start a family, and now they were expecting their first bundle of joy.

Lucia had told him that she'd work part-time, but she wanted to be available full-time to care for their child.

"Just because I know doesn't mean that I'm going to tell you," he said, taking a bite of the strawberry.

"I thought we agreed not to know what it was," Lucia said.

"No, you thought it would be a good idea. I needed to know if I should brush up on my football training or learn how to shoot."

"And which is it?" she asked, raising a brow.

"You said you didn't want to know."

"I didn't want to know, but now I feel left out and with the fact I'm getting bigger each day, I'm feeling more left out. I can't even see my feet anymore. Do they look swollen to you?"

"No, you look more beautiful every single day."

"What are we having?" she asked.

He sighed, intending to deny her request.

When she pouted and her eyes went wide, he knew he was losing.

"A girl," he said.

Her eyes seemed to go wider at the news. "We're having a little girl?"

"Yes, a bouncing baby girl who I hope has your brown eyes and hair."

"What about your blue eyes and nose?"

"So long as she doesn't have my attitude like I did when I was a boy, we'll be okay."

"We're going to have a baby girl," she said.

"Yes, I was going to paint the nursery pink, if that's okay."

"I'd like it pink," she said.

"You're crying. You're not supposed to be sad."

"I'm not sad, Jack. Far from it. In fact, I don't ever recall being this happy before in my entire life." She sat up, cupping his face. "I love you," she said. "So much."

He held her close, feeling all the love that he didn't think was possible.

Jack Parker, husband, soon-to-be father, and completely, totally smitten with his wife. The rebel in him was finally tamed by the right woman.

Five months later, holding his wife and staring into his daughter's blue eyes, he knew there was no way life could get any better than this, and he had at least another fifty years to go.

The End

www.samcrescent.com

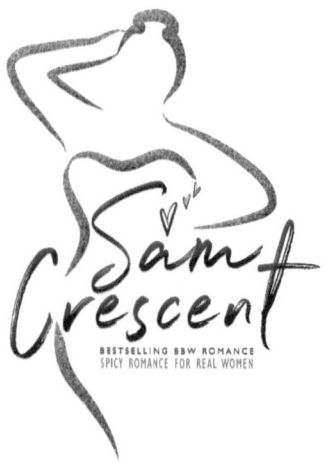